The Alliance Saga - Clouded Moon #1: Shifting Roots
Avalon Roselin, Star Cat Studio

Copyright © 2024 by Roselin Books and Star Cat Studio

All rights reserved. No portion of this book may be reproduced in any form without written permission from the publisher or author, except as permitted by U.S. copyright law.

Roselin Books
California
www.roselinbooks.com

This is a work of fiction. Names, characters, places, and incidents are a product of the author's imagination. Any resemblance to actual people, living or dead, or to businesses, companies, events, institutions, or locales is completely coincidental.

Cover, maps, and interior art designed and illustrated by T. Flowers and T. Pilgrim
Edited by E. Mugdan

Based on the story by T. Flowers and T. Pilgrim

Discover more at www.roselinbooks.com

The Alliance Saga - Clouded Moon #1: Shifting Roots /Avalon Roselin —1st ed
ISBN 979-8-9869284-1-8 (paperback)

While no list of content warnings can completely cover all material that readers may find upsetting, readers sensitive to the following topics should proceed with caution: Ableism, Abuse, Animal Injury and Death, Anxiety and Depression, Chronic/Terminal Illness, Harassment and Bullying, Murder, Religious/Cult Indoctrination, Suicidal Thoughts, Violence, Xenophobia

Acknowledgements

With Special Thanks To:

M. Boucher, H. Groves, M. Hawkins, K. VanNorman, A. Wolfgang
C. Conway, K.B. Cook, E. Finnegan, C. St-Pierre, J. Hinderman, T. Roget
and everyone else who supported this project.
We could not have done it without you!

In loving memory of Sara-Jane (Tusofsky),
may your Spirit always be with us.

Contents

1. Glossary — 1
2. The Ancestors' Law — 3
3. Maps — 4
4. Members of the Alliance — 12
5. A Warning on the Wind — 22
6. The Moonlight Meeting — 39
7. Deadly Discovery — 48
8. The Broken Bond — 60
9. Across Borders — 76
10. The Monster in River Colony — 88
11. The Beast in Marsh Colony — 97
12. Spirits to Come — 106
13. The Invasion of Oak Colony — 113
14. The Loss of Field Colony — 122
15. The Clouded Moon — 135
16. Meeting at Half Moon — 149
17. The Chosen — 159
18. Those Who Follow the Wind — 171

19.	The Price of Trust	177
20.	The Lake of Lost Souls	184
21.	Mages of Death	191
22.	Long Road	198
23.	Familiar Forests	214
24.	Field and Follower	220
25.	Unbound Magic	232
26.	The Calm Before the Storm	238
27.	A Mother's Pain	246
28.	The Prophecy	259
29.	Epilogue	267
30.	Bonus Short - Memories of Whitebelly	269
31.	Bonus Short - Cut Prologue	275
32.	Bonus Short - Relentless Storm	280
33.	Bonus Short - Schemes in the Unbound-lands	284
34.	About the Creators	289

Glossary

Common Terms
Colony - A group of cats who live together as an organized group.
Mage - A cat who is capable of wielding magic.
Molly - A cat who identifies as female.
Quinn - A cat who identifies as neither male nor female.
Tom - A cat who identifies as male.
Unbound - Cats who do not belong to any colony. Sometimes called renegades, outsiders, or other derogatory names by Alliance cats.
Unbound-lands - Territory not claimed by any group of cats; outside of Alliance Lake.

Roles Within the Alliance Colonies
The Alliance - A group of colonies living together in peace around Alliance Lake.
The Spirits Beyond - The spirits of cats within the Alliance who have passed on, representing the colonies' ancestors. They are represented by the moon, especially the full moon.
The Spirits to Come - A symbolic term used to reference future generations. They are represented by the sun, especially at dawn.
Captain - The leader of the colony. They consult with the Council to make final decisions about how the colony is run, lead the colony into battle, and perform ceremonies.
Second in Command (Second) - The cat who is next in line to become Captain. They work closely with the Captain and Council to manage the colony.
Council - A group of cats consisting of Elders, Envoys, and the Second who advise the Captain on major decisions and act for the good of the colony.
Elder - A ranger who has retired from active service to the colony after many seasons, and may serve on the colony's Council.

Envoy - Select rangers who are chosen for their potential to be leaders. They are made members of the Council and carefully trained by the Captain and Second.

Herbalist - Select rangers who learn how to make and use medicine from plants.

Mentor - Select rangers who oversee the training of all new-claws.

Keeper - Select rangers who remain in the colony's base to attend to the upkeep of dens, watch after kittens, and so on.

Ranger - Adult members of the colony who take up a number of different daily tasks like hunting, scouting, training new-claws, fighting to defend the territory, and so on.

New-claw - A young cat who has entered field training.

Kitten - A young cat who has not yet entered their field training, ranging from newborns in the nursery to months-old kittens who have begun base training.

The Ancestors' Law

I. The Colonies of the Alliance shall meet at the Moonlight Island on the night of the full moon to exchange important news and honor the Alliance. Failure to attend the Moonlight Meeting risks a colony's removal from the Alliance. (*Original Law*)

II. A ranger's first loyalty is to their colony, then to the Alliance. (*Original Law*)

III. The presence of magic is prohibited in the Alliance Lake territory. Any suspicion of magic is to be reported at once. (*Original Law*)

IV. Every colony shall be led by a Captain, who represents the colony at the Moonlight Meeting. Every Captain shall have a Second, to whom leadership of the colony will pass if the Captain is killed or unable to perform their duties. They shall be guided by a Council. (*Added by Captain Quietspring, the Wave of Wisdom*)

V. Only the Second, Envoys, and rangers who have retired to become Elders after the completion of their service to the colony shall be eligible to join the Council. The Second shall be the leader of the Council. Elders shall hold higher rank in the Council than Envoys. (*Added by Captain Quietspring, the Wave of Wisdom*)

VI. The Council has the right to reject any decision made by the Captain if they feel that the Captain is not acting in the best interest of the colony. This includes refusing to send rangers on dangerous missions, or rejecting the Captain's choice of Second. The decision to reject a Captain's order must be unanimous among the Council members. (*Added by Captain Quietspring, the Wave of Wisdom*)

VII. No cat shall be made a ranger without approval from the Spirits Beyond on the day of the full moon. (*Added by Captain Brightmoon, the Sage Seer*)

VIII. A ranger must be an Envoy for at least one season before they can be chosen as the Second. (*Added by Captain Longtooth, the Spring Sapling*)

Maps

The Alliance holds a covetous piece of territory on the western coast. Surrounding it on three sides are barren wastes and dry, rocky deserts. At its other edge lies the vast ocean which is credited for its temperate climate, with mild winters and warm—but not dry—summers. The land around Alliance Lake hosts four distinct biomes: open field to the south, wetlands to the north, dense oak forests to the west, and semi-tropical rainforests in the east. The variety in habitats has lead to an abundance of prey and ample prosperity for the cats fortunate enough to call it home.

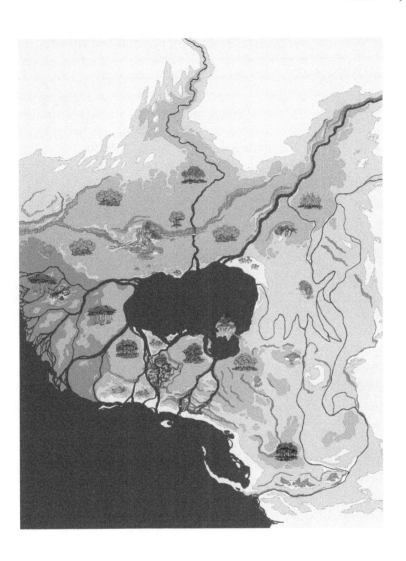

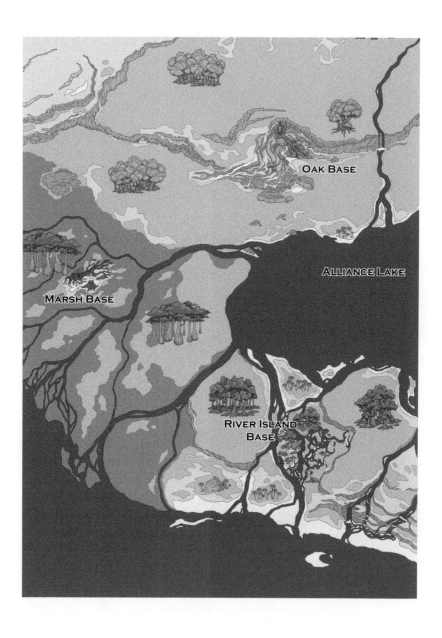

MAPS 7

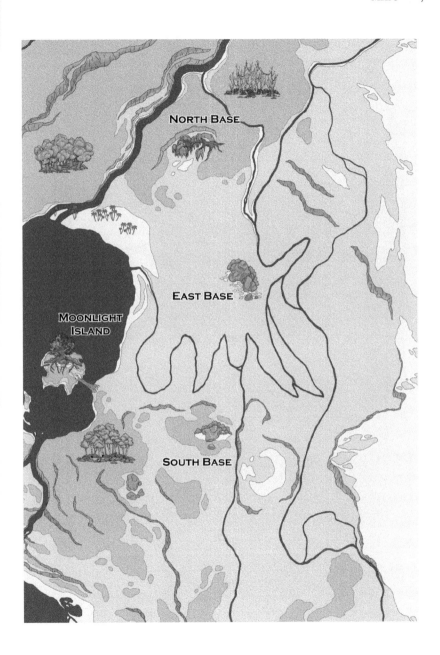

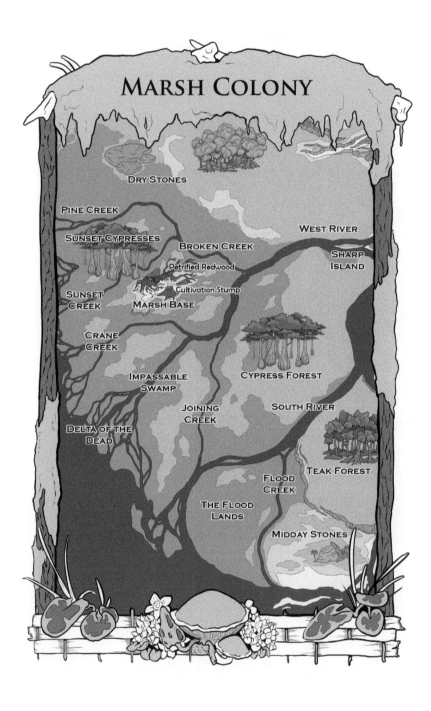

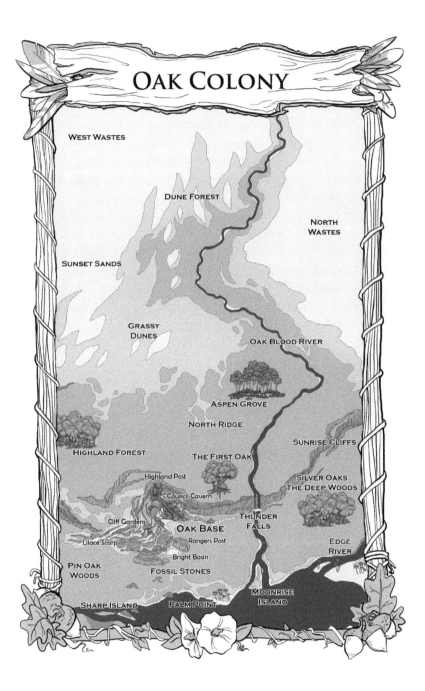

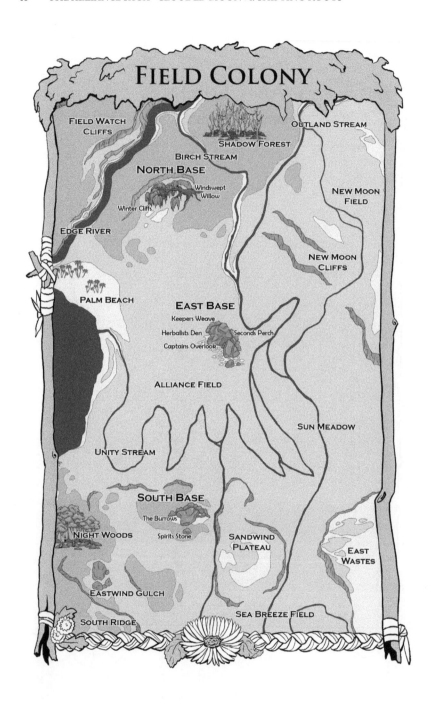

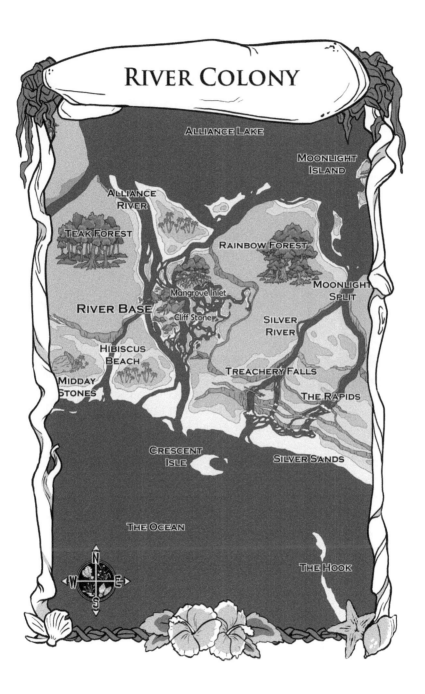

Members of the Alliance

Field Colony

Under the leadership of **Captain Hazelfur, the Reliable Earth**, Field Colony is a secluded colony that manages their own affairs quietly. Field Colony has several bases that are used at different times throughout the year to ensure that none of the fields are over-hunted.

Council: Forestleaf (Second), Swifttail (Elder), Mistysnow (Herbalist), Goldenpelt (Envoy)

Mentors: Mudnose, Spottedshadow, Timberleg (in training)

Keepers: Missingfoot, Meadowleap, Jaggedstripe, Ambereyes, Clayfur (in training)

Rangers: Fleetfoot, Graymist, Shadowclaw, Volefur, Fernface, Nightpool, Lilyfire, Thrushspots

New-Claws: Peach, Stone, Horse, Tabby

Kittens: Dark, Dawn

Field Colony

Marsh Colony

Under the leadership of **Captain Hawkshell, the Soaring Protector**, Marsh Colony has continued to closely follow the Ancestors' Law and its own traditions. The rangers of the marshes tread carefully to avoid threats both natural and superstitious.

Council: Leafstorm (Second), Whitefire (Elder), Rosethorn (Elder), Bramblefur (Elder), Mousetail (Envoy), Indigoeyes (Envoy), Kestrelsnap (Envoy), Sunfire (Envoy)

Mentors: Breezeheart, Birdflight, Wildfur (in training)

Herbalist: Smallpebble

Keepers: Shrewbelly, Starkpath, Frostshadow (in training)

Rangers: Blueflower, Crowstalker, Mudtrail, Tigerstripe, Halfmask, Falconswoop, Snowstorm

New-Claws: Boulder, Red, Ice, Pool

Kittens: Fog, Night, Lichen

Oak Colony

Under the leadership of **Captain Elmtail, the Steadfast Branch**, Oak Colony has gained influence in the affairs of the other colonies, particularly Marsh Colony. Always eager to prove themselves, rangers of the Oak-lands are often friendly and competitive.

Council: Brackenfoot (Second), Yellowflower (Elder), Birchwhisker (Elder), Redleaf (Envoy), Vinestripe (Envoy), Dawnfrost (Envoy), Hailstorm (Envoy)

Herbalist: Wrensong

Mentors: Stagcharge, Stonestep, Tornleg, Rowanstorm (in training), Snowfeather (in training)

Keepers: Gorseclaw, Finchflight, Dustclaw

Rangers: Frondsway, Swiftshadow, Thornheart, Shrewpelt

New-Claws: Lark, Aspen, Black, Frost, Oak, Moon, Fox

Kittens: Lilac, Orange, Sand

River Colony

Under the leadership of **Captain Rainfall, the Shimmering Star**, River Colony has rapidly undergone changes in its ranks. Many formerly respected rangers have seemingly left the colony, replaced by newcomers who are absolute in their loyalty to Captain Rainfall.

Council: Iceclaw (Second), Frozenpool (Elder), Creekbend (Elder), Rockyshore (Elder), Pineclaw (Envoy)

Mentors: Rapidsnap, Mistyclaw, Cherryrill, Ferneyes, Swiftmask (in training)

Rangers: Ripplepelt, Willowshade, Piketail, Silverblaze, Wolfthorn, Sedgestorm, Gillstripe, Eagledive, Skyfeather

Herbalist: Orangebrook (in training)

Keepers: Ashencreek, Blueriver, Minnowgill

New-Claws: Frozen, Talon, Falcon, Gray, Ivy, Moss, Lily

Kittens: Pine, Umber, Snow

A Warning on the Wind

"Be as sturdy as an ancient oak, as wild as an open field, as adaptable as a flowing river, and as guarded as the deepest marshes."
Alliance Lake Proverb

Summer announced its arrival with a gentle breath of dry air. The abundant season of warmth was on its way to Alliance Lake, the Green Moon finally full on the horizon. When it reached its zenith in the sky that night, the Moonlight Meeting would bring all the colonies together upon Moonlight Island to celebrate days of easy hunting and lazy nights spent under the stars.

The warm season was especially welcome in the shady forests of Oak Colony, where cats climbed trees and scaled cliffs as easily as they put one paw in front of the other on the ground.

Dawnfrost was not given to such things as omens or signs—she left that business to Thornheart—but even she would admit to being in brighter spirits than usual. Ever the early-riser, spring often meant returning from her duties with dew soaking her paws. Now the leaf litter beneath her feet was crisp and dry as she led her group along the highlands of Oak Colony's territory. Sunlight touched the Scrub Oak Terrace before it reached the more densely wooded areas in the lowlands, and Dawnfrost could already hear the chorus of songbirds rising from their nests to greet the morning.

Four cats followed her: Thornheart, her humble and trusted friend; Lark and Aspen, the new-claws they had trained together over the last several months; and Tornleg, the Mentor. Tornleg would oversee the final task the new-claws were to complete in order to earn their full names and ranks as rangers of the Oak-lands. This ritual had not changed since Dawnfrost's time, nor since Tornleg's, nor Captain Elmtail's. It was a tradition that spanned memory, all the way back to the first cats who had made the Oak-lands their home, who might be watching over them now—if one were given to believing such superstition.

Their pace slowed as they made their way up the cliff, careful not to give away their presence. Once they found feathers at their paws and the tantalizing smell of a flying feast in their noses, Dawnfrost signaled for the company to stop. She and Thornheart found dry places to sit and watch while Tornleg explained the challenge to Lark and Aspen.

"You may work together with your fellow new-claw to achieve your goal. In fact, teamwork is encouraged," Tornleg said. "You must bring back the following: a crow, black as night; a warbler, gold as day; a jay, blue as the sky; a sparrow, brown as the earth. You have until noon. Once the task begins, you are forbidden from speaking to any ranger until it is done. Do you have any questions?"

Lark's tail flicked up. Tornleg nodded to give him permission to speak. "Do we have to stay on the terrace," Lark began, "or can we range further into the Oak-lands?"

"You may leave the area, though all the species you need to hunt can be found here."

Lark shot a quick glance at Dawnfrost, who blinked her eyes slowly in a show of approval. Of the new-claw siblings, Lark was the thinker who asked questions and Aspen was the motivator who took action. Before they'd even begun, Lark was already calculating where in the territory it would be easiest to find each kind of bird.

"If there are no more questions, you may begin," Tornleg said. "Bring your collection to me when you are ready to stop."

At once, Lark and Aspen discussed their strategy, just loud enough to impress the rangers without being mistaken for asking advice.

"Sparrows and jays are plentiful right here. We'll get those out of the way first, then split up to get the others," Aspen said.

"I'll head to Copper Rock for the crow. My fur will blend into the shore better than yours," Lark said. "You get the warbler from the lowlands. The closer to the Marsh Colony border, the better—those ones are sure to be 'gold as day.'"

The sibling team butted their heads together, then slunk away into the bushes to track down the sparrow and the jay.

Once they were out of earshot, Thornheart let out a purr. "Remarkable. I think we came up with that exact plan of action when it was our turn. Only *you* had to show off by getting every kind of bird on your own, too!"

Dawnfrost curled her tail neatly around her paws and responded with only a smile. It was no secret that she'd had her sights on leadership from her first steps out of the nursery. The faster she was made an Envoy, the faster she would achieve her goals, and that meant standing out early and often.

The call of a crane pulled her from her reminiscing. She pricked up her ears, making sure she'd heard correctly. They were a long way from any free-flowing source of water where cranes might gather.

The high-pitched clattering sounded again, grabbing Thornheart's attention. He started to rise with an uneasy look on his face, but Dawnfrost beat him to it. "If that bird is so desperate to be caught, I think I'll try my luck at it. I want to do my part for the celebration, after all."

"If you're sure." Though still bemused at her reaction, Thornheart sat down again.

"Try to catch a finch for me, would you?" Tornleg said, then flopped inelegantly onto a sunny patch of ground.

Dawnfrost waved her tail in acknowledgement and headed down the terrace, toward Lilac Scarp. The delicate purple flowers interwoven in the dense blackberry thicket were sure to block out the smell of anything—or, rather, any*one*—caught on the wrong side of Alliance Lake.

"Not the most subtle sign," she remarked to the pale tabby tom who greeted her there.

His yellow eyes flashed with affection at her gentle scolding, and he responded in his usual laid-back tone as he stepped out of the thorn vines. "Hello, Dawnfrost. It's been a while."

"Wolfthorn." Despite her curt greeting, Dawnfrost could not deny herself the small pleasure of touching her nose to his once he was close enough. "You smell of River Colony. I suppose that means you didn't find a suitable place outside our borders for us to live?"

"I did. Several, actually. Alone and with other colonies." Wolfthorn lowered his voice. "We could leave tonight, if you wanted."

Dawnfrost should have hissed in disgust, but Wolfthorn's presence always made her reconsider what she wanted most. One path led her to greatness as Oak Colony's Captain, respected and admired by her fellow rangers. The other led her not to greatness, but to happiness as Wolfthorn's mate, free to pursue whatever kind of life they desired beyond colony borders.

She knew it was foolish. Only a kitten lovesick for romances from Elders' stories would consider it. But she had been young once, and Wolfthorn had captured her heart from the moment she'd met him at her first Moonlight Meeting. Though she had dreamed of leading a colony even then, she had allowed her mind to wander beyond Alliance Lake. There were other colonies out there. Who was to say that she and Wolfthorn couldn't lead one of them, or create one, with their own rules and beliefs? In Oak Colony, she would be part of a long history of leaders. In the lands beyond their borders, she could become a legend all her own.

Dawnfrost took a breath to prepare for her answer. She was not a new-claw anymore, and in the year since she had last seen Wolfthorn, her life had changed. It would soon change again. "Brackenfoot is sick."

"I'm sorry." Wolfthorn lowered his head. "But you didn't say that because you're worried about your father, did you?"

"No." Dawnfrost pressed her ears forward, determined. "Why must we leave the territory to be together? You could join Oak Colony. Captain Elmtail would welcome you once you completed the Sundown Challenge."

"No!" Wolfthorn's sharp hiss made Dawnfrost draw her ears back. He licked her cheek in apology. "We won't be safe here."

"You said that before, but you never told me what we wouldn't be safe from," Dawnfrost countered. "I'm an Envoy, Wolfthorn. An elite ranger. I'm strong; my colony is strong. What are you afraid of?"

Instead of answering, Wolfthorn rubbed his muzzle along Dawnfrost's neck and shoulder before turning back to the undergrowth. "I respect your choice, Dawnfrost. If you ever change your mind, I'll be ready." He glanced back one last time over his shoulder. "Please, stay safe."

"Wait!"

The moment Wolfthorn slipped into the shadows of the blackberry bush, his presence vanished from the forest, and Dawnfrost knew she was alone. She raised her nose to the wind to try to catch a lingering hint of Wolfthorn's scent, but found something foul in the air. She turned her head toward it and opened her mouth to inhale deeper, despite her nose wrinkling in disgust.

Something musky and rotten was drifting on the wind from Marsh Colony.

The gentle breeze drifting over the wide fields did little against the growing heat of the bright sun. Spottedshadow did not mind; her focus was on the two young cats in front of her as they sized each other up and planned their attacks.

Though she had been training Peach for more than two months, Spottedshadow had focused on hunting first. A ranger couldn't fight well on an empty stomach, and hunger was a crueler and more efficient killer than any predator. Plus, now that Stone was big enough to leave the safety of the Keeper's Weave and had been assigned to train under Timberleg, Peach finally had a suitable partner to spar with.

Peach feinted to the right. When Stone moved to meet her pretend-attack, she smacked his shoulder and gave him a hard shove. Stone tried to balance on his hind paws, but Peach headbutted him. His forepaws flailed uselessly as he fell into the tall grass. Peach sprang back, paws splayed and tail raised like a kitten at play.

"Good job, Peach! Solid first strike, and excellent follow-up," Spottedshadow said encouragingly. The thick mane of fur that ringed Peach's neck and chest fluffed out as she purred with pride.

"Back on your paws, Stone!" Timberleg, Stone's teacher, trotted over to the young tom and gave him an encouraging lick between his ears. "Can you tell me where you went wrong?"

"Umm..." Stone mumbled, batting at the grass and not making eye contact. "I, well, I got nervous..."

"Nervous? What for?" Peach tilted her head to one side. "It's just practice!"

"But the Spirits are watching!" Stone exclaimed, nodding up at the full moon that hovered in the sky. "What if they don't think I'm worthy of the colony? What if they send Mistysnow a sign to tell me to leave?"

Timberleg chuckled. "Oh, is that all?" He gave his ward a good-natured nudge. "The Spirits Beyond are always watching over us, and they are not looking for us to fail. I'm sure they, in all their wisdom, remember what it was like to be a young cat on his first day of field training."

"I think the Spirits Beyond are a lot more charitable than Hazelfur or Forestleaf would have you believe," Spottedshadow added. "After all, they allow outsiders to join the colony. Why would they cast out a cat who was born here? We're all cats of the Alliance, and every ranger makes the Alliance stronger."

Timberleg looked like he was about to agree with Spottedshadow, but instead he cut himself off and bowed his head. Stone followed his example, nearly shoving his nose into the dirt in his haste. "Good day, Forestleaf. Goldenpelt."

Spottedshadow whipped her head around, hoping the prickly Second hadn't heard her comments. The last thing she needed was to be in trouble with the Council again.

"Good day, Timberleg." Forestleaf arched her tail high above her head. "How lovely to see our newest Mentor hard at work training the next generation."

Spottedshadow's eyes widened. Was Forestleaf actually *praising* her?

"I trust \you will make our colony proud, Timberleg," Forestleaf continued.

Spottedshadow lowered her ears. She should have expected as much. Forestleaf would never offer praise for her, let alone to her face.

"Thank you, Forestleaf, but I'm still training to be a Mentor," Timberleg replied, looking as awkward and off-kilter as Stone. "You know, Spottedshadow has been a great example. I'm learning so much from her. She has a way with young cats that really brings out their potential! You should have seen Peach just now."

Forestleaf looked at Spottedshadow as if only just noticing her granddaughter's presence. "Quite." She cleared her throat. "I see you two have been busy. Captain Hazelfur sent me to inform you both that–against my better judgment–you and your new-claws will be attending the Moonlight Meeting tonight. Use your time this afternoon to prepare."

The tortoiseshell molly started away, but the golden tabby tom stayed behind. He nodded to Timberleg with approval. "You're doing a great job,

Timberleg. I expect nothing less from my former new-claw." His expression remained smug look when he turned to Spottedshadow, but his tail swept through the grass. "Spottedshadow. I hope you've been well. It seems I hardly see you at the base anymore."

Spottedshadow calculated her answer carefully. Whatever she said would make it back to Forestleaf, and her so-called *better judgments* were likely shared by the Envoy. "I've been helping the Keepers with the nursery during my spare time. Nightpool's kittens are due soon."

"I wish there were more kittens to play with *now*," Peach whined. "Horse and Tabby are going to start field training soon, so they don't want to play games anymore. All they talk about is which ranger they hope they're assigned to."

Goldenpelt's amber gaze softened when he looked at the young molly. He decided not to bring up the fact that his niece had *also* spoken of nothing else when she'd been in base training. "I'm sure they want to be the best rangers they can be. Just like you, right, Peachy-keen?"

Peach ducked her head into her thick mane of fur. "Don't call me that in front of Stone!"

"What? Too grown-up for that nursery name? How about Peachpit? If it sticks, it could be your ranger name."

"Uncle Golden!" Peach groaned, and he and Timberleg shared a look before snorting with laughter.

An amused purr built in Spottedshadow, along with a fondness for Goldenpelt that she had all but forgotten. The Envoy was usually so serious, always treading on Forestleaf's tail in his eagerness to do her bidding. It was hard to remember he could be fun, or that they had once shared restless nights talking about their dreams and playing games when they'd been new-claws themselves.

"Goldenpelt!" Forestleaf called, and the tabby tom stopped laughing at once. Spottedshadow nearly rolled her eyes at his abrupt change in attitude.

"On my way!" Goldenpelt shouted back. He lowered his voice and locked eyes with Spottedshadow. "It *is* a shame there aren't more kittens in Field Colony. Though there have been rumors regarding your recent absences from the Moonlight Meeting…"

The fur between Spottedshadow's shoulders bristled. "I will gladly prove the rumors false tonight."

Peach and Stone glanced worriedly between the rangers. Timberleg coughed loudly. "Well, it was good to see you, Uncle Golden. You'd better go before Forestleaf gets impatient. You know how she can be. We'll finish up and head back to base soon." He paused, thinking. "I suppose they can skip sprint drills for today, since they'll need their energy to stay awake tonight."

"Of course. I look forward to seeing you later."

Goldenpelt started down the hillside after Forestleaf, not breaking eye contact with Spottedshadow until the last possible second. She huffed, releasing her frustration in a single breath before giving Peach a smile.

Whatever Goldenpelt and Forestleaf's intentions, they were going to the Moonlight Meeting at last.

Wolfthorn extended his claws in a long, luxurious stretch as he slid from the shade of the mangrove forest. He sharpened his claws on a tangle of roots before slipping into the water. A quick swim across one of the many tributaries of the Alliance River that defined River Colony's territory brought him to the island that served as their base.

Though he'd been born there, Wolfthorn surveyed the area like he was investigating new land. The pale sand was uncomfortably hot under his paws in comparison to the soothing shadows he had come from moments before; after a day of baking in the sun, its trapped heat made it too intense to stand still on for long. The base itself was tucked away in the heart of the island, sheltered by boulders. It, too, was irritatingly sunny, but at least there was sparse grass to cool his paws and hibiscus bushes to curl up under for a nap.

Wolfthorn crept around the edge of the base, taking note of all the cats present. Blueriver sat by the new nursery, struggling to weave reeds and cattails into cover for her kittens. Captain Rainfall was no doubt lounging comfortably inside what *used* to be the nursery; she had recently announced the Spirits Beyond decreed it should be *her* den instead. Minnowgill attempted to help Blueriver, but as far as Wolfthorn could tell, she was quickly becoming frustrated with the fledgling Keeper. Wolfthorn couldn't blame her. Rainfall and Iceclaw had discouraged rangers from becoming Keepers, and even reassigned former Keepers to other roles. What few experienced Keepers remained hardly had time for weaving or tool-making, and less time to teach it to others. Blueriver was trying to build a whole new nursery and care for her young litter almost entirely on her own.

The kittens themselves weren't making things easier. Pine whimpered loudly any time a beam of light broke through the slapdash weave and struck his sensitive eyes. His fussing always made Umber and Snow cry, too.

Mistyclaw approached to offer help, but Blueriver took one look at her large, pregnant belly and sent her away to sunbathe beside Gillstripe. A quick exchange of words between them had Gillstripe taking his mate's place, holding reeds still while Blueriver's adept paws strung thin cattail stalks between them. Unable to match her, Minnowgill watched closely to learn her technique.

Blueriver's own mate, Pineclaw, sat some distance away, looking self-important. He barked orders at a pair of new-claws who were trying to enjoy a fish in the shade of one of the sunning boulders. They jumped to their feet at once to carry out his command, but Wolfthorn could see the unhappiness on their faces as soon as Pineclaw's back was turned. Wolfthorn didn't know their names. Much had changed in his months-long journey away from home; cats he'd known had died or mysteriously left, while others had been born. Then there was Pineclaw himself, a former Unbound who had joined the colony from outside.

A deep mew drew his attention, though he showed it with only the tilt of one ear. "Where have you been all day?"

"Nowhere, really." Wolfthorn adopted his usual easy manner of speaking to respond to Swiftmask. The gray pointed tom was a little more loyal to the rules than Wolfthorn would have liked, but they had known each other since they were kittens. If Swiftmask ever became a threat to him, then there was no hope left for River Colony.

"Iceclaw was asking about you," Swiftmask said. "I know you've only been back a month, but you need to get used to being in a colony again. Leaving without permission doesn't look good. I don't know if I'll be able to keep covering your tracks."

"You worry too much," Wolfthorn replied, though in all honesty he wondered if maybe Swiftmask should be worrying more. He trusted Swiftmask, but Wolfthorn didn't know if he could trust Swiftmask *enough* to reveal all he knew. At worst, Swiftmask might raise his concerns to Rainfall in a well-meaning but disastrous show of colony loyalty. At best, Wolfthorn might make Swiftmask into a target for their Captain's cruelty. Wolfthorn couldn't expect Swiftmask to lie or pretend nothing was wrong as easily as he could.

Swiftmask frowned. "You should at least be here for Gray."

Wolfthorn gave his pelt a noncommittal shake. If anything, staying away from Gray was the best thing he could do for the new-claw. He had no doubt Rainfall had paired them to either keep an eye on Wolfthorn, or to provide a convenient excuse to get rid of Gray should the need ever arise.

"River Colony, meet at the Sentry Stone!"

Wolfthorn's ears flattened at Rainfall's piercing yowl. Swiftmask pretended not to notice and pushed him toward the throng of cats answering the speckled silver molly's summons. Once she had her audience, Rainfall continued.

"During the full moon, the Spirits Beyond speak to me even more clearly. They have sent me a sign!" She paused, allowing gasps of surprise and anticipation to ripple through the crowd. "It is my great pleasure to relay their message to you, my colony. Swiftmask, come forward!"

Wolfthorn bristled. Swiftmask brushed his tail against Wolfthorn's shoulder as he moved closer to the Sentry Stone and Rainfall. Those already there made room for him, leaving him to stand alone against the Captain and Second.

"Congratulations, Swiftmask," Rainfall purred. "The Spirits Beyond have chosen you to be River Colony's newest Mentor!"

Again she waited for the wave of shocked reactions and uncomfortable cheers to flow through the River-landers. Wolfthorn dug his claws into the soft ground. Everyone knew Swiftmask wanted to be an Envoy, not a Mentor. Even if he never boasted or acted superior—unlike some other Envoys Wolfthorn could name—his natural leadership and genuine care for every member of the colony made his path clear to anyone who knew him. He hadn't even trained a new-claw yet; it made no sense to make him a Mentor.

"Oh–I'm honored, Captain Rainfall! I will do my best to serve River Colony and train our young cats," Swiftmask answered.

"I trust that you will not let me down. After all, I see just as well as the Spirits. Your efforts in managing Gray's training have not gone unnoticed." Rainfall curled her tail around her paws and looked over her colony. Wolfthorn met her icy stare with his own, a message passing between them in the brief seconds before Rainfall moved on from him. Swiftmask's appointment as a Mentor was *his* fault.

Rainfall's gaze snapped forward again. "Moss!"

Wolfthorn glanced over to see Sedgestorm and Willowshade nudge a brown tabby molly to her feet. She stumbled forward to a chorus of laughter from the other young cats, and stood uneasily beside Swiftmask. "Y-yes, Captain Rainfall?"

Rainfall cleared her throat dramatically, making sure she had every cat's attention.

"I have been watching you, and it is time for you to begin your field training as a ranger of River Colony." Moss perked up right away when she heard that. "Swiftmask, I am placing you in charge of Moss's training. I have every confidence that you will teach her to be as loyal and hard-working as you are. You are both dismissed to begin training at once. Moss will be presented to the Alliance at the Moonlight Meeting tonight, and I want her ready."

Swiftmask lowered his head as a show of acknowledgement and respect, but Moss was too excited for that. She ran back to Willowshade and Sedgestorm. "Mom! Dad! I'm going to the Moonlight Meeting!"

Sedgestorm sighed before giving his kitten's cheek a lick, and Willowshade whispered something to Moss. The new-claw ducked her head in embarrassment and mumbled a reply that Wolfthorn couldn't hear.

The rest of the meeting was more of Rainfall's grandstanding, and a complete waste of Wolfthorn's time. He kept an ear out for his name during the announcement of which cats would attend the Moonlight Meeting–and was surprised to hear it actually called. Other than that, he could have thought of a dozen better things to do than listen to Rainfall go on and on about how the Spirits had blessed the colony.

"I suppose we will be training new-claws together from now on," Swiftmask said when he rejoined Wolfthorn, putting on a happy face. There was no time for disappointment when a rambunctious young molly was waiting for her first task. "Moss and Gray will get along well, I think. Should we take them for a quick lesson?"

"Sure," Wolfthorn answered. "Let's head up to the Marsh Colony border. I thought I smelled something odd over there earlier." He neglected to mention that he'd been on Oak Colony land at the time. He signaled to his own new-claw to join them, and Gray gave a quick goodbye purr to his father before trotting over.

"Marsh Colony?" Moss gaped, then broke into a wide smile. "Ha-ha! Did you hear that?" She sneered at a calico new-claw who had laughed at her earlier. "*I'm* going to check out another colony *and* go to the Moonlight Meeting on my *first day* of field training!"

Effortlessly, the calico retorted, "Good thing you have the half-Marsh going with you!"

Wolfthorn narrowed his eyes at the jab, but Gray gave no indication that he heard her teasing. He gave his thick, bushy pelt a shake and fell in line beside Wolfthorn.

"Lily is so *rude*! I mean, why would being half Marsh-lander even matter?" Moss grumbled as the four cats swam the short distance to the mainland.

For a moment Wolfthorn's heart was unexpectedly light. If young cats like Moss and Gray would guide the future, perhaps there was still a chance for River Colony to be *truly* great. Evidently, Moss didn't believe Rainfall's yowling about the superiority of River Colony over the rest of the Alliance, or the horrible rumors she spread to discredit her rivals.

Then Moss continued. "Captain Rainfall lets you stay, so you must be a loyal River-lander, not like your mother–"

"Moss!" Swiftmask snapped.

Again, Gray showed no indication that he'd heard the not-so-subtle taunt. Wolfthorn resisted a sigh of contempt as his hopes were dashed.

Dusk crept along the western shore of Alliance Lake like a predator prowling through the undergrowth. The Green Moon blazed as bright as the sun, transforming the shadows in the Marsh-lands into something deep and dangerous, like the quicksand that littered its swamps and bogs.

Wildfur was content to lurk at the edge of Marsh Colony's base. While the rest of the colony had woken from their daytime slumber to eat, groom, and excitedly prepare for the Moonlight Meeting, Wildfur lowered his chin to his crossed paws. No one was going to ask anything of him that night, so he saw no point in waking at all.

Unfortunately, the incessant chatter of the Marsh-landers stopped him from getting back to sleep.

"I hope I get assigned to Birdflight!" a white-and-gray molly squeaked.

"You can have them. I want Breezeheart to train me!" Another kitten–her brother, if Wildfur had to guess–exclaimed far too loudly.

Wildfur turned his head away and covered his ears with a frustrated groan. There were so few young cats in Marsh Colony, he had almost forgotten that the full moon meant more than just the Moonlight Meeting. They would begin their field training that night, and be taken to their first Moonlight Meeting to be presented to the Alliance.

Wildfur was pleased at the idea of having a mostly empty base to himself, if only they would hurry up and leave.

"Oh! There's Captain Hawkshell!" the molly squealed.

"Be on your best behavior, you two," Kestrelsnap mewed.

"Of course! We'll make you proud!" the tom kitten purred.

Wildfur stood to move further away, even if it took him beyond the border of the base. He couldn't block out their voices, so he'd go somewhere he didn't have to hear them.

Bitterness twisted his gut, stinging like thistles. He was distantly aware that this was a problem he should talk to someone about, but who in the Marsh-lands could he possibly turn to? Captain Hawkshell was far too busy to trouble herself with the emotional needs of a low-ranking ranger. Leafstorm had never liked him, and had even less patience for him now that she'd been named Second. Smallpebble was a skilled healer when it came to physical wounds, but was otherwise absorbed in her own little world of cultivating fungi. He hadn't been able to talk to his parents, Blueflower and Crowstalker, without devolving into a shouting match since before he'd been made a ranger.

There was only one cat he could open up to. Almost without meaning to, Wildfur looked toward the lake, even though he couldn't see it through the trees. All the way across the lake, there was Spottedshadow–his one true friend and mate. She would listen to his troubles and confide her own to him, and they'd each know they weren't as alone as they felt in their own colonies.

"Where do you think you're going?"

Wildfur rolled his eyes at the sound of Leafstorm's demanding mew. He didn't dignify her question with a response, and she didn't wait for one. "Captain Hawkshell is about to speak to the colony. We all need to be present."

The temptation to resist was strong. Whether Wildfur was chosen to attend the Moonlight Meeting or not mattered little to him, since Spottedshadow hadn't been there in months. He would either sit by himself at the edge of the base or sit by himself at the edge of Moonlight Island. However, getting into a fight with Leafstorm required more energy than he had to give.

"Fine," he muttered, following the pale brown tabby toward the Captain's Den, where Hawkshell made her announcements. At one time it had been a massive redwood tree, but lightning had felled the forest giant and petrified its wood. The other rangers slept under the fallen remains of that same tree, and a few hollowed out branches provided shelter for Marsh Colony's kittens and Elders. Now, the whole colony sat among the exposed roots in front of the opening of the Captain's Den to listen eagerly.

Wildfur kept to the outside of the meeting, one paw barely touching the end of a root. Leafstorm scoffed at his halfhearted gesture before making her way to Hawkshell's side.

For once, there was a bit of warmth in Hawkshell's commanding yowl.

"It is my privilege as your Captain to announce that tonight, two of our young cats will take their first steps toward becoming rangers. I have discussed plans for their training with our fine Mentors, Birdflight and Breezeheart." Her one eye scanned the crowd and she nodded to Birdflight, then blinked in surprise when she failed to find the other Mentor. "Where is Breezeheart?"

"I saw him and Sunfire leave the base this morning. Maybe they decided to sleep out-of-base and are on their way back," Falconswoop said.

Unease spread through the crowd despite Falconswoop's confident suggestion. Sunfire missing a meeting was nothing out of the ordinary, but Breezeheart hadn't stopped trying to prove he belonged in Marsh Colony since the day he and Crowstalker had joined. Breezeheart had also never stopped bothering Wildfur about being a more outgoing ranger, worrying over the actions of his nephew like they would reflect on his own status in the colony.

As if sensing the unrest, the dusk scouting group returned at that moment with a sharp cry of, "Captain!"

"Report, Halfmask," Hawkshell answered, her claws sliding out of their sheaths on instinct. Wildfur's pelt bristled despite himself, the few matted patches pulling at his skin with sharp pricks of pain.

"There's been an attack," Halfmask answered between panting breaths. "We followed Sunfire's trail along the Oak Colony border, and we found..."

He shuddered. "I'm sorry, Captain. We found Sunfire and Breezeheart dead."

"Sunfire..." Hawkshell's single eye clouded with grief for a moment. "Are you suggesting Oak Colony is responsible for this?"

"No. Their wounds were too severe to have come from any cat, and there was an odd scent in the area. It was unlike anything I have ever seen or smelled before." Halfmask's fur still stood on end, despite his attempts to keep his voice calm. "Tigerstripe and Snowstorm are bringing their bodies now. I had Blueflower hang back to cover the trail, and I will help her as soon as I'm dismissed."

"Go now," Hawkshell said. Halfmask dipped his head before fleeing up the fallen log and out of the base again. The Captain cleared her throat before continuing. "Until we know more about this threat, no one is to leave the base alone. I will warn the other colonies tonight at the Moonlight Meeting." She paused again, until her voice gave away no hint of emotion. "Captain Elmtail has told me that Oak Colony weaves thorns into their nursery's defenses. I would like us to do the same until the danger has passed. Keepers, see to it."

"At once, Captain Hawkshell!" Shrewbelly said, rushing to the nursery where his young kitten was blissfully asleep, unaware that anything was wrong.

"I want two Envoys to stay in the base when Leafstorm and I are not here. Indigoeyes and Mousetail, I'm afraid you will have to miss the Meeting tonight," Hawkshell went on.

"It's no trouble, Captain. We'll keep Marsh Colony safe in your absence," Mousetail said.

Indigoeyes nuzzled the white-and-gray kittens who had been eagerly awaiting the announcement of their field training. "Sorry I won't get to be there to introduce you to the other colonies, but you'll have your mother and Birdflight."

"Yes, what about the new-claws?" Birdflight asked.

Hawkshell blinked, her gaze distant. "Birdflight, you're our only Mentor now, so you will have to oversee their training yourself, and personally train Ice."

Earlier in the evening, this would have probably made Ice emit a high-pitched shriek that would have hurt Wildfur's ears. Now she only shifted to stand by Birdflight, and the older white-and-gray-spotted cat curled their tail around Ice. The other kitten looked around nervously. Without Breezeheart to train him, who would he be assigned to?

"Wildfur."

The shaggy-furred tom pinned his ears back. Was this it? Had Hawkshell finally decided he wasn't worth keeping around, that banishing him from the colony was the best choice? If only Field Colony accepted full-grown outsiders into their ranks, he would have left of his own accord ages ago.

"The Mentors and I spent some time discussing it this morning, and we agreed you will be the one to train Pool as your first task toward becoming a Mentor."

Pool's mouth fell open. "What? But, but I–!" The white-and-gray tom stopped his sputtered protest at Leafstorm's warning growl.

"Hold on. Why wasn't I asked about this?" Wildfur demanded. He had never wanted more than the life of a simple ranger, and he'd barely wanted that to begin with. What was Hawkshell thinking by making him a Mentor?

"Are you questioning your Captain's orders?" Leafstorm hissed.

"Yes, I am," Wildfur snapped back.

Hawkshell silenced Leafstorm with a glare before the small molly could get into an argument with Wildfur in front of the whole colony.

"The original plan was to have Breezeheart monitor your training of Pool and decide afterward if you would be a good Mentor. Now, there is no choice; Birdflight cannot do all of a Mentor's duties by himself. They will need help, and despite your...hesitance, I think additional responsibilities will serve you well," Hawkshell explained.

Pool practically trembled when Wildfur looked at him. Wildfur snorted. "If you say so."

"I do," Hawkshell said.

Rustling near the top of the hollow announced the arrival of Tigerstripe and Snowstorm. They did not come too close to the fallen log that led into the base, just in case the reek of blood drew predators into the heart of Marsh Colony. Besides, the bodies had a long journey to make it to the Delta of the Dead; it wouldn't be sensible to drop them in the hollow only to drag them back out again.

Leafstorm looked up at her Captain. Hawkshell's age rarely showed, her naturally gray fur and stern expression hiding the signs of passing time. Now, with sorrow weighing more heavily on her than gravity ever could, the fading of Hawkshell's dark gray fur to silver around her muzzle and the frayed patches around her shoulders were more apparent.

"Leafstorm, please announce which cats will attend the Moonlight Meeting. Kestrelsnap, Falconswoop, Crowstalker, and I shall deliver these fine rangers to their final resting place before meeting you at the Crossing Log tonight."

"Yes, Captain." Leafstorm took Hawkshell's place to address the colony as the burly gray molly ran up the log and out of the base, her selected rangers following close behind. No one wanted to be out in the funerary swamp after dark any longer than was necessary.

The small Second was keenly aware of how out of place she was standing in front of the Captain's Den. She raised her voice and barked out the orders.

"Guarding our home is top priority until we know what happened. Wildfur and Pool will come to the Moonlight Meeting; we can't risk both Mentors leaving at the same time. I'll lead our group to the Crossing Log to meet with Hawkshell's group. Everyone else, help the Keepers reinforce the base and stay alert for anything out of the ordinary."

The crowd dispersed to their tasks, leaving behind the cats who were to attend the Meeting.

Pool stared enviously at Birdflight and Ice, the pair already chatting amicably about training and what they would do the following morning. Birdflight broke from their pep talk and gave Wildfur a pointed look, nodding toward Pool.

Wildfur grumbled under his breath, "Might as well, I guess." Louder, he called, "Hey. It's Pool, right?"

"Y-yes?" The scrawny kitten nearly leapt out of his fur.

It occurred to the big tom that he didn't know the first thing to say to the young cat. He settled on a straightforward introduction. "I'm Wildfur."

"I know...?"

Wildfur sighed. The coming months were going to be far too long.

The Moonlight Meeting

"One is a target, two is a pair, three is a team, four is an alliance."
  Alliance Proverb

"Countless generations ago, the world was ruled by magic.

"For a time, everything flourished. Lush forests and fields sheltered more prey than you could ever dream of hunting. Though it never rained, creeks and rivers ran with the coolest, most refreshing water you could ever hope to taste. Winters were short and summers gentle. All was at peace.

"But, as always happens when there is plenty, some began to covet more than they needed. Certain colonies learned they could use magic to make their pelts hard as stone, their claws burn like fire, their teeth venomous as a snake's. The magic that once made the world bountiful and beautiful was used to scorch the land, raise impassable mountains, and yes, my dears, even kill without cause.

"Some colonies had no magic at all. They were seen as inferior creatures, and were hunted without mercy. Though it is our nature to fight for what is ours, our Ancestors knew they stood no chance against such fearsome powers. They were forced to flee, far from their home, until they could run no further.

"When our Ancestors were met with the ocean, they knew they would have to stand and fight. They called upon the Spirits of those who had come before, in the name of the Spirits who would come after, to help them win the fight against their terrible foes.

"Then, the miracle happened. While they took refuge on this very island, preparing to defend it with all their might, the sun turned dark! The moon had come in front of it, casting a mighty shadow across the land. Wherever the moon's shadow touched, magic failed its wielders. Without their unearned advantages, the enemy quickly fell to our Ancestors' humble teeth and claws. But our Ancestors were not cruel; they allowed the enemy to retreat into the barren wilderness they had created for themselves. The mages blamed each other, and their groups fell apart. They became Unbound, and wandered the wastes alone.

"We named this land Alliance Lake, in honor of the colonies who came together to protect each other. Ever since that day, our colonies have shared this territory as the Alliance."

Yellowflower lifted her graying muzzle toward the fallen tree that served as the bridge from the mainland to Moonlight Island. "And here they come, now. Can you tell which colony these cats belong to?"

The Oak Colony new-claws sitting around the old molly jumped to their feet, nearly knocking themselves over as they spun to follow her gaze.

If the young cats could not have guessed from the grassy smell of the hills and the smear of pollen that clung to the newcomers, the long-legged black molly who stepped down from the log with dainty paws would have given them away. Field Colony was known for being sleek and slender, and Spottedshadow was an exceptional example–the fluffy orange-and-cream calico bouncing at her side, less so.

Captain Elmtail purred in greeting from his perch in the great tree that grew from the center of the island. At this time of year, its many different leaves were spread wide to welcome all. What the tree had originally been, no one could say; when the Alliance had first formed and banished magic from the land, the tree itself had transformed. Oak, eucalyptus, cypress, and maple leaves sprouted side by side on the ancient, twisted branches. Elmtail had chosen his place on a thick branch beside a clump of oak leaves, to honor his colony.

The old tom adjusted his position to let Captain Hazelfur ascend to his post more easily. Despite leading Field Colony, the cream tom was of much shorter and squatter stature, and his permanent scowl dared anyone to mention it. He preferred a lower perch; Field-landers liked to be as close to the ground as possible. He acknowledged Elmtail with a curt nod and curled his thin tail over his paws.

"I am pleased to see you again, Captain Hazelfur," Elmtail started in an attempt to strike up friendly conversation. "I was surprised that Oak Colony was the first to arrive tonight, given your usual punctuality."

"There was a disagreement over which rangers should attend," Hazelfur answered in a tone that informed Elmtail the conversation was to end there. However, Elmtail had not received his rank for no reason. He followed Hazelfur's line of sight to his Second-in-Command, Forestleaf.

Forestleaf was not so inelegant as to *sulk* at the roots of the tree, but she had certainly made her foul mood known to the red patched tom whom she assumed must be Elmtail's new Second-in-Command, as old Brackenfoot was nowhere to be seen. Her green eyes narrowed on her insolent granddaughter, who was already chattering away like a spring sparrow to two Oak-landers.

In Forestleaf's opinion, Spottedshadow had not earned the right to return to the Meeting for exactly this reason. She was too open with cats from other colonies, and the last thing Forestleaf wanted was for her new-claw, Peach, to pick up that bad habit. Hazelfur, however, had insisted that Spottedshadow return when rumors began to spread that she was absent because she was carrying Goldenpelt's kittens.

Forestleaf had seen no reason to discourage the rumors. Field Colony had not been blessed with many kittens in recent months, since the few litters that were born had been smaller than average. From a practical standpoint, the Council should encourage those who could to have more kittens. It wasn't as though Forestleaf had asked Spottedshadow to take Goldenpelt as her mate forever.

Regardless, the white-spotted molly had not taken kindly to Forestleaf's logical suggestion, and Hazelfur had taken Spottedshadow's side. Now the senseless molly was present with impunity, purring and rubbing her pelt with cats whose names she should *hardly* remember, and being a horrible example to Peach. As a Mentor, Spottedshadow should be showing Peach how to properly behave at a Meeting, how to listen for hidden meanings in reports from the other colonies, and how to best represent the Field-lands, as Timberleg and Goldenpelt were doing with Stone.

While the tortoiseshell molly silently fumed, Redleaf tried his best to look composed and noble. This was his first Meeting as Oak Colony's Second-in-Command, and he was determined to fill the pawprints that Brackenfoot had left. While the sable-pointed tom had never been the most popular cat in the Alliance, he had been respected throughout the colonies for his practical sense and skill in strategizing. Redleaf felt he was the complete opposite: well-liked, but perhaps not well-respected.

He had been aware of Dawnfrost's eyes on him since they arrived. Though the ginger pointed molly was now talking with her friends, Thornheart and Spottedshadow, she kept stealing glances at the position the Seconds took at the base of the tree. Redleaf knew how badly she'd wanted to take her father's place as Second, and he was sure she would be a great Captain someday. He'd known that ever since he'd overseen her field training. However, she was still young. She had many years left of service in her, and at least a few to spare before she had to bear the responsibility of caring for an entire colony.

If Dawnfrost had been having such thoughts—and she most certainly had—she set them aside when the flood of River-landers, including Wolfthorn, arrived. Thornheart subtly excused himself so Wolfthorn could join their group while Thornheart himself went to talk with Wrensong and Smallpebble. Dawnfrost's interest was further piqued when she saw that Wolfthorn brought a few other River-landers with him.

Moss was so taken with her surroundings that she hardly paid any mind to the rangers' greetings. From afar, the island almost looked like a pawful of the Oak-lands had been clawed away and pushed across the water. Up close, it was so much more than that.

The stars came down from the sky as fireflies, spreading warm light throughout the treetops that lined the central clearing. The air was heavily scented—not just with the smell of the other colonies, but with the aroma of dozens of flowers in full bloom. Bushes and ferns offered plenty of places for cats to challenge each other to hiding and stalking games. Moss could already spot some new-claws and young rangers chasing each other around. An Oak Colony new-claw had found a crab, and a group had formed to take turns seeing who dared get their paw the closest to its pincers. She longed to join them, but she'd been instructed by Captain Rainfall to stay close to Swiftmask and Wolfthorn. She didn't want to mess up on her first day as a new-claw; what if the Spirits changed their minds and sent her back to base training?

"Come on, Moss, introduce yourself!" Swiftmask poked her side with his cold nose.

Moss whipped her head around so fast, Swiftmask worried she might have hurt herself. She blinked up at the unfamiliar rangers and offered a shy nod.

"So, did Wolfthorn say that right, Swiftmask? You've been made a Mentor?" Dawnfrost asked.

"I just started training," Swiftmask answered, shuffling his paws on the sandy ground. "Spottedshadow, you've been inducted as a full Mentor, haven't you? If you have any pointers, I'd appreciate it. I want to show Rainfall she was right to trust me with this position."

"Well..." Spottedshadow paused, and Moss's attention slipped away from the rangers. She knew she should be listening and learning, but there was far too much happening around her to focus on the normal and, frankly, boring conversations of adults.

"Finally, Marsh Colony is here!" an Oak-lander farther inland announced.

"A little late, aren't they?" Dawnfrost murmured to Wolfthorn, who gave a hasty nod.

Spottedshadow abandoned her advice to Swiftmask mid-sentence, and instead searched the crowd of burly Marsh-land cats for her tom. Wildfur was never difficult to spot, with his larger-than-average size–even for a Marsh Colony cat–and cinnamon calico pelt.

A purr rose from her chest and through her throat as he stepped off the Crossing Log. His brow was knit in his usual scowl, until he saw her. As soon as they made eye contact, Wildfur transformed into a different cat entirely, one free of the troubles that plagued him while in his colony. Spottedshadow wondered if she, too, looked more youthful and carefree when he was near her. If she had bothered to ask Peach, who was giggling at the sight of their obvious affection, she would have known the answer to that question.

Wildfur walked directly to the slender molly, not bothering to acknowledge anyone else on his way. Spottedshadow touched his nose with hers. "It's good to see you, Wildfur."

"You're finally back." Wildfur purred, a deep rumble, and brushed his cheek against hers. Spottedshadow leaned into him, ignoring the uncomfortable expression on Dawnfrost's face and Swiftmask's scoff at their display. "I was starting to think you would never come again."

Dawnfrost cleared her throat. "I see you have a new-claw too, Wildfur."

Spottedshadow's attention was immediately on the small gray-and-white tom standing nervously behind Wildfur. "That's fantastic! Hawkshell has never put you in charge of training before."

"Hawkshell came up with some scheme behind my back to train me up as a Mentor. Guess she decided it was time I started contributing more than prey." Wildfur shook a bit of moss from his thick pelt. "We'll see how that goes."

"What's your name? I'm Peach, from Field Colony!" The fluffy calico charged right into a conversation with the thin tom, who immediately relaxed upon talking to someone his own age.

"My name's Pool–" he started, but was swiftly interrupted by Moss.

"Why are you so small?" the brown tabby demanded. She looked Wildfur up and down before turning to Pool with an accusatory tone. "Shouldn't Marsh Colony cats be big and scary?"

"I just started field training today!" Pool shot back, though he tried to stand taller all the same.

"So did I, but I don't look like a scared mouse," Moss teased.

"*Moss!*" Swiftmask scolded.

"Sorry!" Moss said, but she was still laughing under her breath. Even Peach couldn't resist a little chuckle.

Pool didn't find it funny at all. He muttered angrily, "How would a River-lander even know what a mouse looks like?"

Gray broke the tension by giving Moss a gentle swat, which started the two of them play-fighting. Peach jumped in at once, and after Pool observed for a moment, he joined the tussle. Wolfthorn watched with a pang of nostalgia, remembering when he, Spottedshadow, and Dawnfrost used to play the same way. Whatever else was going on around them, at least the young cats could still have fun at the Meeting. Perhaps too much fun, if the yelp from the beach and the raucous laughter that followed from the River Colony new-claws was any indication.

"Attention, cats of the Alliance! The announcements are about to begin!"

Cats who had been exploring the island returned to settle beneath the ancient tree in the clearing. The new-claws paused their play fighting. Usually there was more time for the colonies to mingle and the Captains to talk amongst themselves before the announcements, especially during spring and summer, when the weather was fair. Moonlight Meetings lasted as long as the moon shone overhead; some lasted only a few moments in the calm of a passing storm, while others went on until nearly sunrise.

Ever impatient, Captain Rainfall went first. Even Spottedshadow, who respected most cats from other colonies, couldn't help but bristle at the River Colony Captain's haughty attitude when she spoke.

"River Colony *prospers* this spring! How could it not? Mistyclaw and Gillstripe are expecting a large litter to be born soon. We will have to start expanding the new-claws' den! I've had to name Swiftmask as a Mentor to keep up with our *flourishing* colony."

As a show of unity, all present cats cheered for the success of River Colony. Wolfthorn, however, remained silent. For as many rangers-in-training as there were in the River-lands, he knew there should be more. He had heard whispers of kittens being pushed to start swimming too soon and dying from it. No one wanted to talk about it, but every so often one of the new-claws' parents would slip up and mention their lost children. Wolfthorn had tried to commit their names to memory, but there were too many to keep track of when they had not even been grieved properly.

Not to be outdone, Hazelfur raised himself up next. "Spring brings blessings to all of us, not just River Colony. We are ready and waiting to welcome Nightpool's kittens within the coming month, and Mistysnow has assured me it will be a large litter. Clayfur and Thrushspots completed their border watch during the last full moon, and are here now at their first Moonlight Meeting as rangers of the Field-lands. Our new-claws in field training, Peach and Stone, are here tonight for the first time as well."

Peach almost disappeared into her fluff when the other new-claws enthusiastically called her name and brushed against her. Spottedshadow gave her an encouraging lick on the ear and she poked her head out like a turtle. The sight made Moss roll with laughter.

Elmtail glanced at Hawkshell to see if she would like to speak next. When she remained silent, he began his own announcements, his creaking voice reminiscent of a tree branch moving in the wind. "Oak Colony is blessed with two new rangers guarding our border tonight: Larkwing and Aspenbreeze. They have trained with the best to become rangers of the Oak-lands, and we have high hopes for their futures.

"However," Elmtail continued in a more somber tone, "we have also suffered a loss today. Our Second of many seasons, Brackenfoot, has joined the Spirits Beyond due to a longstanding illness. I have chosen Redleaf to take his place and become my next Second."

Few rangers could bring themselves to call out his name in enthusiastic cheers, given the circumstances of his promotion. Most settled for a more reserved, "Congratulations," which Redleaf accepted with a bowed head. Dawnfrost quietly curled her tail over her paws.

"We have chosen to take the timing of his passing as a good omen, though we welcome any cats outside Oak Colony to mourn with us on the new moon if they so desire," Elmtail finished. "Captain Hawkshell, will you please conclude the announcements?"

Hawkshell rose to her full height slowly. Though she was nearly as old as Elmtail, she rarely looked it. That night, the moonlight seemed to highlight every dulling gray hair around her muzzle.

"Cats of the Alliance, I do not bring any good news tonight."

Several cats' eyes widened, and a few shot quick glances at Wildfur and Pool. The shaggy tom did not seem bothered by the Captain's words, nor did Pool complain. Instead the gray-and-white tom's gaze was fixed on Hawkshell, taking in her every word as though the Spirits themselves were speaking.

"There is danger in our midst," Hawkshell declared, her long claws sinking into the maple branch. "Two rangers were killed today: Breezeheart and...and Sunfire." She broke off, giving herself time to breathe, and the cats beneath her a chance to express their surprise and grief, before she continued. "We do not know what killed them—"

"It was a badger! We ran one from our territory just this morning," Rainfall huffed.

"Hold your tongue, you prideful toad!" Hawkshell roared, the fur along her back rising. "Could a mere badger maul a ranger until his *own mother* could barely recognize him?"

Shocked gasps and worried whispers filled the crowd. Wolfthorn snorted under his breath, "If the badger's name is Iceclaw..."

"Shh!" Swiftmask hissed. "This is serious, Wolfthorn. Two rangers are dead!"

"I'm being serious," Wolfthorn replied, and Swiftmask shook his head in disbelief. The pointed tom glanced at Moss, hoping she hadn't heard Wolfthorn. The tabby molly was transfixed by the arguing Captains, oblivious to the cats she was meant to be watching.

Despite the balmy weather, a chill raced through Spottedshadow. Sunfire and Breezeheart hadn't been inexperienced rangers fresh out of their new-claw training. Breezeheart was a wise cat, and Sunfire commanded respect across the Alliance for his skill and bravery in battle. Their deaths made the whole Alliance weaker. She leaned into Wildfur's side, and he rested his chin on top of her head to soothe her.

The fireflies took shelter under leaves and dimmed their glow. Thin, wispy clouds crowded together above, blotting out the moonlight. Soon, the island was swallowed by shadows.

Elmtail shook out his unkempt fur. "The Spirits send a sign. This Moonlight Meeting must be at an end."

"Please, I urge you all to make your way back to your homes quickly, and guard them well," Hawkshell warned.

Rainfall scoffed once more. "The River Colony base is *always* well-guarded." Not bothering with any kind of formal farewell to the other Captains, she leapt down from the tree and headed for the Crossing Log. Her brutish Second, Iceclaw, followed close behind, snarling at anyone who stood in their way.

Hazelfur was next to leave the tree, though he wasn't in any hurry to return to the Field-lands. Marsh Colony lay on the opposite side of the lake, and their troubles concerned him least when it came to getting involved in other colonies' affairs. Whatever had attacked the unfortunate rangers would need to travel through Oak or River Colony to reach the Field-lands, and he would have plenty of warning before it arrived.

Once the other Captains had departed, Elmtail approached Hawkshell. He could see the way she trembled, her claws leaving gouges on the bark. He lifted his muzzle under her chin, and she allowed herself to rest and accept comfort from her old friend. The mere thought of anything happening to his own son struck Elmtail with fear and anguish; he could only imagine what agony Hawkshell was going through in losing her only child.

"Marsh Colony will stay strong," Hawkshell said.

"And Oak Colony will support them," Elmtail replied. "For now, I'd best get my rangers home. One of my Envoys picked up an odd scent coming from the direction of your border earlier today–it may have come from whatever is responsible for your rangers' deaths. We will investigate in the morning."

"We shall walk with you. I do not feel up to traveling through the River-lands at the moment."

The two Captains leapt down, signaling for their colonies to join them at the Crossing Log.

Were it not for Pool, Wildfur would have ignored the summons to steal a few more moments with Spottedshadow, but the young tom looked anxious enough as it was. Wildfur settled on touching her nose with his. He brushed their cheeks together, taking in as much of her as he could while she wreathed herself around him.

"Please take care of yourself," she whispered.

"We will see each other again. This reunion was too short," he answered with a purr.

Somehow he dragged himself away, crossing the bridge and following after his colony, each step like wading through thick mud. He looked back over his shoulder only once, but instead of Spottedshadow's beautiful green eyes, he was met with Goldenpelt's venomous amber glare.

Deadly Discovery

"The measure of a colony's strength is the safety of its most vulnerable member."
Captain Surefoot the Swift of Oak Colony

The cats of the oak forest were safe within their base. High, steep cliffs rose around it on nearly all sides, and it wouldn't be easy for anything larger than a cat to squeeze through the thick tangle of bushes and tree roots that protected the opening. On occasion a particularly bold fox did poke its nose into the base, but there were always rangers on guard duty to deal with that. If anything got past them, then the Oak-landers had the advantage of high ground and training to climb the rock faces. Only they could safely navigate the sheer stone.

However, no one stayed within the safety of their well-sheltered home all day. Prey had to be hunted, the territory needed to be scouted and kept secure, and it was the perfect time to gather what few herbs couldn't be grown in the Cliff Gardens. Elmtail and Redleaf had ordered extra guards for both the day and night watches, but otherwise life in Oak Colony had continued as normal.

That morning, the base was its usual bustle of activity. Stagcharge touched his nose affectionately to Elmtail's before taking Fox out for hunting practice. They were joined by Snowfeather, who spotted her own new-claw, Moon, trying to sneak away after Wrensong on her way to the Cliff Gardens. There was no doubt Moon would be an Herbalist someday, as Snowfeather assured the young molly—but until that day, she had to learn to hunt and defend herself like every other ranger in the colony. Shrewpelt and Swiftshadow stood guard, and Shrewpelt stood especially tall and proud. Ever since Redleaf had been named Second, he'd doubled his efforts in getting his father's attention so he might take Redleaf's place on the Council as an Envoy.

All was safe and well.

Heat had blazed through the early morning mist, leaving the air thick with the promise of rain. Dawnfrost wished it was only the humid air that made her so uncomfortable as she lay near the entrance of the Council cavern. Despite the extra guards, no one seemed overly concerned with the misfortune that had befallen Marsh Colony. Dawnfrost, however, couldn't get Hawkshell's warning out of her mind.

At first, Dawnfrost had almost been willing to believe the beast was an overly aggressive badger. They could be nasty, though they usually didn't attack unless provoked. Sunfire, confident to the point of arrogance at times, might have picked a fight. But this confidence wasn't unfounded, and he had not been alone; Sunfire and Breezeheart were both experienced fighters who worked well together and knew their territory better than their own pelts. Then, on the walk back to the base, Hawkshell had mentioned deep claw marks left high up in a pine tree to Elmtail.

What could have taken Sunfire and Breezeheart by surprise, and left both them and the surrounding pines so damaged?

An unspoken worry lingered: *magic*. If an Unbound mage lurked in their lands, it was only a matter of time before the Alliance lost another brave ranger.

"Moon is going to be a great Herbalist one day, but a pawful until then," Wrensong mewed as she sat beside Dawnfrost, not quite shaking the ginger pointed molly from her thoughts.

Dawnfrost rose to her feet. "I'm going to have a look around."

The golden tabby rolled her eyes. "You *are* already an Envoy. You don't need to keep proving yourself." When her teasing got no response from Dawnfrost, Wrensong added in a more serious tone, "Take some rangers and make this an official investigation. There's no need for you to do it alone."

Dawnfrost nodded and bounded toward the rangers' sleeping quarters. The large currant bush had been pruned into a dome and the ground beneath had been dug out by generations of Oak-landers to give the rangers more room. Woven honeysuckle and creeper vines locked out wind and rain in the winter and kept the den cool and fragrant in the summer. Feathers lined the ground within the den to make it more comfortable. Of all the dens in the base, the rangers often boasted that theirs was the best, though they all did their part to keep the Elders and kittens just as cozy.

The ginger-pointed Envoy slipped under the tight branches to find Larkwing and Aspenbreeze still sleeping after their long night watch on the Field Colony border. They were rangers now, but coming to wake them for their duties made Dawnfrost purr at memories of the early days of their training.

She hadn't had a care which border they guarded a day ago. Now she was glad Elmtail had taken her report of a strange scent coming from the Marsh-lands seriously, and had assigned them to watch the Field-land border.

Thornheart raised his head at her approach. No doubt he'd woken when Snowfeather left his side, and his eyes glinted knowingly. "I wondered if you would wait for Redleaf to assign you to the border watch, or if you'd assign yourself."

"You know I won't be satisfied until I see for myself that Sunfire's killer didn't cross into the Oak-lands," Dawnfrost answered.

"*Yes!*" Aspenbreeze jolted up as if she'd been struck by lightning, accidentally kicking feathers onto her brother. "Our first real mission as rangers! Get up, Larkwing!"

"Come on, Aspenbreeeeeze," Larkwing yawned, then tucked his nose under his forepaws. "We sat out in the open all night, and I thought Yellowflower would never stop talking during the celebration ceremony. I just want to sleep!"

Aspenbreeze pressed a paw into his side while she imitated Yellowflower's aged mew. "Oh Larkwing, I remember when you were just a li'l baby kitten! You've grown into such a handsome young tom!"

"Stop it, Asp!" Larkwing swatted at her, and she bounced away with a laugh. Thornheart chuckled at their antics, recalling a time from their training days that had played out exactly like the scene in front of him. It would be hard to see them as full rangers for a while.

"It will be noon shortly. If you don't come with us now, Redleaf will be in here to wake you for an assignment any moment," Dawnfrost pointed out.

"See? Let's go, you lazy lump of fur!" Aspenbreeze cheered.

"Alright, alright, I'm going." Larkwing yawned again and gave his pelt a shake, ridding himself of the down Aspenbreeze had kicked over him. "But not because we were your new-claws! We don't *have* to do what you say anymore."

Dawnfrost tilted one of her ears to the side. "How odd. I could have sworn I just heard some young cat volunteer to help the Keepers clean dirty bedding out of the nursery for the next month. Was it you, Larkwing?"

"What are we waiting for? Let's go!" Larkwing bolted out of the rangers' quarters with Aspenbreeze right behind him. They waved their tails to Shrewpelt as they passed Sentinel Point and dove into Pin Oak Woods, where the trees grew taller and dappled the ground with light and shadow.

Running under the branches of the massive oaks, maples, and birches of the lowland forests was as natural to the Oak-landers as breathing. Dodging tangles of berry bushes and ivy, darting over boulders by leaping into the trees and then to the ground again, and bounding across narrow creeks without breaking stride were the first skills new-claws mastered. Aspenbreeze and Larkwing had learned well, and kept pace with Dawnfrost as they made their way to the Marsh Colony border. Thornheart ran at the back of the patrol, alert for signs of danger but still enjoying their race through the territory.

Trees swayed in the rising wind and the clouds grew heavier and darker above, but their paws were steady and sure on the uneven ground. Not even the purpose of their mission could dampen their spirits or dim the sheer joy of knowing, to the very core, that they were where they were meant to be. Dawnfrost could hardly believe she had ever seriously considered going away with Wolfthorn when the forest was in her every breath and heartbeat. She loved him, yes, but she loved Oak Colony—its cats, its lands, its history—more and more with each passing day.

The first raindrop fell onto Dawnfrost's nose, prompting her to slow and look up at the canopy of ancient, interwoven branches. The forest had been massive when the Ancestors first settled near the lake, and had only grown larger and stronger since—just like her colony. If the trees had ever been small saplings, then the lake must have once been a puddle.

The scouting group came to a stop near a shallow stream. They'd come far from the base, and with the rain picking up, Dawnfrost wasn't sure she wanted to take them much further. Thunder rumbled in the distance. It would be a proper storm, which meant any unusual scents would soon be washed away.

Three of the Oak-land rangers lapped water from the stream. Aspenbreeze looked up and opened her mouth wide, letting rain drip into it from the leaves overhead.

"You're so weird," Larkwing teased, splashing water at her. The drops missed her by a wide margin, but she leaped back with her tail arched and fur fluffed out to humor him.

Thunder roared again, somehow closer to the ground than before. Thornheart pricked up his ears, his amusement at the younger cats' antics draining from his face. With less sunlight, the shadows under the trees grew larger and deeper. It would be dark far sooner than it should be.

Larkwing shivered, flicking water from his paw. "I've been thinking. If it's as bad as Hawkshell said it was, should we be looking for whatever killed those two rangers without backup?"

"I heard no one knows what did it," Aspenbreeze added. "What if it was magic? Maybe there's a cat out there who can turn into a monster, or make themselves really big!"

"Yeah, I'm sure *that's* it," Larkwing said, pushing her shoulder.

"If the culprit has reached the forest, we need to know right away. It could save lives," Thornheart answered. "Doubly so if it's an Unbound cat."

"Wrensong knows where we went, and I'm sure she relayed it to the rest of the Council. If we're gone too long, a search and rescue party will be sent out," Dawnfrost answered. "We're close enough to the Marsh-lands now. Let's have a quick look around and report back to base with our findings. If you see something–or someone–*don't* engage. Fall back and report."

Dawnfrost didn't put much stock in the legends of cats outside the Alliance borders who used magic, but she was willing to entertain the idea for the sake of caution. When dealing with an unknown enemy, it was best not to rule out any possibility—even if her current theory was that a group of Unbound renegades had ambushed the rangers and left strange claw marks to cover their tracks.

Dawnfrost set the pace at a brisk walk. Larkwing was right; they shouldn't linger here when they knew danger could be lurking. However, they were a group of four rather than two. Dawnfrost didn't know any animal that would openly attack that many healthy and alert adult cats. Even a group of invaders wouldn't risk an altercation when one might escape to raise the alarm. As long as they stayed together, and didn't try to instigate a fight, she was sure they would be fine.

Thornheart walked at Dawnfrost's shoulder, sniffing the air carefully. Despite their focus, it was hard to discern the direction of any scent as the rain continued, leaving everything smelling fresh and clean.

"The weather's getting worse. We should go home," Thornheart whispered.

"It isn't too bad yet, and this could be our last chance to find clues about what happened," Dawnfrost replied.

Thornheart shook the rain from his fur and kept pace beside Dawnfrost, but he was unable to rid himself of the creeping doubt that settled like a tick between his shoulders.

The rain dampened Marsh Colony's scent, but there was no mistaking the way the ground started to squelch between their toes at the border. The trees thinned in front of them, swaying dangerously in the gale as the swampy earth struggled to hold their roots. Half a dozen fallen trees from years past created the solid barrier that marked the edge of Oak Colony's territory.

Black clouds crashed together overhead, leaving the world blinding white for a moment as lightning jumped between them. The boom of thunder was so loud that Dawnfrost could not hear Thornheart speaking right beside her. The wind pushed against Dawnfrost's face, forcing her to narrow her eyes and lay her ears flat. Rain pelted her and she turned, leading her group back into the cover of the trees.

A low, echoing rumble made Thornheart's hackles stand on end. Dawnfrost unsheathed her claws. Between the two of them, they knew every tree in the Oak-lands, every bush and boulder. They could scale any cliff or crag, and knew all the best places to find prey or herbs. Dawnfrost knew how tall the mighty oaks were. She had climbed to the very tops to look out over all the Alliance territories. Not until that moment had she ever felt so small, ever been so keenly aware that everything around her was massive and old and would not remember a little cat if she suddenly disappeared.

"Our mission is complete. We're going back to base. Larkwing, Aspenbreeze–" Dawnfrost turned to address the younger rangers, but Aspenbreeze's black-and-white pelt seemed to have vanished into the shadows. Dawnfrost hissed at Larkwing, "Where is Aspenbreeze?"

Larkwing lowered his head. "She smelled a squirrel and went after it. I know she should have waited, but hunting will be poor today and we haven't had a chance to eat. She said she'd only be a moment."

Dawnfrost narrowed her eyes, but Thornheart's widened.

"No," he breathed, and bolted into the woods.

The next flash of lightning was paired not with a clap of thunder, but a yowl that chilled the blood in Dawnfrost's veins to ice. A growl lingered in the air. Dawnfrost tensed her forelegs, not sure if it was thunder or some monster lying in wait behind the nearest tree. The torrential downpour made it almost impossible to pick up Aspenbreeze's scent even as they followed their own trail back into the cover of the forest. Thornheart must have found some faint hint of his former new-claw, or else the Spirits guided his paws; either way, Dawnfrost followed her friend through the sudden dark, to a small clearing where squirrels often stored their acorns in the fall.

What they found there was worse than any monster could be.

Thornheart hardly felt his paws touch the ground as he approached, his sides heaving. Before him lay the torn, broken body of Aspenbreeze. Only when her warm blood touched his paws did he jerk back with a harsh cry.

"Aspenbreeze!" Larkwing staggered toward his sister's motionless form. "This can't...this can't be happening." He ignored the blood pooling around her, placing a dripping paw gently on her side. She did not stir. "No! You can't join the Spirits yet!" He shook her shoulder. Dawnfrost winced when his movements revealed her ribs, where her pelt had been torn. "We just got our ranger names! What about all our plans? Hunting, exploring, training new-claws together, spoiling each others' kittens? Aspenbreeze!"

Dawnfrost forced herself to look away. Thornheart, still trembling, stumbled back. Dawnfrost stood at his side, facing the opposite direction. If whatever killed Aspenbreeze came back, it would not find them unprepared a second time.

"Did you see anything?" she asked.

"No. Whatever it was came and went too quickly. We..." His voice cracked with pain, "...We need to get her back to base."

Dawnfrost examined the broken foliage around them, judging whether it would be safe to carry a fresh carcass through the woods. Above Aspenbreeze's body, higher than any cat or fox could reach, there was a gash in an alder tree that seemed to bleed as much as the young molly on the ground. The gouge was as deep as Dawnfrost's paw could have reached.

Anger surged through her. The beast was obviously too big to be threatened by a lone cat, and it hadn't taken her for prey. It had killed Aspenbreeze for no reason.

"We've got to get out of here, now. We can't handle this on our own," Thornheart insisted, leaning against Dawnfrost's side. "We need to report to Elmtail and Redleaf."

The Envoy shuddered at the thought of standing before the Council and explaining what happened, then taking her place beside them to discuss what should be done. As if she had any right to speak now. Maybe Elmtail would remove her. She would deserve it.

Larkwing had sunk to the ground beside Aspenbreeze. He did not cry out again; he only lay there with his muzzle resting on her shoulder.

"I'm sorry, Larkwing," Dawnfrost said at last. "I never should have asked you to come with us. It was too dangerous."

Larkwing hardly looked like the same cat she'd trained when he turned his empty blue eyes on her. "What am I going to do without her?"

Dawnfrost did not dare speak. She carefully grabbed Aspenbreeze's scruff in her jaws. Thornheart and Larkwing found other still-intact places to hold so they could lift her body, limp like prey, and carry it home.

Somewhere in the trees, a squirrel ran to its hole to shelter from the rain.

Shrewpelt and Swiftshadow nearly called out a warning to the base when they smelled the blood. Their eyes widened at the sight of one of their own being carried inside before they lowered their heads. The storm had grown in strength, washing away much of the trail, but the guards would trace it back as far as they could to bury whatever remained in the mud.

Dawnfrost withstood the stares of her colony as she helped carry Aspenbreeze to the center of the clearing. Several cats had hidden in dens and caves to avoid the worst of the rain, but the scent of fear roused most of them from their beds.

Redleaf's cheerful greeting mew was cut short at the sight of them. "What happened?"

Dawnfrost set Aspenbreeze gently on the ground before releasing her scruff to answer. For a moment, the wind ruffling her fur made it look like she was breathing still, but the body was already becoming cold. She took a breath, only for a horrified wail to steal it away from her.

"Aspen, no! No!"

Vinestripe darted out from the cover of the rangers' quarters and nearly knocked Thornheart off his paws in her haste to get to her daughter. Her blue eyes were wild with disbelief and panic at the sight of Aspenbreeze's wounds and Larkwing's blood-stained fur. She glared accusations at each of the cats around her. "Don't just stand there! Fetch Wrensong!"

"Ma..." Larkwing pushed his head against Vinestripe's shoulder. "She's gone, Ma."

The touch of her living kitten woke Vinestripe from her denial. Dustclaw approached from the nursery, sparing only the briefest of glances at his dead daughter before comforting his mate. Looking any longer would have been too painful; Dawnfrost could barely stand the sight herself.

"We need to call the Council together," Dawnfrost said at last. She forced herself to move to the cavern so she wouldn't have to hear Thornheart's departure prayer for Aspenbreeze:

"Spirits, please guide this ranger to your resting grounds. Let her find peace and fulfillment in the Beyond. Oak Colony will never forget her bravery and enthusiasm. Oak-landers will cherish her life and tell her story so that Spirits to Come will know of her sacrifice. Spirits, forgive us for failing her. Guide her where we could not, and may she guide our paws in turn..."

Dawnfrost waited in the darkness of the cave, listening intently to the patter of raindrops on the ground outside. She was distantly aware that she should groom herself, if only to lick away some of the blood that had smeared onto her fur.

She had hardly drawn her tongue over her shoulder when Yellowflower and Birchwhisker arrived. Though they spent most of their time sleeping and telling stories to the kittens since they had retired, they were still honorable rangers who had served the colony since before Dawnfrost's parents had drawn breath. Their input on the situation would be invaluable, as they carried the colony's history. If anyone had knowledge of any similar past incidents, it would be them.

Yellowflower touched her tail to Dawnfrost's ear as she moved to the back of the cavern, where it was warmest and driest. Hailstorm guided Vinestripe up the cliff. The gray molly was not expected to attend the meeting in light of what had just happened, but she was an Envoy as well as a mother, and she had a job to do. Vinestripe took her place next to Dawnfrost while Hailstorm lay on her other side to accommodate her pregnant belly.

At last, Redleaf and Elmtail arrived. The full Council of Oak Colony was gathered.

Elmtail didn't pause on his way to the back of the cavern, where he and Redleaf would take their places on the raised stone. As soon as he entered the cavern, he asked, "Dawnfrost, what happened to Aspenbreeze?"

Dawnfrost curled her tail over her paws. Elmtail's tone was as patient as ever. "I'm sorry, Captain. Aspenbreeze was killed on our patrol to Marsh Colony's border, most likely by the same creature that took Sunfire and Breezeheart's lives. It has moved into the forest."

"Did you see it? What was it?" Redleaf was unable to sit down. He started toward Dawnfrost, but halted at Birchwhisker's polite cough. Redleaf forced his haunches down.

The presence of the cat who had raised her did not calm Dawnfrost's nerves. "No, we didn't see it. Aspenbreeze was hunting alone when it attacked her. But this is nothing I've seen before, I can say that much for certain."

"How can you be so sure?" Elmtail asked.

"It left claw marks on the side of a tree, as long as a cat, and deep."

Vinestripe whimpered, and swiped a paw over her whiskers to try to hide it.

Redleaf was on his paws once more before anyone could stop him. "That's impossible! A creature that large?" He looked to his Captain for guidance. "Elmtail, what kind of beast is that?"

The old tom's eyes were dark with uncertainty. "I don't know."

"We need to take further measures to protect the base," Hailstorm said, shifting to sit up. "We should weave more thorns into the cliff opening, and establish a rotation of guards so two cats are *always* on duty. Rangers shouldn't go out in groups of less than three."

"And any new-claw not nearing the end of their field training should be kept to base duties," Yellowflower added.

Elmtail nodded at the suggestions. "Are there any other details you can share, Dawnfrost?"

"No, Captain. I'm sorry."

Elmtail stood slowly. His scruffy fur tickled Dawnfrost's whiskers when he rested his muzzle between her ears. "Then go and get some rest." He turned to Vinestripe and licked her ear. "You as well, Vinestripe. Aspenbreeze's death is a loss for the whole colony. We will mourn on the new moon, but you two have your own grieving to do. You are relieved of all duties for the rest of today and tomorrow."

"Thank you, Captain." Vinestripe wasted no time leaving the cave and racing back down to the central clearing. The rain had eased up, and more cats were emerging from their dry beds to see what had happened.

Dawnfrost retreated to the quiet of the rangers' quarters, not to sleep, but to wait.

By nightfall, the storm had blown over and moonlight shone through the scattered clouds. Thornheart, Vinestripe, Dustclaw, and Larkwing had not abandoned their vigil for Aspenbreeze. As her closest family members and teacher, they would stay awake and offer prayers to the Spirits Beyond to accept her into their ranks. They would bury her before dawn, so the first light of the Spirits to Come could shine on her burial place and complete her transition from life to death.

Dawnfrost watched from a secluded spot near the base entrance before turning to leave. Her pelt snagged on the extra thorn vines that had been added to the tunnel, but she forced her way through, not caring if she got scratched.

She was barely out of sight of the guards when a concerned mew stopped her. "The Dawnfrost I know, would know better than to wander off alone right now." She looked over her shoulder, unable to keep the guilt from her face now that she was alone with Redleaf. The ginger-patched tom stood at her side and lowered his voice. "I understand if you need some time away. I can go with you."

"It's fine. I'm just going for a walk to think."

"Why doesn't that put me at ease?" Redleaf pawed at a drying spot of ground, prompting Dawnfrost to sit beside him. She did her best not to get comfortable, but every muscle in her body had been tense since she returned to the base, and her legs ached for a proper rest. "You can talk to me about anything, Dawnfrost. Always."

"There's nothing to talk about. I have to make this right somehow."

Redleaf touched his muzzle to her ear. "It isn't your—"

"It is!" Dawnfrost snapped. "I should have taken experienced rangers with me, not two cats who just graduated! If I'd been smarter about who I chose for the scouting group, then Aspenbreeze wouldn't have...!"

Her chest tightened like she had been buried under a rock slide. Redleaf licked her forehead the same way he would comfort one of his frightened kittens. Dawnfrost shoved her head under his chin to hide her face in his fur, taking in his familiar scent.

"And after everything, I don't have any answers," Dawnfrost whispered. "If I can't find out what it was, then Aspenbreeze will have died for *nothing*."

Redleaf purred, low and comforting, while she leaned into his chest. He hadn't seen her this upset since she'd been a new-claw in his care, the first time she had failed to catch a bird she'd been stalking. Although she'd still had a squirrel to bring home from their hunting trip, she had been mortified that she had failed at something. Brackenfoot's disapproving look at her bringing in only a single piece of prey had not helped matters.

"You don't have to do everything on your own. That's what being a colony cat is about," Redleaf reminded her. "I've been worried about you lately. You've seemed distant ever since Brackenfoot..."

"This isn't about Brackenfoot."

"Then what is it?"

Dawnfrost glanced back toward the base, a small sigh of disappointment escaping her. Silence widened the short distance between them, tearing into the connection they'd once shared. Dawnfrost's mother had died not long into her kittenhood, and Brackenfoot had always cared more about being a Second than being a father. Redleaf had been the one to show pride in Dawnfrost's achievements. He'd listened to her whenever she got in an argument with other new-claws over something silly. If she needed an adult cat on her side, she would go to Redleaf. She was practically Shrewpelt's littermate, sibling rivalry included. After Lilac, Orange, and Sand were born, Redleaf had allowed Dawnfrost to meet them before they were presented to the colony.

Still, they had both been Envoys on the same Council. They had both given their input on important matters as equals. Redleaf would have trusted any of the Envoys with the position of Second, but he knew Dawnfrost had a hunger for it unlike any other in the colony.

"Try to be patient a while longer," Redleaf said finally, offering his signature optimism. "Your time will come, and you will fix this, but right now you're needed here."

His voice was full of care, but Dawnfrost recognized an order when she heard one. He led her back into the base, licking her forehead before departing for the nursery to check on Stonestep and their young litter.

Dawnfrost approached Aspenbreeze's body with the last bit of resolve in her sore muscles. The black-and-white ranger had been arranged to conceal the worst of her injuries. Moss and flowers around her hid the sight and smell of her blood. If Dawnfrost looked at her from the right angle, it seemed Aspenbreeze was merely sleeping. She could imagine Aspenbreeze looking up with a twinkle in her eye and asking Thornheart what they were going to practice that day.

She sat between Thornheart and Larkwing, then tucked her paws under her body and curled her tail around her former new-claw. Vinestripe bowed her head to Dawnfrost and whispered, "Thank you for joining us. I know Aspen would appreciate it."

"Of course."

Dawnfrost touched her nose to Aspenbreeze's intact flank. The others did the same, murmuring apologies and wishes for a better future into the dead ranger's fur. Each of them vowed the same thing. They had failed to keep Aspenbreeze safe; they would not allow another Oak-lander to be killed by the same beast that had taken her from them.

The Broken Bond

"Fighting within the colony becomes fighting outside the colony."
Thistlewort, Herbalist of River Colony

Spottedshadow surveyed Field Colony's eastern base, her long tail swaying with the gentle breeze. Seeing her colony at peace warmed her pelt as much as the late afternoon sun that shafted through the lingering clouds.

Jaggedstripe rolled Dark and Dawn over, purring as the kittens squealed and battled against their father's steady paws. Nightpool watched nearby, contentedly lying on her side and occasionally smoothing the fur on her large belly. Meadowleap wove grass stalks to expand the Keepers' Weave in preparation for Nightpool's kittens while her youngest litter, Tabby and Horse, listened to Missingfoot and Swifttail tell stories of noble Captains leading Field Colony to victory against outsiders. Graymist and Fleetfoot shared a rabbit in the shade of the Captain's Overlook, and Mistysnow emerged from the herb storage at its base to join them. Volefur was on guard duty, watching the fields for any sign of danger, though all he could see was Timberleg and Lilyfire sparring with Stone. The rest of the Field-landers lay among the fragrant heather and mustard flowers, enjoying a peaceful afternoon.

Spottedshadow nodded to herself in satisfaction. Everyone was safe and accounted for, except–

"Hi, Spottedshadow!" Peach exclaimed from beside the spotted molly's shoulder, making her jump in place. The young cat bounced on her paws in delight. "Did I really catch you off guard? I've been practicing my stalking all morning!"

"You did," Spottedshadow mewed, smoothing her fur back down with long licks. Just as Peach started to lower her guard, Spottedshadow hooked a paw around Peach's shoulders and dragged the younger molly to the ground, tumbling her over a patch of wild sage.

"Spottedshadow! Peach!" Mudnose called from the small rise that led to the wide expanse of Sun Meadow. "Goldenpelt and I are going hunting. We could use some extra paws."

Peach looked at Spottedshadow with wide, expectant eyes. Despite her reluctance to spend any more time with Goldenpelt than absolutely necessary, Spottedshadow could not deny Peach's silent plea. She relented with a nod.

"Coming!" Peach bounded over excitedly, looking like a rabbit herself the way she lifted her paws in half-hops. She nearly barreled into Goldenpelt. "I'm ready!"

"Save some of that energy for chasing rabbits. Otherwise, they'll out-hop you!" Mudnose teased.

"Out-hop *me*? Never!" Peach declared, trotting in a circle around Mudnose. He pushed her over with a strong shove, only for her to roll back onto her feet with ease.

"Very good!" Mudnose purred. "Did Spottedshadow teach you that?"

Peach raised her tail with pride. "Yes! I've learned so much from her. Soon no one will be able to stand against the mighty Peach–rabbit, cat, mage, or monster!"

Goldenpelt sighed fondly. "I miss having a new-claw to train."

"Really? I seem to recall that *I* was the one managing most of Timberleg's training, while *you* showed off to the Council," Spottedshadow said with a note of teasing.

"Well, I do have a lot to show off," Goldenpelt smirked. He arched his back and splayed his muscular legs, claws extended, in a long stretch. While Peach giggled, Spottedshadow could only manage a groan in response as her attempt at friendliness was transformed into an attempt at flirtation.

"Save it for later, you two," Mudnose said. "Let's get going before the heat drives all the prey back into their burrows."

The tall grass of Sun Meadow tickled Spottedshadow's nose as they walked. The faintest trickling of a creek soon reached her. She took a long step over the drying waterway that snaked down the slope toward the lake. When heavy rains came in the cold season, the creek would swell, cutting off access to much of the hunting grounds. It was important that the Field-landers take advantage of the land in the spring and summer, when they could run freely to chase down the rabbits that made their burrows in the hillside. During the fall and winter, the rabbits would have a chance to recover their population in peace. This was the way of hunting in Field Colony; careful rotation of fields kept prey plentiful all year long.

With a pointed nod, Goldenpelt broke off from the patrol to scout the area for fresh burrow entrances. The rabbits were always moving around underground, making new openings and closing old ones. Knowing where they were could not only save a hunt, it could save a cat's legs. Not a single new-claw started field training before hearing a dozen horror stories of rangers who had their forelegs snapped or their back legs snagged and twisted by an unseen rabbit hole.

Spottedshadow signaled for Peach to stop walking. In a low voice, she said, "You've done well in group hunts. Today I want you to try by yourself. While we usually hunt in pairs, you won't *always* have someone nearby to help you."

"You've got it!" Peach flicked her tail this way and that. She had known practicing her stalking skills would pay off. "I'm going to bring back a big, fat rabbit for Nightpool."

"That's the spirit!" Spottedshadow mewed. Peach's consideration for others made her wonder if she might train to be a Keeper once she received her ranger name. "When hunting alone, you must use the land around you to herd your prey into the right position. I'll keep an eye on your technique, so stay close–"

Before Spottedshadow could finish, Peach raced into the swaying grass, cutting a straight trail through the growth. The grass rustled noisily. The young molly had to bound forward in a leap more than once, unable to find a decent path any other way. Spottedshadow shook her head and placed her paws carefully in pursuit.

"Now, don't tell me you're tired already," Mudnose chuckled behind her. "I seem to recall a certain new-claw who kept me on my feet all hours of the day. Where did that vim and vigor go?"

"If that's your way of asking for an apology, you aren't getting one!" Spottedshadow laughed back at her old teacher. Her humor faded when she saw Goldenpelt stalking around a heather bush. "Though sometimes, I do worry if Peach takes her training seriously. I'm glad she has fun, but hunting and sparring aren't games."

Mudnose only smiled in response, and Spottedshadow took a moment to appreciate his apparent approval. She had certainly put him through a lot when she was a new-claw, but he had guided her through every difficulty with patience. It was thanks to him that she'd become a ranger at all, and then a Mentor. There were few cats Spottedshadow trusted as much as Mudnose, and almost none of them were in Field Colony.

"How about you focus on your strengths for now?" Mudnose offered. "You're good to others. You treat new-claws with respect, and they respect you back. Captain Hazelfur would not have made you a Mentor if you weren't up to the task." He licked one of her ears. "Now, let's go catch some rabbits!"

Spottedshadow nodded and let Mudnose take the lead. From high on the hilltop of Sun Meadow, she could turn and see all the way across the lake, to the marshes and forest and beach, even out to the rolling waves of the ocean. There was so much land, and even more beyond their borders. She wondered if she would ever see it someday.

Peach had disappeared into the tall grass, but a triumphant yowl led them right to her.

"I got it, I got it!" Her plumed tail flashed over the greenery as she pounced. "Ha-hah!" Dirt and dust billowed into the air as her paws came down, followed by a small screech of rage and fear from the rabbit. "Caught you, you silly rabbit! You can't outrun me! I'm a *Field-lander!*"

"Peach!" Spottedshadow hissed, hurrying to her new-claws side so she could talk more privately. "All the *other* rabbits can still hear you!"

Goldenpelt's glowering face appeared over the grass. "My prey just ran off, thanks to you!"

"Oh, pigeon feathers." Peach ducked her head, hunching into her own mane. In a loud whisper she said, "I'm sorry, Uncle Golden! I'll catch another to make up for it!"

Spottedshadow sniffed at the rabbit Peach had killed. It was a large buck, with plenty of meat on his bones to feed not only Nightpool, but Meadowleap's kittens too. Spottedshadow gave her new-claw a satisfied nod. "It's a good catch, but we'd better go somewhere else now."

"What should I do with my catch?" Peach asked, undaunted.

"We aren't too far from the base yet. Take it to Nightpool and join us near the south base when you're done. Make sure you go *quietly,*" Spottedshadow answered.

Peach grabbed the limp rabbit by its neck and started for home. The buck was nearly as big as she was, but she managed to pull it along without too much trouble. She had taken care to kill the rabbit with a clean break to its neck, as was Field Colony tradition; there would be no dangerous blood trail to lead any hungry predator back to their base. Unlike the other Alliance colonies, Field Colony did not have sheer cliffs, dense bogs, or streams to shield their home from the elements or other animals. They had to be more clever about defending themselves and their most vulnerable members.

While she headed to the east base, Mudnose turned his distinct brown-furred muzzle to the south and led their party that way. The south base was closest to River Colony, and though it didn't offer great hunting at any time of the year, they would have their best chances now, when the creeks were at their narrowest and the ground dry enough to reach top running speeds.

"We'd better hurry, if we want to catch anything," Goldenpelt huffed.

"Don't be angry with Peach. She's young and excited, that's all," Spottedshadow said.

"I'm not angry at her. I'm angry at *you* for not teaching her better!"

Spottedshadow glared at him. "She learned her lesson and will do better next time."

"Learning that lesson cost Field Colony a meal," Goldenpelt snapped, stopping to let Mudnose continue ahead of them and out of earshot. "If this is how you intend to carry out your Mentor duties, I think Forestleaf and Hazelfur might reconsider your position."

"And you just *love* getting me into trouble with Forestleaf, don't you? Has that been an amusing game to you these past months? Spreading rumors about me, questioning everything I do, and making sure it all goes back to your powerful friends?"

"If you would just listen to me, you wouldn't get into trouble," Goldenpelt shot back, stopping so he could turn and face her. "You defied direct orders at the Moonlight Meeting to go hang around with those *outsiders* again. That's what got you banned in the first place!"

"Then why go at all?" Spottedshadow exclaimed before lowering her voice to a growl. The last thing she needed was the shame of Mudnose seeing them quarrel. "And I'm not an idiot. Captain Hazelfur might not actively seek friendships with other colony cats, but he understands the value of having allies. Those orders came from you and Forestleaf."

"Last I checked, *I* was the one trained to handle diplomacy with other colonies, not you. You turned down that opportunity and decided to focus on training young cats how to be good Field-landers. That means putting Field Colony first."

He sighed. "I'm only trying to keep you safe, don't you realize that? We're at peace *now*, but anything could happen. Marsh Colony and Oak Colony have warred with each other in the past. River Colony's actions will increase tension on all borders. Could you be loyal to your colony if you had to fight against your friends?"

Spottedshadow snarled as if he'd struck her. "I *am* loyal to Field Colony!"

"Then prove it and stop nuzzling *that tom*!" Goldenpelt yelled.

"Enough!" Mudnose's sharp yowl silenced them. "I am very disappointed in both of you. I had hoped that rangers, *adults*, would be able to set aside their grievances for the sake of their colony's welfare. I see now that I overestimated your abilities."

Goldenpelt and Spottedshadow lowered themselves, their ears pinned back in shame. Mudnose was not satisfied. "You will return to the east base while I wait to hunt with Peach. Spirits above, she might even learn something without the two of you squabbling like kittens!"

Without another word, Goldenpelt turned and walked as fast as he could away from Mudnose. Spottedshadow followed him. Despite their scolding, the dark-furred molly was not yet done with the conversation. She caught up to him quickly and demanded, "Why can't you let me choose my own friends?"

"You take things too far. There's friendship, and then there's that...*disgusting* display. It's an embarrassment to the whole colony!" Goldenpelt's skin crawled like he'd slept on an anthill whenever he thought of Wildfur and Spottedshadow at the Moonlight Meeting. The worst part of it was how happy she had looked.

"My relationship with Wildfur is none of your business, nor anyone else's." The fur along Spottedshadow's spine stood on end. "Field Colony has my loyalty, always. If you knew me at all, you would know my word is the only proof needed."

Goldenpelt did not dignify that comment with a response.

If he did not know her, then no one did. They had grown up together in the same nursery; they had started field training on the same full moon. They had been inseparable, Shadow always following right behind Golden, just as her namesake would. No one had doubted they would become Envoys and mates, that they would rule the Field-lands together the way Hazelfur and Forestleaf did.

That had changed when strange white spots had appeared on Shadow's pelt. She had been kept under the watchful eye of the Herbalist for weeks. When Mistysnow had finally determined that it was not dangerous and Shadow could return to her training, fate had struck to separate the friends again. Shadow's parents had been attacked by a fox, her mother killed and her father wounded so badly he'd had to retire from ranger duties. Shadow had stayed by her ailing father's side to nurse him back to health and grieve their loss together.

From that moment on, Shadow had been different. She stopped following Golden and abandoned their talks of the future. Instead, as each white spot appeared on her fur, she seemed to form another connection outside their territory: Dawn, the ambitious Oak-lander she'd sparred with in secret; Wild, who had captured her heart in a way Golden never could; Wolf, the mysterious River-lander who had fed her stories of the world beyond Alliance Lake.

Every cat she'd met outside the Field-lands led her further and further away from her old friend, and the life he'd expected them to have.

When they had finally finished their training and earned their names, Spottedshadow and Goldenpelt were near strangers to one another. The ambitious molly who'd tussled with him over who would be Captain and who would be Second was replaced with a fickle cat who always looked beyond the fields, who had no interest in Field Colony leadership, who only ever talked about cats he'd met briefly in passing.

It terrified him to think she might one day follow her wandering heart, and be lost to him forever.

Other voices reached Goldenpelt then. He lifted his nose and sniffed, ears pricked up to identify where the sound was coming from. Beside him, Spottedshadow stopped and did the same. A purr began in her throat; Goldenpelt rushed forward with a snarl. The air was split by his furious caterwaul and a screech of, "*Look out!*"

Goldenpelt leapt, claws outstretched, at Dawnfrost. The Oak-lander was tired, but ready to meet the other Envoy in combat. She tensed her legs, preparing to dodge and counter.

The golden-furred tom never touched her. Spottedshadow tackled him out of the air. The two of them careened across the ground, rolling into a patch of yarrow.

"Leave them alone!" Spottedshadow snarled, driving her paws into his shoulders to keep him pinned beneath her. A small trickle of blood oozed from a cut on her chest.

"What are you *doing*?" Goldenpelt kicked her belly with his back feet, hard enough to knock the breath from her. The moment she let up the pressure, he wrenched free and pushed her off. She gasped more in shock than pain when he left another bleeding scratch on her shoulder.

"I could say the same to you," Dawnfrost snapped. "Attacking allies without provocation? Is this how Field Colony operates these days?" The ginger-pointed molly helped Spottedshadow to her feet. Spottedshadow stayed close to Dawnfrost, twining her tail with her friend's in greeting. "Are you alright, Spottedshadow?"

"I'll be fine," Spottedshadow answered, licking the blood from her fur.

Stagcharge stood at his full height and stared down at Goldenpelt. "We are here with a message from Captain Elmtail. It is urgent that we see Captain Hazelfur to deliver it."

"So urgent you couldn't wait for an escort? That *is* the standard practice here," Goldenpelt pointed out, regaining himself.

"We did wait. Then we saw you coming this way and thought to meet you in the middle. As Stagcharge said, it's an urgent matter," Frondsway offered more delicately, putting herself between the two growling toms.

Goldenpelt flicked an ear. In his annoyance, he was half-tempted to make them give him the message and send them away, but he doubted they would trust him to deliver it now that he'd attacked them. As much as he disliked it, he would have to concede.

"Follow us quickly and *silently*." He glowered at Spottedshadow on the last word, then turned toward the base with the Oak-landers behind him.

Dawnfrost pulled her ears back and narrowed her eyes, but Spottedshadow brushed against her in a calming gesture. Goldenpelt could make demands and dole out orders, but he couldn't stop them from simply enjoying one another's company. They walked side by side the entire way to the base, walking slowly to let Goldenpelt get a little bit too far ahead to hear their whispers.

Spottedshadow gave a friendly mew to the red-and-white molly walking at Stagcharge's flank. "You're a new-claw, aren't you? Is this your first time in the Field-lands?"

"It is," Stagcharge answered for her. "This is Fox."

"I've heard all about you," Fox said.

Spottedshadow blinked for a moment, failing to recognize her, until she gasped, "You're Thornheart's little sister!" She purred. "You've gotten so big! I remember when you were born. Thornheart was *so* excited it was all he could talk about for the entire Meeting."

"Oh, *Spirits*." Fox swiped a paw over her ear self-consciously, and Stagcharge laughed.

"And Moon is just like Wrensong," Dawnfrost added. "She gives Snowfeather the run-around to follow her big sister to the Cliff Gardens all the time. In fact, she did it again just...the other day."

Dawnfrost's tail drooped to the ground. Frondsway ducked her head under Dawnfrost's chin to keep it from falling, too. They were in the Field-lands on official business, and Dawnfrost was representing Oak Colony as a member of the Council. They couldn't let personal feelings get in the way, no matter how much Frondsway sympathized with what Dawnfrost was going through at the loss of Aspenbreeze.

The rest of the walk was silent after that. Goldenpelt stopped them at the edge of the eastern base and went ahead to alert Hazelfur of their visitors. When the small cream tom took his place on Captain's Overlook, Spottedshadow gave the Oak-landers the signal to go inside.

"Greetings, Oak-landers," Captain Hazelfur called down from his perch. "What brings our neighbors to visit us this afternoon? I hope it is important, as our time is precious."

"Thank you for allowing us into your home, Captain Hazelfur," Stagcharge answered. "I am afraid we have brought unfortunate news. One of our rangers, Aspenbreeze, was killed yesterday. We believe the killer is the same one responsible for the deaths of Sunfire and Breezeheart."

He nodded to Dawnfrost, who took a deep breath before adding, "We have additional details to report about the creature. Its scent is unknown to us. Based on the claw marks left in the trees around Aspenbreeze, it is at least three times as tall as a cat, though I suspect it is even bigger than that. Aspenbreeze's injuries were inconsistent with any known predator."

Startled mews erupted from the clearing. Frightened squeaks sounded from the dense woven walls of the base as Meadowleap nudged Dawn and Dark back into the cover. Horse and Tabby kept close to their mother, and she gave them reassuring licks once the littler ones were tucked away.

"We have come to inform Field Colony of this tragedy, and ask for support," Stagcharge continued. "Though we recognize Oak and Marsh Colonies are currently the most affected, there is no guarantee that this monster will not move onto the Field-lands. We have not been able to track it to any den, and we do not know its current location." He took a long look around the large, open base. "Captain Elmtail has doubled our guards. We suggest other colonies do the same, and ask that rangers from all colonies be ready to deploy into battle if the beast strikes again."

Hazelfur curled his thin tail around his paws. "Field Colony's Council will consider Oak Colony's request. Please return to your territory so we may begin our discussion. We will send a messenger with our decision."

"Do not send them alone," Frondsway said. "Three adult cats is the smallest size of any ranger patrol in the Oak-lands currently. Please, for the safety of your colony, send no fewer than that."

"Noted." Hazelfur jumped down from the boulder in the center of the base. He joined the Council members who were already gathering in a circle around him.

Spottedshadow licked Dawnfrost's forehead. "I'm so sorry, Dawnfrost."

"I will be fine," Dawnfrost said, licking Spottedshadow's cut in turn. "We're going to make sure this doesn't happen to anyone else. That's the best I can do for Aspenbreeze now." She signaled to the rest of the Oak-landers, and they set off toward their territory at a run.

Spottedshadow approached the small Field Colony Council, which consisted of Captain Hazelfur, Forestleaf, Goldenpelt, Mistysnow, and Swifttail. Though she was a Mentor, and therefore not a part of the Council, Spottedshadow had to make her thoughts known. Goldenpelt and Forestleaf always dominated the Council meetings, steering the colony's actions toward their own ends. She simply couldn't let that happen when her friends' lives were in danger.

Goldenpelt was already nodding along with Forestleaf's rejection of the request. "Oak Colony is asking us to take a big risk, with no apparent offer of compensation. We would be putting our lives on the line for the sake of a colony that outnumbers ours. What happens if someone gets hurt, or worse?"

"'Or worse' has already happened, and it will keep happening if we don't do something," Spottedshadow argued, ignoring Forestleaf's intense glare. "The longer we wait, the fewer rangers we'll have to take action. Oak Colony isn't asking us to send them rangers to wait on standby in hostile territory; they're asking for our help if and when they find the creature responsible and have a plan to face it. If we do as Captain Elmtail has asked, we'll be facing the danger together as a larger, stronger group. If we refuse, and it does somehow arrive in the Field-lands, we'll have to fight alone."

She expected hostility or annoyance in Goldenpelt's eyes when she met them. Instead, Goldenpelt considered her words carefully. He had always followed Hazelfur and Forestleaf's policy of keeping Field-landers out of other colonies' business, but Spottedshadow made a fair point. Using Oak

Colony's numbers to their advantage to stop a threat before it reached Field Colony was a sound strategy.

Before he could say as much, Forestleaf's expression hardened further. "Field Colony lives are more important. If Oak Colony can't handle this themselves, what difference will sending our rangers to die make?"

"You assume defeat," Mistysnow pointed out. "Field Colony's inclusion in this battle—which I remind the Captain, may or may not even come to pass—could make all the difference and save Field Colony lives in the long run. The risk is justified."

"That's two votes against, one vote in favor. Swifttail, your thoughts?" Hazelfur asked.

The old, patched molly licked her paw thoughtfully. "Hm...it's a difficult situation. I'm not sure our rangers have the right training to be of much help in the woods. It may be an unnecessary risk. Still, there's no guarantee we will have to fight, and it would be cowardly to decline. We do not want to appear weak to the other colonies. I suppose I'm in favor."

Spottedshadow's belly tightened with anxiety. Two versus two, meaning Hazelfur would be the deciding vote–and Hazelfur always leaned toward whatever Forestleaf said, as a dutiful mate would.

Missingfoot shuffled away from his place by the nursery to sit at his daughter's side. Spottedshadow curled her wiry tail around him.

"Wait," Goldenpelt said. "Despite her outburst being improper, Spottedshadow raised a solid counterargument. I would like to change my vote to support Oak Colony."

The spotted molly was not the only Field-lander to gasp in surprise. Goldenpelt *never* voted against Forestleaf, especially not when it came to Field Colony's relations with other members of the Alliance. The Second's jaw was agape at the betrayal of her trusted Envoy.

Hazelfur, undisturbed, simply nodded in acknowledgement and said, "Then, at a three to one vote, the request is approved." He looked at the sky, painted red and gold as the sun sank toward the horizon. "It is too late now for our messengers to return before nightfall. Fleetfoot, Graymist, and Thrushspots, please take the message to Oak Colony at dawn."

"Approved, just like that?" Forestleaf challenged. "I remind you that Oak Colony has offered us nothing in exchange for our help. If we are going to agree to this recklessness, I think compensation for Field Colony casualties is in order." She sneered down at Spottedshadow. "After all, what good is solving Oak Colony's problem if it leaves us unable to handle our own?"

"A reasonable amendment," Hazelfur nodded. "What do you suggest?"

"If I may," Mistysnow cut in before Forestleaf could speak again, "I think assistance caring for our injured would be enough. There are a number of valuable medicines that grow only in the Cliff Gardens. If Field Colony is called to fight, we should be allowed a portion of those herbs to help our injured rangers recover."

"I vote in favor of the amended agreement," Swifttail said.

"As do I," Goldenpelt said, still avoiding Forestleaf's eye.

"Then we are agreed."

Satisfied that the meeting was adjourned, the gathered cats began to depart for their previous activities. Forestleaf's sharp yowl stopped them in their tracks. "Now, for the matter of Spottedshadow's punishment."

Spottedshadow winced. She had known it would happen if she spoke out, but Goldenpelt's change of heart had shocked her so much that she forgot.

"Yes," Hazelfur sighed. "Spottedshadow, you are aware that only Council members are meant to speak during these meetings. We allow the rest of the colony to listen, and will ask for input if we are undecided. Your interruption was out of line. You will not attend the Moonlight Meeting next month, and will take over the night watch until it passes."

Spottedshadow lowered her head. "Yes, Captain Hazelfur."

At last the Council dispersed, but Forestleaf's anger had not yet burned out. Missingfoot pressed closer to Spottedshadow to offer comfort as the Second stood before them.

"Have you not embarrassed this family enough?" Forestleaf hissed. "First you turn down the position of Envoy. Then you take a mate outside the colony. Now you dare assert yourself in a place that is not yours, that you *denied*, so you can put your friends' lives ahead of your colony?"

Spottedshadow knew she shouldn't answer, but she couldn't resist. "What I do, I do for the good of the Alliance and Field Colony. My personal relationships have nothing do with this, grandmother."

The lash of Forestleaf's tail burst a nearby dandelion seed pod. "Don't you dare lie to me."

"Forestleaf, please. What's done is done, and Spottedshadow is being punished for her misconduct," Missingfoot said.

Forestleaf spat at him before walking away. Spottedshadow confounded and frustrated her; despite it all, she did have some love in her heart for Whitebelly's daughter. The same could not be said of Whitebelly's mate, who had been too slow or too cowardly to save Forestleaf's only child from the fox attack. Losing his foreleg in the attempt was not enough to stir pity from the Second, as it was for many of the Field-landers.

"It's late. You should get some rest, Dad." Spottedshadow licked Missingfoot's cheek.

Mudnose and Peach had been successful in their hunt, much to the relief of Spottedshadow's grumbling stomach. She plucked the soft feathers out of a pigeon to give to the kittens as playthings and bedding, before sinking her teeth into the still-warm flesh. Any uneaten food had to be cleared from the base shortly after sundown, and Spottedshadow was pleased to do her part.

"May I join you?" Goldenpelt asked.

Without a word, Spottedshadow tore off a wing and nudged it toward him. She did not carry the rest of the pigeon away, and Goldenpelt lay down so he could easily hold the meal with his forepaws.

"I'm sorry I scratched you, earlier," Goldenpelt said. "I didn't mean to turn my claws on a friend."

His use of that word–*friend*–hurt Spottedshadow almost more than the cut had. She could not think of them that way knowing that, to Goldenpelt, friendship meant compliance.

When Spottedshadow didn't answer, Goldenpelt dropped any attempt to start a conversation. Eating together was the best they could do for the time being, and he wasn't going to push his luck further than that.

The way she had spoken up during the meeting reminded him of the old Spottedshadow's ambition. If she'd become an Envoy, they would have been an unstoppable team. Still, she was suited to being a Mentor, and Field Colony needed cats like her to guide the next generation of rangers.

They finished their meal in silence.

It was only when Spottedshadow began to climb up Captain's Overlook to begin her night watch that Goldenpelt finally found the words to express what he wanted to say.

"I'm not your enemy, Spottedshadow," he said.

She glanced back, opened her mouth to speak, then closed it and finished her climb. She sat stone-still on the top of the boulder, eyes and ears alert for any danger. He sighed and started for his own bed, a clump of clover and feathers not too far from the edge of the base.

"She doesn't deserve you."

Goldenpelt nearly jumped out of his skin, but he calmed himself when he recognized Fernface's raspy voice. Her brother, Volefur, gave a hearty nod.

"She thinks she's something special," Fernface's eyes gleamed despite the dimming light. "But you actually *are* special. You're the future Captain of Field Colony. Maybe she needs a reminder that you aren't to be taken lightly."

"I appreciate the thought, but I can handle Spottedshadow myself. Good night," Goldenpelt said with a smile.

Fernface's claws, which never seemed to retract, kicked up small bits of grass and flowers as she walked to the nest by the nursery that she shared with Volefur. Despite being her mate, Jaggedstripe did not share a nest with her; rather, he slept inside the nursery with their kittens. Goldenpelt glanced at his own lonely bed before following them to theirs, curling up with the brown tabby siblings for the night.

Truth told, he wasn't sure he *could* handle Spottedshadow anymore, not when she was walking down such a dangerous path. Even the most capable ranger was as defenseless as a kitten if her heart wasn't behind her claws and teeth. Should Wildfur ever leave Marsh Colony—which seemed more and more likely every time Goldenpelt listened in on the Marsh-land Envoys—Spottedshadow wouldn't be able to chase him away from the Field-lands. She might even go away with him, led astray to the miserable life of an exile.

Goldenpelt wouldn't let that happen. Even if she hated him for it, he would protect her. That was what good leaders did.

If she had fallen for any other cat, even an outsider like Dawnfrost, Goldenpelt wouldn't have to worry so much. But for some reason only the Spirits could possibly know, she'd chosen that lazy, good-for-nothing mange-pelt called Wildfur.

The last thing he saw before he closed his eyes was Spottedshadow's outline against the sunset, the nearly-full moon still drifting through the sky above her.

Guard duty was considered a miserable chore by most rangers. Sitting exposed on the hard stone for hours on end, unable to lie down, buffeted by any stray wind, was not a pleasant experience. Guard duty at night was even more tedious, as there were rarely ever any patrols coming or going to offer distraction.

That meant Spottedshadow had a month of long nights on an uncomfortable rock with only her thoughts for company to look forward to.

Still, sitting on Captain's Overlook stirred distant dreams in her mind. What if she had become an Envoy? She shivered uncomfortably at the thought. Goldenpelt had become little more than Forestleaf's lackey since he'd taken the position. She knew the job wouldn't be worth it if she had to fight with the Second daily, especially once she became Captain and

Goldenpelt was promoted to Second. No one had any doubt that leadership of the colony lay in his future. Though there were other Envoys, Forestleaf had made her favoritism clear. And if Spottedshadow had pursued a place on the Council, she'd be under even more scrutiny than she already was. She'd have to say goodbye to her friends in the other colonies, and she would never give them up, not for every star in the sky.

Spottedshadow had tried to become an Herbalist, but Mistysnow had denied her request for training. She did not have the spiritual gift that Field Colony required of its healers. Still, the two of them had bonded while Spottedshadow took up brief residency in the healer's den after the appearance of her white spots, and then the tragedy that befell her parents. She had thought the older molly might want her around after that.

"Oh, dear. Your heart has gotten you into trouble again." As if she had heard Spottedshadow's thoughts–and perhaps she *could*, with the Spirits' blessing–Mistysnow hauled herself onto the boulder to sit beside Spottedshadow. She licked the top of Spottedshadow's head. The dark-furred molly purred, happy for company.

"Is my friendship with other cats really so concerning? Does it make me...disloyal?" Spottedshadow asked, getting right to the point.

"You wouldn't be my Spottedshadow if you didn't care about others. It's who you are. And you contribute your share," Mistysnow answered. "Though, I do worry what would happen if we ever did have to face other cats in battle. I can imagine you trying to talk things through with an Unbound and getting yourself hurt."

"That's not as reassuring as I hoped it would be," Spottedshadow replied with a soft laugh.

"I have to see a wound to treat it." Mistysnow looked up, spotting the first star to appear in the sky. Spottedshadow followed her gaze, leaning against the gray molly. Her long fur tickled Spottedshadow's ear. "I have never lied to you. It *would* be easier if you could love Goldenpelt, but not even the Spirits can control someone's heart. Especially not a heart as big as yours."

"Have the Spirits sent you any signs about what's happening?" Spottedshadow asked.

"It doesn't work that way, as much as I wish it would," Mistysnow answered. "This is but one trial of many that the Alliance has faced in its long history, and this too shall pass. The rangers of every colony are strong, skilled, dedicated cats. We have all we need to solve this problem."

"I wish someone would tell Hazelfur and Forestleaf that," Spottedshadow sniffed.

"Didn't you?" Mistysnow chortled. With a groan, she lay down, her body curled around Spottedshadow's. "I may be getting on in years, but I think I can stand this for one night, at least. I expect Missingfoot and Peach will keep you company on others." She lowered her head to her paws. "You are not alone, Spottedshadow. Remember that."

More and more stars began to dot the sky above as the sun finished its descent. No matter where in the Alliance Lake territories her friends were, they could all look up and see the same sky she looked at now. Her heart unexpectedly light, she shifted to get comfortable on her paws. A month of night watch might not be so bad, after all.

Across Borders

*"Forevermore, Forest Colony shall be divided into Marsh Colony and Oak Colony,
and our borders will be defended."*
Captain Deepmarsh the First of Marsh Colony

The sun had long since begun to set, and Wildfur was still asleep. It was well known in the Alliance that while the sun first touched Field Colony, Marsh Colony were the first to wake; and while the sun set over River Colony, Marsh Colony were the last to sleep. The dim, gray twilight suited them best, be it dawn or dusk. Few rangers remained in the Marsh Colony base after their daytime rest, and those who did were there on Captain Hawkshell's orders to defend it.

Pool stared nervously at the twitch of Wildfur's paws and muzzle, hesitant to move closer. His own nest was at the far end of the den, with the other new-claws. It was not his place to cross the invisible barrier of social convention to the rangers' side, but what else was he to do?

"Wildfur?" Pool called. He hated how his voice wavered, and repeated in a too-shrill hiss, "Wildfur!"

Wildfur jerked awake with a deep breath, like he'd just fought his way up from the bottom of the swamp. The panic in his eyes calmed to confusion, then annoyance, when he saw Pool's face instead of whoever he had been dreaming about.

"Uh, sorry, I...um..." Pool looked anywhere but the ranger as Wildfur stood to chew at a tangle near the base of his tail. "The sun is almost all the way down. Leafstorm wants you to take me to battle practice this morning before it's too dark. Everyone else is ready to go." He swallowed nervously. "Actually, they've already left for the mossy hollow."

"Suppose that's as good a reason as any to wake me up." Wildfur stretched. "Next time, just throw a pinecone at my head."

Pool responded with a nervous laugh. "I don't think the other rangers would appreciate me throwing pinecones into their bedding."

"Hey, who's the Mentor here? It's a Marsh Colony custom to throw pinecones at sleeping rangers. You should try it." Wildfur bumped Pool's shoulder with his own, nearly knocking the new-claw off his unbalanced paws. Pool's answering laugh was more strained than the first, and Wildfur sighed, dropping his attempted friendly facade. "Let's get moving, then. Wouldn't want to give Leafstorm another reason to be unhappy."

Wildfur tried to remember anything useful from his own new-claw days as they walked to the training grounds. It only served to put him in a dour mood. His own teacher, Tigerstripe, had expected nothing less than perfection from his new-claw from day one, and had reacted harshly whenever he was reminded that he needed to *teach* first. Most of Wildfur's combat training had come from fending off Tigerstripe's frustrated blows, and he was an almost entirely self-taught hunter. Other, more promising new-claws had taken the attention of the Mentors at the time, leaving Wildfur to figure it all out on his own.

He'd barely spent any time at Marsh Colony's training grounds as a young cat himself. The thick, spongy patches of moss offered natural padding to practice the throwing and pinning techniques Marsh Colony rangers prided themselves on. Wildfur had nearly walked past the place when he'd first shown Pool the important areas of the Marsh-lands. He had only truly remembered it because the ground was drier there, safer. The riverside swamp banks made it nearly impossible to fish, as Wildfur had learned in the harshest of ways as a new-claw. Moss tricked the mind into thinking there was solid ground below; thick mud trapped a cat's paws and sucked them down, into the water. A grim joke among some rangers was whether slowly drowning, choking on mud, or being eaten by a gator or a gar was the preferred method to meet one's demise.

The thought brought Wildfur's nightmare to mind. He wondered what his brother, Patch, would have preferred—not that he'd gotten a choice. All for an undersized catfish that would barely have sated their appetites if he'd caught it.

Tigerstripe had denied any responsibility for the drowning of the young tom. After all, he had not been in charge of watching Patch, and Wildfur's struggle to save his brother had been born of insubordination. Young Wild had been meant to be cleaning out the dirty nesting material from the nursery and bringing back fresh supplies. If he hadn't gone with Patch, if he hadn't been there to show off to and tease, if he hadn't complained he was hungry, maybe Patch wouldn't have gotten such a fungus-brained idea in the first place.

Wildfur gritted his teeth. Patch probably would have been a better Mentor to Pool—but at least Wildfur wouldn't be as bad as Tigerstripe had been.

Halfmask, Falconswoop, and their new-claws–Boulder and Red–were already practicing in the mossy hollow when Wildfur and Pool arrived. The burly young toms sized each other up, then rose onto their hind legs to grapple with their forelegs. Boulder tried to use his size to overpower Red. Red took advantage of his lower center of gravity to step back and pull Boulder down. Paws still hooked around his shoulders, Red managed to force Boulder's head to the ground and twist, rolling the larger tom onto his side where Red could pin him.

"Good show, Red!" Falconswoop cheered.

Boulder did not take his defeat with grace. When Red shifted his weight to let the pale gray tom rise, Boulder kicked hard with his hind legs and caught Red in the stomach, knocking the wind out of his sparring partner. Red collapsed with a wheeze and Boulder slammed him down further with a cruel sneer.

Falconswoop yowled, "Control your new-claw, Halfmask!"

"Battle can be unpredictable. A ranger should never lower his guard." Halfmask shrugged, giving Boulder an approving glance while Red dragged himself out of the practice area.

Pool's mouth dried when Halfmask beckoned him closer. "Shall we start the next round?"

Wildfur narrowed his eyes in response. "Where's Birdflight?"

"Our colony's only current Mentor is unfortunately busy assessing Ice's skills," Halfmask drawled. Pool flinched; he knew Ice was doing well, but to be assessed so soon was unheard of. Then again, so was carrying out a battle training session without a Mentor present. With a haughty sniff, Halfmask added, "But that's alright now that you're here, isn't it, Wildfur?"

Wildfur growled at the challenge. Were it just the two of them, he wouldn't have a second thought about cuffing Halfmask around the ears and reminding him who'd won their few sparring sessions when they were new-claws.

"Pool, let me give you some pointers," Falconswoop said, not missing a chance to shoot Halfmask a dirty look. She crouched beside her little brother so only he could hear her. "First, don't let him get in your head. They know you're new, they know Boulder is bigger than you, and they're counting on that. Before you ever meet an enemy in combat, you have to defeat the opponent in your own mind."

"Right!" Pool nodded fiercely. "How do I do that?"

"By knowing you're bigger on the inside."

Pool blinked at Falconswoop, hoping it was one of her bad jokes. Her expression was completely serious. She offered nothing else before clearing the sparring area to sit by Red.

"Ready?" Halfmask asked.

"N–"

Boulder did not wait for Pool's protest. He charged, completely forgoing the custom of observing an opponent and assessing their weaknesses before a fight. He raced forward like Pool was a sizable piece of prey, not an equal opponent.

Pool froze, and Boulder struck him hard. The gray-and-white tom's feet left the ground and he sailed through the air before tumbling to a stop at the edge of the moss covering.

He didn't have a chance to stand before Boulder was upon him, pushing him over with a single paw. Instead of pinning Pool the way Red had done to him earlier, Boulder grabbed the new-claw by his scruff and flung him away. Pool gasped in pain when he landed on his back, paws churning in the air like a kitten trying to stop his guardian from grooming him.

Boulder ignored his weak swipes and placed a claw to Pool's throat, standing over him with a demeanor more bored than triumphant.

"Alright, that's enough, Boulder. Get off him," Halfmask called.

"*That's* enough?" Falconswoop shrieked, but Halfmask did not turn an ear to listen to her complaint.

Boulder gave Pool one last shove and scoffed, "A twig could put up a better fight!"

"It's my first time!" Pool protested. He swiped a paw across his cheek, though it did little to clean off the mud. A brown streak was left behind, smeared under his eye to give him the appearance of a frustrated raccoon.

"Why do I have to train with him? Why do I have to train at all? I should be a ranger by now!" Boulder groaned. Wildfur almost wanted to remind him that his attitude was exactly the reason why Hawkshell hadn't granted him a ceremony yet. "Come on, Halfmask. This is a waste of time. Let's go hunt or check the River Colony border instead."

Halfmask halted the overgrown new-claw's whining with a glare. "You're supposed to show that you're ready for the responsibility of being a ranger. That means more than winning fights and catching prey. Rangers are colony cats, and that means taking care of each other."

As he spoke, his harsh gaze drifted toward Wildfur and his voice grew more and more condescending. Wildfur would have bristled at those comments, if he'd thought bullies like Halfmask and Boulder were worth getting riled up over. "Any tips for your new-claw, Wildfur? You are supposed to be the Mentor here." His smirk was echoed on Boulder's face. "Though I guess you can't be blamed, since you only took this job to avoid being kicked out."

Wildfur shifted his shoulders, if only to remind both Halfmask and Boulder that he was a great deal larger and stronger than they were. That was all they seemed to respect. Still, after giving it a moment of thought, he said, "I have to agree with Boulder. It's idiotic to make these two train together when they're at such different levels. Pool hasn't grown into his paws yet, and Boulder has been an adult for months."

Before Boulder could react to the barbed comment, Pool cried out, "I can do it, Wildfur! Let me try one more time!"

"Now *there's* a Marsh-land ranger in the making!" Halfmask said with eyes gleaming in fiendish glee. "Besides, Red still needs a moment. He can be Pool's partner once he catches his breath, but there's no sense in wasting time waiting."

Wildfur rolled his eyes. "Fine!" He motioned Pool over and hooked a paw over his scruff, pulling him in close. "I want you to use your size to your advantage. Focus on dodging his attacks. Being small means you can make yourself a harder target to hit. Keep your balance, and don't let him knock you around. If you can avoid getting pinned, that'll be a marked improvement."

Pool and Boulder faced each other in the middle of the training grounds for what would hopefully be the last time that day. *Ever*, if Wildfur had his way. Pool dug his claws into the moss beneath his feet, feeling the thick tufts between his toes. He took a deep breath.

"Fight!" Falconswoop signaled.

Pool hurled a chunk of moss at Boulder's face. "That's for the last time!" he shouted, circling behind Boulder as the larger tom wiped the dirt and debris off his nose with a snarl.

The light gray tabby charged again, but Pool danced out of the way on his long, nimble legs, always keeping to Boulder's side or back. Once, Pool managed to land a hit on his side. It wasn't a strong blow, and Boulder probably wouldn't have noticed if Falconswoop hadn't let out a triumphant whoop, but it was something.

Pool was putting distance between him and his training partner again when Boulder snapped, "Dodging might work, but it makes you a coward! A real Marsh-lander can take any blow and get back up on his feet."

He lunged again. This time Pool tried to meet his attack head-on, only to be knocked out of the air the moment they met. Boulder easily overtook him, pinning the smaller new-claw to the ground. Boulder ground Pool's face into the dirt before strutting back to Halfmask.

"Guess you're not a real Marsh-lander, huh?"

Wildfur winced and shook his head. "Pool..."

Pool kept his head down even when he shook himself off. His long tail remained in the mud.

"We're finished for today," Falconswoop said. "Red, you did well. Head back to base and get something to eat. You've got the evening to yourself." She nudged Pool and whispered to the young tom, "Next time I'll make sure you get here on time so you can practice with Ice. I should have gotten you when I realized Wildfur wasn't planning to show up."

"I don't need you to be my Keeper," Pool sniffed, but he leaned against her anyway, until Boulder whispered something nasty to Red and they both laughed.

Wildfur resisted a sigh and wondered what Spottedshadow would do. Halfmask might have been being sarcastic when he described the duty colony cats had to each other, but Spottedshadow embodied it. She always knew how to make a cat feel better, even as miserable a cat as Wildfur. She would know just what to say to Pool, the right advice to give, the best way to encourage the young tom's spirit. That's why she was a Mentor, and Wildfur was only an imitation of one.

The sharp snap of a twig distracted him from any more thoughts of his love across the lake. At the unexpected sound, Falconswoop pushed Pool behind her, and Red joined her to defend the smaller new-claw. Boulder dashed forward with a wild frenzy in his eye at the thought of a real fight, Halfmask close behind to give orders. Wildfur inhaled, then gestured for

Falconswoop and Red to relax when he caught the aromatic scent of Oak Colony. Pool had already fluffed his fur out until he was twice his usual size, and would likely be that way for the next hour.

A golden tabby molly with a white underside emerged from the bushes. Wildfur did not take notice of many cats outside the Marsh-lands, but he did know Wrensong. He knew her less as Dawnfrost's friend, and more as Smallpebble's surprisingly aggressive mate who was impossible to ignore–especially when a romantic rendezvous with Smallpebble was interrupted.

Boulder came to a skidding halt at Halfmask's bark of, "Herbalist! Stand down!" His claws remained unsheathed, however, when he saw Wrensong was not alone. With her were Thornheart, Snowfeather, and Moon.

"Oak Colony spies!" Halfmask hissed. "Trying to steal our battle tactics, are you?"

Wrensong hardly looked impressed at the accusation. "I wasn't aware shoving kittens into the mud counted as a battle tactic." Entertaining no further distraction, she said, "Captain Elmtail sent us as messengers. We must speak with Marsh Colony's Council at once." She gave Boulder one look, taking note of his aggressive stance, before adding, "Save your strength to fight the monster."

Even Boulder and Halfmask had the sense to be concerned about that. The fur that had just begun to flatten on Pool's back and tail fluffed out again.

"I'll take you to the base," Wildfur said. "The rest of you, go on ahead and let Hawkshell know we're coming."

"We don't take orders from you," Boulder argued.

"I am the oldest ranger here, and technically the only one with a rank beyond ranger. So yes, you do." Ordinarily Wildfur would have loathed the idea of throwing his weight around like some brute, but he had to admit it was satisfying to watch both Boulder and Halfmask's egos deflate at the realization that they had to listen to a cat they considered beneath them. Falconswoop certainly appreciated it, giving Wildfur an encouraging, if awkward, smile.

Pool hung back, trying desperately to look like anything but a frightened kitten. He only looked smaller and more scared when he stood next to Wildfur. "I'll stay with you, since I'm your new-claw...if that's okay?"

"Do what you want," Wildfur said, shrugging.

Thornheart looked at the small Marsh-lander with pity while the Oak-landers formed a line behind Wildfur.

"Hey, don't worry. You'll get the hang of it," Thornheart offered.

"Uh...thanks," Pool answered shyly.

"If I could become a ranger, any cat who tries can do it," Snowfeather laughed. When Pool gave her a quizzical look, she added, "I used to be Unbound. I lived with my mother in the wastes, until she decided I was old enough to fend for myself. I wasn't." Snowfeather waved the memory away with a flick of her tail. "Oak Colony took me in when I was a little older than you and trained me."

"Really? *You* were Unbound?" Pool gaped. "But you're pretty! I thought Unbound cats were more like..." He tried to stop his eyes from wandering toward Wildfur. "Like Crowstalker and Breezeheart. Scruffy."

"Some are, certainly. But some are very lovely," Thornheart said.

Snowfeather giggled at his praise while Moon rolled her eyes. She had thought they were cute when she was a kitten, but now that she had to put up with their flirting during training, she was tired of it. She wished she could train under Wrensong as an Herbalist right away. She knew enough about fighting and hunting, in her opinion. She was hardly an expert, but she could catch a bird or two for those who were bound to the base, and a scratch was a scratch no matter how the fur split.

"Maybe Captain Hawkshell and Captain Elmtail might let us train the new-claws together," Snowfeather suggested. "Oak and Marsh Colonies used to be the same, didn't they?"

"Ages ago," Pool said. It was one of his favorite Elder stories. "But then there was a war. It started with River Colony deciding to give up their swamp land, leaving it unclaimed. Some cats from Forest Colony wanted to take over the marshes, others wanted nothing to do with them. It ended up splitting the colony in two, and they had a bitter rivalry that eventually got so bad, they spilled each others' blood on sight! They couldn't even be at the Moonlight Meeting at the same time; Oak Colony would show up first, say their announcement, and leave, then Marsh Colony would come. Captain Elmtail and Captain Hawkshell finally ended the grudge for good."

Snowfeather blinked. "Is all that really true?"

"Maybe," Thornheart laughed. "I like to think it's exaggerated for excitement. I hate to think of Alliance cats killing each other for no reason. In the end, I think it's good we have our own territories, and there's a colony ranging the marshes. We wouldn't want dangerous predators settling here." His voice slowly faded to a whisper and Snowfeather licked his ear sympathetically.

"Has the monster been seen in the Marsh-lands again?" Wrensong asked Wildfur at the head of the group.

"Not yet, but it only seems to be a matter of time, if you listen to Hawkshell. Double scouting patrols and guards on duty all day and night. Have you seen it in the forest?"

Wrensong's eyes clouded with grief.

"Did someone get hurt?"

Thornheart swallowed a deep breath before answering, unable to keep his voice from wavering. "Aspenbreeze is dead."

"Oh." It was a stupid thing to say in response–it wasn't even really a reply–but Wildfur didn't know what else to offer. He knew how useless words were in the face of grief.

"*Aspenbreeze*? Didn't she just become a ranger?" Pool gasped. When no one answered, he lowered his head and took a place at the back of the group without another word.

Wildfur cleared his throat. "You don't think it'll go to the Field-lands, do you?"

"I doubt it. Dawnfrost's scouting group encountered it near your border, so it must be living somewhere between the marsh and the forest," Wrensong replied. She jostled the bag she had slung over her back. "In any case, I have a shipment of herbs for Smallpebble. They'll help treat any possible infections, since we don't know what we're dealing with."

Wildfur glanced into her bag and saw a clump of violets sitting on top of the pile. He somehow managed not to laugh in her face. "*Only* herbs?"

"Alright, herbs *and* a little gift, to let her know I'm thinking of her," Wrensong quipped. "It's not easy, being in a separate colony from a mate. Especially during dangerous times. I'm sure you understand."

"I do." Wildfur paused with a paw raised in the air. They were nearly at the base, and he could already hear voices rising from within as the Council gathered. "She won't be at the meeting. If you think Thornheart and Snowfeather can handle delivering the news, it might be your only chance to spend some time with her."

Wrensong purred in gratitude. "Good idea."

Once the Oak-landers entered Marsh Colony's base, Wrensong sniffed out the calico molly. As usual, Smallpebble was hard at work studying the mushroom clusters on the Cultivation Stump, one of the few facets of Marsh Colony's base that had a specific name–even if it was admittedly literal. The holes dug into the stump were perfect for both growing medicinal fungi and storing plants that would mold if left exposed to the humid swamp air.

The two Herbalists nuzzled each other in greeting. Smallpebble tucked the violets into her thick fur with a loud purr, then placed the rest of the herbs in the cavities of the stump. She sliced a few white mushrooms and placed them in Wrensong's bag. "These will help with Hailstorm's pregnancy!"

Though Shrewpelt was the father of their coming litter, Wrensong was as much Hailstorm's mate as the red tom, and she would take an active role in the lives of the kittens. Smallpebble would be a distant aunt to them, but she was still excited to meet them at the Moonlight Meeting when they were old enough.

Their business done, the two mollies snuggled close together to listen in on the meeting.

Hawkshell sat with her Council at the base of the broken tree where she made her den. Thornheart and Snowfeather took their places among the roots while Moon sat by Pool and Ice. Despite his protests, Ice groomed the dirt from Pool's fur.

"It has been some time since Oak Colony sent a proper messenger group to Marsh Colony. What news could not wait at the border?" Hawkshell asked with concern rather than contempt.

"It is dire, Captain Hawkshell. Oak Colony has experienced the same grief as our neighbor and ally," Snowfeather explained. "Yesterday, a scouting group explored the land near the border to see if they could track down the source of the mysterious scent we picked up on the day of the full moon. While they were searching, one of them was attacked and killed. Judging by the smell and the damage done to the area, we suspect it was the same beast responsible for Sunfire and Breezeheart's deaths."

"This is most troubling," Indigoeyes said. "If it has developed a taste for cats..."

"Aspenbreeze was not eaten," Thornheart said. Anger and sorrow choked his mew. "She was mauled, and left to rot. A senseless death."

Kestrelsnap nodded. "Further evidence that it was the same creature."

Hawkshell's claws slid in and out of their sheathes as fear warred with her thirst for revenge. "Was the scouting group able to track it to a lair? A den?"

"No. Its scent trail was washed away by the storm, and the surviving rangers did not see it," Snowfeather said. "We suspect it's living somewhere on the border, which makes it the problem of both our colonies. Captain

Elmtail has also dispatched an Envoy to Field Colony to secure an agreement to fight it together."

"You think it will take more than the combined might of Marsh and Oak Colonies to deal with this?" Mousetail asked.

"We're not taking any more chances," Thornheart answered. "Maybe it will leave on its own. Maybe it will have to be run out, or killed. There is a lot we don't know, but what we *do* know is that the Alliance has lost three rangers in less than a week. We won't underestimate it again."

"What of River Colony? Has Captain Elmtail sent a request for their aid?" Hawkshell asked.

Thornheart and Snowfeather exchanged a glance. "He did not think it a good idea to send rangers so far from home at the moment," Thornheart answered.

"And we all know what Rainfall's answer would be," Whitefire snorted. "I doubt we'll send word to them, either. The last thing River Colony needs is news that other colonies are under attack. Rainfall will turn it into an omen from the Spirits before you can blink."

Hawkshell narrowed her eye for quiet, but did not dispute the Elder's claim. "Oak Colony can count on Marsh Colony's support. Likewise, Marsh Colony expects that Oak Colony will come to our aid, if this monster reveals itself on our land."

"Of course. Marsh Colony messengers are welcome to Oak Colony's base, unquestioned," Snowfeather mewed. She looked behind her shoulder at Moon, who stood to join the young Mentor. "It seems we are in agreement. We'll return to our base now."

"Not so fast," Leafstorm yowled. The brown tabby molly was eclipsed by Hawkshell, and had to stand up to make herself noticed. "It will be quite dark soon. Due to our increased guard we do not have spare rangers to see you home safely." She looked to Hawkshell, who nodded in approval. "You may stay the night here, and I will personally escort you to the border in the morning."

"We accept Marsh Colony's generous offer!" Wrensong exclaimed. She curled her tail around Smallpebble, who rested her chin on Wrensong's paw.

Wildfur glanced at them with an unwanted flare of envy. There was no way Spottedshadow could cross the treacherous marshes to see him, even if they tried to meet between full moons. Her delicate paws would be caught in the muck and mire and she would be dragged down, her long legs only trapping her faster as she struggled.

Flashes of his nightmare from that morning surfaced in Wildfur's mind again, and he crept off to his place at the edge of the rangers' den, hoping he could hide there for a while.

Instead, Pool followed him. "Can we go back to training now?"

"Aren't you dirty enough?" Wildfur returned.

"I'm not going to improve if I don't keep trying!" Pool complained. "I'll listen this time, I promise. I don't want to give up! We barely did *anything* this morning, either."

Wildfur tucked his paws under his chest. "Knowing when to give up is important. Trust me, you'll have plenty of other chances to fight bullies like Boulder–not that cats like him will help you become a better ranger."

"But they're Marsh-landers," Pool pointed out.

"So are cane toads."

Pool gave him a measured look. Wildfur wondered if he was going to force a laugh or take him seriously, and which reaction he wanted the new-claw to have. His words might have been sarcastic, but they were also true.

With no response, Wildfur finally added, "We'll try again when Birdflight is ready to supervise. They're better at this whole Mentor thing, anyway. For now, get something to eat. If you want something to do after that, go check on the nursery or the Elders. With all this double-guard stuff, they're probably being overlooked."

Though Pool didn't seem particularly enthused by his words, he at least looked less like a kitten who had lost his favorite toy. "Alright. What do you like to eat?"

"Food," Wildfur answered. At least *that* earned him another half-hearted chuckle from the gray-and-white tom. Pool nodded and ran off to get something for the two of them to share.

The Monster in River Colony

"Never forget that the cat beside you has teeth and claws of their own."
Captain Poolglare the Still Water of River Colony

Moss looked up to see a cloudless sky, as usual. The hot sun on the sand and stones was made comfortable by the cool ocean breeze and crystalline water that flowed from the lake to the sea. Bright hibiscus flowers bloomed at the base of mangrove trees, outdone only by the collage of color in the rainbow eucalyptus trees.

As the colony basked in the warm sunshine and sweet smells of their home, Moss thought of how lucky she was to have been born into the greatest of the Alliance colonies. She had to do her best to be worthy of the River-lands and Captain Rainfall.

She cursed when the smelt she'd scooped from the stream danced away from her paws and struck the water again with a loud splash. "Oh, come on! Stupid fish. I was sure I had it!"

"I think you were a little too early. And you let your shadow hover over the water for too long," Gray explained, unbothered by her yowl of frustration.

"So was I too early or too late?" Moss groaned. "There's so much to remember!"

Gray chuckled. "Don't worry, you'll get it eventually. Wolfthorn had to show me lots of times before I made my first catch. At least you touched it this time."

Moss looked over at Wolfthorn, who lay nearby on a basking stone, eyes closed. The only indication that he wasn't sleeping through their lesson was the occasional twitch of his ears, and the fact that Swiftmask kept nudging him. She, like most of the colony, couldn't help but feel bad for Gray. Having such an unreliable teacher couldn't be easy, but Gray had stepped up and worked hard to keep pace with the other new-claws. Perhaps putting him in Wolfthorn's care had been a test from Rainfall, to see if either of them were truly capable of being rangers.

Moss was too young to remember Gray's mother, but she had heard plenty about her from the older cats. Lakespeckle had been a highly skilled Herbalist, the best in the Alliance, respected among all the colonies. The rangers of the River-lands had been shocked and dismayed when Iceclaw had reported that she was killed by a coyote on her way to visit Mistysnow. Many had demanded her body be recovered and given proper burial. However, that had ended when Rainfall received a warning from the Spirits that Gray's father was Unbound, and had been hiding on their territory for months with Lakespeckle's help. No sensible cat had mourned her on the new moon after learning of her disloyalty.

Lakespeckle's conspiracy to hide her mate instead of inviting him to join the colony only made sense if he was cursed with magic. He would never have been allowed to stay if that was true. If Gray ever showed signs of carrying his father's curse, he too would have to be exiled. Thankfully, Lakespeckle's betrayed River Colony mate, Rockyshore, still cared for Gray and treated him like a son.

If Gray was sad about what happened with his mother, he never showed it. There was no point. All he could do was try to prove that he would never betray River Colony the way she had, even if some cats within the colony were wary of him.

Moss didn't mind Gray's dubious parentage. He was kind and patient with her. She couldn't imagine he was secretly evil. Frankly, she didn't think he was *interesting* enough to be harboring secret magical powers.

"Maybe you should ask Swiftmask for help?" Gray suggested as Moss stared into the water, willing another fish to appear.

Her paws worked at the sand, digging up and reburying a small clam shell. She glanced at Swiftmask a few times, who was whispering something into Wolfthorn's ear with a sharp expression. She didn't want to interrupt, or make Swiftmask explain the exercise again, but even Gray could see she was struggling.

"Swiftmask, could you, um, show me again? Please?" she finally squeaked out.

With a nod and smile, Swiftmask crouched between the two new-claws. Both of them perked up and tried to copy the stance he adopted with practiced ease.

"First, crouch to keep as much of your shadow away from the water as possible, but don't let your haunches become stiff. When you strike, you do it with your whole body. Make sure you have a good view and stay on your toes." Even his breathing slowed as he settled into the perfect position. Moss's whole body trembled as she waited for another fish to come. A few minutes of silence and stillness later, Swiftmask's claws darted out, and he lunged to scoop a rainbow trout out of the water and into his waiting jaws.

Rather than try to hold it there, Swiftmask tossed it farther onto shore, away from the water it struggled to return to. Moss gasped when the trout's tail almost struck her face as it flew through the air. Swiftmask pounced, pinning the fish to the ground, and delivered a clean killing bite before it could flop to the stream again. He lifted it with triumph.

Moss bounced on her paws. "You make it look so easy! Wow, that's a big one, too!" She raced back to the edge of the stream. "Okay, I think I've got it now!" She crouched with her tail high and her nose nearly touching the water's surface. Gray looked to Swiftmask and shook his head before taking a seat next to her.

"It's my turn, Moss. I need to make at least one catch before you scare all the fish away," he teased.

"Hush, you! I'm in my element!"

Gray's long, bushy coat hid Moss from Wolfthorn, but he could imagine the water dripping from her whiskers after another loud splash and a frustrated growl reached his ears. He lowered his eyelids again, content to listen to the young cats as they practiced.

Swiftmask had other ideas. He carried the trout to Wolfthorn and set it down at the base of the stones.

"Show off," Wolfthorn mumbled with the quietest of purrs.

Without missing a beat, Swiftmask replied, "If our new-claws need a lesson on lazing in the sun, I'll send them your way." He settled onto the stone beside Wolfthorn, releasing a deep breath as he soaked up the warm light. "I still can't believe Rainfall gave us both new-claws. And making me a Mentor...I've waited so long to move up in the ranks!" He nudged

Wolfthorn. "We've got a pair of good young cats to teach, too. I can tell Gray thinks the world of you."

Wolfthorn knew what Swiftmask wanted him to say. If not a cheerful and enthusiastic confirmation, he would at least expect some kind of joke or friendly jab about how they were getting older, or how there were so many young cats in River Colony–yet still, somehow, not enough–that Rainfall had been left with no choice.

As much as he might have liked to; as easy as it would have been, Wolfthorn couldn't bring himself to do it. Rainfall did have a choice. She always knew exactly what her choices were and where they would lead, and she followed only the path that benefited her most. She might have been a noble Envoy once, someone whose paw prints he'd been excited to follow, but that Rainfall was long gone.

"She made you a Mentor to spite you and keep you in your place. You should have been an Envoy months ago, instead of being made to settle like this so Pineclaw could be the only one speaking in Council meetings. You deserve better," Wolfthorn answered, undaunted by Swiftmask's wince at the reminder of what they both knew to be true. "As for me, most of the River-landers still don't trust me to be in the colony at all, let alone train a new-claw." He lowered his voice, though Moss and Gray were making plenty of noise to cover them. "There's a reason Rainfall gave me Lakespeckle's son to train. She has her own agenda."

Wolfthorn chanced a glance at Swiftmask to see his reaction. At first he thought the gray-pointed tom might acknowledge the unfairness of his situation. Then the moment passed, and Swiftmask put on the happy face Wolfthorn was starting to think he'd been named for.

"Well, with River Colony having such a bountiful spring, we need all the help we can get training new-claws. Even oddballs like you!" He laid his tail over Wolfthorn's back, but the pale tabby didn't return the gesture. Swiftmask's words were the kind of thing Wolfthorn would have said if he was only interested in small talk. If he didn't want to really *say* anything. "The Spirits will unite the colony again. Maybe us getting new-claws is a sign of that."

Wolfthorn couldn't help but scoff. Rainfall was the one who had split the colony. She'd found excuses to banish anyone who didn't show complete loyalty to her wishes, or made them so miserable that they fled in the night without a word. "The Spirits can do nothing for us. We've got to think for ourselves and do something before Rainfall breaks the Alliance completely."

"Rainfall is doing what she thinks is best. And the Spirits Beyond think Rainfall is the right cat to lead the colony." Swiftmask raised his head, looking down at Wolfthorn. "I'm not talking to you about this again."

Wolfthorn stood and stretched, pretending to be the nonchalant and laidback tom the rest of the colony thought he was. "Let me know when you come to your senses." He slipped off the stone and grabbed the trout, taking it away to eat. Swiftmask's shadow briefly fell over him as the pointed tom prepared to launch into a lecture about colony loyalty or the Ancestors' Law or some other nonsense, but a much louder splash from the stream distracted him.

"*Spirits, take me*!" Moss yowled as her head popped back out of the water.

"*Moss*!" Swiftmask scolded, hurrying over to help the brown tabby back to shore.

"It wasn't her fault. I startled her," Gray said as Swiftmask guided Moss back onto dry land.

"Why would you do a foolish thing like that?" Swiftmask demanded. When he shook, water droplets flew off his short but dense outer coat. Moss, who had yet to lose all her kitten fluff, remained sopping wet and trembled on the sand.

In answer, the ear-splitting shriek and furious caterwauls of a battle reached their ears. Gray winced, staring hard at his paws. Moss tried to make herself bigger, but her wet fur stuck to her frame.

Like the Envoy he should have been, Swiftmask wasted no time in running toward the commotion–worryingly, toward the base.

Wolthorn paused at Gray's side before following. "Find somewhere safe for you and Moss to hide. I'll come get you when it's over."

Gray gave a terse nod and gripped Moss's scruff before she could take off after Swiftmask. Her protests soon slipped away from Wolfthorn's ears.

The chaotic sounds of a fight drew Wolfthorn into the very center of the base, beneath the Sentry Stone where Rainfall looked on with cruel approval as Iceclaw pinned another cat beneath his terrible talons. Pineclaw held down an even smaller cat, who wailed for the other and struggled to reach them. Gillstripe looked on impassively, though his ruffled fur proved he had been part of the fray, as well.

Wolfthorn slowed, choosing to slip around the clearing and stay in the shade of the undergrowth to observe. Just in case he needed to make a quick escape.

Swiftmask stood before Iceclaw, Pineclaw, and their captives. He was still panting from the sprint, but his voice held a measured authority–just enough to demand attention, without threatening the superior rank of those he addressed. "What is the meaning of this?"

"We caught these two Mange-landers trespassing on River Colony land." A thin trickle of blood ran down Iceclaw's muzzle as he smiled. His sharpened claws edged closer to the neck of the gray-and-white speckled cat in his clutches.

Wolfthorn seriously doubted that. It was more likely the Marsh-landers had simply strayed close to the border, and Iceclaw and Pineclaw had cut them off from retreating, forcing them farther into the River-lands until they could claim it was rightful capture. He didn't know why they bothered with the farce.

"We weren't on River Colony's side of the border!" the speckled cat protested. "The Floodlands belong to Marsh Colony, and we weren't even hunting. I was showing my new-claw the territory!"

"*Our* territory!" Iceclaw snarled, pressing the cat's face deeper into the sand until they sputtered and coughed. He looked up at Rainfall. "What shall we do with them, Captain? Should we send a message to Hawkshell that she needs to keep a closer eye on her rangers?" He turned his murderous gaze back to the speckled cat. "If you've trained your new-claw well, she'll find her way back without you."

Swiftmask shifted on his paws. This was far beyond what should be done for a simple border crossing. A single ranger and a new-claw did not constitute a show of force, merely a reminder of the border's limits and an escort back. If they had a message for the Captain or were visiting a mate or parent in another colony, there was even less reason to retaliate. To drag them into the base against their will to stand before the Captain, and to threaten them with possible execution–it was unheard of.

"A warning is surely sufficient," Swiftmask said before he could stop himself. "They have broken no law, and their current wounds show we are not to be trifled with. There is no need for cruelty!"

All the other River-landers who had come to see the commotion fell silent. Any sound might draw the massive white tom's attention. At the moment, Iceclaw was focused squarely on Swiftmask—an unenviable position. Though the white tom's eyes were wild, Swiftmask did not waver. He adjusted his weight ever so subtly, shifting it to his hind legs in case he needed to raise his paws to defend himself.

Wolfthorn abandoned his hiding place. "I agree with Swiftmask. We can send a message to Marsh Colony without killing one of their rangers. There's already something killing cats around the lake; we wouldn't want to have all of the other colonies' attention on us at the wrong time."

Rainfall arched her back, taking her time to stretch her legs and toes before speaking.

"I suppose River Colony is hardly threatened by two measly Marsh-landers straying out of their ugly little swamp. We don't want to overreact and give the wrong impression." She yawned and curled her tail around her paws neatly. "But, we also don't want them to forget that River Colony takes trespassing *very* seriously. Iceclaw, mark the new-claw."

"Wait–"

Gillstripe took Iceclaw's place to keep the Marsh-land ranger pinned. Though Iceclaw sauntered toward the younger cat with confidence and ease, his excitement was clear to everyone watching. Iceclaw drew back his paw and struck. The young molly shrieked and blood stained the sand.

"Stop squealing, runt! I let you keep *one* of your eyes," Iceclaw snapped, cleaning the blood from his claws with relish.

The ranger let out a yowl of rage and tried to get up, to fight, but Gillstripe held them fast.

"Don't make this worse," he grunted into their ear before letting them up. "Go home now."

The speckled cat did not waste another second. They pulled the new-claw to her feet by her scruff and hurried away from the base, forcing their way through the shallow stream. They ran for the Marsh-lands, for home and safety, as fast as they could.

Gillstripe made sure to glare at Wolfthorn before walking away, as if it was his fault that Iceclaw and Rainfall were monsters. Wolfthorn didn't bother to glare back; Gillstripe could hate him all he wanted. It wasn't like they'd had much to do with each other since they were new-claws.

Since before their father died.

The official story was that Brightscale, the brave Envoy who might have been Captain Poolglare's choice for successor, had died defending the colony from a dangerous Unbound mage. Only Wolfthorn knew that was a lie.

The rest of the River-landers went about their business, unaware of the awful truth, helpless to save themselves. At a glance, the base was a paradise. Cats lounged in the sun and chatted in small groups, with plenty of fish to go around. If anyone looked closer, they would realize the base was gripped in the claws of unease. Groups sat too close together and whispered too quietly, afraid of being overheard. Rangers stood guard not only at the designated posts that had stood for generations, but at the entrance to every den and gathering place. No one could even leave the base to relieve themselves without having to report it and get permission first.

With the exception of Wolfthorn, none of them knew why. Any reason at all was kept to River Colony's esteemed leaders: Captain Rainfall; her brother and Second, Iceclaw; their father, Frozenpool; and Pineclaw, who had been allowed to take the rank of Envoy far sooner after joining the colony than anyone should. There were noble colony-born cats, cats like Swiftmask, who had waited and worked for the opportunity. Iceclaw had simply brought Pineclaw back with him one day from the Unbound-lands and declared he was a ranger, without having to receive training or complete a Sundown Challenge.

Creekbend and Rockyshore were still a part of the Council as Elders, but their votes counted for little when they were so easily outnumbered. There had been nothing Rockyshore could do when his mate, Lakespeckle, had been accused of mating with an Unbound and producing Gray from their affair. Anyone with an ounce of thought or willingness to defy Rainfall could clearly see the resemblance between Rockyshore and Gray, and Rockyshore refused to be absent from his son's life despite the vicious rumor that had taken Lakespeckle from them.

Creekbend, for his part, was simply old and not up to fighting the desires of his colony's leaders. He had been a close friend to Poolglare, and the loss of the former Captain had taken its toll on him.

Ousting Rainfall and Iceclaw would have been far easier if there was support from the Council, but they had efficiently usurped their power. Frozenpool would never rule against his children, and his voice echoed in their nefarious plots. Pineclaw's placement ensured that the best the Council could ever come up with was a draw, which Iceclaw could then tip to Rainfall's favor.

Wolfthorn slipped away into the shade of a hibiscus bush. Was there any point in trying to revive the old River Colony anymore? He hadn't been able to convince Swiftmask to help him, even though it was obvious the pointed tom didn't like what was happening. Swiftmask's hope of being an Envoy who could actually *do* something about Rainfall and Iceclaw was officially dead.

Wolfthorn thought again of Dawnfrost and their dreams of a life beyond Alliance Lake, but that too was gone. She would never leave Oak Colony. She would never set aside her desire for power and prestige. Not for him.

He could escape on his own. It would be lonely at first, but Wolfthorn could rejoin the cats he'd met in the Unbound-lands. They would accept him into their ranks once he proved he would stick around and contribute. He would have to learn new customs and hunting techniques, but he was nothing if not adaptable. He'd do whatever it took to survive, and his heart could tear itself out of his chest if it didn't like that.

And yet, the River-lands had called to him during his time away. He had seen many things, met many cats with histories all their own, but nowhere had truly felt like home. The River-lands carried *his* history, all the places he'd experienced life for the first time. He'd learned to swim in *that* pond; he'd caught his first fish from *that* creek.

He had watched Rainfall kill his father from *that* reed bed.

The Beast in Marsh Colony

"A change of name is a significant event in a cat's life, whether it be to honor a fallen friend, accept a new role in the colony, or declare a new identity."
Truetongue, Envoy of River Colony

The heat of midday lingered in Marsh Colony even as the sun began to set, and Pool had never been more grateful that his colony slept during the hottest hours of the day. The moisture lingering in the air made his pelt feel heavy. His skin itched under his fur, which did little to ease the sting of the cut on his side. Boulder claimed his claws had *slipped* and that he hadn't had time to file them, but Pool knew he'd been scratched on purpose. It was a little thing, but the fact that it still hurt after his nap put him in a sour mood.

Pool settled on plucking feathers out of a heron wing as a distraction. Though it was generally thought of as Keeper work, and he would have to assert again that he was *not* interested in becoming one, it was worth it to get soft lining for his bed and easier access to the meat on the wing.

He appreciated the Keepers. They did an important job, and a colony could never have too many cats looking out for the kittens and fixing up their home. But Pool was tired of Marsh-landers taking one look at him and *kindly informing* him that he'd be a *perfect* Keeper. He would be an Envoy, if only to prove them all wrong.

Ironically, he thought Wildfur might be a better Keeper than a Mentor. It was obvious the burly tom hated leaving the base. He could not relax for a single moment when he took Pool out hunting, always on alert for danger. That wasn't a bad thing for a Marsh-lander to be, but Pool could sense Wildfur's overwhelming anxiety, especially when he got close to the muddy riverbanks or waded into stream beds. Despite everyone claiming that Wildfur only cared about himself, he frequently had Pool check on the Elders, bring food to Smallpebble, and mind the kittens. From what he had seen, Pool knew Shrewbelly could use the help of another Keeper, if only to have a second set of eyes watching Night and Fog. The siblings were still months from starting their field training, but they liked to pretend they were already new-claws.

Pool looked at the outer reach of the sheltering branch, expecting to see Ice yawn and stretch. Her bedding was bare, and her scent was growing stale. She hadn't come back to base since she and Birdflight had left that morning. He had been disappointed when she left, since it meant any battle training would be unproductive.

Ice was brilliant when it came to fighting. She had mastered the grappling maneuver already, and could even roll Red over onto his back. Before too long she'd be able to take on gigantic foes like Boulder with little worry. She would have no trouble reaching the rank of Envoy, if she wanted to be one.

"Red's a toad-brain who couldn't fight his way out of a rotting log without someone telling him each move to make. It doesn't matter how heavy *he* is," Pool had said in his own defense that morning when Ice had teased him about it.

She hadn't been bothered, shrugging a reply. "Ah, well, we haven't been new-claws for very long. There's still time." Then she'd headbutted his shoulder to cheer him up before Birdflight called her for training.

Before she'd gone off to scout the River Colony border–which, Pool noted with a scowl, he hadn't even gotten to *see* yet–she had stopped short with her eyes wide and her mouth open wider. "*Whoa!*"

"What?" Pool had jumped to his feet, looking around with his back and tail arched in alarm. He hadn't seen anything out of place. "What is it?"

"Your fur is messy." Ice had given him a fond smirk and swatted the out of place tuft on his head. Then she'd darted out of reach before he could hook a paw around her forelimb and drag her into a wrestling match. "See you later!"

Pool glanced at the sky, where the sun was already drifting lazily toward the horizon. That exchange had taken place hours ago. Had Birdflight and Ice found somewhere comfortable to rest while they were out? Was there such a place so close to River Colony and their attack-first, ask-questions-never rangers?

He'd hardly taken two steps out of his nest before Smallpebble was upon him. The short calico molly pushed him toward her workspace like an errant kitten, not uttering a word as she slathered his scratch with medicine.

"*You* come to *me* next time," she huffed when she was finished.

"Y-yes, Smallpebble," Pool stuttered, slinking with his head and belly low to Wildfur's side. Though the shaggy tom still had the most unorthodox training schedule, he had gotten better about being awake when Pool was up.

"Can't hide anything from Smallpebble. Learn that, and you'll be able to walk around the base without her swooping on you like a hungry owl," Wildfur teased.

Pool wrinkled his nose against the pungent odor of the salve. "What are we doing tonight?"

"Well–" Wildfur paused, narrowing his eyes at something over Pool's shoulder. Just when the young tom had thought his day couldn't get any worse, he had to scramble to look presentable as Captain Hawkshell and Leafstorm approached. Though his parents were close with the Captain–both of them being Envoys, and Kestrelsnap being Hawkshell's only niece–Pool had not seen much of her during his base training, except from a distance. Even from across the base Hawkshell had always seemed larger than life, and when she stood in front of him, Pool knew that she *was*. Her every movement exuded power, control, and intimidation.

Pool was so in awe of the Captain that he missed what she said. Wildfur, however, caught every word, as well as the condescending concern hidden in them.

"Leafstorm will accompany your training for an assessment."

Wildfur frowned. His training as a Mentor certainly hadn't lasted long before they'd decided he wasn't good enough. At least this assessment would give him a chance to show them how one-sided so many of Pool's training sessions had been. He was sure Boulder would not turn down a chance to shove Pool into the mud, and Halfmask was almost as eager to prove his superiority over Wildfur as a teacher.

"Let's go. We're battle training tonight," Wildfur said flatly.

"*Battle* training?" Leafstorm scoffed. "We just watched Smallpebble treat an injury from your battle training. No, he'll work on hunting tonight."

Wildfur hunched his shoulders, walking with his head low. "Alright, then. Let's go *hunting*."

Pool tried to shake off the worry, but it filled him the way the stench of the bitter medicine filled his nose. He could hardly smell the cats in front of him, much less prey!

Just as Leafstorm suspected, Wildfur had little to offer in guiding the new-claw to an appropriate hunting ground. She corrected him no less than three times.

Leafstorm carefully watched the way Wildfur's pelt bristled along his spine, his voice more of a growl every time he uttered, "Yes, Leafstorm," and changed directions. If he could be patient, perhaps he could make it as a Mentor—but she doubted he would be able to hold his temper for long.

Finally, he stopped in his tracks. "So, the West River is no good, the Marsh Fork is too risky, and Pine Creek is too far. Can we hunt *here*? Or should we just cross the River-lands border and try our luck at catching fish?" Wildfur snapped.

Leafstorm gave their current surroundings a scrutinizing look. *Here* was the west bank of Joining Creek, where the water was slow, nearly stagnant in the summertime. That meant more bugs, and therefore more frogs and bats that ate those bugs.

"I suppose this will do," Leafstorm conceded at last.

Wildfur nodded to Pool. Before the new-claw could start sniffing for prey, Leafstorm interrupted with a hiss. "Aren't you going to instruct your new-claw at all?"

"He's done this before," Wildfur stated, giving another nod to Pool. The young tom almost perked up at Wildfur's faith in his ability, until Leafstorm spoke again.

"Do I *really* have to do this for you?" Leafstorm stood at her full height, which wasn't much in comparison to Wildfur's stature. She barked, "Pool! Tell me what you can smell around here."

"O-okay." Pool looked to Wildfur for reassurance, but the scruffy tom had turned away, tail twitching in irritation. Pool couldn't blame him. "I think some of the prey might have been scared away..." The gray-and-white tom withered under the fiery heat of Leafstorm's glower. "But I smell a few birds, and an otter, too." Pool lowered his head when Leafstorm did not relent, shuffling his paws and trying to figure out what she wanted from him. He took another deep breath, letting the musty air linger in his nostrils. "There's some really old badger scent, too. Possibly the one that River Colony chased off during the full moon. And–" A new scent, fresh and burning, filled his nostrils. "Blood! There's blood nearby!"

Wildfur let out a growl and breathed in deeply. Pool was right; the smell of blood was getting stronger with each passing second. His first thought was that a hawk or owl had dropped its catch, perhaps losing it in a midair battle, but any prey with an injury that bad would hide somewhere, as still as it could be. The source of this smell was moving.

Someone was hurt.

"Ice?" Pool gasped, rushing down the length of the creek. "Ice!"

Following the scent, Pool raced around the trunk of a dogwood. Among the clusters of white flowers, breathing heavily, was Birdflight. They dragged Ice's bloody body, both their pelts streaked with dirt and tangled with leaf litter.

"We need to get them back to base," Leafstorm said, a stammer threatening to disrupt her words.

"Obviously," Wildfur snapped. He grabbed Ice's scruff and slung her up and over his back, her paws not even reaching the ground when he stood tall. Birdflight gave him a grateful look, though the quinn was too tired to speak their thanks. They leaned against Leafstorm, limping and bleeding, but not nearly as badly hurt as Ice.

Pool walked beside Wildfur, licking Ice's face and paws whenever he could. "Don't worry, Ice! We're going to get you home. Smallpebble will fix you right up."

Once, Ice slipped her eyes open, only to moan weakly in pain before they fluttered shut again. Pool almost demanded they stop so he could make sure his sister was still breathing.

As if she had received a messenger ahead of time, Smallpebble was waiting at the entrance to the base, moss and webs and medicines at the ready beside the fallen tree.

Leafstorm hurried down the log and rushed into Hawkshell's den, where the older molly had spent most of her time since Sunfire's death. "The assessment is over, Captain Hawkshell," Leafstorm reported, trying to sound bigger than she felt.

"So soon?" Hawkshell drawled, hardly bothering to raise her head. It was almost painful to see the once powerful and imposing Captain this way, but Leafstorm had a job to do. Then she could let Hawkshell rest and grieve in peace.

"We found Birdflight and Ice. They're badly hurt," Leafstorm said.

That grabbed Hawkshell's attention. She surged to her paws, hackles rising, her one eye wide and burning. "Is it the beast? Has it come back?"

"I don't know. They're both alive, so they can tell us what happened," Leafstorm said. She hoped Ice would live, but the amount of blood the little molly had left trailing behind them, dripping down Wildfur's pelt, made her reluctant to say for certain. She would pray to the Spirits tonight and beg them not to take another life from Marsh Colony so soon.

"Show me," Hawkshell demanded, storming out of her den.

Even a Captain would not interfere with an Herbalist at work. Hawkshell watched from a respectable distance as Smallpebble wove Ice's torn flesh back together with wrappings and antiseptic powders. Once Birdflight had gotten a chance to drink and catch their breath, they told the Marsh-landers everything.

"We were watching the River Colony border. We weren't even close to crossing it when we were ambushed by a group of rangers." Birdflight shook. Their sister, Blueflower, offered comfort until they could continue. "Iceclaw wouldn't let us leave. We would have run home, but we were captured and taken to River Colony's base." Birdflight's shivering only got worse the longer they spoke. "Iceclaw was going to kill me, but some of the rangers convinced Rainfall to let us go. Then Iceclaw did *that* to poor Ice, to send a message..."

"How badly wounded is she?" Hawkshell raised her voice to ask Smallpebble.

The Herbalist's response was curt as she focused on her work. "One eye has been removed, deliberately. The rest of her face is badly maimed; the bridge of her nose is cut to the bone. The other scratches and bites will heal, but those are the most dangerous."

Pool shuddered. How could anyone hurt his sister like that? She was just a new-claw, not a threat! Even if she and Birdflight *had* been trespassing on the River-lands, it would not have warranted a response like this.

"The Council moves for a declaration of war!" Indigoeyes said.

"I second!" Kestrelsnap yowled.

"Denied," Hawkshell responded flatly before turning her attention back to Smallpebble. "Do you have what you need to treat the injuries, or should we send for supplies?"

"I'd like some more bloodseal from Oak Colony, if we can spare a few rangers to fetch it. Wrensong should have plenty in stock right now."

Indigoeyes stomped a hind foot. "Dammit, Hawkshell, that's my *daughter!* You have no right to deny us justice if the Council votes for war!"

Hawkshell fixed him with an icy stare that chilled Pool's blood. It was rare for his father to disagree with Hawkshell on anything, and rarer still that he voiced dissent. Sensing the scolding Indigoeyes was about to receive, Kestrelsnap pressed herself against her mate's side, standing tall with him against the Captain's ire.

"You forget that you are not the only family in this colony, and River Colony is not our only concern," Hawkshell said. "What would we gain by declaring war? Do we have the strength and numbers to overwhelm River Colony and command a swift victory, or would we be dragged into a conflict that could last months, if not years? Perhaps you think I could call upon my friendship with Elmtail for support, but because of that friendship, I know Elmtail would never be swayed to open hostility against another colony. And the day Hazelfur acts for the sake of any colony but his own is the day he will step down as Captain. All this, while our rangers face an unknown threat within our own territory." Hawkshell stepped forward and rested her muzzle upon each of their foreheads. "I understand your frustration, your anger, your desire for vengeance. Iceclaw and his colony *will* be brought to justice for this—but not now. We must choose our battles wisely."

Before he could utter a retort, Hawkshell added, "What is most important for the time being is that we save Ice. Smallpebble has requested bloodseal, and I imagine you need something to do right now. Will you lead a group to Oak Colony?"

Pool watched his father in awe as Indigoeyes shook off his anger and took control of the situation, the way a good Envoy must always be ready to do. "Falconswoop! Crowstalker! Let's go!"

The rest of the colony dissipated back to their duties; someone still needed to keep watch, make sure everyone was fed, clear out old bedding, mind the kittens. Smallpebble finished wrapping Ice's injuries and sat back to look over her work, tucking in mushroom powders and leaves where she thought they were needed. Kestrelsnap groomed what patches of her daughter's fur were exposed, and Pool settled in beside her to receive his own bath without complaint.

Hawkshell returned to her den, Leafstorm close behind.

"Was that a wise decision?" Leafstorm asked, once she was certain the rest of the colony could not hear. "Ice is a popular young cat, and many of our rangers were fed up with River Colony's actions *before* this."

"I will not have you question me on this."

"As your Second, I *must* question you," Leafstorm countered. "River Colony is becoming more persistent. If we don't take action now, Rainfall will think she can do whatever she pleases. You heard Birdflight—they weren't even near the border. River-land rangers invaded *our* territory, captured *our* ranger and new-claw, and assaulted them. If not war, then surely some other retribution is in order!"

"Not now, Leafstorm! Our priority is on finding and eliminating Sunfire's killer. Everything else can wait," Hawkshell hissed.

Leafstorm pinned her ears back, but she did not argue further. If Hawkshell would not be swayed to act on behalf of her own kin, then nothing Leafstorm said would change her mind.

In the following days, Ice was never without at least one family member by her side. Pool, Kestrelsnap, Indigoeyes, Falconswoop, and even Snowstorm made regular visits to her in the patients' den, each time hoping her pain would ease enough for her to have a full conversation. The bloodseal stopped her wounds from becoming infected, but she faced a long road to recovery. One of the bites on her back had been deeper than Smallpebble initially realized, and Ice had difficulty moving her hind legs. The Herbalist had hope that Ice would regain better control of her legs as treatment continued, but it was a worrying symptom that did not make Ice's recovery any easier, nor her family any more pleased with Hawkshell's inaction.

Hawkshell hardly left her den at all, retreating further and further from the colony. Leafstorm spent most of her time outside the entrance to the Captain's den, giving out orders and receiving reports to relay to Hawkshell. Her own unhappiness with the situation was apparent, but she minded her tongue around the Captain and tried to consider it a blessing in disguise. She had been the newest member of the Council when Hawkshell had named her Second; this was valuable experience in running the colony.

Nearly a week passed before Ice raised her head and uttered a full, coherent sentence. She called out for Kestrelsnap, and asked her mother to bring Captain Hawkshell to see her. Whatever else was happening, the Captain could not deny a request from a young cat in pain. She sat beside Ice and listened in silence as the young molly made her case.

"I don't want to be called Ice anymore," the new-claw stated. "I don't want to share any part of myself with that *monster*."

"Have you given thought as to what your new name will be?" Hawkshell asked.

"Yes. How soon can we do the ceremony?"

Smallpebble cleared Ice to leave her nest—for just a few moments—that very night. Under the light of the waning moon, Ice dragged herself away from the patients' den and into the heart of Marsh Colony's base. Wildfur did not dawdle or lurk on the edges when the summons came for the colony to gather for Ice's naming ceremony. He seated himself near the center of the group for the first time in years so he could be with Pool.

"We gather under the light of the Spirits Beyond to give this cat a new name," Captain Hawkshell said, recalling the words from her own renaming ceremony so long ago, and from Falconswoop's transition to a molly more recently. "In light of the recent tragedy–and the name of the cat who caused it–Ice has asked that she be reborn, under a new name and identity. Henceforth, she shall be known as Osprey."

Osprey lifted her chin, though it made pain lance through her face as the wrappings tugged her fur.

She had chosen her new name carefully. Her great-aunt was named after a hawk; her mother, a kestrel; her older sister, a falcon. As Osprey, she would join them and be as fearsome as her namesake.

Others might criticize Hawkshell's stance on River Colony, but Osprey was grateful. She would rise on new wings, she would soar over those who hurt her, and one day she would sink her talons into Iceclaw's heart. Vengeance, justice, was *hers* to deliver.

Spirits to Come

"The Spirits Beyond and the Spirits to Come are one and the same. They are the cycle of birth, life, death, and rebirth. We are the Spirits, and the Spirits are us, and we are whole."
Gentlestar, Keeper of Marsh Colony

Peach observed the placement of Stone's paws carefully, waiting for the telltale shift of weight that preceded his charge. Sure enough, just after making a small wiggle to balance his weight, he lunged at her. Peach flopped onto her back and caught Stone under his chest with her hind feet. With a mighty kick, she flipped Stone clear over her. A short roll and hop later, Peach was back on her feet and Stone was shaking heather out of his fur, unharmed. Timberleg didn't even need to move to help him to his feet; the young gray tom already raring for a second chance.

"A great start! Your form was perfect, but you let Peach use your own strength against you. Try not to think too long before you move or you'll give yourself away."

"Sure thing, Timberleg. Can we try again?" Stone replied, meeting the in-training Mentor's eyes with a smile.

It was Peach's turn to wiggle in excitement. "You want to get rolled again?"

Stone answered by dropping into his battle stance, noticeably still this time.

"You did an excellent job, Peach, but remember to use that move with caution. If Stone were a larger cat, or if he hadn't had quite as much momentum, he could have crushed you," Spottedshadow warned.

"Indeed," Timberleg laughed. "Don't you worry, Stone. Once you get this down, no Unbound renegade will be able to lay a claw on you. Let's go again."

The new-claws returned to the proper starting positions and began their spar. The point of a Field-lander's fighting style was to use their small bodies and speed, diving in for quick strikes and forcing the opponent to keep moving, keep turning, keep twisting and dodging and striking empty air. Eventually, their enemies would be too exhausted to continue the fight and either give up or slip up. Then the Field-landers took their victory.

Peach's thick fur meant she didn't have the slighter frame of most Field-landers, but Spottedshadow had shown her how to use that to her advantage. Most Unbound invaders would go for her throat, and Peach's mane offered plenty of protection. She could get in close and throw them off when they found that their claws harmlessly passed through nothing but fur.

Stone tried his lunge again, this time without delaying. Instead of dropping down and kicking him, Peach sprang up, leaping clear over her training partner in classic Field-land style. Stone skidded to a halt trying to catch her hind leg, but she was already turning.

She glanced to Spottedshadow and Timberleg to see if they saw her pull off the jump-and-turn, which had been giving her trouble the last time they'd trained. She'd kept falling over on the turn, leaving herself open, but this time she'd managed to keep her paws under her and move out of the way of Stone's next swipe with ease.

But Peach saw that Timberleg and Spottedshadow weren't watching the new-claws. They were in the midst of a heated discussion, their faces intense even as they whispered. Peach kept her eyes on Stone, but turned an ear toward them.

"I hate seeing you two fight. When Nightpool and I were new-claws, you and Goldenpelt were always there for us. You taught us *everything*. Seeing how you worked together to teach us made me want to be a Mentor too. But now..."

"It's more complicated than that. There's a lot you don't know, and a lot you didn't see back then."

"I know he's sorry he hurt you."

Peach stumbled through her next dodge. Stone's paw grazed her ear, which was ringing with the Mentors' words. Had her uncle hurt Spottedshadow? Peach knew they didn't always see eye-to-eye, but she'd never thought the two would fight each other. They were both Field-landers, both cats she cared about deeply. How could this happen?

"It's not about a scratch, Timberleg," Spottedshadow sighed. "It's about trust."

"I probably shouldn't tell you this, but Goldenpelt said almost the same exact thing."

Stone crashed into Peach's side, sending her rolling across the field before she slammed into a clump of sage. She sneezed as the smell of it filled her nostrils.

"Peach, I'm sorry!" Stone shouted as he ran over.

"I'm fine, I'm not hurt," Peach answered. "Should have been paying attention. Sorry!" As she stood, a sharp pain pricked her paw and she brought it back up with a yelp. "Ow!"

"Are you okay?" Spottedshadow asked, trotting over. She stopped short. "Oh, no. Here, Peach, come around this way." She waved her tail, showing Peach a trail back through the sage. Peach didn't understand why, until she looked down at the ground. She had landed in a cluster of dwarf thistles. Her paw stung every time she stepped on it.

Spottedshadow stood at her new-claw's side once Peach was clear of the thistles. She nosed her paw, and Peach lifted it for inspection.

"I knew there was a reason we avoided collecting from this patch of sage..." Spottedshadow mumbled to herself. She licked the paw pad clean, then nodded in satisfaction. "The good news is, there aren't any spines stuck in your paw. The bad news is, there isn't any mint around here, so you'll have to wait until Mistysnow can see you to put ointment on it."

"I'll be alright. It only hurts a little," Peach said, wincing when she took another step.

"I'm really sorry," Stone murmured.

"Don't be. We should have been paying attention." Timberleg licked Peach's cheek in apology. "It won't happen again. Now, let's get you back home. It's getting late, anyway."

By the time they walked all the way back to Field Colony's eastern base, Peach was limping along on three feet. Her injured forepaw stayed tucked up whenever she could manage it, but there were times she had to set it down, and it burned as soon as it touched the ground. She hoped Mistysnow had plenty of mint salve. She didn't know how she'd sleep with it itching and hurting all night.

Given her sunny disposition and energy, most cats assumed Peach preferred daytime, but evening was her favorite time of day. Once the sun went down, the base was calm and quiet. Rangers shared meals and watched the stars, telling legends from long ago as they found mythical figures in the constellations. It was the time when Peach's whole family—her older siblings, mother, and uncle—would gather together to share news and jokes.

Tonight, there was a quiet buzz of activity, like a bee colony had built a hive in the middle of the base. Hazelfur sat outside the Keepers' Weave, while Forestleaf herself stood guard at the top of Captain's Overlook.

"Spottedshadow, good, you're here!" Ambereyes mewed as soon as they arrived. "You too, Timberleg! And Peach, it's always good to see my baby." Ambereyes spared a moment to give her youngest kitten a lick on the cheek. "Now, Spottedshadow, I have news. Nightpool and Mistysnow are asking for you."

"For me? Why?" Spottedshadow's tail stuck out straight. "Is something wrong with Nightpool?"

"Just the opposite! Her kittens are coming. Two arrived late this afternoon, but there are more on the way," Ambereyes purred. She noticed Peach holding her paw up and sniffed at it. "What happened here?"

"Thistle," Peach answered. At her mother's concerned look she hastily added, "I can manage it myself! Nightpool needs Mistysnow more than I do right now."

"The mint salve is just inside the medicine storage. The smell is unmistakable," Spottedshadow told Ambereyes, crossing the base in what felt like a single step to reach the Keepers' Weave.

Ambereyes nudged Peach toward the Healers' den. The golden-brown eyes she'd been named for flashed with surprise when Timberleg followed. "Aren't you going to watch over Nightpool?"

"I want to make sure Peach is alright, and you might need someone to reach the high shelves if the mint is up there," Timberleg said. He flicked an ear self-consciously. "Why?"

"I thought she was having *your* kittens."

"What? No!" Timberleg stammered. "Nightpool is a friend, a great friend, but we've never—I mean, you would be the first to know if I was going to be a father! We aren't mates."

Ambereyes let out a small laugh as she gathered the mint salve, which was kept in an abalone shell—a relic from generations ago when Field Colony's

Herbalist had joined them from River Colony. Peach dipped her paw in it, sighing as the cool gel instantly relieved the thistle sting.

"I don't know if I'm disappointed that I'm not a grandmother, or if I'm glad to have some more time to feel young," Ambereyes teased while she wrapped Peach's paw in a grass bandage. "So it isn't you, and it isn't Goldenpelt…"

Peach snorted. "Someone thought Uncle Goldenpelt was the father?"

"Well, there aren't many other available toms in the colony at the moment." Ambereyes replaced the salve and curled her tail over her paws. "Perhaps I shouldn't be thinking of toms *in the colony.*"

"You don't think Nightpool is disloyal, do you?" Peach gasped.

"Oh, nothing of the sort," Ambereyes said. "She's a Field Colony ranger through and through, of course. She's been here since she was a kitten and she knows the Ancestors' Law as well as anyone. But she *is* from the Unbound-lands…"

"Whoever the father is, Field Colony will care for Nightpool and her kittens," Timberleg said. He had already been forced to witness how cats treated Spottedshadow for having a romance outside the Field-lands' borders, even though her mate was still in the Alliance. He wouldn't allow his best friend to endure the same, especially when it was only a rumor. Whether or not Nightpool disclosed the identity of her litter's father was her decision alone. And if the father *was* an outsider, that didn't mean she would abandon the colony. She was still loyal. Her kittens would be, too.

"Of course," Ambereyes nodded, and brushed her cheek against his shoulder. Peach rubbed her head against his other side, and he sighed.

"Let's get a rabbit, yeah? I plan to relieve Spottedshadow from guard duty tonight, so I'll need a full stomach," Timberleg said.

By the time Peach, Ambereyes, and Timberleg had chosen their meal and settled in to eat beside the entrance to the Keepers' Weave, more tiny mewls had joined the chorus of newborn crying. Jaggedstripe had moved Dark and Dawn out to give Mistysnow more space to work, and the little ones were tumbling over themselves in excitement at the prospect of new playmates.

"I wonder if there will be more toms or mollies," Dark squealed.

"I wonder if any of them will have *magic*!" Dawn squeaked.

"Doubtful," Captain Hazelfur said, and they sat up to listen to him. He chuckled in response. "Nightpool has never shown any signs of it–and if the mother doesn't have magic, the kittens won't, either."

"Besides, colony cats like us wouldn't use magic even if we had it," Jaggedstripe said. "We have the Ancestors' Law, the Spirits, and each other.

We don't need dangerous things like magic, and we're happier without it. Aren't we?"

"Yeah!" Dark cheered.

Dawn didn't look as convinced. "Is magic really that bad?" the pale tortoiseshell-tabby kitten asked.

"It's unnecessary," Hazelfur said, his tone slightly more clipped than usual when he spoke with kittens. "Magic makes some cats think they're better than others, which leads to fighting that could be easily avoided. As Jaggedstripe said, we've no need for it here." He sat up. "All that matters is that Nightpool's kittens are healthy members of our colony, and they will learn our ways."

Mistysnow appeared to spare them any further lectures. "Four healthy kittens, and one tired but healthy mother!"

"Four? That's wonderful! A blessing from the Spirits to Come!" Hazelfur purred. "River Colony has out-numbered us for a while now. These kittens are our path to a more secure future."

"Nightpool will thank you not to add the future of the colony to her worries," Mistysnow laughed.

"Nightpool will have nothing to worry about," Hazelfur said, no laughter in his voice. "Kittens are the lifeblood of this colony, and we will all be here to help her raise them into fine rangers."

Not long after Mistysnow emerged, Spottedshadow stepped out of the Keepers' Weave to join Peach and her family for their meal. She tore into the rabbit as voraciously as if she had just given birth herself, and Peach glanced toward the den. She wished she had been invited to see the kittens be born, but Spottedshadow was the closest thing Nightpool had to a mother. There was a reason she'd been asked to see them.

"I can't wait to meet the new kittens," Peach said. "Shame they came now, though. Just another week and they could have been born on the Solstice!"

"I'm sure the Spirits to Come won't mind," Mistysnow remarked as she sat with them. Before she could crane her neck to groom her long silver tail, her head whipped up again.

"*HELP!*"

Hazelfur emerged from the woven grass tunnel so fast that Peach was scared something had happened to the newborns, but his eyes and ears were pointed outside the base. Forestleaf had already leapt down from her post and was rushing to intercept whoever had shouted.

A black-and-white Oak-lander stood just beyond the shelter of the heather bushes, panting and shaking.

"What's happened? Why are you here?" Hazelfur demanded.

"It's back! That giant beast...that monster...it's in our home! Please send help, quickly!" The Oak-lander sank to the ground, trembling. After a quick look from the Captain, Mistysnow disappeared into her den.

Fernface snarled. "I'm not dying for a bunch of tree-climbers! It's their problem, not ours."

"Oak Colony's base is so well-guarded, how could we possibly help?" Jaggedstripe wondered.

"Please, we can't get rid of it on our own. You promised to send aid. Do it for the sake of the Alliance, if nothing else will sway you!" the Oak-lander pleaded.

Despite the angry and fearful yowls of the Field-landers, Hazelfur nodded. "We will honor our agreement and do what we must." With a powerful leap, he launched himself onto the top of the Captain's Overlook. "Forestleaf, gather our most battle-fit rangers and follow this cat back to the Oak Colony base. I'll assemble my own team to lay an ambush for the beast. Tonight we will drive it away, once and for all!"

Timberleg rushed forward, and Ambereyes almost wanted to pounce on him and keep him down. As rangers, it was their duty to protect their home, but she couldn't help wanting to protect her son, too.

"I'll go!" Timberleg said, and Forestleaf nodded.

"Timberleg, Stone, Volefur, Fernface, Shadowclaw, with me," Forestleaf commanded. She nudged the Oak-lander back onto his feet, and they were off toward the fight. Peach stared anxiously up at Hazelfur, wondering if he would call her name.

"Spottedshadow, Goldenpelt, Mudnose, and Thrushspots, follow me," Hazelfur said. He met Peach's eyes and she shuddered. "Ambereyes, Peach, and Meadowleap, help Mistysnow. We're bound to have injuries when we return."

Despite knowing she wouldn't be in the fight, Peach didn't feel any relief. So many cats she loved were running into danger, against an unknown monster—something so bad that Oak Colony had to ask them for help. Timberleg, Stone, Spottedshadow, Goldenpelt...what would she do if any of them didn't come back? She was too stunned to even say goodbye before they vanished into the brush.

Ambereyes licked her between the ears, purring to calm her. "Come along, Peach-pit. It's going to be a long night."

The Invasion of Oak Colony

"The secret to victory is not who you fight against, but who you fight beside."
Captain Skyfang the Victorious Scar of Field Colony

Earlier That Day

Rowanstorm and Stagcharge watched with worry as Elmtail choked down the herbal concoction Wrensong had placed in front of him. Though it stopped his coughing fit and eased him into sleep, they could not tear their eyes or ears away from him. His wheezing was so loud, it would be a wonder if the whole colony did not hear.

"How long does he have?" Stagcharge asked, straight to the point.

"It's hard to say. If he were an ordinary cat, I would say...a month, maybe two?" Wrensong sighed and lowered her head, her nose nearly touching the Captain's. "But he is blessed by the Spirits. They might keep him going for a few more months. I'd like to promise it will be long enough to see Oak Colony settle into Redleaf's reign, but nothing can be certain at this point." She spat in frustration. "It would be easier if I could travel freely to Marsh Colony. Smallpebble cultivates a mushroom that supports the immune system far better than anything I have."

Wrensong found herself missing the little calico molly more and more lately. Her time spent with Hailstorm was cherished, of course. However, it didn't replace what she had with Smallpebble. Their shared passion for medicine, and for each other, could not be replicated with any other mate.

She set aside her personal feelings for the moment. Guards could not be spared to escort her to Marsh Colony whenever she wished and Oak Colony demanded her attention from sunrise to sunset. The sooner Moon earned her ranger name and began training as an Herbalist, the better.

"Thank you for your efforts. I doubt any medicine would be enough to save him now." Stagcharge curled his paws underneath his body so he could lie beside his mate. "I'll stay with him until he wakes."

Rowanstorm met Stagcharge's eyes briefly. It was neither selfishness nor possessiveness that dwelled behind Stagcharge's stoic gaze, but understanding. While inevitable, losing a loved one was never easy. Stagcharge was giving Rowanstorm permission to go and make his peace with the fact that his father would soon be gone, rather than stay and be forced to put on a brave face for Elmtail.

Rowanstorm took his leave after brushing his tail over both toms' shoulders, walking side by side with Wrensong. Redleaf waited outside, pacing along the cliffside path and occasionally sending a pebble skittering to the bottom of the canyon.

Redleaf started toward them, his mouth open, but he swiftly closed it and lowered his tail when he saw their faces. Wrensong and Rowanstorm's distress told him everything.

It was not a secret that Elmtail was one of the oldest cats in the Alliance, nor was it a secret within Oak Colony that he had suffered breathing issues which had worsened every spring and summer over the last few years. However, after the shock of losing Aspenbreeze and the looming threat of *something* in the woods that was capable of massacring rangers and escaping unnoticed, anxiety about the Captain's health had doubled. Most Oak-landers trusted Elmtail to get them through the crisis; if they lost him, too, they might very well lose everything.

In Elmtail's absence, Redleaf took his place atop the Council Ledge to address the colony and see that afternoon chores were assigned. Rowanstorm knew this would soon be the norm of Oak Colony, but it was strange to see another cat standing there. He seated himself beside Dawnfrost, who watched Redleaf with the same intense focus she showed everything nowadays.

"Gorseclaw, take a few new-claws to fetch more weaving supplies. I want the walls of the healing den reinforced." No doubt because Elmtail's coughing fits disturbed the entire base. "Shrewpelt, organize a scouting group and head to Thunder Falls. It's going to be hot today, so you should find plenty of prey there, too. Vinestripe, I want you to take another group with new-claws to the edge of the lake to practice tree hunting."

One by one, the named cats chose their companions. Gorseclaw gestured to Fox and Oak, though it was unlikely Stagcharge or Redleaf would be available to join them. However, despite the rule that any group leaving the base have at least two full rangers, the vines used for weaving were barely outside of the base. If any trouble arose, a single yowl would summon immediate aid. Shrewpelt chose Frondsway and Stonestep for his patrol, while Vinestripe selected her new-claw, Frost, along with Snowfeather and Moon.

Dawnfrost let out a frustrated sniff when she realized she'd been overlooked for any duties. Rowanstorm turned a sympathetic ear toward her, but neither of them had to wait long for Redleaf to approach Dawnfrost for a private conversation. He leapt down from the rocky façade and gestured with his tail for her to follow.

Without hesitation, Dawnfrost followed Redleaf around the edge of the healing den. She could hear Elmtail's labored breathing through the evergreen shrub wall. Redleaf spoke in a low voice, one that would not be overheard. "I'm sure you already know this, but Elmtail is very ill." Redleaf's hunched shoulders and serious expression made him look like a completely different cat. "He isn't going to get better."

Dawnfrost bowed her head. She knew as well as anyone that Elmtail could not live forever, but so soon after losing Aspenbreeze and Brackenfoot...

"Oak Colony must be prepared to meet this darkness," Redleaf continued. "The less time spent in confusion, the better. That is why I want to speak to you now, before the storm is upon us." He stood up straight and tall, striking the figure of a Captain giving the order to charge into battle. "I want you to be the next Second in Command of Oak Colony."

Dawnfrost's heart pounded loudly in her chest. She had known it was likely, and it was what she had always envisioned for herself, but hearing those words spoken aloud silenced all other sounds except her heart.

Before she answered, she found her eyes slipping toward the shadows of the bushes, looking for a pale tabby pelt. She forced herself to look back at Redleaf.

"I accept, Redleaf. I will serve Oak Colony and you with all I have."

Redleaf rested his muzzle on top of her head. "I know you will." He brushed his cheek against hers, drawing a short purr from her. "Oh, Dawnfrost. I hope you'll forgive me for putting you in such an unenviable position. What will we do without Elmtail?"

"We'll protect the colony he loved," Dawnfrost answered. "And we'll miss him terribly." She swiped his ear with a paw. "Now, go get some rest. You look like a dour Marsh-lander."

"That bad?" Redleaf laughed, a little forced, and shook himself. "I suppose you're right. I've been so busy that Lilac, Orange, and Sand must be forgetting what I look like."

He flicked Dawnfrost's nose with his tail as he left. He knew she would not openly celebrate just yet, not wanting to alarm anyone about the state of Elmtail's health–no matter how obvious his decline. But her closest friends were all still in the base, and he passed Thornheart on his way to the nursery. He would surely be the first to know, and would spread the news to Dawnfrost's circle of companions.

Redleaf pushed through a new wall of blackberry thorns, careful to make sure he didn't accidentally track any into the nesting material that covered the floor. He wished Stonestep had not gone hunting, but it was good for her to spend time with their grown son now that their second litter no longer needed her constant presence.

The trio still had their soft kitten fluff, but they were growing steadier on their legs every day. Soon they would be ready to begin their base training under the watch of the Keepers. Once they'd mastered scaling the sheer walls of their home and climbing through the trees to chase birds, they would be assigned to teachers and start their field training to be full rangers. They would be among the first rangers Redleaf would name, once their training was done.

For now, their steps were still clumsy as they adjusted to their rapidly growing bodies. Their eyes were wide with delighted surprise when their father entered the nursery. Judging from the way Sand's fur was ruffled and Lilac looked ready to pounce, Redleaf guessed he had interrupted an argument between the two. No doubt Lilac was planning to sneak out after Stonestep, and Sand was doing everything in his power to make his sister behave. Orange had already flopped onto Lilac's tail, keeping the feisty kitten from leaping at Sand.

Redleaf knew better than to try and keep Lilac inside if she wanted out. He would have to satisfy her curiosity in a safer way.

"Who wants a tour of the base?" he asked cheerfully as the kittens barreled into his legs, bundles of softness and excitement.

"Show us the Rangers' Post!" Lilac mewed.

"The Cliff Gardens!" squeaked Orange.

"The Council Cavern, please, please, please!" Sand pleaded.

Redleaf was relieved none of them asked to see the healing den. They didn't understand how sick Elmtail was, or even that their great Captain could be near the end of his life.

However, the Cliff Gardens and Rangers' Post were still too far for kittens who hadn't begun base training. Reaching them unassisted was one of the final assessments to prove an Oak-land kitten was ready for field training and full new-claw status. He normally wouldn't risk taking them that far, let alone now that all the Oak-landers' steps felt as though they were stalked by something hiding in the dense woods.

He waited for them to quiet down, then laid out their plan like he was talking to a troop of rangers going into dangerous territory. The trio leaned in close, both silly and serious, the way only playing kittens could be.

"First we'll have to sneak our way around the new-claws' sleeping quarters. We don't want to alert Black; you know he'll be as mad as a snake if we wake him. Then we'll climb the fallen tree, up past the Elders' den–remember, we can't disturb them, either–all the way up to the Highland Post. Once we're up there, we'll look around, then head down halfway and get off on the Council Cavern level."

"Yes!" Sand cheered. "We get to see where Dad sits on the Council!"

"Booor-ing!" Lilac groaned. "I want to see where the rangers do stuff!"

"We're going to see Highland Post," Orange pointed out, placating the gray tabby.

Any further protest was silenced when Redleaf crouched and began to slink out of the nursery. The kittens followed, doing their best to sneak out behind him. Anyone lingering near the dens could see them–including Rowanstorm, Thornheart, and Dawnfrost, who were sharing a plump dove–but the rangers politely looked away and pretended not to notice their Second and his little ones at their game.

Lilac tried to copy her father's stance and take quiet steps across the base. Her attempt at stealth was somewhat ruined by her singing to herself: "*We are the Oak-landers, fierce and stro-o-ong! We can hunt and fight all day lo-o-ong!*"

"Shh, Lilac!" Sand scolded as Orange began to hum along. Redleaf tried his best not to break into laughter and ruin the atmosphere completely, but he couldn't keep a wide smile off his face.

Redleaf led the trio to the base of tangled branches that sheltered the new-claws' sleeping quarters. Usually it was the most open of the dens, as the Keepers put less effort into its upkeep. Shielding kittens, Elders, and the ill was more important, so Keepers focused on maintaining the nursery, Elders' den, and healing den. The rangers' keep was where the vast majority of cats spent most of their nights, and it was well managed by the rangers. But new-claws didn't seem to mind where they slept, too eager to get to the next day's training and one step closer to joining the adults. They huddled near the center of their den when it rained and stayed mostly dry, and wind rarely disturbed the base. Now, even the new-claws' den had extra thorn vines loosely woven around the branches. It was not enough to make walls, not like the other dens had, but it was a sad reminder of the times.

Perhaps Redleaf shouldn't encourage the kittens to slink around. They were safer in the heart of the base. But if he didn't take them out, they'd go out on their own, and that was far more dangerous. At least he could recognize danger and defend them until help arrived, should something happen. Even brave Lilac would probably freeze up in the face of a real threat, or hesitate because she worried about getting in trouble more than being killed, the latter being so far beyond her scope of experience that it wouldn't even register as a possibility.

Redleaf tested the fallen tree, then picked each kitten up by the scruff, pulling them onto the log. He held each one until their small, sharp claws found purchase in the bark.

Orange lifted his tail high. "It's like we're going to the Moonlight Meeting!"

"Can we play Moonlight Meeting?" Sand asked, apparently forgetting that they were supposed to avoid anyone noticing them as they climbed up the old oak. "I want to be Captain."

"No, *I'm* Captain!" Lilac hissed.

"I didn't finish! I want to be Captain of *Field* Colony. You can be Captain of Oak Colony," Sand replied.

"Good, because Oak is better than Field anyway," Lilac said.

"We already know all about Oak-landers! It's boring to be one when we play, too!" Sand said.

"I guess I can be River Colony's Captain," Orange offered. "Yum, yum, fish! I love water! Splash, splash!"

"You're so weird," Lilac laughed.

Redleaf kept them moving along the tree, making sure they stayed balanced on the wide trunk. This was one of the most basic of base training tasks, one they were old enough to complete, *if* they were paying attention to where they put their paws. "So does that mean I'm Captain of Marsh Colony?"

"Hmm..." Sand shook his head. "No, you aren't scary enough. Orange, you be Marsh Colony Captain and Father can be River Colony Captain."

"So I'm not scary enough, but Orange is?" Redleaf mumbled to himself. Then, louder, he said, "Yum, fish."

The farther they went along the tree, the wilder the game grew. Lilac had claimed mages were waiting on the Oak-land border to invade, which Sand argued was nonsensical because if there were going to be Unbound amassing anywhere it would be on Field Colony's border, which Lilac said was impossible because Field Colony was too boring to want to take over. Orange mostly ignored them, and struck up a conversation with Redleaf about why Marsh Colony didn't eat fish even though they could also reach the ocean from their territory.

"It's because they're swamp-ocean fish," Orange said sagely, channeling all the stories he'd heard of Captain Hawkshell into his stiff walk and stern face. "No good for eating."

"Oh, definitely," Redleaf agreed. "Everyone knows swamp-ocean fish are terrible."

Orange nodded. "Lake fish are better."

Distracted by their game but kept on track by Redleaf, the kittens soon reached the end of the log. Sand crouched low, digging his claws in with a whimper when he looked over the side and realized how far from the clearing below they were. Acting quickly, Redleaf lifted him by the scruff and set him on solid ground on top of the cliff. Lilac and Orange carefully climbed around the roots next. Redleaf made sure to grab them when they got near the edge so they didn't slip. It was a long, long way down for a small cat who hadn't been taught how to land safely yet.

Lilac bounded toward the forest before stopping suddenly, her tail sticking straight up and doubling in size. "Something's there!"

"Stop kidding around, Lilac," Sand growled.

Redleaf took a deep breath. "No, she's right. Something *is* there."

Sand darted under Redleaf's belly and curled into a tight ball. "Is it the monster? Is it going to get us, like it got Aspenbreeze?"

At Sand's words, Lilac ran back to Redleaf and hid behind him. Orange fluffed himself up and pressed against Redleaf's side. The red-patched tom leaned down to lick the kittens' ears.

"You'd better come out, before they're petrified," he said.

Stonestep emerged from the bushes, leading to a litany of high-pitched mews from the kittens.

"*Mother!* You scared us!" Sand whined.

"I wasn't scared," Lilac said.

Orange shook out his thick fur. "It's okay to be scared, you know."

"But I wasn't!"

While the young ones made enough noise to scare off all the prey in the woods, a silent message passed from Stonestep to Redleaf. After hunting, fighting, and sleeping next to her for so long, he knew every twitch of her whisker and turn of her tail.

Danger was coming their way, fast. He had to get their children to safety.

He picked up Sand, knowing the cautious tom-kitten would be reluctant to clamber back onto the log. He didn't set Sand down until they were halfway along, nearly level with the turn-off for the Council Cavern. Stonestep followed with Lilac dangling from her jaws, the kitten loudly protesting that she could walk. Orange steadied himself between his parents, claws chipping away minuscule bits of bark as he walked.

A triumphant yowl echoed from the top of the cliff.

"We've got them! We've got them cornered!" Shrewpelt whooped, "Oak-land rangers, hurry! To battle! This ends now!"

Redleaf looked up after curling around Sand to see a pair of strange, dark-furred animals standing atop the cliff. They looked more like canines than badgers, but they were far burlier than any fox or coyote. They had short nubs for tails, round ears, and long, wicked claws on wide-set paws. Each of them was easily four times larger than a full-grown cat.

A strange, heavy odor struck Redleaf's nose and made him hiss. It stank of meat and moss and mud, blood and death and decay.

The drop to the base lay behind the beasts. In front of them were Shrewpelt and Frondsway, with more reinforcements racing up the slope. It seemed the beasts were captured, and by sheer numbers Oak Colony would defeat them easily.

Then one of them took a step back.

Its hind paw slipped on the edge of the cliff, sending pebbles raining down into the clearing.

It tumbled after them.

The beast rolled over and over, a startled howl tearing from its throat as it rolled down, flailed over a ledge, and kept sliding. Those long claws snagged stray branches, slowing its fall before its weight snapped them and kept it moving down, down, down.

Straight into Oak Colony's home, where it landed, unharmed.

It got up, shook itself off, and let loose an angry bellow. The second beast cautiously leaned one foot over the edge of the cliff and slid down to join it. Both of them stood in the heart of Oak Colony and roared for blood.

The Loss of Field Colony

"When all else fails, it is our unity that will save us."
Captain Goldengorse the Brilliant Sun of Forest Colony

Shrewpelt stared in horror as the beasts slid and tumbled down the cliff, too fast to stop, but too slow to die from the force of impact upon landing. His victorious charge, his plan to corner them, claiming victory for the Alliance and an Envoy title for himself, had just put everyone he loved into terrible danger.

He should have listened to Frondsway when she suggested going back to the base as soon as they discovered the beasts wandering the woods. She'd always had a knack for knowing when things were about to go horribly wrong.

"No, stop them!" he screamed, throwing himself down after the beasts he had chased straight to his home.

Shrewpelt's yowl jerked Dawnfrost's attention to the ridge in time to watch the bulky, black-furred beasts slide down the slope and lumber into Oak Colony's base, one after the other. The rangers who had rushed to aid Shrewpelt followed them down, hissing and spitting curses all the while, but the beasts only stared with eyes as dark and unfeeling as night.

Dawnfrost couldn't place what they were. For the moment, it did not matter.

One of the creatures let out a warning bellow and loped toward the nearest cover it could find–the Herbalists' den. Toward Elmtail, Wrensong, and Stagcharge.

Dawnfrost's blood chilled.

Thornheart screeched a battle cry fiercer than such a gentle cat should make. He raced past Dawnfrost's shoulder, two more rangers close behind. Though they were all competent in battle, they were small compared to the mass of black fur stubbornly rooted in front of the den. The beast sniffed around the edges of the bush that concealed the entrance, pushing onwards despite the hisses and yowls of the cats inside.

"Form a line!" Redleaf called, leaping down into the clearing and waving his tail high. "We must work together! Stand with me, Oak Colony, and hold them back until the base is evacuated!"

The rangers rushing to the Herbalists' den skidded to a halt, letting the rest of the colony's fighting force catch up to them and spread out. Forming a wall of claws and teeth, they kept the beasts pinned to the cliff, preventing them from advancing on the nursery or the Elders' sleeping quarters. Stonestep guided her litter into the safety of the Council Cavern, standing guard at its entrance, while Dustclaw roused the Elders. Gorseclaw, Fox, and Oak checked the rest of the dens for any dozing cats not yet awoken.

The Herbalists' den was not without its own protection. From within came the furious snarl of a cat fighting for his life, and the beast that had pushed its head in reared back on its hind legs. Blood spilled from scratches on its nose. It crashed back to all four massive paws, crushing part of the den's outer wall under its feet.

The other saw its companion bleeding and let out a furious roar, then charged.

Shrewpelt leapt with claws outstretched. "Bastards! Brutes!"

"Shrewpelt, no!" Dawnfrost hissed, racing after him. When she moved, so did the rest of the rangers, following as one unit. She could only hope that would be enough to give the Keepers time to evacuate. One moment, Rowanstorm and Thornheart were at her side; the next, they stood with Shrewpelt, keeping the beast away from the healing den.

"Get back!" Shrewpelt snarled, swiping at the beasts with reckless, uncoordinated strikes. Finally he landed a blow, shearing black fur from one beast's muzzle, close to where Stagcharge's scratch had made its mark.

All it earned Shrewpelt was a bark and a lunge from the animal. Its fanged jaws closed with a snap where Shrewpelt's head had just been. It reared onto its hind legs again, ready to crush the cats or the healing den–whichever was in its way.

"*No!*" Redleaf howled. "Defend the den!"

Dawnfrost dashed ahead of the line and dug her claws into the beast, climbing it as easily as she scaled cliffs and trees, until she gripped its muzzle. It tried to shake her, but she kept a firm hold, sinking claws into its face and biting its ear. It stumbled backward into its companion and toppled over. Dawnfrost barely managed to jump clear, nabbing a low branch with her front paws while her hind legs churned in the air above the beasts' heads.

With the entrance to the Herbalists' den clear, Wrensong and Stagcharge led Elmtail out between them. They could not make it to the fallen tree; instead, they guided Elmtail up the cliffside, toward the Cliff Gardens.

Though Elmtail could barely breathe, he turned his head toward his colony, claws unsheathed. "Fight on, Oak-landers! Fight on!"

The beasts were not satisfied with the destruction they'd caused. One slammed its paws into the ground and barreled toward the new-claws' den, breaking through the line and crashing against the fallen tree. The cats climbing to safety froze, clinging on with all their might to avoid slipping down to their dooms.

It had made one mistake, at least: the beasts were now divided, if only by the length of a single cat or two, and Oak Colony's rangers worked quickly to widen the gap. Shrewpelt and Larkwing followed Dawnfrost's example, using the beast's size against. They leapt and clung on with teeth and front claws and batter it with their hind claws. Tornleg, Frondsway, and Black rushed to meet the beast that was destroying the new-claws' den. They danced around its legs, drawing its attention and giving the fleeing cats a chance to make their escape. For a moment they had the advantage; then, with a single swipe of a massive paw, the beast scattered them. Tornleg struck his old wound and let out a yelp. Frondsway and Black hurried him away.

Dawnfrost pulled herself onto the branch and planned her next leap, aiming to take their place. If she timed it right, she could land on its neck–then she would sink her teeth in until it stopped moving. She didn't know if her teeth could get that deep, but she knew she had to try.

Once her feet left the branch, the beast pounded its legs on the ground, lowering itself by several inches. Dawnfrost slashed its back, but couldn't hold on, falling to the side. She intended to scramble out of the way once she landed, but her claw caught in the creature's thick, tangled fur. She was left hanging there, struggling to wrench her paw free. The beast reached for her with its mouth open, drool flying in her face as it let out a roar.

"Dawnfrost!" Rowanstorm cried.

"Rowan–" Dawnfrost began, but her shout was cut short when he was struck in the chest by the beast's hind leg and sent sprawling to the wall of the base. He struck the stone and fell into an unmoving heap.

Dawnfrost's paw finally came loose, but she hit the ground hard, the air knocked from her lungs. Before she could stand and run to check on Rowanstorm, before she could defend herself, before she could *think*, she became aware of the shadow towering over her. The caterwauls and shrieks of her colony faded into silence against the sound of her own pulse.

Just as the beast moved to crush her, a lithe, dark shape flew into its head, knocking it off balance so its paws landed on either side of Dawnfrost. The ginger-pointed molly took as big a breath as she could, then raced between its hind legs to where Rowanstorm still lay. She nosed his fur and was relieved to see his chest moving and his open eye focused.

"I think I dislocated something," he groaned. Dawnfrost helped him up with a purr she wouldn't have expected of herself.

The evacuation was nearly complete. Dustclaw and Hailstorm helped cats make the final steps onto the clifftop. Yellowflower and Birchwhisker shouted encouragement beside them. At some point in the fighting, Vinestripe's group had returned. She and Frost stood with Larkwing against one of the beasts while Snowfeather and Moon helped Tornleg into the Council Cavern. Frondsway and Black joined Stonestep in defending the cave.

Gorseclaw approached Dawnfrost and Rowanstorm with his belly low to the ground, eyes darting quickly to make sure they were, for the moment, safe. "I can take Rowanstorm up to the cavern."

"Dawnfrost, too," Rowanstorm said, his mew coming out strained and awkward. Dawnfrost prayed the kick from the beast had not broken any of his ribs. Flashes of Aspenbreeze's corpse filled her mind before she shook them away.

"I can still fight. Besides…" Dawnfrost glanced back at the beast that had nearly killed her, and the sleek-furred tortoiseshell molly currently tearing its fur out in chunks. "We have guests."

Forestleaf gave the beast one last tear through its ear before she sprang away, landing nimbly on her delicate paws. She looked over her shoulder at the cats cowering near the ground entrance. "Don't just stand there! Get over here and help!"

"What on the sun-scorched earth is *that thing?*" Fernface whimpered.

"It doesn't matter what it is. We need to get it out of the base!" Redleaf answered. "The evacuation is all but complete. We can shift the line now to drive them out."

"Understood." Forestleaf raised her tail and dropped it, and the Field-landers fanned out, clearing the entrance from which they had come. The beasts were too clumsy to climb back up the cliffs, so they would have to be pushed into the dense woods. Once out of Oak Colony's base, they could be tracked back to their lair for a rematch on the Alliance's terms.

"Oak Colony, back away!" Redleaf commanded. "Reform the line to block off every route but the main entrance! All injured, report to the Council Cavern."

Dawnfrost stepped into place between Shrewpelt and Thornheart, waving her tail at Redleaf before he tried to make her leave. Her paw might be hurt, but she knew it was not broken–a torn claw, maybe, but nothing so serious that she needed to abandon the fight. Not when she was proving herself the right choice to be his future Second in Command.

With Field-landers replacing the injured Oak-land rangers, the beasts were soon surrounded on all sides but one. A squalling, hissing barricade of cats kept them away from any of the dens or from following vulnerable members of the colony up the fallen tree. Together, the rangers backed the beasts toward the entrance. The creatures were tiring, bleeding from a dozen scratches. Their dark eyes drooped and they breathed heavily, more and more effort going into every half-hearted counter-strike.

"*Oak Colony stands tall!*" Redleaf yowled, joining the line. Soon the cheer was taken up by all the Oak-landers. "*Oak Colony stands tall! Oak Colony stands tall!*"

Bewildered even more by the unified chanting, the beasts stumbled back faster, letting out startled whines and rumbles of their own.

"That's the way!" Birchwhisker whooped from above.

"Just a little more," Yellowflower added. "Give them something to remember us by!"

With a final, triumphant growl, Redleaf rushed forward, making an impressive leap with his claws outstretched. Dawnfrost recognized it from her days as a new-claw, when she'd watched him do the maneuver in mock-battles with other Envoys. He would land on the back of the beast with all his claws, roll to slash four sets of cuts through its flesh, then leap clear.

He never landed.

A massive paw struck him from the air, slamming him into the ground with a horrible, sickening crack.

Dawnfrost knew without doubt that he was dead.

The two beasts made happy grunts as a monster more than twice their size dropped onto four legs and let out an ear-shattering roar. The line of cats faltered. Once the first fled, the rest scattered in sheer terror. Some did not run fast enough to avoid the swipe of the beast's claws.

Spottedshadow's eyes darted from one panicked, screaming cat to the next. Her legs trembled and her muscles tensed to jump into the fray. The reek of blood hung in the air like an unpleasant fog.

She had expected things to be bad when Swiftshadow had come to Field Colony for help, but even her worst nightmares could not have conjured the scene in front of her. Redleaf lay motionless at the end of a crimson smear on the ground. Other rangers she didn't know well enough to name dragged themselves toward cover.

Dawnfrost had clung to the beast's face, trying to blind it, but had been thrown clear. Thankfully, Thornheart had managed to drag her up the cliffside—but she was limping badly, and the cliff was hardly any safer than the ground when the beast stood on its hind legs.

A sick feeling of helplessness clawed Spottedshadow's heart and filled her veins with fire. "Captain, we have to help them!"

"No! We need to wait for more reinforcements from Marsh Colony. Going down there now would be a meaningless waste of Field Colony lives," Goldenpelt argued.

Hazelfur watched Forestleaf and her group, who fared no better than the native Oak-landers against the gigantic creature stampeding through the canyon base. Its claws came down dangerously close to the nursery, and one of the smaller beasts rushed toward it. It jammed its face into the den, only to pull back with a pained cry as its nose was stuck with thorns. The larger beast huffed angrily and raised a massive paw.

Horrid visions of dead kittens that looked far too much like Nightpool's newly born litter flooded Spottedshadow's mind. "That thing is going to destroy the nursery! We must act *now*," she pleaded.

Hazelfur glanced quickly between Spottedshadow and Goldenpelt, two of his most brilliant yet most divided rangers. He set his jaw and pinned his ears back. "Field Colony rangers don't let kittens die. Attack!"

Together with Spottedshadow and Thrushspots, Hazelfur lunged down the rock face and raced toward the nursery. Despite his misgivings, Goldenpelt's paws landed only seconds after theirs, and he was soon at Hazelfur's shoulder.

"Take the kittens to the cliffs. I'll join our rangers here to distract the enemy," Hazelfur ordered.

"But Hazelfur–"

Goldenpelt didn't finish voicing his rebuttal. Hazelfur fixed him with the most ferocious glare he had ever seen on the cream tom's face. He doubted even Forestleaf was capable of a look that venomous.

"*That was an order!*"

Hazelfur joined Forestleaf as she struggled beside the Oak-landers to hold off the beasts. A line had reformed to try to keep them from pushing further into the base, to force them back to the forest, but there were wide gaps. All the rangers were panting from exhaustion and most were bleeding. Timberleg's left side was drenched in blood that poured from a deep slash on his neck.

"About time," Forestleaf snapped, though Hazelfur did not miss the way her green eyes shone with relief, nor the brush of her tail against his back.

Hazelfur stood his ground, as he had done all his life. Before anything else, he needed to bolster the line's morale. Without the will to fight, they were already defeated. "Alliance rangers! We must be strong. The Spirits are with us, and they will not see us fail. Move as one and push them back! They may have size, but we have numbers and skill!"

Yowling, hissing, and spitting, the rangers made as great a show of force as they could, weaving between each other to let their stripes and spots blend together. They were one force, united—one Spirit against any challenge. For a brief second, Hazelfur noticed apprehension in the great beast's dark eyes as it realized the cats had them surrounded and more were rejoining the battle, their wounds patched up to the best of Wrensong's ability. Perhaps, with their size and strength, the beasts could kill every cat in the base, but it would cost them everything to do so.

"Run!" Hazelfur commanded them. "Run and find somewhere else to live!"

The smaller beasts looked to the larger, grumbling nervously. Hazelfur stepped forward, confident that the creature would realize its mistake and retreat.

A single step was all it took for the largest beast to strike.

A massive paw hurtled toward Hazelfur.

"Look out!" Forestleaf screeched. She leapt in front of him, and for a heartbeat he saw only her. Beautiful, determined Forestleaf, who had been his partner in all things.

Hazelfur was aware of his paws leaving the ground. In that brief moment, he prayed his body would shield Forestleaf from the impact as she was thrown through the air after him. She had always brought him good fortune; he could only hope the Spirits would allow him to give a little back to her. Then his head struck the stone wall of the quarry, and he knew no more.

Clouds of dust rose under Wildfur's paws as he raced across the dry Oak Colony ground. Pool snuffled beside him as dirt got in his nose, but the new-claw put his long legs to use to keep up with his Mentor. Wildfur had protested taking a cat so young into battle, but Hawkshell had made clear that Pool would be a lookout and messenger, not an active combatant.

"Just a little farther!" the calico Oak-lander panted ahead of them. She had run all the way to Marsh Colony's base and back, hardly pausing to catch her breath when she'd told the Council what was happening. It hadn't taken many words; the only reason Elmtail would risk sending one of his rangers into the Marsh-lands alone was if the danger was already in the Oak-landers' home.

Hawkshell ran at the Oak-lander's flank, followed by Indigoeyes and Birdflight, then Snowstorm and Falconswoop. Wildfur and Pool took the rear, and would stay there unless the worst happened.

"Mind if I join you?"

Pool nearly jumped out of his fur at the arrival of a pale tabby tom at the back of their group. He thought he'd been on alert, watching and listening for any sign of Oak Colony abandoning their base or monsters approaching, but the River-land ranger had come out of nowhere. If the other rangers noticed, they said nothing about the extra set of claws beside them. Wildfur would have shrugged if he hadn't been busy running for all his paws were worth. Wolfthorn went where he liked and did as he pleased. If Wildfur were slimmer and didn't get his fur snagged in every bush and bramble, he would do the same.

"Sunfire, witness your vengeance!" Hawkshell howled in fury as they at last burst through the entrance to Oak Colony's base. She hardly paused to assess the damage in front of her before she gestured for her rangers to fan out. One of the smaller beasts turned to face her and she struck with as much ferocity as she could across its snout, causing its head to whip to the side as it stumbled. Wasting no time, the Marsh Colony rangers pounced and dug their claws in to drag it down.

Wolfthorn found the fastest route to Dawnfrost's side, climbing up and over the giant creature. His hind claws raked its ear as he leapt clear of its snapping jaws to land in front of her. "I'm here," he said, and all fatigue lifted from the Envoy.

"Vinestripe, Thornheart, Stagcharge, help the Marsh-landers! Perhaps if we do enough damage to the small ones, the larger will retreat," Dawnfrost commanded.

Together with the remains of her rangers and Wolfthorn, she rushed the giant monster. She dodged its paws to keep it busy while Hawkshell and the Marsh-landers corralled the smaller beasts toward the entrance with harsh strikes. They whimpered and wailed in fear, and Wildfur could practically see the frustration and weariness radiating from the great animal when it was kept away from them.

"Go up there," Wildfur told Pool, nodding to the safety of the cliffs. "We need a better view so we know when to go for help, if we have to." He already smelled the fresh, light scent of Field Colony in the base. Who would they go to for help, if it came to that? Rainfall had made her stance clear on how useful River Colony would be, and Wolfthorn was surely there on his own orders. He supposed they could get reinforcements from Marsh Colony, but he knew Hawkshell didn't want to risk more of her rangers. If they lost this fight, Marsh Colony would need all their rangers ready to defend their own home.

As they climbed, Pool let out a sharp gasp. Wildfur looked ahead to see a dark, lithe shape lying on the edge of the cliff. Blood soaked the slender molly's fur.

Wildfur's heart thundered in his ears. A patch of orange in the molly's fur stood out as he stumbled closer. His whole body shook with relief. Forestleaf, not Spottedshadow, lay dead in front of him.

"Keep climbing," he told Pool. If the beast could reach the cliff, they had to go higher. He would not let his new-claw die in his first battle.

The beast stood on its hind legs and the rangers scrambled away, clearing the path for it to rejoin the small ones by the base entrance.

At last, the creatures retreated.

Hawkshell spat and sliced her claws through the shaggy fur on the back of the fleeing beast's haunches before Indigoeyes managed to pull her back. They hurried away, and Hawkshell yelled in fury at the dark sky. "I will kill them! I will!"

"It was not the right time." Indigoeyes soothed her by licking her shoulder. "Next time, Captain. Next time we will line our nests with their fur."

Before Wildfur could stop him, Pool rushed back down into the base. "Falconswoop, are you okay?" The stocky gray-and-white molly had a scratch on her flank that oozed a streak of red down her leg, but it was not as deep as it appeared. Pool purred in relief and groomed the blood from her fur.

"*I'm* fine, thank you very much," Snowstorm grumbled.

With the new-claw safely reunited with his family, Wildfur was free to search the crowd for the one cat he most wanted to see. He found his mate butting her head against Dawnfrost's.

"Thank the Spirits you're okay. I mean...*are* you okay?" Spottedshadow asked.

"I'll be fine, but..." Dawnfrost heaved a sigh. Wolfthorn touched his muzzle to her ear, and she did not pull away from him.

"Spottedshadow," Wildfur breathed. The fear and despair he'd felt when he saw Forestleaf shook him again, until he could barely remain standing. Spottedshadow had not died, but she could have. She so easily could have.

When he could not move his legs, Spottedshadow ran to him. She brushed her cheek along his neck, his shoulder, the whole length of his body, both of them taking in as much of the other's scent as they could. They searched for the stench of blood on each other, and didn't stop until each was sure the other was unhurt.

"I thought–" Wildfur could not bring himself to say it. He nearly knocked Spottedshadow over when he buried his face in her shoulder.

"You thought what?" Spottedshadow asked.

Wildfur drew away from her, nodding toward the half-crushed nursery and the bodies being lowered down the cliff with as much care as the exhausted rangers were capable of. The rest of the Field-landers had regrouped there, surrounding the broken forms of Forestleaf and Hazelfur.

"Oh!" Spottedshadow gasped. "Oh, *no.*"

Wildfur steadied himself, ready to walk her to the bodies of her Captain and Second–her grandparents–when a quaking voice cried out from up on the cliff.

"H-help!" Stone called out as he tried to assist Timberleg down the fallen tree. The brown ranger was bleeding heavily, barely standing, and the gray new-claw couldn't support his weight. He slipped, long legs flailing as he slid over the side.

Spottedshadow moved so quickly that Wildfur hardly realized she'd left his side. She used her body to soften the ranger's fall and helped him back onto his feet, ignoring the soreness in her shoulder from where he'd landed. "Hang on! We'll get you to Wrensong."

"Are you completely daft? We aren't staying in this Spirits-forsaken forest! We should never have come at all!" Fernface spat. "Let's get out of here before those *things* come back to finish off Oak Colony."

"Timberleg needs treatment now!" Spottedshadow snapped.

"Like Field Colony needed to attack *now,* to defend an *empty* nursery?" Goldenpelt shot back. He raised his voice to an authoritative yowl. "Field Colony is going home. Volefur, carry Hazelfur. Shadowclaw, carry..." He paused to avoid choking out the name. "Carry Forestleaf. Spottedshadow and Stone, help Timberleg. I will *not* leave him here."

There was no time for Spottedshadow to argue, or even point out that the odds of Timberleg making it to Field Colony's base were getting lower by the second. The golden tom had spoken, and all the other Field-landers were on his side. She looked longingly back to Wildfur, and he nodded. They would speak again soon, even if he had to fight Goldenpelt and all his lackeys himself to get to her.

Heart heavy with regret, Spottedshadow followed her colony out of the broken base, whispering reassuring words to Timberleg in the hopes that he would make it home.

"Marsh Colony, we're going after them!" Hawkshell announced. "We will track the monsters to their den. We may not be able to chase them out of our territory tonight, but we will not go home with nothing to show for it."

"Finchflight and Swiftshadow, go with them," Dawnfrost ordered. "They're likely hiding somewhere near the border. We stand a better chance of finding them if we work together to check both sides."

Though Finchflight and Swiftshadow were still breathing hard from running to get aid, neither had been injured in the fight. They nodded and joined the Marsh-landers as they marched out of the base.

Wildfur gently pushed Pool after them. "Go, stay with your family. Hawkshell won't start another fight tonight, not without a lot more rangers."

"What about you?" Pool asked.

"I'm staying here to help. I'll be back soon." Wildfur might not be a Keeper, but Oak Colony had suffered its share of casualties in the fight, and an extra set of paws to fix dens and carry supplies were always useful.

Elmtail emerged at last from a cavern high on the cliffside, his eyes clouded with grief as he looked over the base. He started to open his mouth, perhaps to give some kind of rallying speech, but instead lowered his head until his nose nearly touched the ground.

A light gray molly sprang from the den, leaving a trio of kittens hiding behind Elmtail as she jumped all the way down to the forest floor. "*Redleaf!*" She fell onto the former Second's body, shoving her nose into his side to try to rouse him. When Frondsway tried to approach, she lashed out with claws unsheathed, barely missing the former Herbalist's muzzle. "No! No, this isn't happening! Come on, Redleaf, wake up! Wake up, now! You're scaring the kittens!"

Wildfur shuddered. It was too easy to see his mother in Stonestep's place, to remember the way she'd screamed and hissed when it was time to mourn Patch at the new moon ceremony.

One by one, Oak-landers turned their expectant gazes from Elmtail to Dawnfrost. They were waiting to be told what to do. Waiting for *her* to tell them what to do, as she had with Finchflight and Swiftshadow.

"No. Not like this. I can't," Dawnfrost whispered. When she had accepted Redleaf's offer to be Second, she had done so with the promise of being *his* Second–not his replacement. Still, there was little choice left. The colony had decided for her. Even Elmtail, silenced by sorrow, was looking at her now.

She turned to Wolfthorn for support, only to find the pale tabby had vanished, as if he'd never been there at all.

She alone was Oak Colony's guiding light now.

The Clouded Moon

"The ranger cried out to the Spirits Beyond to make him strong, and brave, and resilient against all the ills that could harm his colony. When they answered, he was blessed by their wisdom and power, and he endured many pains in the place of those who followed him."
Alliance Folktale, *"The First Captain"*

Timberleg was dying.

Goldenpelt pushed onward through the night, urging the tired and injured rangers to move faster, but Spottedshadow knew it was already far too late for the brown tom. Even if Timberleg had received treatment from Wrensong, the odds of him surviving that much blood loss were slim to none. Spottedshadow had left his side only once to gather moss and cobwebs to form a makeshift tourniquet. It was soaked through with his blood almost as soon as she applied pressure.

Stone hadn't blinked once, terrified that Timberleg would perish the moment he took his eyes off his Mentor.

Worst of all, Timberleg knew it himself. His pace slowed as his heart struggled to beat. His paws lingered closer and closer to the ground with every step. Soon he would not be able to lift his feet at all.

"Stone, I'm so proud of you." Timberleg's voice was too quiet. "You didn't let fear stop you, even when older rangers fled. You're going to be great. Wish I could see it with my own eyes..."

"Don't talk like that, Timberleg!" Stone tried to nudge Timberleg forward with his shoulder and nearly knocked him over. Timberleg leaned heavily against Spottedshadow, unable to find his footing again.

Spottedshadow looked ahead. Goldenpelt's eyes and ears were alert in every direction except theirs. He refused to glance back at Timberleg and see the obvious: his former new-claw, his *nephew*, was dying, and they needed to stop so he could do it in peace. Or perhaps it was the lifeless bodies of Forestleaf and Hazelfur being dragged along with them that Goldenpelt was avoiding.

Once they were clear of the trees, Goldenpelt barked, "Thrushspots, run back to base and tell Mistysnow we're on our way. Don't tell anyone about Hazelfur and Forestleaf yet. We don't want to cause a panic."

Thrushspots was only too eager to comply, racing away with speed rivaling that of the wind itself.

"Field Colony has nothing to fear with you leading us," Fernface purred in his ear.

Goldenpelt hissed at her praise. "You say that while we are carrying back a dead Captain and Second!" He let out a long sigh, eyes drifting up to the waning moon. "What do we do now? The Ancestors' Law is clear on what to do if a Captain or Second dies, but not both at once..."

Fernface replied, smugly as ever, "I think it's obvious. *You* should be Captain."

Murmurs of approval rose from the rangers. It made sense: Goldenpelt was the only Envoy in Field Colony. Even if there had been others, it was obvious that Forestleaf had always favored him as her choice of Second. What other option was there? More and more voices added to the praise Fernface heaped upon Goldenpelt, until he no longer bothered to feign hesitance.

The thought of it made Spottedshadow's heart sink lower. Perhaps she had been foolish to encourage Hazelfur to join the fight, but how could she have known the nursery was empty? Goldenpelt spoke as if it were obvious—but like her, he'd only realized it had been evacuated after the fighting calmed down. And even if the kittens hadn't been there, how could she have known some other cat, frightened and hurt, hadn't taken temporary shelter there?

More than that, it was his insistence that Field Colony lives were more important than others that she couldn't get out of her head. Goldenpelt might be a good Captain for Field Colony, but what about the rest of the Alliance? Especially now, when they needed to be united more than ever?

Goldenpelt's chest rose with pride until he looked back to meet Spottedshadow's eyes. They were dim with worry, and Timberleg was barely standing.

"If you can talk, you can walk. Let's hurry," the golden tom snapped at his admirers.

Thrushspots had completed her task. Mistysnow had already assembled the rangers guarding the base and instructed them on how to manage light scratches and bruises. They would manage the rangers who had received mild injuries while she focused on those who were more heavily wounded–namely, Timberleg.

The brown tom was still clinging to life when Mistysnow guided him into the healing den to see what could be done. Spottedshadow gestured for Stone to stay outside while she went in to help.

Timberleg collapsed on a pile of ferns and let out a bloody cough. "Don't waste medicine on me, please."

"We have to try," Spottedshadow protested, though she knew he was right. She reached for better bandage material than she'd been able to scavenge in the forest, but Mistysnow put a paw on her shoulder to stop her.

"His Spirit is departing for the Beyond. There is nothing more to be done."

Spottedshadow thought she had accepted the inevitable some time during the too-long journey to get back home. Now, looking down at Timberleg's not-yet-still body, a surge of defiance coursed through her.

"No!" She leaned in closer to his ear. "You can't go, Timberleg. Stone needs you. Your family needs you. Field Colony needs you!"

Timberleg did not raise his head or open his mouth to answer. His only response was a pained smile. His eyes met hers for a moment before the light faded from them. With a choked cry, Spottedshadow smoothed a patch of fur on his leg and pressed her muzzle into his neck. Seconds later, Ambereyes, Lilyfire, Peach, and Stone crowded around Timberleg's body beside her.

Spottedshadow thought she would be permitted to stay and grieve with the family and Timberleg's new-claw, but Mistysnow gently pulled her aside. Before Spottedshadow could argue that she deserved to mourn before the new moon, Mistysnow whispered to her, "You need to get out there. The colony is confused and distraught, and I need to oversee the care of the wounded."

"Me? What can *I* do?" Spottedshadow shook her head. "Without Hazelfur and Forestleaf, you're the closest Field Colony has to a leader, other than Goldenpelt. They need *your* guidance. Let me take care of the injured rangers while you talk to them."

Mistysnow's ears pulled back. "No. You belong out there."

Spottedshadow blinked in surprise at the older molly. It had been ages since she'd taken such a stern tone, back when Spottedshadow was still a new-claw helping the Herbalist with chores. After Spottedshadow's parents had been attacked by the fox, she had spent more and more time helping, until she'd finally asked if Mistysnow would train her as an Herbalist. For some reason, Mistysnow had refused outright. Spottedshadow had assumed it was because she didn't have a special connection to the Spirits; now she wondered if there was another reason.

She looked toward the center of the base, where the colony had gathered around Hazelfur and Forestleaf's bodies. They bowed their heads to pay their respects, touching their noses to the dead leaders. From their hushed mews, Spottedshadow detected more fear and worry than sorrow.

Mistysnow gave Spottedshadow a lick on the cheek. "The Spirits will guide you. Now go."

Spottedshadow took a deep breath. As she held it, she thought back to her youth. Those had not been days of joy or comfort, yet she could not help longing for the time she'd spent at her injured father's side, helping him grow strong again under Mistysnow's watchful eye. She wished, desperately, that the Herbalist was going with her now to face the colony–yet she also sensed that whatever she was walking into, it was important to take those steps alone.

She released the breath. It was time to face whatever would come next.

"There you are! How's Timberleg?" Goldenpelt demanded. He put on a show of bravado, of hope, but Spottedshadow knew he was well aware of Timberleg's fate after his ludicrous order.

"He is a ranger all cats in the Alliance will honor for his skill and bravery," she said.

Goldenpelt lowered his head, glaring at the ground. "I see. Excuse me." He pushed past her, heading into the already crowded den to join his grieving family. Spottedshadow mustered some pity for him, but she would not forget that he had put his pride over helping Timberleg.

"Spottedshadow!" Missingfoot called, hurrying to her. "I'm so glad you're safe."

"*Father.*" Spottedshadow curled against him, resting her head on his back. He sat, letting her sink all her weight onto him. She was so heavy, so full of grief and concern that she did not know how she would ever stand on her own four paws again. "We did all we could for Oak Colony."

"I know you did your best, my kitten. I know. Hush, now. What's done is done, and we will figure it out in the morning. Right now, you need rest," Missingfoot purred.

"I can't," Spottedshadow murmured. She inhaled again, her nose picking up not only his comforting scent and the fresh summer breeze blowing over the fields, but also the panic beginning to seize the colony when Goldenpelt vanished from their sight. "Not yet. I have to speak to them. But, after, can I spend the night in your nest, please?"

"Of course, always." Missingfoot stood and stepped back, making way for her. "Do what you must. I will be right here."

Spottedshadow smiled, only for her expression to sour when Fernface's voice reached her ears.

"We're vulnerable without a Captain to command us. Goldenpelt has to take charge and name his Second as soon as possible! The other colonies could take advantage!" the split-faced molly caterwauled, whipping the colony into a frenzy.

"We need a leader!" Shadowclaw shouted.

"We need Captain Goldenpelt!" Jaggedstripe joined in. "Goldenpelt! Goldenpelt!"

Once they started chanting, it wasn't long before the rest of the colony followed. Fernface poked any cat who stayed quiet with a single sharp claw, until the whole of Field Colony was yowling Goldenpelt's name.

Spottedshadow leapt onto the Captain's Overlook with her back arched and fur on end. "*Enough!*" Her tail lashed behind her as she sat down. "Moon's sake, everyone, please settle down! Losing Hazelfur, Forestleaf, and Timberleg is a tragedy. But we can't lose our heads, too. Or our faith in the Spirits to guide us through this."

To her surprise, many of the cats below looked at her with rapt attention. Even Goldenpelt's most loyal followers stopped their screeching, if only to grumble in displeasure at her interruption.

"What happened tonight has shaken us. We have lost much, and we face a great challenge," she continued. "But Hazelfur, Forestleaf, and Timberleg are still with us, watching over us. Let them see that we are still the colony they were proud to serve. We shall honor them tonight, and deal with the rest tomorrow."

Spottedshadow glanced toward the Herbalists' Den to see Mistysnow and Goldenpelt sitting at the entrance. Mistysnow practically glowed as she offered Spottedshadow an approving nod. Goldenpelt jumped up beside her on the boulder, nearly shoving her off in the process. They couldn't both stand atop it without pressing against each other.

"Thank you for your encouraging words, Spottedshadow," he said. "Rest assured, everyone, our colony will not be vulnerable. Fleetfoot, gather a group of fit rangers to check the River-lands border. Rainfall won't catch us off guard. As for who should lead us...I know it is unusual for an Envoy to become Captain without first serving as Second, but I am sure the Spirits will understand our situation and visit me tonight to give me my blessings and title. Until then, I cannot name a Second. We must be patient and vigilant. We will overcome these trying times! In the meantime, there is still much to do."

Spottedshadow did not linger to listen to Goldenpelt's orders, nor did she join the colony in sharing the prey that Graymist and Clayfur had caught. She returned to Mistysnow, who did not ask her to address the colony again. Instead, the old molly let her bundle herbs together to make medicines that would guard against infection and speed recovery for the injured. Spottedshadow's paws moved almost on their own, carefully piling dried flowers and leaves, stamping them with honey, then passing them along to Mistysnow as she moved in and out.

When Mistysnow told her she could stop, Spottedshadow dragged herself out, away from Peach, Ambereyes, and Lilyfire, to her father's nest near the edge of the Keepers' Weave. He was already asleep, so she carefully settled in beside him, tucked her paws over her nose, and wept until she drifted into dreams.

Spottedshadow was no longer beside Missingfoot, but back in the Herbalists' Den. She turned to see the sleeping forms of Mistysnow, Peach, and Ambereyes; Lilyfire must have left some time during the night, perhaps to mourn without waking her mother and sister.

When Spottedshadow's eyes fell on Timberleg, she let out a startled gasp. He was standing, his wounds glowing with silvery moonlight.

"Timberleg! Oh, thank the Spirits, it's a miracle!" she said–or rather, tried to say. When she opened her mouth to speak, no sound came out.

Timberleg shook his head slowly and touched a paw to the cold body still lying in the nest of ferns—*his* body. Without waiting for her mute apologies,

Timberleg walked out of the den, his paws passing through Ambereyes without disturbing her slumber.

Field Colony's base glowed in the light of a full moon that was closer and brighter than Spottedshadow had ever seen. Cats walked around the clearing, greeting each other in silence or grooming twitching rangers until their restless paws stilled into deeper slumber. Kittens tussled and rolled over each other, playing games with shards of moonlight and glowing bugs. Spottedshadow glanced toward Graymist, who was on guard duty. The molly didn't seem to notice any of the glowing cats. The Field-landers that Spottedshadow knew, with their solid shapes and duller fur, slept on without noticing the activity around them. She could even see herself slumbering beside Missingfoot.

Spottedshadow ran to her body, and with great relief discovered it was warm to the touch. She was still alive, no matter how much her grief threatened to tear her heart out.

A familiar scent wreathed itself around her. Spottedshadow went rigid as longing, despair, love, and pain all burst forth with a single silent shout: *Mother!*

Spottedshadow tackled Whitebelly, the two of them rolling over and landing in a heap of purrs and licks. Whitebelly pulled Spottedshadow against her with one paw over her back and licked her ears, just as she had when Spottedshadow was small. Taking comfort in her mother's presence, Spottedshadow almost forgot her confusion at her surroundings. She was drawn back into herself with the sound of a growl.

Forestleaf glared down at her from the Captain's Overlook, Hazelfur sitting at her side. They fit together in that space much more easily than Spottedshadow had with Goldenpelt.

Words had always been Spottedshadow's strength. It was not easy to communicate in this place–in the Beyond–without them. Yet, without a single utterance, she knew what she had to do. Claws unsheathed, back arched, teeth bared, she made a bold jump onto the Captain's Overlook and took her place there. It was crowded and uncomfortable, but she refused to stand down, just as she had when Goldenpelt invaded her space.

Within moments, Hazelfur stepped down, his thin tail brushing over her back. Only Forestleaf remained. The two dark-furred mollies stared at each other with the same green eyes. They were not the only inheritance Forestleaf had given Spottedshadow, and with a lightning-fast strike from her paw, Spottedshadow reminded the former Second that she was just as stubborn and driven as her grandmother. With a glare, Forestleaf yielded at last, leaving Spottedshadow alone atop the Captain's Overlook.

Spottedshadow looked over the cats of Field Colony, living and deceased, with new resolve. This was her home, the lives within it her responsibility. Perhaps Goldenpelt would have been a great leader, and perhaps he still would be someday—but he wasn't the Captain that Field Colony needed now. They needed a cat who would work together with the other colonies against a mutual threat.

She knew she was an unusual choice for Captain, that her succession would be the talk of the Alliance for years, that some of those sleeping peacefully under her watch would not accept her. In time, she might even step down from the role and let Goldenpelt ascend to Captain as they had all expected. But for the time being, she could not allow him to lead.

She would protect Field Colony without abandoning the rest of the Alliance. She would strengthen their bonds and lead Field Colony into a better and brighter future.

Slowly, the base and its living cats faded. Even many of the Spirits winked out of sight, leaving behind stray beams of moonlight. Soon only a few cats remained, standing before Spottedshadow. She raised her head, determined to be worthy of their blessings.

Hazelfur came forward first. Once they made contact, he disappeared in a burst of light, and a faint glow formed around Spottedshadow. She hadn't realized how tired she felt until her fatigue vanished, leaving only the strength and determination to protect and guide her colony.

Whitebelly nuzzled Spottedshadow's cheek, and she returned the gesture. The glow around Spottedshadow grew brighter, and she knew her love for Field Colony would be as endless as a mother's love for her child.

Timberleg approached next. Before Spottedshadow could attempt an apology for failing to protect him, failing to heal him, he touched his nose to her forehead and joined her Spirit.

Now she shone as brightly as the Spirits who had yet to give their blessings. The glow made it hard to see the cat who stepped forward next, and she blinked in surprise when she recognized Breezeheart. He touched her paw with his, and she knew that even from across the lake, the Alliance was united. Marsh Colony's problems were Field Colony's problems, too.

Another cat came forward, one who smelled of mud and marshes. Spottedshadow did not recognize him, yet she felt like she should know who he was. The pale calico tom beckoned her to lean down, and when she did, he licked her cheek. With that simple gesture, Spottedshadow felt her strength and determination grow.

Aspenbreeze was next, again stopping Spottedshadow with a look when she tried to apologize for the young cat's short life. Now was not the time for regrets and sorrow; now was the time to move forward into a new and better tomorrow, where such tragedies would not repeat themselves.

Spottedshadow was shining so fiercely that the rest of the Spirits were now dimmer than her. She felt like she was so much bigger than her body, and wondered at how she had managed not to burst into light. It was a Captain's duty to shine more brightly than any other cat, to lead their colony in times of darkness. It was a duty she was honored to fulfill.

Only Forestleaf remained.

The older molly did not approach Spottedshadow, did not touch her to give her a blessing. Instead she raised a paw toward the moon, and its light faded as clouds moved to conceal its glow. It was not completely obscured–patches of the moon could still be seen–but the meaning was clear. This was Spottedshadow's title.

She was Captain Spottedshadow, the Clouded Moon. She would guide Field Colony through hardships the likes of which no one had ever seen, and she would have to fight every step of the way. Her determination and resolve must pierce through the clouds of doubt, or they would all be left in darkness.

Spottedshadow woke to the light of dawn creeping over the horizon and Mistysnow staring down at her. The spotted black molly sat up, feeling a thrum of energy in her legs. She was sure she could have run all the way to Oak Colony and back in the time it took most rangers to make it to the lake. She could have leapt over the Captain's Overlook with all the effort it took to scratch a flea. She was greater than herself–but it was still her own heart, her own Spirit, that beat in her chest.

"Did you know?" Spottedshadow asked.

"I had my suspicions," Mistysnow answered.

Before they could say more–if more needed to be said–Fernface bolted up from her nest and ran to Goldenpelt, meowing loudly enough to wake the entire base.

"Well? What title did the Spirits give you, Captain Goldenpelt?"

"Quiet, Fernface! You're acting like an excited kitten on the Summer Solstice. And anyway, I–" Goldenpelt yawned, rising from his bed and shaking out his fur. Spottedshadow realized she didn't feel tired at all, and couldn't ever recall seeing Hazelfur yawn, either. From the amount of bedding stuck to his fur, Goldenpelt must have been tossing and turning all night.

"I bet it's something amazing. Goldenpelt the Gleaming Light, maybe?" Jaggedstripe suggested.

"If you would stop–"

"Captain Goldenpelt! Captain Goldenpelt!"

Goldenpelt hissed. "I didn't receive my blessings or title!"

A collective gasp of surprise escaped every cat in the clearing.

"Then, who...?"

Spottedshadow dipped her head to Mistysnow, who licked her shoulder as she passed. Missingfoot, confused and half-asleep, purred out a low, "Go get them, Shadow."

The dark-furred molly walked through the clearing with her head high. In a single, graceful jump, she landed on top of the Captain's Overlook. She tried to remember how Forestleaf had looked in her dream and copied her stance, curling her tail over her paws to show she was not going anywhere.

"Good morning, Field Colony. I am Spottedshadow, the Clouded Moon–your new Captain." Before the colony could react negatively, she continued with confidence that was no longer artificial. "I know this must be a shock for all of you. It was for me, as well. And I won't deny that it is unusual. However, the Spirits Beyond have chosen me to lead this colony, and I plan to follow their guidance, as Field Colony cats always have."

Goldenpelt stood and marched forward, quieting the worried whispers that had begun to stir among the colony. Every pair of eyes followed him, tracking the movements of his high-held tail, twitching ears, and intense eyes. At last he lowered his head to acknowledge Spottedshadow's rank.

"What do we do first, Captain Spottedshadow?"

Relief washed over Spottedshadow as the attitude of the assembled cats began to shift. She might hold the title of Captain, but Goldenpelt's penchant for leadership was undeniable.

If only he had not continued to speak.

"As your Second, I'll see to it that every Field-lander follows your orders." Spottedshadow pinned her ears back at his comment. "I did not say you were my Second."

Goldenpelt's most ardent followers tensed, and Fernface dared go so far as to hiss a curse at the newly named Captain. Spottedshadow ignored it.

Perhaps it would have been easier to allow Goldenpelt the rank of Second, but she knew down to her core that he was the wrong choice. Increasing his authority now, in any way, would lead to Field-landers seeking his orders before her own. She could not afford to doubt her choices now, when she was establishing herself and her reign.

"Is every Field-lander gathered?" Her eyes scanned the crowd and the faces poking out from the cover of the Keepers' Weave, confirming their attendance. "Good. There is much work to do, and it begins now. Every Captain needs a good Council, and I think it's time Field Colony's Council expanded. From now on, Mudnose will join Mistysnow, Swifttail, and Goldenpelt as a Council member, and lead it as my Second."

Many gaped in surprise, Mudnose himself among them. Meadowleap prodded him forward, a loving purr rising in her throat. Thrushspots and Clayfur sat up straighter as their father passed them to stand at the base of the Captain's Overlook.

"I certainly never expected this," Mudnose said. "I have always been a Mentor at heart, and never considered becoming an Envoy, let alone Second. That said, I have only ever wanted to serve my colony. If you feel that being your Second in Command is the best way I can do that, then I accept."

"This is most strange," Swifttail commented, "but I've known Mudnose to be a capable ranger for many seasons." Her gaze slid toward Goldenpelt with a hint of apology. "If no one else objects, I'll allow it."

Mistysnow said nothing. Goldenpelt, still reeling from the rejection and chided by his mother's words, did not speak against Mudnose's appointment either.

With all the anger and indignation Spottedshadow had expected, Fernface snarled, "This is *nonsense*! You can't name a Mentor as a Second. It goes against the Ancestors' Law! Goldenpelt is the Envoy, he should be *Captain*! Second is a step down from what he deserves, and you dare deny him even that?"

"I have a different plan in mind for Goldenpelt. One that honors his strengths," Spottedshadow answered breezily. "Goldenpelt, you are Field Colony's only Envoy, and we are facing dangerous times. We need more cats prepared for leadership, should the worst happen, and Stone is now without a teacher."

She did not conceal a brief flare of accusation in her gaze. The golden tom looked away, meeting Stone's eyes instead.

"I ask that you take over Stone's training, as you once trained Timberleg, and guide him in becoming Field Colony's next Envoy. I believe he has what it takes to be a leader someday, if you show him the way."

Suppressing a growl and the wrongfulness of the situation pricking his skin like bug bites, Goldenpelt finally nodded. "It would be an honor to train this new-claw in Timberleg's stead. I will teach him all he needs to know, and I accept Mudnose as the Second of Field Colony in *my* stead."

Spottedshadow did not push her luck any further. "Thank you." She waved her tail in a wide sweep and stood, changing the tone from somber to joyous in a single motion. "There are two more new-claws who are ready to begin field training. Though they will not be officially presented to the Spirits until the full moon, I believe they can start learning the basics. Field Colony will need to make a strong showing at the next Moonlight Meeting." Her eyes fell on two of the cats closest to Goldenpelt. If she was right, their promotion would help ease the sting of his being denied leadership. "Jaggedstripe and Ambereyes, I would like the two of you to instruct Horse and Tabby in the ways of hunting and fighting. Meadowleap and Clayfur should be able to help Nightpool with her kittens and keep the base in order, should either of you decide to change careers to full-time Mentors. We will need more soon."

"Oh, well..." Jaggedstripe shifted awkwardly under the glare of his mate, Fernface.

"Thank you, Captain. We'll do our best," Ambereyes said for him.

Spottedshadow purred in approval. Of all Goldenpelt's followers, Jaggedstripe and Ambereyes had always been the most agreeable toward her. As Keepers, they were already familiar with Horse and Tabby.

"Lastly, Fleetfoot and Lilyfire, please take word to the other colonies. Do not cross into their territories if you can help it. Pass the message along with a border scout, instead. This battle took a heavy toll on all of us; I want to call an emergency Meeting to assess the damage and make a plan to move forward. We will meet on the half-moon at Moonlight Island. Be swift!"

"*Lastly*?" Shadowclaw sneered. "Haven't you forgotten border checks?"

Inwardly, Spottedshadow winced. That was the kind of thing a cat who had trained as an Envoy would have planned for right away. However, she could not show a moment's hesitation when she responded.

"There will be no further border checks today. All cats who were in the battle, your orders are to guard the base and recover. There may be another battle soon, and we will need as many ready rangers as possible. Those who were not in the battle, or who are unhurt, should hunt for those of us who can't."

She hoped no one noticed how she relaxed when she saw groups of rangers forming hunting parties, following her orders.

"Peach," she called, "let's hunt together. Ambereyes, why don't you and your new-claw join us?"

Ambereyes was more apparent in her relief at not having to take Tabby for her first hunting lesson alone. Secretly, she was also happy to hunt beside Peach. She had taken the few times she'd caught rabbits with Timberleg for granted, always assuming she would have another chance to spend time with her son. She would not make the same mistake with her youngest kitten, and she would be sure to share her meal with Lilyfire when her older daughter returned. In truth, she was grateful for Spottedshadow giving her something to do so she would not be bound to the base and her grief all day.

"What about me and Horse?" Jaggedstripe asked.

"You can help Mistysnow tend to injuries here. If she needs anything, you can show Horse around the territory and collect herbs."

Horse looked a bit disappointed to miss out on hunting, but Jaggedstripe gave him a friendly lick on the head. "No long face, now–you aren't *really* a horse, you know!"

Spottedshadow turned away, facing the open fields. For a moment, she let herself forget she was Captain and sank into a fantasy that the previous day hadn't happened. She was only going hunting with her new-claw as a Mentor.

She blinked, and the moment ended. "Mudnose, you're in charge of the base while I'm gone."

"Of course, Captain."

Her dark shape slipped away into the tall grass, and Mudnose watched from Captain's Overlook.

Goldenpelt was not so easily swayed. Once Spottedshadow turned her back, his mask of acceptance slipped away, revealing bitterness and anger. He found his expression mirrored on the faces of Volefur and Fernface.

"Don't worry, Goldenpelt." The brown molly unsheathed her claws, tearing a dandelion out of the ground by its roots. "That traitor can't keep you from your rightful position for long."

"Keep your voice down!" Goldenpelt growled. "This isn't the end of the world. Mudnose is old and will retire soon. In the meantime, I'll prove that I should be the uncontested leader of this colony."

"You have nothing to prove! You are our Captain, no matter what the Spirits have done," Fernface insisted. "Leave it to us. We'll make things right."

Goldenpelt's growl transformed into a low purr at her praise. "If you have faith in me as your Captain, then trust that I will handle this my way. Spottedshadow will see reason soon enough." He turned away and shouted in a bright and cheerful voice, "Stone, let's get a move on!"

The young gray tom jolted from his place beside Timberleg's body, which would soon be taken for burial with the other dead Field-landers. Stone looked around warily, his hunched shoulders and low tail hiding his size. Goldenpelt owed it to his nephew to train this meek cat, but he knew Stone would never be an Envoy.

Goldenpelt would become Captain and appoint a more suitable Council long before things came to that.

Meeting at Half Moon

"Unusual problems call for unusual solutions."
Quickwit, Elder of Field Colony

"Report from the border, Captain!" Swiftmask called as he bounded over the stream that separated the base from the mainland in one easy leap. Moss's hind paws splashed into the water when she followed, and she paused to kick the droplets off before hurrying up the sandy bank.

Rainfall looked up from her grooming warily. Any news was bad news when it came to borders.

"Captain Spottedshadow of Field Colony has extended an invitation for River Colony to attend a meeting," Swiftmask continued. "It will be held at Moonlight Island, on the night of the half moon."

At this, Rainfall found her eyes widening ever so slightly. *Captain* Spottedshadow did not sound correct. If Hazelfur had passed on, it was her former rival, Forestleaf, who should be Captain. As she recalled–and it did take some effort; she struggled to care about Field Colony much at all–Spottedshadow was not even part of their Council.

Clearly, *something* momentous had happened without Rainfall's notice, and that was unacceptable. Thoughts buzzed through her mind like a swarm of angry bees. Had there been some kind of uprising in Field Colony? Had Hazelfur and Forestleaf been killed by a sickness that might spread to the River-lands? Could the meeting be an ambush, this 'Captain Spotted-shadow' a clever ruse to pique her curiosity? Was this supposed Captain a renegade interested in joining their glorious colony, and if so, what could they offer?

Rainfall did not let a single uneasy thought show on her face, her posture and tone remaining in elegant repose.

"I suppose I can deign to attend their silly meeting," Rainfall replied, her voice as smooth as a fish swimming with the current. When she tilted her elegant muzzle upward and slid her gaze away from Swiftmask, it appeared she was unbothered—bored, even—by the news. No one would notice the way she glanced toward her father, Frozenpool, for approval. The old tom watched her every move, as he always had, and seemingly found no fault with her response so far. "If we don't go, it will hardly be worth anyone's time."

The rest of the River-landers chuckled, offering the appropriate nods and comments of River Colony superiority. She knew some rangers were forcing themselves, doing their best to blend in lest they draw unwanted attention from her *true* followers. The new-claws, though, lapped up her words and repeated how lucky they were to belong to the best colony in the Alliance. *They* meant every word, directing their complete and total adoration toward Rainfall. She basked in their praise, and an idea surfaced in her mind when she spotted one new-claw in particular.

"Thank you for delivering the message, Swiftmask. Why don't you enjoy some time off? I can take Moss fishing this afternoon."

Moss lit up as Swiftmask stammered out a response of, "Thank you, Captain. I'll do just that."

Rainfall purred her approval. Swiftmask had been too boring to be noticed by her for months, until Wolfthorn had returned and started chatting with the broad-shouldered tom. She was sure his appointment to Mentor had halted any possible rebellion Wolfthorn might be plotting. A complacent cat like Swiftmask would never dream of starting anything on his own, and Wolfthorn had backed off when he realized Rainfall had her eyes on his friend.

The sudden appearance of the light tabby had disconcerted her at first, but Frozenpool had assuaged her worries. It was best to keep enemies close. As long as Wolfthorn was living within River Colony borders, he couldn't move against her without her knowing well in advance. The fool might have raised an army of outsiders to help him overthrow her, but he had not thought of it.

Moss pranced blithely after Rainfall, trying to place her paws exactly where the Captain had trod. Just that morning Lily had been bragging about a catch she'd made, shoving it in Moss's face to remind her that she was still a poor fisher. Now Captain Rainfall herself was taking Moss for a private fishing lesson! Even if it was because news had traveled to the Captain that Moss wasn't doing well, she felt special. The Captain never had time to give individual attention to the new-claws.

They walked deeper and deeper into the mangrove forest, until at last they stopped on a twisted tangle of roots that reached into the aquamarine water of a quiet stream. They were far from the base now. Moss's ears pricked up for the sounds of any other cats nearby. She detected none.

"I've been meaning to speak with you privately, Moss," Captain Rainfall said. "How are your lessons with Swiftmask going?"

"Okay, I guess," Moss answered, then hastily added, "I mean, Swiftmask is an amazing Mentor! He's taught me so much and he's always patient with me. I do my best every day."

Rainfall smirked. "Yes, I thought so. Swiftmask has always been a dedicated ranger. But what about Wolfthorn and Gray? They hang around quite a bit, don't they?"

"Gray is a good training partner," Moss said, feeling the need to stick up for the quiet tom. "He reminds me of Swiftmask, actually. They're both really patient."

"And loyal?" Rainfall pressed.

Moss smiled, a little awkwardly. "Of course! Who wouldn't be loyal to River Colony?"

"Who, indeed?" Rainfall sighed. "I hate to cause you worry, Moss. You have such a bright future ahead of you in this colony. And yet it's because of that, I think you should know..." Captain Rainfall lowered her voice. Moss leaned in. "...I believe there may be a traitor in our midst, working to weaken our great colony."

"What? No!" Moss gasped. "Who would ever betray our colony? Betray *you*?"

"I know it's hard to believe," Rainfall went on, nodding sympathetically. "However, I have reason to believe it. The Spirits watch over me and warn me with secret signs. My most loyal rangers are always on the alert, and they've heard whispers and rumors that some cats aren't happy with my leadership. They think it would be better if someone else were Captain, and they may even plan to...oh, I shouldn't say it. You're so young."

"To what?" Moss's hackles raised in indignation. As quietly as she could manage, she hissed, "You don't mean they plan to *kill* you?"

"It's possible." Rainfall curled her tail over her paws. "That's why it's important that I have loyal rangers–loyal cats like *you*, Moss–who keep an eye on things for me. I'm so busy managing the colony and communing with the Spirits about their plans, it can be difficult to know who these traitors might be." She licked Moss's forehead. "You'll do that for me, won't you? Keep a close eye on the Mentors?"

"Yes!" Moss shouted. "Of course I will, Captain Rainfall!"

She couldn't imagine Swiftmask was one of the traitors. He was her Mentor, patient and kind and most definitely loyal to the colony and their Captain. Although Cherryrill mostly trained the older new-claws, Moss knew she had also been a loyal ranger her entire life. No one had a bad word to say about Cherryrill, except for maybe Iceclaw—but Moss couldn't think of a single cat who Iceclaw liked other than Rainfall. And Ferneyes could be nothing *but* loyal if she was willing to put up with Lily all day.

Could the traitor be Mistyclaw or Rapidsnap? Mistyclaw was about to have a litter of kittens. She'd be too busy to do anything horrible to Rainfall. And Rapidsnap–Swiftmask's own mother–could not have raised so noble a son without a fair amount of nobility herself.

That left only Wolfthorn.

Wolfthorn was mysterious. He disappeared from the base sometimes without telling anyone where he was going. He fraternized with cats from other colonies, even outside the Moonlight Meetings. Recently, Moss had caught him returning to the base at odd hours, smelling of the Oak-lands. He'd also had the scent of blood on his fur. Could he be conspiring with Oak Colony against Rainfall? Oak Colony might not have anything to gain from hurting River Colony, but they were close with Marsh Colony.

Moss shuddered. She knew Marsh Colony was jealous of River Colony, but could they really persuade Oak Colony to join forces and attack them? Would Wolfthorn really endanger the lives of his friends and family to take down Rainfall? Why would he *want* to?

As Rainfall watched suspicion and fear swim in Moss's eyes, she smiled. "I'm glad I can count on you, Moss. There may be a place on my Council for you someday–but don't tell the other new-claws I said that. Wouldn't want anyone to accuse you of showing off, would you?"

Moss shook her head. She would *not* be a braggart like Lily.

"Right. It's our special secret." Rainfall struck the water so quickly that Moss hardly saw her move. Her hooked claws sent a rainbow trout sailing through the air. She killed it with a quick pounce, then offered it to Moss. "Congratulations on your catch, Moss. I see you'll rise up the ranks quickly."

Moss bit into the bleeding flesh of the fish and carried it back to the base without another word. She brought it to Mistyclaw, then looked for Wolfthorn. She found him dozing in the shade of a hibiscus bush beside Gray.

She was onto him now. She would watch Wolfthorn's every move and make sure he did not bring destruction upon her colony, or her beloved Mentor.

Gone were the fireflies and the gentle, balmy comfort of the full moon that usually greeted the Alliance cats at the Moonlight Meeting. At only half its strength, the silvery light of the moon could not penetrate the canopy, leaving the clearing shrouded in shadow.

Spottedshadow had only brought Mistysnow with her; the rest of her rangers guarded the base and kept a watchful eye for any sign of the beasts, along with the usual predators. Dawnfrost had come in Elmtail's stead, the old tom still too tired–physically and emotionally–to make the journey. With her were Thornheart and Larkwing. Smallpebble and Indigoeyes sat at the base of the ancient tree as Marsh Colony's only present rangers, aside from their Captain. River Colony had the largest group: Rainfall, Iceclaw, Pineclaw, Blueriver, and Orangebrook.

Spottedshadow did her best to put the unease out of her mind as she climbed onto her perch beside the other representatives. "Thank you all for coming. I know it isn't an easy time to be away from our colonies. I've called this meeting to discuss what we plan to do about the beast that attacked the Alliance–"

"Excuse me," Rainfall interrupted, her mew sickeningly sweet, "who *are* you?"

"I-I'm Spottedshadow, Captain of Field Colony," the black-and-white molly stuttered, and cursed herself. She needed to make a good impression in her first appearance before the other colonies as a Captain.

Rainfall wasted no time in exploiting the opening. "My, my! Field Colony has truly fallen on hard times if a cat with no leadership experience is in charge. You *must* tell me how this tragedy came to be." Rainfall glanced at Dawnfrost. "Oak Colony's change in leadership needs no explanation. I presume the sack of skin and bones you called a Captain has *finally* stopped moving, and Redleaf couldn't be bothered to show up."

"Show some respect!" Dawnfrost snarled. "A tragedy has befallen the Alliance, one that you would already know about if you had bothered to join us in battle."

"And share in it, I presume?" Rainfall licked a paw and drew it over her face, utterly unimpressed. "I fail to see how this issue is River Colony's problem, just as I did when you first cried for our help. Why should I risk *my* rangers' lives to help *your* colony?"

"You are a disgrace!" Hawkshell hissed. "The Alliance exists for our colonies to help each other. You have only ever helped yourself!"

"And how have the Marsh-landers helped us in our time of need?" Rainfall shot back. "We have more kittens and new-claws than any other colony, but you've refused to give up an inch of your wetland territory to help feed their hungry mouths—territory which *rightfully* belongs to us!" She turned up her nose with a haughty sniff. "If you want us to help you, we expect the same in return. River Colony will fight when Marsh Colony gives us access to their hunting grounds."

"That's ridiculous!" Indigoeyes gaped. The land Rainfall coveted was nearly useless to River Colony, something he had told their rangers many times when they tried unsuccessfully to hunt there. The land dried up for most of the year, only forming temporary creeks when winter storms flooded the lake and rivers. The banks were unstable, and the land practically unusable for fishing. The only benefit it would serve would be swimming practice, but River Colony already had many more suitable pools and shallows for that.

"No more ridiculous than expecting us to fight someone else's battle," Rainfall quipped.

Indigoeyes snarled, "How *dare* you make demands, after what you did to my daughter?"

"If you've only come to this meeting to make trouble, then you can leave now," Hawkshell snapped.

"No, wait!" Spottedshadow yowled, but it was too late. The rest of the assembled cats had had their fill of Rainfall, and without the usual decorum and understanding of the Spirits watching from the full moon, they were not shy of letting her know it.

"Go back to the River-lands!" Smallpebble yelled.

"How can you be so selfish? Don't you have any compassion at all?" Thornheart asked, genuine dismay in his warm eyes.

"Only fools would risk their lives for nothing, and that is what you all are; nothing!" Iceclaw replied.

"We'll see about that the next time your territory floods," Indigoeyes shot back.

"Cowards! Traitors!" Larkwing hissed.

Claws unsheathed and fur spiked. Only Rainfall's calculated leap down from the tree stopped Iceclaw from slicing the nose of the nearest ranger.

"It won't make a difference," she said smugly over her shoulder to Hawkshell. "Either you'll give us the land and have a chance of survival, or we'll take it when your colony is no more. Your choice! Until the next Moonlight Meeting–if you live that long."

The light silver molly kicked her hind feet like she was burying excrement, then left at a brisk trot toward the Crossing Log, her rangers following behind. Only Orangebrook delayed, giving the remaining cats a sympathetic look. He opened his mouth as if to utter an apology, but thought better of it when he saw how the others glared at him. He hurried off after the rest of the River-landers.

None of them noticed the pair of pale yellow eyes that watched from the shadows beneath the bridge.

Spottedshadow's whole body shook. She had known that trying to appeal to Rainfall was a risk, one not likely to pay off, but she had let herself hope the self-centered Captain would see reason when confronted with how the other colonies had suffered. Clearly she had underestimated the lows to which Rainfall would stoop in the pursuit of her own ends. That was a mistake she would not make again.

Frustration worked through her paws. Biting back a curse, she slashed at the trunk of the ancient tree. "What now?"

As if in answer to her question, the wind began to rise. First it shifted the dust at their paws, bringing scents of cats who had long ago traveled to the island to their nostrils. The gust circled the gathered cats, becoming a gale that whipped at their fur and whiskers and pushed them closer together. The trees shook violently, forcing Spottedshadow, Dawnfrost, and Hawkshell to jump down or be thrown from their place in the ancient branches. They joined their rangers in a huddled mass, standing together to support each other against the unseasonably icy wind.

Unite.

A single word echoed in each of their ears, and then the wind was gone as suddenly as it had come. The cats looked at each other in bewilderment, then awe.

"Was that the Spirits?" Dawnfrost asked, turning to Mistysnow and Thornheart.

"I can't imagine what else it could have been," Thornheart answered. He shifted his weight on his paws uneasily. "Yet, it was strange...I've never known the Spirits to communicate that way." The signs of the Spirits were subtle, and sometimes so vague that Thornheart questioned if they were truly signs until he saw them two or three times in the same day. The Spirits' presence was always distant, lest cats lose their minds seeking their lost loved ones.

"Nor have I," Mistysnow agreed. "But like you, I cannot think of anything else it could have been. At the very least, they have made their message clear: we must unite in order to survive."

"Yes." Thornheart nodded. "But...perhaps not with River Colony."

"What do you mean?" Spottedshadow asked.

Thornheart met her eyes, then Hawkshell's, then Dawnfrost's. "What I mean is, I don't think it's a coincidence that the sign came *after* River Colony left. This beast came from somewhere. Maybe there are others who know more about it, how to fight it. We could send a few rangers to ask *them* for help."

"You're talking about thieves and mages!" Smallpebble gasped.

"I'm talking about cats more likely to help us than River Colony. Not all Unbound cats are terrible," Thornheart asserted, thinking of Snowfeather. The gentle and beautiful molly had once been Unbound, and though her mother had chosen not to join Oak Colony, Snowfeather had trained and hunted and fought beside them for most of her life. He would gladly challenge anyone who dared to say she didn't belong simply because of where she'd been born.

Thankfully, Hawkshell nodded. "There have been plenty of noble rangers who were born outside of the Alliance. Breezeheart was among them. However, even if what you say is true, how would we find these cats and convince them to help?" She shook her head. "It seems too much like a kitten story to me, and Marsh Colony needs all its rangers for protection now."

"We might as well go crawling back to Rainfall to beg for help," Smallpebble agreed.

"But it's as you say–every colony, at some point, has accepted outsiders into its ranks. We can ask *them* about where those monsters came from. Someone must know *something*. They might tell us where we can find other colonies, or even lone Unbound cats, who will help us. We have to try," Thornheart insisted.

"But *will* they help us, and ask for nothing in exchange?" Dawnfrost asked. "Oak Colony already promised medicine to Field Colony. We don't have much else to trade away at the moment."

Spottedshadow had forgotten that deal in the wake of all that had happened since. Though Spottedshadow herself did not wish to take anything from Oak Colony when they were already so vulnerable, she could not go back on the agreement without looking weak to her rangers. She would have to send someone agreeable to collect the payment in the morning—Fleetfoot and Graymist, most likely.

"I'm sure it will cost us something." Spottedshadow raised her head. "But I'm willing to shoulder that burden. If it comes down to bargaining, Field Colony will accept responsibility on behalf of the Alliance."

Her words did not inspire the confidence she had hoped they would. Most of the gathered cats' eyes flashed with resentment and questioning. Who was *she* to put herself forward as the representative of the entire Alliance? Those who knew her worried for other reasons. She would not be popular among her own colony if she started giving land away, and a Captain only remained Captain if she had the support of her Council. Dawnfrost forced the fur between her shoulders to lie flat, and for her mouth to stay closed before unbidden advice could fall out. She would not help her friend by questioning her in front of the other colonies, even if she knew Spottedshadow's lack of experience was getting the better of her.

After some thought, Hawkshell relented. "I may not like this, but if the Spirits have spoken, then it shall be so. I am willing to do whatever it takes to prevent more lives from being lost. Let me discuss this with my Council. Marsh Colony will choose two rangers for this task, and they will be ready to depart on the night of the new moon."

"Thank you, Captain Hawkshell. And what of Oak Colony?" Spottedshadow asked.

"If it is the only way—and no one else has offered a better plan—we'll do it. And I agree with Hawkshell; each colony should nominate two rangers to go, and see them off at the new moon. That is all the time and resources we have to spare." Dawnfrost waved her tail to gather the Oak-landers and headed for the bridge. "Make your choices carefully. We all depend on their success."

The Chosen

"Four claws are better than one."
Alliance Lake Proverb

Though there was plenty of time until the new moon and the beginning of Captain Spottedshadow's risky mission, Captain Hawkshell could not rest. Whenever she closed her eye she saw the face of the beast that had taken her son from her. When she groomed her paws, she imagined its rank fur caught between her claws, its bitter blood between her fangs. If only she had brought more rangers with her to answer Oak Colony's call for help, perhaps they could have killed the creatures that night.

Instead, the monsters had escaped. The Alliance scouts had tracked them as far as Dry Creek, nearing the shared edge of Marsh and Oak Colony territory, before the trail simply vanished—as if, they had reported with troubled expressions, by magic.

Gigantic animals with sharp claws and teeth were bad enough. If they could also use magic...

It occurred to Hawkshell that, if they were truly magical, they might not be unknown beasts at all. Perhaps they *were* renegade mages, disguising their shape through unnatural transformation. She had never put much stock in the old tales of magic, but she could not imagine Sunfire and Breezeheart being caught off guard by ordinary means. They would have run, she told herself over and over–they would have run. They *should* have run. She should still be waking up to her son's bright smile and cheeky bravado as he regaled her with some exaggerated story of his daily activities.

One way or another, Hawkshell was now in the unenviable position of choosing which of her beloved colony members would have to face the dangers of the Unbound-lands.

She discounted any member of her Council. Mousetail was getting too old for such an ambitious journey; Leafstorm needed to learn the finer points of leading a colony before Hawkshell's age caught up to her; Indigoeyes and Kestrelsnap were simply too important to risk losing. Hawkshell considered sending Halfmask and Boulder, giving the oversized new-claw a chance to prove himself and finally earn his rank as a ranger, but the fact that he still hadn't was proof enough that he could not be trusted to behave. Falconswoop and Red didn't get on well enough with each other. Birdflight was the only full Mentor left in the colony, plus they were caring for Osprey day and night. Crowstalker had some knowledge of the Unbound-lands, but he was busy looking after Night and Fog.

Every ranger who had a reason to go had a greater reason to stay. Tigerstripe would be too self-destructive if left to his own devices, and Frostshadow–the one cat who might be able to control those tendencies–was currently training to be a Keeper. None of the Keepers' skills lent well to tasks outside the base. Mudtrail was still nursing Lichen. Snowstorm was an option, but who would be willing to accompany the aggravating tom?

Hawkshell's ears twitched at the sound of approaching steps. Leafstorm cleared her throat outside the moss curtain that obscured the entrance to Hawkshell's den.

"Captain Hawkshell, a ranger wishes to–" Leafstorm cut herself off with a hiss when Wildfur barged into the den.

There was plenty of room for the both of them—the ancient trunk could accommodate the entire Marsh Colony Council for meetings—but Wildfur carried a weight that filled the space around him. He was, perhaps, Hawkshell's greatest failure. She had gotten too confident in her decisions, too complacent that life would always be prosperous. She had forgotten the dangers of the marshes, and Patch had paid the price with his life. Wildfur, too, had died that day. The hollow-eyed cat who had returned to base to announce his brother's death was not the brash and confident tom who had left that fateful morning.

"I heard you're choosing cats to leave the territory on a mission," Wildfur said.

"Yes. The Council will make that choice this evening," Hawkshell replied, deciding it herself at that moment. She could not decide, so she would defer to the wisdom of her closest advisors.

"Don't bother. I'm going." Wildfur stood in a wide-legged stance, for once raising his head above his shoulders to tower at his full height. It briefly astonished Hawkshell to remember that he was the same size as her. So often he made himself small and slunk around the edges of the base, unsure if he truly belonged or if he was a trespasser who hadn't been noticed yet. To see him looking like a Marsh-lander was a pleasant change.

When Hawkshell did not answer, Wildfur continued, his mew insistent. "You're always asking me to prove my worth to this colony. When will there be a better chance? Besides, whether you give me permission or not, I'm going."

"This isn't a game!" Leafstorm protested. "Marsh Colony is *depending* on this to work, and you're one of the least dependable rangers I know."

"It is interesting that you've become motivated to volunteer for once," Hawkshell said. "How do I know you'll return? That this isn't an easy way for you to abandon Marsh Colony in our time of need?"

Wildfur bristled at the insinuation. "If I wanted to run, I'd have done it by now. Besides, I'm taking Pool with me. Think what you want about my skill as a ranger, but I wouldn't do anything to hurt a new-claw."

"Except take him into Unbound territory!" Leafstorm screeched.

"Hawkshell?" Whitefire's hoarse voice called from outside. "We can hear Leafstorm yowling across the base. Should the Council convene *now* to settle this matter?"

Hawkshell almost smiled for the first time since before the full moon at her sister's suggestion. She sometimes found herself wishing Whitefire was still her Second, and she was sure the old molly thought the same at times, but being on the Council was good enough for both of them most days.

"We may as well," Hawkshell answered. Whitefire came inside and sat beside her, followed by Indigoeyes and Mousetail. Either Indigoeyes or Kestrelsnap were always with Osprey to soothe her and help her with exercises; it must be Kestrelsnap's turn at the moment.

Wildfur did not move from his place, forcing each Council member to walk past him as they took their seats. They cast confused glances in his direction, each of which he met with what he hoped was a look of determination.

"Wildfur has volunteered himself *and Pool* to be Marsh Colony's representatives for the mission," Leafstorm summarized. When she spoke the new-claw's name, she rolled her eyes to Pool's father. "I would not loathe to be rid of Wildfur for a while, but endangering a new-claw?"

Indigoeyes tensed, and Wildfur curled his tail in. If it weren't for Osprey's condition, he could imagine the Envoy being much more supportive of his idea.

"Back when we were new-claws, it was customary to prove yourself with an act of great skill or courage. Perhaps Pool deserves the same opportunity, since he hasn't been able to stand out much around here." Whitefire's amber eyes glinted. "Perhaps Wildfur will finally find himself, as well."

"I will admit, I would be comforted by having our strongest rangers remain here to guard the base. And perhaps the lands beyond our territory will be safer for Pool right now," Mousetail added.

"That's two votes in favor and two against. Of course, we can assume Kestrelsnap would be against it, too—so that's three against," Leafstorm said. She smugly nipped at an itch on her shoulder.

"I didn't say I was against it," Indigoeyes snapped. He rounded on Wildfur with a low growl. "You had better promise to bring my son home in one piece."

"Anything that wants to hurt him will have to get through me first," Wildfur said.

While Leafstorm stammered out more reasons why Wildfur could not be trusted, Hawkshell gave a firm nod. "It is decided. Wildfur and Pool will represent Marsh Colony. Indigoeyes, I'll leave the joy of telling Pool he's been assigned to a special mission to you."

"After we grieve our losses on the new moon, I am leaving on a journey that will help us against this new, dangerous threat, and I need another cat to join me. We can't afford to fail this mission."

Dawnfrost felt strange making the announcement outside the Council Cavern, Elmtail standing shakily at her shoulder. They had agreed privately that her direction and drive were a must to see the mission through after she'd brought news of the decision back to him. The choice for her companion was less obvious. They had waited a few days, hoping Thornheart might receive another vision or sign from the Spirits that would make it easier.

The base was on its way to being rebuilt, but the scars of the attack would linger for seasons–some, forever. The loss of Redleaf was felt by every Oak-lander in some way. Stonestep had become withdrawn, and her behavior toward her young kittens changed directions from obsessive attention to a complete lack of effort as abruptly as a hummingbird could turn. Shrewpelt had to be forced to rest. Elmtail's condition worsened by the day, grief taking a physical toll on him.

Though Dawnfrost had been ready to take Redleaf's place when it came to assigning daily duties and providing the colony with clear directions, she could not replicate the ease with which he invited cats to speak about their problems. As an Envoy, she had not minded the distance so much; she had her friends and kept up with their lives and issues, offering advice where she could, but knowing their choices were ultimately not her business. As a Second and soon-to-be Captain, she *needed* to know anything that could lead to conflicts, beyond her circle of friends, and be ready to intervene if necessary.

Several cats approached the base of the cliff below Dawnfrost, offering themselves up as potential partners on her journey. Vinestripe and Larkwing she discounted at once–they were still grieving Aspenbreeze, now Dustclaw as well. She would not further endanger their family. Snowfeather and Stagcharge were among the volunteers, but Dawnfrost would not take either of them from their new-claws, especially now that Oak was training under Snowfeather's guidance.

If it were her choice to make alone, if it were her feelings alone that mattered, she would choose Thornheart to walk with her into the unknown. They had trained together as new-claws, and then trained their own new-claws together. She knew how to work with Thornheart, and she could not deny it would be nice to have a cat with a connection to the Spirits along to remind her their ancestors were with them even in the Unbound-lands. However, that was exactly the reason he needed to stay. If there were any more signs, Elmtail needed to know at once.

Rowanstorm, too, would make a fine companion. He was resilient and agreeable. She might not know him quite as well as Thornheart, but they had been friends for many seasons, and she knew she could hunt and fight at his side without worry. However, he was still recovering from an injury sustained in the fight, and while he hardly limped anymore, she did not want to strain the healing wound. She also didn't want to take him away from Elmtail when any day might be the old tom's last.

"Dawnfrost!" Shrewpelt shouted, leaving Hailstorm's side to approach the cliff. The gathered cats parted for him. "I'll go with you."

The sight of Hailstorm halted Dawnfrost's agreement. The spotted molly was heavy with an unborn litter that would arrive soon. "This mission is dangerous. Would you risk leaving your kittens without a father?"

"Better no father at all, than a coward who did nothing while his colony suffered."

"He wishes to prove himself. Can you work with him?" Elmtail whispered. Dawnfrost gave the Captain a curt nod, and he announced, "With my blessing, Shrewpelt will accompany Dawnfrost into the Unbound-lands after the new moon."

"Spottedshadow, are you sure about this?"

"Yes." A flicker of doubt flashed in Spottedshadow's eyes before she blinked it away. "I have to be."

Mistysnow groomed her chest, hoping the gesture would quell the rapid pace of her heart. To have Spottedshadow leave the Alliance territories was nearly unthinkable–and given that she was Captain now, it was unprecedented. Mistysnow could not decide if taking Goldenpelt with her made that better or worse. Goldenpelt was among the most skilled rangers in the Alliance, and had been trained from his youth to make difficult choices and lead missions. He was an obvious candidate for a serious mission, yet...

"I hope the two of you can come to an understanding," Mistysnow murmured. "All the same, be careful. I won't be there to heal you."

"Don't worry. The Spirits are with me, wherever I go—and so are your teachings."

To emphasize her point, Spottedshadow lifted the small bundle of herbs between her teeth and carried it to the heart of the Keepers' Weave. Though Field-landers preferred to see in all directions, the snug cavern of woven grasses was nonetheless nostalgic. All Field Colony rangers started their lives in similar dens, comforted by the soothing scents of heather and lavender as their parents purred them to sleep with stories of great warriors and clever hunters.

Nightpool's black fur cut a sharp outline against the soft shadows behind her. Four tiny kittens squirmed at her side, vying for the best place at her belly to nurse. Spottedshadow set the herbs down at Nightpool's paws, and the new mother lapped up the medicine. It would give her strength and energy to keep up with the demands of the newborns. Even with the Keepers around, the first few weeks of kittens' lives took their toll on the birthing parent.

"And to what do I owe a visit from the Captain?" Nightpool smiled, her tone light and teasing. She had not seen much of Spottedshadow lately, but visits from the Captain—and her former Mentor—were more than she'd expected.

"I'm sorry to admit it isn't merely a chance for me to admire the new kittens," Spottedshadow said, feeling a greater swell of pride and hope when she looked at them than she had ever experienced. That must be Hazelfur's influence, she decided. He had always been known to have a special place in his heart for kittens; now Spottedshadow had it, too. It calmed her, somehow, to be connected to her grandfather in a way she had never been in life. "As you know, the Alliance is sending a group of cats to seek help from outsiders. And, as you know *I* know..."

Nightpool looked down at her babies. The Spirits to Come had blessed her with three daughters and a single son, and she did not know how she could love them any more than she did in that moment—yet, she would find herself amazed the next moment when she did. The only way her life could have been more complete was if their father could have been present.

She had put her hopes for that aside long ago. She knew she had only been accepted into the colony because she had been found on its edges as a kitten, left by a mother who had declared she was old enough to care for herself. Captain Hazelfur would not have allowed her mate to join the colony, and likely would have banished her for having such an affair after the kittens were old enough to live without her.

Only Spottedshadow had ever known the truth. Nightpool had needed to tell at least one Field-lander the true identity of her kittens' father in case anything went wrong, and she'd known Spottedshadow would understand and protect her secret. She had never been more sure that she'd done the right thing.

"I have not been able to send word of the birth, but he must be expecting to hear about it," Nightpool said, lowering her voice to a whisper. Spottedshadow had chosen to see her when the Keepers were busy with other duties, for good reason.

"Did he ever tell you about the Unbound-lands?"

"Not much. It wasn't a popular topic." Nightpool found it hard to take her eyes off her litter. "I remember enough from my first months. It was a hard life, and it made cats' hearts just as hard. It wasn't like it is here, with all of us looking out for each other. There was little food and water to be had, not enough to support more than a few cats, so we either had to move frequently or be ready to fight to defend our claim."

It was not by coincidence that Nightpool's mother had left her where she did. For all the pain the decision had caused her, Nightpool had a better life in a colony than she would have as a lone renegade struggling to survive in the wastes. She was grateful her kittens would grow up as safe as they could ever be.

"Stay close to sources of water," Nightpool said sternly. She remembered her mother telling her that water was important above all else, and the way her siblings' skin had stretched taut across their bones when they died from lack of it. "*Waste no scraps, and bury all bones*–that was something my mother used to tell me. There was a story, I think, about bones becoming possessed by the wind and chasing careless hunters. I'm sure it was really a warning about vultures."

Vultures. Spottedshadow had seen them once or twice in the hazy, distant skies–great, ugly birds, twice the size of the hawks and owls that hunted over the fields.

"I will use the utmost caution," Spottedshadow assured her. "After all, I need to give these precious little ones their ranger names when they grow up. Have you decided what to call them for now?"

"The tom is Spot." Nightpool licked the fluffy head of a white-and-black spotted kitten. Next was the brown-and-cream molly, whom Nightpool introduced as Sky. Berry shared her mother's dark fur with splashes of what must be her father's ginger tabby, and Hunter was brown with a white muzzle. Each of them mewled in turn when they were licked. "If we're discussing ranger names, I would like Sky's given name to come at the end—and perhaps one of them could be called Catcher, after their father? But please don't take Sky's name away completely, or Spot's. That is a very special name to me."

Spottedshadow tested a few names in her mind: Berrycatcher, Summersky, Cloudspot, Huntermoon. After she had spent some time lost in thought, she realized the rest of what Nightpool had said.

"You mean you've named your son after *me*?" she gasped.

"Why wouldn't I?" Nightpool nuzzled the spotted kitten. "He'll be a great ranger someday, just like you."

"Right." Spottedshadow let herself forget about names. These young Field-landers had their whole futures ahead of them to show which name would suit them best. It was her duty now to make sure they lived to see that future, safe and happy. "Thank you for your advice, Nightpool. I'll try not to be gone too long."

Wolfthorn looked out at the ocean as the sun sank behind it, the sky orange and streaked with purple-shadowed clouds. Water splashed onto his paws from Troutleap Falls, the rushing sound of water filling his ears. The heady smell of plumeria, passion flower, and hibiscus wreathed him in the comfort of fond memories.

Brightscale had brought him and Gillstripe to that very spot after their first day of field training. Wolfthorn remembered how he had been struck by the vastness of the horizon, the ocean reaching endlessly into the unknown—just as he was now.

He wished he could show Dawnfrost this view. Though the setting sun was stunning anywhere, it was especially beautiful in River Colony.

He would be leaving it behind once again.

The rustling of the hibiscus bush told him he was not alone. His claws slid out, expecting to see Iceclaw or Pineclaw come to deal with him at last. He sheathed them when he saw Gray.

"Be a little louder next time, would you? I'm not a fish. You won't scare me off," Wolfthorn chuckled.

Gray did not respond right away. The two of them eyed each other in silence for an uncomfortable amount of time. Gray was not a particularly outspoken cat, but he rarely hesitated to say what was on his mind when they were alone. Unease prickled at Wolfthorn. Had something happened? Was Gray in trouble? He had thought of himself as a distant and watchful Mentor, but he could not deny that he cared for Gray as a trusted friend.

"Take me with you!" Gray blurted at last.

Wolfthorn blinked. "Take you with me, where?"

"Wherever you're going." Gray lowered his head. "I know you're leaving, and I want to go, too."

"Who else knows?" Wolfthorn asked.

"No one, as far as I'm aware." He tipped his ear. "Maybe Swiftmask."

Wolfthorn huffed out a laugh. Swiftmask always knew more than he let on.

"I can't stop you from following me if that's what you're set on doing, but I want you to think about a few things first. It's a miracle that Rainfall let me return to River Colony after I left once–I can't guarantee she will allow me back again, and it's clear she already has her eyes on you. If you go, there's a chance you will never be able to come back. You might never see your father again," Wolfthorn said.

Gray curled his tail over his paws, and Wolfthorn was reminded that the large tom was still only a new-claw. Wolfthorn rested his muzzle on Gray's head. "I know that life in River Colony has been hard for you, but it was not always like this. My hope is that it might not be this way for too much longer. I won't stop you from coming with me, but I think you should stay."

"Are you going to come back?"

Before he answered, Wolfthorn looked back over the sunset, listened to the falls, inhaled the scents of the tropical flowers, and felt the soft, sandy ground under his paws.

"Unless I die," he answered with a grin.

Though it was meant to be a joke, Gray's eyes widened in fear. "You haven't told me where you're going."

"That's because I don't know. Rainfall has kept the details of the recent meeting a secret from most of the colony. All I heard from Orangebrook is that a group of cats from across the Alliance are going to look for help in the Unbound-lands, and I mean to go with them."

Gray breathed a sigh of relief. "So you aren't wandering again." He stood, his tail sweeping up. "In that case, I will stay and wait for you to return. Someone needs to keep a watch on things here. Count on me to keep track of things while you're away."

"I'm not leaving right now. Come, let's get in some hunting practice–though I doubt you need any help with stalking," Wolfthorn purred with pride.

The moon was a slender claw slicing through the darkness of night. Rainfall groomed her own claws until the light shone from their talon-sharp tips. Disappointment tugged at her skin, stretching it too tight across her muscles and bones. Captain Hawkshell had been so obsessed with the oversized badger running amok that Rainfall had been *sure* the old fool would send her best rangers away on the mission. Finding out from her own rangers that the chosen cats were Wildfur and Pool instead–names that only brought to mind the question of *who?*–was a snag in her plans to reclaim the flood-lands.

Iceclaw paced beneath her perch, his tail lashing in restless fury. "I don't know why we have to go to those stupid meetings. It doesn't matter what the other colonies do. If they cross us, we'll slaughter them!"

"It's good to keep eyes on our enemies, and rewarding to hear their misfortunes. I'm sure we'll soon have plenty to laugh about, if they're still set on this ridiculous plan." Rainfall stretched her legs and settled with a yawn. The balmy night air was comfortable, much more than the inside of her too-warm den. She didn't know how the kittens had ever stood it. Truly it was a blessing that she had taken the nursery for her own.

Iceclaw purred at the reminder of bloodshed. "Maybe we *should* get involved. I'm sick of fighting minnows–I want to take down a real opponent! How else am I to prove my strength to the Spirits?"

"You'll get your chance." Rainfall twitched one ear at the sound of approaching footsteps, then wrinkled her nose at the smell of dry grass. "Sooner than I thought, even."

Swiftmask, Cherryrill, and Frozen appeared, escorting a brown tabby molly between them. Rainfall would have set Iceclaw upon her at once, but she did not carry herself like a captured ranger humbled by defeat at the claws of superior River-landers. Her half-masked face was defiant and she pinned her scarred ears back in indignation, but her yellow eyes glittered with excitement. She twitched the end of her tail in the droll Field-land custom.

"Good evening, Captain Rainfall. I hope you will accept my humble request for a meeting."

Rainfall groomed her claws again before answering. "I admit your boldness interests me–but little else. Who are you, and what do you want?"

"My name is unimportant," the Field-lander answered, which was certainly true from where Rainfall stood. "As for what I want, I would like to make a deal that I think will be beneficial for both our colonies. Were you aware Captain Spottedshadow will be leaving the territory soon?"

That drew Rainfall's full attention. She cleared her throat, and Iceclaw sheathed his claws. The rangers who had brought the strange molly to the base stood at attention to wait for their orders.

"Please excuse us–this is private business between our guest and the Council." Rainfall ushered the brown molly into the musty old nursery-den. "Now, *do* go on..."

Those Who Follow the Wind

"When the wind calls, the Followers answer."
Followers of the Wind Proverb

The land had many names.

To the cats of the Alliance it was the Unbound-lands, or simply the wastes. It was an endless desert of harsh stone, scraping sand, and prickly bushes that offered no shelter. What little rain fell on the land gathered in thin creeks that choked and died in the blistering heat. Only the toughest prey–venomous snakes and crunchy, dehydrated lizards–survived in the desolate landscape.

Cats who wandered the wilds alone each had their own names for it, too: the Dry River, the Windswept Desert, the Expanse, the Passing-By. To them it was a land once lush and rich, now dry and brittle; an obstacle on their way to somewhere better that they'd heard about in a story once.

To Ardentwind, it was *home*.

The breeze lifted her paws like a playful littermate as she ran under a cerulean sky. Dust clouds danced in her wake. She could not say, exactly, what led her to run so far that morning. Her grandmother would not be pleased to find the young molly gone from her family's camp. Thoughts of the scolding she would get kept Ardentwind moving, determined to find whatever called her, in the hopes that it might make her punishment less severe.

As she raced the sun across the desert, she practiced what she would say. "It isn't *my* fault, really!" Those words failed the test as soon as they were spoken. Matriarch Dragonfly would never accept such a pitiful excuse.

"The wind called me, and *when the wind calls, the Followers answer.*" That sounded much better in Ardentwind's ears. She was not a rambunctious kitten disobeying out of boredom; she was a young Follower, doing what Followers did best.

At nine months old, Ardentwind considered herself old enough for her first adventure away from the watchful eyes of the gust. She had practiced tracking her family with Dragonfly and Zephyrwillow until she was sure she could find her way home with her eyes closed. Her brother Trueflight might need a little more practice, but Ardentwind was ready. The spirits of the wind clearly agreed with her, or they wouldn't have woken her so early with the promise of *something* waiting for her to discover.

She could hardly be called a kitten anymore. She was twice as big as Lavaplume, and already had plenty of survival experience. She had not even cried when the flash-flood last spring had washed her father away. As future leader of the gust, she knew better than to waste time crying over things she couldn't change.

Sometimes Kestrelsight asked Ardentwind if she missed her father. She lied and said she didn't remember him well enough to miss him. When other members of their gust told stories about Bravesong, Ardentwind pretended he was some cat she'd never met, not the father she loved and missed more than anything.

Though it was impossible to know which spirits were leading her–if, indeed, there were any individual spirits at all–Ardentwind liked to think it was Bravesong who guided her paws. There were so many things he'd wanted to show her once she was old enough to leave the safety of the camps, so many adventures they'd never had the chance to share. He would not have scolded her for running off; he would have asked her what she'd seen, and if she'd had fun.

The wind shifted, and the dust clouds that had trailed behind her blew to her front. Ardentwind skidded to a halt, more dust rising and settling around her in the now-still air.

"Here?" Ardentwind asked. Though the spirits never spoke in words, she found that vocalizing her questions usually led to answers.

She pricked up her ears, opened her eyes wide, and drew in the scents of the surrounding area. There was a small creek not far away, marked by the twisted palm tree that grew on its banks. The tree's branches swayed in a gentle breeze, beckoning Ardentwind to trot into its shade. She had come a long way. A drink of water and a short respite from the sun would be welcome while she continued her search.

Now that summer had well and truly arrived, the creek was nearly dry. Ardentwind could count every pebble at the bottom of the shallow ravine as she dipped her paw into the warm water and lapped up the drops. Every little bit of moisture brought relief to her dry throat.

The wind died down, leaving Ardentwind to wait beneath the tree. She tried to stay alert for signs like a seasoned Follower, but her attention soon wandered. The ground beside the creek was soft and sandy, and her coat was due for a good washing. She flopped onto her side and rolled through the silt, then shook out her pelt and groomed the patches where dust had stuck to her spotted yellow fur.

The breeze had not returned, but the fronds overhead still swayed.

Ardentwind hardly saw the shadows shift before the heavy, scaled body of a snake fell across her back. She hissed in surprise and tried to spring away, but the snake's crushing weight stopped her from moving. By the time her claws were out, the snake was already coiled around her, squeezing her tight.

Ardentwind struggled against the snake's hold. A strong gale whipped grains of sand at its hide, but the snake was not bothered. Its mouth gaped in front of Ardentwind's face, impossibly wide. She stared down its throat, imagined herself being swallowed, suffocated, crushed–and she screamed.

A furious yowl answered her.

A streak of red-brown fur and muscle slammed into the snake's head, forcing it to the side. The snake uncoiled just enough for Ardentwind to slip free, and she was forgotten as the snake reared back to lunge at her rescuer. Long claws met longer fangs as the two struck each other. Ardentwind was sure she saw the cat's head go into the snake's mouth, and then the snake's lower jaw was ripped away from the rest of its body. It twisted and flailed in the throes of death, until at last the tom gripped its throat and bit down hard enough to end the snake's misery.

The tom dropped the snake's corpse. His sides heaved and as he panted. Gold eyes fell on Ardentwind.

"Is it venomous?" he asked.

Ardentwind looked at the pattern on the snake's brown scales. "I don't think so."

"Good." The red-brown tom sank to the sand and pawed at the fang caught in his ear.

"Don't!" Ardentwind said. "Even if there's no venom, the wound will get infected for sure if you aren't seen by a healer."

"A healer." The tom rolled his eyes at her. "And where am I supposed to find one of *those* in this sun-scorched wilderness?"

His short, dense coat was ruffled by a breeze. The same breeze played with the crest of fur on top of Ardentwind's head, and she understood. She had found what she was looking for.

"I can take you to my gust!" she declared. "My grandmother knows everything there is to know about medicine. She'll help you for sure once I tell her how you saved my life."

The tom gave her another disbelieving look. "You're going to take me–a complete stranger–to your home?"

"It's only fair. You *did* save my life," Ardentwind repeated.

With a grunt, the red-brown tom rose to his feet. He considered her closely, almost like he was sizing up a piece of prey, and for a moment Ardentwind wondered if she had escaped one predator only to fall into the jaws of another. Though it was true that wanderers rarely bothered the Followers, *that* was true because the Followers traveled in numbers. A lone cat was a lone cat, no matter which way the whisker fell.

At last, he spoke. "In that case, I hope your grandmother has enough medicine for a few more injuries. There are others in my group who are hurt worse than me."

The wind twisted the faint orange sand first one way, then another. Dragonfly stared into it, waiting for a predictable pattern to appear. As soon as it seemed the wind spirits had finished, they moved the sands again, endlessly shifting.

Dragonfly understood it to mean one thing: change. And while change was not unfamiliar to the Followers, *this* change was something greater than she had ever encountered before.

It came as no surprise when Galerunner informed her that Ardentwind was gone.

Dragonfly emerged from her den, which was wedged between two tall rocks, to see Kestrelsight pacing back and forth across the ravine their gust called home during summertime. The silver molly's fur bristled with impatience and annoyance rather than worry for her lost daughter. Only

Trueflight, who had yet to master the more basic skills of communicating with the wind, wore a look of concern.

"She's on her way back," Galerunner continued. "She must have gotten up pretty early to make it so far before anyone else woke. That's a first for her."

Galerunner's mate, Darkhaze, narrowed her eyes at him and bundled their two kittens closer to her belly. "Don't give these ones any ideas."

"Only looking at the silver lining," Galerunner purred.

Dragonfly arched her back, then leapt onto the overhang of rock under which most of her gust slept. If anyone noticed the wind helping the aging molly clear the distance, they did not mention it. Her fur was tugged in several directions once she was settled, and the sand at her paws blew into several small piles.

"As we are all aware by now, Ardentwind decided to leave the camp this morning–without permission–and is now returning to the gust," Dragonfly announced. "What may have escaped notice is that she is not returning *alone*."

At this, Kestrelsight's hackles rose on end. "Strangers?"

"Might it be Lacewing's gust?" Blazewind asked.

"No, their camp is two days' journey away," Valorflight said.

"What do strangers want with a kitten?" Kestrelsight hissed. "If they have harmed one hair on her pelt–"

"The spirits would not be so gentle if she was hurt," Dragonfly assured her. Though every Follower was born with *some* wind magic, there were a few–like Dragonfly herself–who had a stronger connection to the spirits that provided their magic. She had sensed the same heightened connection in Ardentwind, and perhaps had done the young molly a disservice in not taking her aside for private training sooner.

She supposed Ardentwind running into trouble was inevitable. Dragonfly would have to keep a closer eye on her granddaughter in the future, and giving her lessons on how to read signs from the spirits was not a bad way to do it.

"I'll keep watch for them," Blazewind offered, knowing the orders that were soon to follow. Dragonfly flicked an ear in acknowledgement and he scaled the cliffside, making an impressive jump over the ledge as soon as he was close enough.

"Cuttingbreeze and Dunebreak, find defensive positions to cover our retreat, if necessary. Darkhaze and Galerunner, stay with the kittens; Trueflight, remain with Kestrelsight; Sunlight, with Blusterstrike. Everyone else should be ready to scatter." Dragonfly gave the directions more as a formality than out of need; everyone already knew what to do in the event that the gust was attacked. Running far in many directions ensured the safety of most of the gust, and with Cuttingbreeze and Dunebreak slowing down any pursuers, they were almost guaranteed a successful escape. They would regroup when it was deemed safe, some distance from their last camp. Only young kittens or those still unable to track with the wind needed to stay close to their parents during the run.

Still, Dragonfly kept her eyes and ears open. She did not want to give up their summer safe haven unless she absolutely had to.

"I see them!" Blazewind called shortly thereafter. The spirits had not given Dragonfly much forewarning about the strangers' arrival–hopefully, that meant none was needed.

"How many?" Cuttingbreeze called from halfway up the craggy cliff, her light cream-and-ginger pelt hidden by a clump of desert marigold.

"Seven, plus Ardentwind."

"And it's *not* a gust?" Trueflight gaped.

While Dragonfly maintained her composure, she shared the spotted gray tom's surprise. A group that size traversing the wastes was nearly unheard of outside of the Followers. A bonded pair with a litter of young kittens *might* get that large–but seven grown cats, together? If it wasn't a gust, Dragonfly did not know what it could be, but she had not received word from any of the other groups of Followers that they were going to be passing by.

"They're hurt," Blazewind reported. At Kestrelsight's hiss, the ginger tom added, "Not Ardentwind! The others. I count two–no, three injured among them. Ardentwind is leading them this way."

Dunebreak began to descend from the rock face. He stopped when Dragonfly growled, "Hold your posts. Four of them are still fit to fight."

The large golden-ginger molly ascended to the top of the ravine.

"I shall go and meet them myself."

The Price of Trust

"Beware that which looks too good to be true; it is often a trap."
Unbound Proverb

The strangers were in worse shape than Dragonfly had expected. Ardentwind was the only one in the group who was wholly unharmed. The red-brown tom she walked beside had an ear pierced by a snake fang, the wound slowly dripping blood down the side of his face. A young gray-and-white tom limped forward, his pads clearly scraped raw; most of them walked with the same aching gait. The golden tom's face was a horrifying vision of blood, but it appeared that little of it was his own.

The two that made Dragonfly's heart pang with sympathy were the scruffy-looking calico tom and the thin spotted molly barely standing beside him. Her green eyes were dull, and his were filled only with worry–only with her. He walked on three paws, one of his front legs barely attached, yet still supported her. Her back was scored with the bite marks of a coyote, and Dragonfly knew in a glance that she was lucky to be alive at all.

Ardentwind ran forward as soon as she was close enough to shout her grandmother's name. "Matriarch Dragonfly, these cats are hurt!"

"So I see," Dragonfly responded wryly. "Are *you* alright?"

"Yes, I'm fine. Shrewpelt–" Ardentwind gestured to the solid tom with the pierced ear, "saved me from a snake. I thought it would be only fair that we help them, too." She lowered her voice. "The spirits of the wind led me to them, Grandmother. I wouldn't have gone off alone otherwise, really!"

Dragonfly doubted her second statement, but she could too easily imagine the wind guiding the inexperienced young cat toward this strange group. They marked a change for her gust, and change was always welcomed most readily by the young.

The breeze ruffled the crest of fur atop her head. If this was what the spirits truly wanted, then Dragonfly would at least hear what the strangers had to say. Whether she would do more remained to be seen.

Gathering her magic, she flicked a paw back toward the ravine to send a simple message to those still on guard: *Stand down, on our way back.*

"Greetings." The strangers had caught up at last, led by an orange-pointed molly and golden tabby tom. The molly continued, "We have traveled far. We will not stay longer than you wish us to, but we *must* rest. Ardentwind offered medicine and shelter as thanks for her rescue."

"That was not her offer to make," Dragonfly replied, her tone sharp as a winter gale. Though she had already made up her mind to give the two most injured cats some help, the strangers did not need to know that. Comfortable strangers became guests who overstayed their welcome.

The golden tom growled in response, but was quickly silenced by a light tabby tom bumping into his shoulder. "Show respect; she's comparable to a Captain," the pale tom hissed.

The word *Captain* sent a prickle of unease running along Dragonfly's spine, but a pained moan from the spotted molly forced her to brush it aside. She would deal with it when the time came. Two cats needed help immediately, or one would lose his leg, and the other, her life.

"Hang on, Spottedshadow. We're almost there." The calico tom winced as he urged her on, and the golden tom rushed to her other side.

"You will follow me," Dragonfly commanded. Though she loathed to turn her back on strangers, she sensed no hostility. Ardentwind certainly was not their prisoner to use for bargaining, and she had led them to the gust of her own will, however foolish. "Ardentwind, make introductions."

"Yes!" Ardentwind's tails and ears shot upward. "Travelers, this is my grandmother, Matriarch Dragonfly. She leads our gust. Matriarch, I already showed you Shrewpelt. The others are Dawnfrost, Goldenpelt, Wildfur, Spottedshadow, Wolfthorn, and Pool."

Dragonfly considered their names carefully. Few revealed any elemental connection. *Pool* and *Dawnfrost* might indicate water magic, but the others were harder to identify. These cats became more mysterious the longer Dragonfly looked at them. Wolfthorn was the only name she recognized–Matriarch Lacewing had mentioned him the last time their two gusts blew past each other. Though Dragonfly was surprised to see him with a different group of cats, he was at least familiar.

"It is nice to meet you, Matriarch," Dawnfrost said.

"Are you the 'Captain' of this group?" Dragonfly asked. "Ardentwind told me your names, but not who your leader is."

"Spottedshadow is our Captain," Goldenpelt asserted. "Dawnfrost and I are the next highest in rank. Dawnfrost only speaks for us while Spottedshadow is recovering."

Dawnfrost narrowed her eyes at him. "We are *not* the same rank."

Before Goldenpelt could contradict her, Spottedshadow let out another low whine. "*Don't leave–!*"

Pool hobbled over to her and licked her forehead. He jerked his muzzle back in alarm. "She's burning up! We need medicine *now*!" The young tom turned to Dragonfly. "I can make it back faster than they can walk. If you tell me what to get, I'll bring back the herbs."

"That's ridiculous! I'll go," Ardentwind replied. "Grandmother?"

Though the travelers were odd, Dragonfly had never willingly let a cat die in her care. "Bring a cluster of the sundrop that grows on the cliff."

Ardentwind's paws hardly touched the ground as she raced to return her rescuers' favor, Pool close behind.

Goldenpelt tried not to show his irritation when so much depended on the mercy of strangers. After a brief stop to apply the sundrop petals, Matriarch Dragonfly had led the injured into what passed for the Followers' healing den: a cleft in the canyon with a floor of soft sand. The beds were dug into the sand, and had no feathers or foliage to insulate the cats from the cold ground

Matriarch Dragonfly worked with a small army of assistants. Ardentwind squeezed a clear gel from a bit of cactus onto the burnt pads of the uninjured. The ointment cooled and soothed their scrapes. A spotted gray tom who introduced himself as Trueflight brought them a fresh-caught hare with instructions to share it, especially the liver and kidneys. A solid ginger tom slathered Wildfur's leg in a poultice, then held it in place while a cream tom bound it to two straight sticks. Then a molly gripped a long cactus needle between her teeth, wove it through thin strands of webbing, and drove the point between layers of Wildfur's broken skin and muscle. If not for the third stick that Wildfur bit down on, his curses would have shaken the canyon like an earthquake.

Dragonfly herself stood over Spottedshadow, a look of concern mixed with suspicion contorting her face into a scowl.

The golden tabby tom watched every movement she made around Spottedshadow, every herb or poultice she reached for–and remarked on the strangeness that she was completely still. While she had been quick to prescribe the treatments for the rest of the patrol, all of which had been carried out without hesitation, Dragonfly simply stared at Spottedshadow.

Spottedshadow's breaths came in short, shallow gasps, and Goldenpelt could practically feel the heat radiating off her from several feet away. He tried to recall what Mistysnow would have treated her with. Sun asters would bring her temperature down. He recalled that mint was good for just about every ailment. Did either exist in this sun-scorched desert?

He felt his hackles rise. He had not come all this way to watch his Captain die from negligence. Despite the pain in his paws and a warning hiss from Dawnfrost, Goldenpelt approached Dragonfly and Spottedshadow.

"Are you going to help her or not?" he demanded.

Dragonfly gave no indication that she had heard Goldenpelt. Her eyes were trained on Spottedshadow; her muzzle moved to form words, but she made no sound. Panic jolted through Goldenpelt like a bolt of lightning when he realized she might be using magic on the dark molly, and his claws reflexively unsheathed.

Wolfthorn was beside him in an instant, gently pushing Goldenpelt back. "Let her work," the pale tabby urged.

"That's my best friend." Goldenpelt hardly recognized his own voice, the desperation foreign to his ears.

"We care about her, too," Dawnfrost said, her voice far sharper than Wolfthorn's. "That is why we are not interrupting. Matriarch Dragonfly's methods might be strange to us, but there isn't anything *we* can do to help Spottedshadow."

Goldenpelt wanted to shove Wolfthorn aside, grab Spottedshadow by her scruff, and drag her all the way home. Instead, he settled into his strange, grainy bed, tucked his paws under his body, and curled his tail over his muzzle. He ignored his portion of the hare, though the others somehow managed to find their appetites.

If only he had not trusted outsiders, this would not have happened. He had done his best over the past two weeks to show Spottedshadow that he was reliable and adaptable. He had tried his hardest to be amiable to her strange friends, though he would never consider them friends of his own. He got on well enough with Dawnfrost, whom he had always respected as a fellow Envoy, and was impressed with Wolfthorn's resourcefulness. Shrewpelt, though prickly, occasionally had good ideas on how to find prey and use their numbers to their advantage to hunt for buzzards and large lizards. Pool achingly reminded him of Timberleg, and while he avoided Wildfur as often as possible, he did admit a begrudging approval for Wildfur's treatment of his new-claw. He would never choose them for friends, but he could acknowledge that they had their merits and the Alliance was better for their cooperation.

He had lowered his guard *once*, and it had cost them all dearly.

He remembered how Pool had eagerly approached him when the party had settled to sleep through an agonizingly hot day. Pool had never been on guard duty–a task usually split between Goldenpelt and Shrewpelt–and had volunteered to take Goldenpelt's watch. With an encouraging nod from Spottedshadow, Goldenpelt had agreed; Wildfur and Pool had taken his post.

Goldenpelt had not meant to sleep so deeply, but after two weeks of travel with little rest, his body had at last overcome his mind.

He had awoken some time later to find they were under attack from a pack of coyotes.

Coyotes were among the most dangerous predators that stalked the outskirts of the Field-lands. Goldenpelt only knew of one story in which a ranger defeated a coyote; all the others ended with a patrol driving the coyote away. Most of the time, the patrol that fended off the attack returned with fewer cats than it started with.

As he'd launched into battle against the fearsome canines, Goldenpelt could not help but think of a story Swifttail used to tell him and his sister in the nursery. Hazelfur's first Second-in-Command, Russetpelt, had kept watch one night, and had seen a coyote targeting the nursery. Before any other rangers could react to the alarm he'd raised, Russetpelt had thrown himself at the coyote and mauled it to death–at the cost of his own life.

According to Swifttail, the Spirits had given Russetpelt the strength to kill the coyote because he was protecting his kittens: Golden and Amber.

Russetpelt must have been watching him from Beyond, and had given Goldenpelt the strength and speed to do what was needed.

He still was not entirely sure what had happened.

One moment, he had seen Wildfur's leg in the mouth of a coyote, being torn and crunched; the next, Spottedshadow had launched a frenzied assault against the beast.

Her unfocused and panicked movements had left her open to counter attack. Once the coyotes had realized they were not going to get an easy meal, the one nearest to the dark-furred molly had sunk its teeth into her. Then the pack had started running back to whatever hole they'd crawled out of.

Goldenpelt had raced after the coyote who'd taken Spottedshadow. He'd leapt onto its back, clinging with his claws as he bit down, harder and harder, until his mouth bubbled with blood and the coyote's paws had faltered. With a final gurgled yelp, it had released Spottedshadow and died, but she, too, was left on the edge of death.

All because Goldenpelt had trusted the Marsh-landers with his duty.

All because he had failed to succeed Forestleaf as next in line to lead Field Colony.

All because Hazelfur had been convinced to help Oak Colony in battle.

All because Spottedshadow had let her love for her friends take precedence over her duty to the colony.

All because she had chosen the Marsh-lander as her mate. He had almost gotten her killed—just like Goldenpelt had always known would happen.

He felt like he was rolling a ball of moss from one paw to the other. Was it Spottedshadow's fault for being who she was, or was it his fault for failing to convince her that her beliefs were dangerous?

There was no vindication in being right, not when she was barely holding onto life. If she died, he would return to Field Colony in disgrace. His rangers would know he had failed to protect his Captain. Perhaps Mudnose would step down and allow him to become leader; perhaps he would serve as Mudnose's Second before assuming leadership. Either way, it would be a hollow victory if Spottedshadow was not there to cheer for him and acknowledge him as Field Colony's true Captain.

At last, Dragonfly moved. She worked with deft paws to scrub the dried blood and pus from Spottedshadow's wounds, then covered them in dainty, white flower clusters. Generous layers of cactus gel kept the medicine in place.

Goldenpelt raised his head. Spottedshadow's breathing eased after the treatment, but it did not seem like enough–hardly more than had been done for Shrewpelt's ear.

"They will survive." There was no triumph in Dragonfly's voice. No joy. "I shall wait until your Captain is awake to speak further."

Wolfthorn sat up straighter as Dragonfly passed and cleared his throat. "Matriarch–"

"I shall wait until your Captain is awake," Dragonfly repeated. "Unless the next words out of your mouth are gratitude for what we have done for you, then be silent."

"I am grateful for your help." Wolfthorn lay down again, his paws tucked under his body.

"As am I. As are we all," Dawnfrost added, though she said no more than that. Her gaze pointedly lingered on Goldenpelt before flicking to Dragonfly and back.

Goldenpelt lowered his head onto his paws again. "I will save my thanks for when the Captain wakes."

Dawnfrost might have glared at him. Wolfthorn might have given an indifferent shrug in response to his attitude. He paid no mind, and they went back to eating the hare. Pool, however, came to sit beside him.

"I know how you feel. When my sister was hurt...it's hard not to be able to do anything for the cats you care about," the young Marsh-lander offered.

Goldenpelt did not have the energy left to tell the gray and white tom how wrong he was. He could not possibly know Goldenpelt's feelings, watching the one he loved most nearly die for a tom he despised. The Envoy only turned away; the new-claw didn't deserve his wrath. He would save it, and let it sharpen his claws against the one who did.

The Lake of Lost Souls

"There is a lake that lies where the sun sets. It appears at first to be a paradise of calm weather, lush greens, and prey that runs into your paws. Do not be deceived; it is a lake of death."
Matriarch Swiftpaws

Dunebreak was the first cat to bring news to Dragonfly that the outsiders' Captain was conscious, though the Matriarch had been listening in on the oddly dappled molly for some time. Hers had been a serious case. There had been times when Dragonfly had thought she might not pull through–but there was *something* around her which would not allow her to slip away so easily. Wolfthorn's presence in their group had given her a clue as to where they'd come from, and the odd energy around the Captain had confirmed it.

"The one called Captain Spottedshadow is awake and lucid," Dunebreak reported dutifully. "Shall I send for the others, or would you like to speak with her alone?"

The sense of unfamiliar discomfort Dragonfly had felt upon first meeting the outsiders intensified with every moment she spent in the Captain's presence, and she did not relish the thought of a civil discussion between them. Dragonfly's instincts told her that she ought to send them on their way as quickly as possible to prevent her gust from getting involved in their affairs.

Unfortunately, Ardentwind had other ideas, and the situation presented as good an opportunity as any to instruct the future Matriarch on how to deal with strange cats asking the Followers for help.

"I will meet her, along with Ardentwind, Dawnfrost, Wolfthorn, and Goldenpelt. Send Ardentwind to me first," Dragonfly instructed.

When Ardentwind arrived, the young golden molly stepped into the cool shade apprehensively. Dragonfly greeted her with silence.

Ardentwind took a deep breath and let it go slowly, the wind smoothing her fur and playing with her whiskers. "The cats I met are here for a bigger reason than I know, aren't they?"

"Yes–and a bigger reason than I know, yet." Dragonfly scooped a pawful of sand into the air. It swirled and twisted as it fell back toward the floor of the den, but never quite settled. "Change. That is what the wind spirits told me to expect."

"A good change?" Ardentwind asked.

"I don't know." Dragonfly sighed, feeling her age in her sore back as she stood. "You are the future Matriarch of this gust, so I want to include you in decisions which will affect that future. I also want you to have the benefit of its past."

"Grandmother?"

"I believe these cats come from the Lake of Lost Souls."

Ardentwind's back arched. "But that's just a story!"

"It is not." Dragonfly licked between the young molly's ears. "It is a very real place. A place I have visited only once, in my youth, and swore I would never return to."

The wind whistled through the stone walls of the den, howling in echo of Dragonfly's pain. Ardentwind nuzzled under her chin, brushing her cheek against Dragonfly's neck and shoulder until the turbulent air stilled. She stayed pressed against her grandmother's side as the story was told.

"It was a harsh winter. We had heard warnings about the Lake of Lost Souls, but we had also heard it was a place of plenty–a forbidden land that tempted cats to enter with promises of plump prey, flowing water, and comfortable shelter. We were starving, freezing. *Desperate.*

"My great-grandmother, Willowwisp, was our Matriarch at the time. Her magic was the most powerful I have ever known, and with it, she found the Lake of Lost Souls and led us there. It was a hard journey, and we lost many. My siblings, my aunt–" Dragonfly paused to compose herself. "It was a risk. We took it in the hopes of finding something better awaiting us at the end.

"There were already cats living around the Lake of Lost Souls. They called themselves the Alliance. We were happy to see others, and we demonstrated how our gifts could be useful to them in the hopes they would offer shelter. Instead, they reacted as if we had declared war. They attacked us, tired and hungry and cold travelers, without mercy. We were outnumbered, and our magic faltered. Even Matriarch Willowwisp was helpless against their forces. They drove us away, and worst of all, they stole our last remaining kitten–my young cousin–as a trophy of their victory, just as the stories said they would.

"After that, we wandered the desert for months. We hoped beyond hope that we might find shelter nearby, that our lost kitten might return to us. Then the wind finally pushed us to move on."

Dragonfly stepped back and looked into Ardentwind's glistening eyes. "I ask you, do you think we should give aid to these cats?"

Ardentwind did not answer right away. Sorrow and indignation warred with compassion in her chest. She had never heard Dragonfly speak with such pain in her voice before, her heart still broken so many years later. She waited until she could speak without sobbing herself to give her reply.

"What happened in the past, what they did to our gust, is horrible. I don't want you to have to go back there if you don't want to. But I want to believe that they have changed–I must believe that they *can* change." Ardentwind placed one of her paws on Dragonfly's. "The wind called me to them. Please give me your blessing, so I know you are with me, even if you do not walk beside me."

Dragonfly licked Ardentwind's ear. She nipped a few more sun aster and yellow spider stems from the cliffside on her way to the infirmary. Even though the Captain was able to stay awake, her wound was surely in need of redressing again. "Let us go and speak to them, and see what they want from us."

Unease, anger, relief, and affection twisted Dawnfrost's stomach into an endless knot.

Spottedshadow was awake. She was *alive*. Dawnfrost had thought the sheer joy of that would overtake the rest of her emotions, but she had been wrong. Looking at Spottedshadow, who was struggling to groom what scant patches of her back and sides were not covered in medicine, made Dawnfrost feel like she would vomit.

What came out of her mouth was not the contents of her stomach, but her heart.

"How dare you!" she snapped, her face mere inches from Spottedshadow's own. "How *dare* you do something so reckless, so brash, so–stupid! The blessings of the Spirits are not to be used for foolish stunts like that! What if you had died? What would your colony do without you?" Her voice wavered and cracked. "Every decision you make from now on will impact the lives of everyone around you. You have to be more than who you've been." She struggled to find the words to explain her meaning. "There are times when Elmtail is *just Elmtail*, the goofy old cat who complains that the rain makes his joints ache, who dotes on his son and loves kittens. But there are also times when Elmtail is *the Steadfast Branch*, the peacemaker and leader who guides us through our hardest trials." She tilted her head to look Spottedshadow in the eye. "Sometimes there isn't room for both. Sometimes the Steadfast Branch has to make decisions Elmtail doesn't like."

Spottedshadow rested her muzzle on Dawnfrost's forehead and purred until the pointed molly's frustration and fear began to fade. They were not gone, merely pushed to the back of Dawnfrost's mind for the time being as relief came forward in their stead.

"Whether I am acting as Spottedshadow or as the Clouded Moon, I will always defend the cats I care about."

"And that is what will make you a great Captain."

Dawnfrost stood tall at the sound of Wolfthorn's voice, a reminder that the two mollies were not alone. Instead of a teasing smirk, Wolfthorn looked at her with fondness. He brushed his tail along her back, and for a moment Dawnfrost felt the way she had as a new-claw, free and burning with passion and ideas on how she and Wolfthorn and Spottedshadow would change everything for the better. It lasted only a moment with Goldenpelt stalking toward the Field Colony Captain, but Dawnfrost held onto it as something to cherish on lonely nights.

"You're awake," Goldenpelt stated simply, then lay beside Spottedshadow and began grooming the places she could not reach before she could protest.

"Where are Wildfur, Pool, and Shrewpelt?" Spottedshadow asked.

"Wildfur is right here, recovering," Wolfthorn answered with a nod toward the large lump of fur sleeping deeper within the infirmary. "They had to give him what they call *stitches* and are treating him for infection. He's past the worst of it, and with luck, he won't lose that leg. The other two are fine. I think they're out hunting with the Followers, actually."

"The Followers?"

"I see your Captain is finally awake." Dragonfly made her way into the den, Ardentwind close behind. Dawnfrost was surprised to see the young molly, but did not protest. She owed her friend's life to Ardentwind as much as to Dragonfly. "I am now ready to discuss whatever trouble you have brought to my gust."

Wolfthorn crouched beside Spottedshadow, explaining quickly. "The Followers are the colony of cats who treated our injuries. I spent some time with a different group of them when I was wandering." He lowered his voice to a whisper. "They're strong, but they might not want to get involved with others' problems. We need to prove that we're worth helping."

Spottedshadow took a deep breath. She looked to Dawnfrost, then to Goldenpelt–two cats who had far more negotiating experience than she did, as Envoys. But Matriarch Dragonfly was looking to Captain Spottedshadow to make the decision, despite her having had no time to absorb their current situation. She would have to do her best and trust that the Spirits had chosen her for a reason. For *this* reason. After all, wasn't it her willingness to hear others out and embrace their differences that most set her apart from the conventional choice of Goldenpelt?

Dawnfrost gave the spotted molly an encouraging nod. She could not think of a more fair-minded cat all the Alliance. As much as it stung Dawnfrost's pride to admit, if anyone could convince the Followers to unite with the Alliance, it was Spottedshadow.

"I'm sorry I wasn't able to introduce myself sooner," Spottedshadow began. "I am Captain Spottedshadow the Clouded Moon, of Field Colony. May I know your names?"

"I'm Ardentwind!" the lithe golden molly chirruped.

"And I am Matriarch Dragonfly."

"It is an honor to meet you, Matriarch Dragonfly, Ardentwind. Thank you for healing my rangers and me, and giving us a safe place to recover. Would I be right to assume a few days have passed?" Spottedshadow continued with her head respectfully lowered.

"Almost a week, yes."

Spottedshadow's ears pulled back. "Then we haven't much time. You were right earlier; we do bring news of trouble, and we left our home to seek aid from other cats." Spottedshadow lifted her chin to meet Dragonfly's eyes, drawing herself up with the proper pride of a leader. "At the beginning of the summer, two rangers in Marsh Colony were killed by an unknown creature. That same creature then attacked Oak Colony, and killed many more cats–including the previous leaders of Field Colony. If it is not stopped, more innocent lives will be lost."

She glanced toward Ardentwind, whose wide eyes flashed with curiosity. Spottedshadow managed a low purr. "Perhaps I should tell you more about who we are. We are from the Alliance, a group of four colonies that live around Alliance Lake. Goldenpelt and I are from Field Colony; Dawnfrost and Shrewpelt are rangers of Oak Colony; Wildfur and Pool came from Marsh Colony; and Wolfthorn lives in River Colony." At the mention of the last colony, her cheerful tone dropped away. "If the entire Alliance had united together against this threat, we might not be here–but River Colony's Captain refuses to help. Wolfthorn is defying orders to try to save the other colonies."

The wind changed directions as Dragonfly's fur rose on end. Ardentwind's look of wonder turned to contemplation.

"We are familiar with the colonies that dwell around the Lake of Lost Souls. Our gust has suffered much because of them," Dragonfly murmured, a growl slipping into her voice.

"I am sorry," Spottedshadow responded immediately. Goldenpelt started to speak, but quieted himself quickly as the other Field-lander continued. "I know the Alliance colonies are protective of our lands. We have feared the power of outsiders, as we do not possess any magic of our own–but I believe in helping others, and in atoning for harm. If our colony has done an injustice to yours, please let me make it right."

Ardentwind stepped forward, looking at each of the Alliance cats in turn. She touched her nose to Spottedshadow's ear. "I believe you, and I want to help. Grandmother?"

With a more skeptical tone, Dragonfly asked, "How would you make it right when you do not know what was done?"

"I am sure I will have time to learn about it. We can come up with a solution together, on the journey back to the lake–if you are coming," Spottedshadow said. "If you agree, I can at the very least promise that you will be welcome in the Field-lands. Our shelter and hunting grounds will be yours for as long as you stay."

Dawnfrost half-expected Goldenpelt to protest, but the tom had the sense not to contradict his Captain during such a delicate negotiation. She found herself needing to bite her tongue as well. If it were Elmtail in Spottedshadow's place, she would want to have a lengthy talk with him and the Council in private about such an offer. Opening the Field-lands to outsiders, mages, for as long as they pleased was a dangerous move that would not earn Spottedshadow any favors in her colony, but if that was how she wanted to handle things, it was not Dawnfrost's place to correct her.

A gentle breeze swirled dust and bits of herbs around Dragonfly's paws. She twitched her whiskers and blinked at Ardentwind. "The spirits of the wind are blowing in the direction of the Lake of Lost Souls. My gust will follow." Her gaze hardened once more. "However, do not presume to give us orders. My gust will follow my command, not yours. We will exchange information on the journey and see what can be done when we arrive."

"Thank you, Matriarch," Spottedshadow purred, lowering her head in gratitude once more. "I shall ensure that you do not regret this."

"Why do you call it the Lake of Lost Souls?" Goldenpelt asked abruptly.

"It isn't as if they have any reason to call it Alliance Lake if they aren't *in* the Alliance," Wolfthorn answered too quickly. Dawnfrost knew well the signs of anxiety in his mew, understated as they were. The fact that he carried his tail low, turned his ears to the side, and had bothered responding at all meant that he was uncomfortable with Goldenpelt's question.

Ardentwind, however, had no reservations.

"Because that's where the death mages live."

Mages of Death

"All living beings with souls have the potential to wield magic."
Matriarch Willowwisp

Ice flowed in Wolfthorn's veins instead of blood. Time slowed to a crawl as he assessed the reactions of the other Alliance cats. Spottedshadow, predictably, blinked in surprise and confusion; Goldenpelt's nose wrinkled in a snarl as he prepared a nasty retort. Dawnfrost looked at Wolfthorn, her eyes asking a devastating question: *Did you know?*

He could only look away, a silent admission.

"How dare you accuse–" Goldenpelt started to yowl, but Spottedshadow stopped him by placing a paw on his shoulder.

"We have myths about the Unbound and mages who live beyond our territory. They must have their own about us," she reasoned. With the same smile a Keeper gave a kitten who had tried a maneuver beyond their ability, she said to Ardentwind, "There are no mages at the lake. The Ancestors' Law forbids magic, so no cat is better than any other."

Dragonfly's mew cut deeper than any scratch when she asked, "Then how are you alive?"

Spottedshadow looked at the poultice that was caked onto her side like mud.

"You should have died long before you made it to me for treatment," Dragonfly stated flatly. "True, my healing skills have helped you recover, but the bite you received should have pierced your lung. You should have been dead in minutes. Instead, miraculously, you survived." The wind rustled her fur, dancing around her. "We have another word for miracles."

"That was the blessing of the Spirits," Dawnfrost argued. "All Captains receive blessings when they take up their position."

"Magic," Dragonfly asserted.

"No, it's different!" Goldenpelt shot back. "Spottedshadow can't have magic! If she did, the Spirits would not have given her their blessing. They would have sent signs to drive her out of the territory. She was born in Field Colony. We grew up in the same nursery. She is *not* a mage, or I would know about it!" Goldenpelt pressed himself closer to her, claws unsheathed to defend his Captain from an invisible enemy.

Dismayed, Dawnfrost looked back to Wolfthorn. He sighed.

"Yes, she is. We all are."

Spottedshadow's voice quavered. "I think you had better explain, Wolfthorn."

The pale tabby settled himself on the sandy floor of the infirmary, well aware of his friends' hostility. Before he began, he stated, "I wasn't sure I entirely believed it at first, either, so don't judge me for not telling you. What good would it have done anyway, if I arrived back to the territories after spending time with *renegades* and *mages*, and started yowling that our history is all wrong? Do you think Rainfall would have let me stick around?

"You grew up on the same story I did. Mages destroyed the world with their power out of jealousy and greed. Our ancestors managed to find Moonlight Island, and somehow sealed their magic to have a fighting chance against them. Maybe some of that is true. Magic works differently around the lake, and it grows weaker the closer you get to Moonlight Island. Cats outside the Alliance have a different story. A few, actually."

Wolfthorn paused, wondering how best to proceed. Some of the stories he'd heard varied widely in their telling. Should he try to share them all as a tangle of vines, with every countering twist and turn? Or should he pluck out only those parts that were consistent across each of them? Which would be the easier medicine for his allies to swallow?

He recalled the words of the strange black tom he had met one night. For days, the tom had followed him through the shadows, and before they had parted ways, he taught Wolfthorn many things. If any version of the story was close to the truth of it all, it would be the one that tom had shared.

"Before the Alliance, mages who wielded control over life and death—necromancers—were the most powerful of all cats. *Some* cats can still receive signs from the Spirits, but they feel distant, like trying to talk through water. Trained necromancers were capable of talking directly to the dead, as easily as talking to a living cat. They could even absorb the souls of the dead to lengthen their own lives. Despite their great power, they ruled over the other mages fairly, and all cats thrived.

"Still, others began to hate them and covet their power. One foolish princess, in an attempt to quell their envy, revealed the secrets of life and death magic to her friends. The necromancers were then hunted to near extinction. A small group escaped, and found Moonlight Island. Only, the territory wasn't as desirable back then as it is now. It was almost the same as the Unbound-lands. The last death mages came together on Moonlight Island and sealed their magic within the ancient tree in order to infuse their power into the land. That is how the Ancestors' Law started: magic wasn't allowed because it had to be given to the tree for the land to thrive. Anyone who refused to give up their magic was driven out and left for dead.

"That's why any cat who dies in Alliance territory becomes a Spirit. That's why Captains resist death; they are given a small fraction of the power we should *all* be able to wield, and use the Spirits to fuel their necromancy. The more so-called *blessings* you receive, the stronger your magic would have been, had our ancestors not sealed it all away." Wolfthorn finished with a shrug. "At least, that's what I've heard. I'm not entirely convinced about any of this, but it makes a lot of sense. What would you call the Spirits Beyond, except magic?"

The fur along Ardentwind's back lifted. "To the Followers, our magic is part of our souls. The idea of giving it up–of casting it out of ourselves–it's unthinkable!"

Dawnfrost, Goldenpelt, and Spottedshadow had remained eerily calm throughout the explanation. Their stillness did little to put Wolfthorn at ease. Spottedshadow stared at her paws as if they were not her own. Of all of them, he had expected her to be the most open to accepting the truth, whatever scraps of it were there. He had not anticipated how she might react now that she was a Captain. She had received blessings and was bonded to the Spirits–the magic–in a way no one else in their group was.

"The other Captains have no idea, do they?" Spottedshadow asked at last.

"I don't think so, no. We are now the only cats in the Alliance who know the truth."

"And Wildfur," Spottedshadow added with a worried glance back at her mate. Though he was still deep in sleep thanks to the medicine, she said, "I will tell him when he wakes up—when he's better. He deserves to know what I am if we are going to be together."

"This is ridiculous. How can you trust anything outsiders say about us?" Goldenpelt demanded. "The only thing in Wolfthorn's kit-story that makes any sense is other cats being jealous of us."

"I know they're right," Spottedshadow replied. She curled her paws in, staring hard at the pads underneath. "I know what I felt that night, when the Spirits blessed me. I know what I feel right now. It *is* magic." She hissed suddenly, "Magic that our colonies do not fully understand or know how to use because our ancestors wanted to bury the truth! They made us live in fear of others, and ourselves!"

"We can't know why they did what they did. For all we know, it was the only way to stay alive. Keeping their magic might have ruined the land. It might still, if you welcome the Followers into Field Colony." Dawnfrost looked lost, and all Wolfthorn wanted was to weave around her and guide her back to safety, to him—but he doubted she would ever want to see him again, much less feel their pelts brush together or speak softly of the future.

"The monster will ruin it first," Spottedshadow said. "Now get it together; we have a long journey ahead of us. Matriarch, in your opinion, how long will it be until Wildfur can walk?"

The golden molly's expression remained unreadable to Wolfthorn as she spoke. "In a day, maybe two, he will no longer need to be sedated. He will have to walk on three legs unless you want to wait a month or more for him to fully recover."

Clearly Spottedshadow did not like the sound of that, but she swallowed her feelings down. "Thank you. I will speak to him about what he wants to do when he is able to discuss it. And thank you, again, for all you have done for us so far, and for agreeing to help our colonies. I look forward to speaking with you in greater detail about our partnership. For now..."

Dragonfly nodded. "I know you are still tired, and quite hungry. Ardentwind, you may stay and speak to them if you wish, but fetch Captain Spottedshadow something to eat before you harass her with questions."

Ardentwind, unbothered by Dragonfly's hasty exit from the conversation, bounded away to greet the returning hunters. Wolfthorn swallowed; Shrewpelt and Pool were back, and had missed quite an important conversation.

"Should we tell—"

"*No.*"

Wolfthorn lowered his ears at the combined responses of Spottedshadow, Dawnfrost, and Goldenpelt.

"I think we need to get more comfortable with this before we tell others," Spottedshadow added. "If we are stressed and uneasy when we explain the Alliance's magic, it will only make others stressed and uneasy too. Shrewpelt and Pool can wait until we get home to learn the truth, along with everyone else. When we're *ready* to tell them properly."

"If we tell them at all. This changes nothing about our way of life. Most rangers will never be Captains, and generations of our ancestors have been perfectly happy without knowing about this. I'm still not sure I believe it," Goldenpelt said.

Dawnfrost did not offer further explanation. She cast hesitant glances Wolfthorn's way once or twice, but said nothing to him or anyone else. She walked away, bumped her shoulder against Shrewpelt's when she passed him by, and walked away.

Doubt and guilt prickled Wolfthorn's pelt, making him feel as if he had slept in a bramble patch. Though he was sure Dawnfrost wanted to be left alone, he could not resist the desire to offer her whatever comfort he could provide. He kept pace with her as she moved farther from the Followers' camp. Once he was sure they would not be overheard by anyone, he asked, "Are you okay?"

"I don't know." Dawnfrost sighed heavily.

"Amazingly, Goldenpelt is right about something. Generations of rangers and Captains have lived and died without magic impacting them—at least, not in any way they'd notice. Magic, blessings, whatever you want to call it, nothing has actually changed," Wolfthorn offered.

"But I know, now," Dawnfrost replied. "When I become Captain, I'll also become a necromancer."

"And?" Wolfthorn leaned in to brush his muzzle against her cheek, but she pulled away.

"And you knew." Indignation burned in her eyes. "You *knew* and you didn't tell me. What's more, how do you know that magic 'works differently' around Moonlight Island?" Her voice lowered to a whispered hiss, "Are *you* a mage?"

"Does it matter if I am? Does it change anything?" Wolfthorn was surprised at the anger in his own response. "And when was I supposed to tell you? We've been traveling together for a while now, but we've hardly talked. You stay close to Shrewpelt and you keep an eye on Goldenpelt, but you spend almost no time with me or Spottedshadow. Why? Have we done something wrong?"

"Of course not." Dawnfrost's mew was clipped. She pushed on through the searing heat of daylight.

Wolfthorn drew his ears back for a moment before pushing ahead of Dawnfrost and sitting down in her path. "Talk to me."

Dawnfrost growled in frustration. "You don't understand. Spottedshadow doesn't understand. I'm Second now—soon, I'll be Captain. I've been working for this my whole life. I have always put Oak Colony first, above everything else! Above myself, above *you.*" She glanced up at the moon, clearly visible even during midday. A constant reminder. "I've tried to be the cat the Spirits Beyond would want me to be. And yet..." Her tail lashed before she sat down and curled it around her paws. Dawnfrost looked away, her mew laced with guilt. "When Spottedshadow and Wildfur were wounded, my first thought was that they were being punished by the Spirits for having the gall to be happy together after all that's changed, because you and I can't be. She almost died, and all I can do is pity myself. I'm an awful friend."

"Don't say that." Wolfthorn put his paw on hers and touched her cheek with his muzzle. "We all have negative thoughts sometimes. The important thing is that you obviously feel bad about it, which means it isn't really what you wanted." He licked her ear. "So much has happened, and you haven't had time to work through any of it. I want you to know that you don't have to be the Second of Oak Colony around me. You can let me in."

"Does that mean you're going to let me in, too?"

Wolfthorn blinked. "What do you mean?"

"Is this what you were so afraid of back then–what you wouldn't tell me about? Is the truth about the Alliance and magic what's been keeping us apart?" Dawnfrost demanded.

"Partially," Wolfthorn admitted. "Was I wrong to hide it? Would you have listened?"

"I–" Dawnfrost hesitated, then said, "I would have listened. I would have supported you, because you're *you.* So, please, tell me the truth."

Wolfthorn curled his tail around himself, and was surprised to find Dawnfrost's tail curled around him as well. Though her frustration had faded quickly, Wolfthorn could almost feel the elevated beating of her heart, the unease and confusion that pushed her toward defensive anger. Only the truth would calm her completely, and give them a path forward.

Wolfthorn raised a paw, as if to groom his whiskers. He contemplated how much he should tell Dawnfrost. Now was his chance to come clean to someone, to tell the cat he should trust most about *everything*. Yet, she had hesitated. She'd said she could not give all of herself to him. Some part of her—and he did not think it was a small part by any means—would always be Oak Colony's leader first and foremost. He could not give her more than she could give him. They were not Wildfur and Spottedshadow. Things had always been and would always be too complicated between them. In another life, perhaps they could have been mates, but that future had long since slipped away. It was time to stop grasping at the ripples it had left behind in their lives.

"Alright, the truth. I spent time among mages while I was wandering, and I don't want anyone in the Alliance to know that. Rainfall is beyond paranoid about magic and if she ever found out I even saw them, she'd banish me, or worse."

"Then...you aren't a mage, yourself? Any more than the rest of us?" Dawnfrost asked.

Wolfthorn looked directly into her eyes, and lied. "No."

Long Road

"The wind always blows toward home."
Matriarch Wanderer

Shrewpelt had not expected to miss Black as much as he had over the days of traveling. The new-claw was not particularly pleasant to be around; he often picked fights with Shrewpelt over the correct way to do things—and worse, sometimes he was right. Yet Shrewpelt did enjoy having someone to hunt beside and practice battle moves with. Black was nearly ready to be a ranger, something that Shrewpelt had been eagerly looking forward to before the past month of trouble.

It was a strange relief to have Pool, Trueflight, and Ardentwind so close by. Ardentwind in particular hung on Shrewpelt's every word, staring up at him with her bright green eyes as if he'd personally placed the stars in the sky. Goldenpelt, too, seemed to hang around the younger cats more than any of the others after Spottedshadow hit her limit of withstanding his company for the day.

Perhaps it was because they were both the sons of Seconds, or because they were both aspiring leaders of their colonies, but Shrewpelt found Goldenpelt easy enough to get along with. Yes, the other tom was arrogant, but he had earned the right to be with his prowess in hunting and fighting—skills he gladly shared with the young cats.

Pool excitedly approached them every time the travelers made camp, eager to learn something new. Ardentwind and Trueflight followed right behind.

Under the growing light of the moon, the young cats tussled and tumbled. Goldenpelt had taken special interest in Pool's training, showing him how to use his long legs and lithe frame to turn in midair, leap straight up from a dead stop, and strike opponents while staying out of their range. Ardentwind and Trueflight were more like Oak-landers in their build, and Shrewpelt delighted in their endurance for running, leaping, and springing after him or any other target he set them upon. Galerunner and Darkhaze often assumed the role of prey in their training sessions, which gave Lavaplume and Blusterstrike the tendency to pounce after their parents' tails, too.

"What are we learning today, Viperfang?" Trueflight asked excitedly one evening.

Shrewpelt stared at him. "Who?"

"Oh, uh..." Trueflight ducked his head sheepishly. "It's just a name we've been...I mean, no disrespect of course..."

"It's because of that fang stuck in your ear." Goldenpelt batted at it, but Shrewpelt jerked his head away.

"I mean, you *did* save my sister from a viper," Trueflight added.

"Pretty sure it was a python, actually," Shrewpelt said.

"Pythonfang doesn't have the same ring though, does it?" Goldenpelt teased. "Viperfang is a good name."

"Hm." Shrewpelt considered it. He had always thought his own name was rather dull. Not everyone could have a standout name, of course; it would be ridiculous if the whole colony was full of cats named things like Sparklingeyes, Lovingheart, or Blazingsunlight. Goldenpelt's name suited him perfectly despite having a blander ranger title, as the tom's golden fur *did* stand out, and his name hearkened back to his father's. However, there wasn't any cat called -pelt in Shrewpelt's family as far as he could remember, and he didn't think *shrew* was all that impressive. Shrews didn't even share his russet coloring. If he was perfectly honest, he was pretty sure Elmtail had run out of ideas after Dawnfrost, Hailstorm, Thornheart, Wrensong, and Snowfeather.

Perhaps Shrewpelt had never stood out...but Viperfang certainly could.

Of all the cats to approach him as the travelers settled into their temporary shelter against the heat of the day, Wolfthorn had not expected Wildfur to sit beside him. The burly tom lowered himself slowly onto the ground, mindful of his injured leg in a way Wolfthorn had never known him to be. He supposed the pain alone would cause Wildfur to take greater care, but he had always seemed to be a cat who paid little mind to things like that. It was not an unpleasant change to see him minding the wound.

One quality that had not changed in the slightest was the Marsh-landers bluntness.

"Would you join Oak Colony to be with Dawnfrost?"

Wolfthorn blinked in surprise at the question, then began to laugh in an effort to disguise just how seriously he had considered that very idea. Wildfur's stern face stopped his efforts, and Wolfthorn sighed. "No. I could never join Oak Colony."

"Why not?"

"I don't belong there. And Dawnfrost...well, I think she'd claw my ears off if I tried it now. She's worked too hard to get over the idea of us ever being together to have me put the option in front of her again. Maybe it could have worked out, if I had joined Oak Colony earlier, but not anymore. Such is life."

"But what if you didn't belong in River Colony either?" Wildfur pressed.

"I'm not sure I do. There's so much more out there." Again, Wolfthorn sighed. When he reminisced on his time away from the Alliance territory, what stood out most was how homesick he'd been. The excitement of visiting new places and meeting new cats with different ways of life had been undercut by the tether pulling him back home. Everything he experienced had been colored by his comparisons to the Alliance, and the knowledge that he would one day return—for Dawnfrost or for River Colony, it did not matter which. "Nowhere has ever felt like *home* quite like River Colony. There are cats I care about, after all." Gray and Swiftmask were waiting for his return, and he at the very least wanted to meet his nieces and nephews, even if Gillstripe never let them be close. "Why do you ask?"

"Because Marsh Colony doesn't feel like home. Spottedshadow does."

"Well..." Wolfthorn bumped his shoulder against Wildfur's uninjured side. "You don't look like a Field Colony cat, but you *are* stubborn enough to fit in." He glanced at Pool, who was talking with Shrewpelt and Goldenpelt. Despite their differences, the three of them were getting along well. Shrewpelt helped groom an unruly patch behind Pool's ear, and Goldenpelt regaled them both with the story of how Forestleaf had chosen him to be an Envoy. "What about your new-claw?"

Wildfur grumbled, "I don't want to leave Pool, but I know I'll never be the Mentor he deserves. If I go, maybe he'll get someone better to teach him how to be a proper Marsh-lander."

Wolfthorn lowered his voice. "It sounds like you've put a lot of thought into this."

"It's all I've been able to think about for a while now. And it's not just for Spottedshadow—it's for me, too. I've never belonged in Marsh Colony. Trying to make me into a Mentor was Hawkshell's last attempt to get me involved before she kicks me out, and Leafstorm is determined to see me fail. I may as well leave on my own terms, rather than in disgrace." Wildfur lowered his head onto his un-bandaged paw. "But how to tell Pool?"

"I've heard honesty and open communication are ideal. Let me know how it goes for you; might be time I tried them, myself," Wolfthorn offered, curling his own paws underneath his body.

The moon's brightness grew steadily each night. Soon it would be full again, for the second time since the start of Pool's ranger training. Though he knew it was foolish, he could not help but wonder at times if any new-claw had experienced so much so soon in their lives.

Life among the Followers was not what he had expected it to be. Stories of mages, Unbound renegades, *any* cat living outside the Alliance painted them as lost souls, miserable drifters who were more likely to commit murder than lend aid to a stranger. Only those who were able to find their way to the Alliance, complete the Sundown Challenge, and swear to leave their old lives behind were worthy of acceptance within the colony. Yet being with the gust eased the ache in Pool's heart for his own family.

Ardentwind was very like Osprey—at least, before she had become Osprey. Kestrelsight reminded Pool of his mother so much that he had accidentally called her Kestrelsnap a few times. Trueflight was as close a friend and brother as Pool could have ever asked for, and he was sure battle training would have been immensely more enjoyable if Trueflight had been around to spar with from the start. He had made tremendous strides under the tutelage of Blazewind and Sunlight, so much so that at times he wondered if he had been meant to be a Follower. His long legs and lithe frame certainly made him more suited to their battle tactics than the Marsh-land ways he struggled with. Even Goldenpelt's instruction on Field-land techniques was easier to master.

Yet, he knew he could never leave Marsh Colony. His family was there—thus, so was his heart.

He sincerely doubted Wildfur felt the same way. It was not as if his teacher had hidden his feelings for Spottedshadow, but Pool had never considered the idea that Wildfur might be happier in another colony. He had always seemed to Pool like the kind of cat who could never be happy anywhere—even in those rare moments when he seemed to genuinely like having the gray-and-white tom around. Over the course of their journey, however, Pool had watched the way Wildfur lit up around Spottedshadow, the way the two of them fit so perfectly side by side. Though they could not be more different at first impression, there was something inside them that was the same, and called to its other half.

Therefore, Pool was not all that surprised when Wildfur beckoned him over with an overly-gruff mew to hide his bashfulness. "Hey, Pool, c'mere."

"Do you need something?" Pool asked, sniffing at his wound briefly. The bitter smell of herbs made him wrinkle his nose, but it was better than the rotting smell of an infected wound.

"Just to talk," Wildfur said.

Pool waited several minutes in silence.

"Well, nice talk," the new-claw laughed before starting back toward Goldenpelt. The Field-lander had promised to show him a pouncing technique that was guaranteed to catch any toad.

"Hold on a second," Wildfur grumbled. "I'm trying to find the right words."

"I know." Pool sat down next to Wildfur and tried to brush out one of the calico tom's mats with his paws.

"I'm…leaving. Going to Field Colony."

Pool blinked in surprise, not because it was a shocking thing for Wildfur to say, but because he would have thought Spottedshadow would be prancing around with joy.

"I haven't told Spottedshadow yet," Wildfur said in answer to his unspoken question. "Guess I wanted your blessing, or something."

"Isn't it supposed to be the new-claw who gets the Mentor's blessing?" Pool teased. One of his claws snagged in the tangle of Wildfur's pelt, and he carefully tugged it free. "You can have it, though. I will miss you, and I wish you didn't have to go so far away, but I've seen how you are with her. I want you to be happy, for once."

"I'll miss you, too," Wildfur admitted. He rested his nose between Pool's ears, which *did* surprise the young tom. "I really will."

"We'll see each other at Moonlight Meetings," Pool said, fighting the wave of sadness that threatened to wash away his unbothered façade. "I'll fill you in on all the dumb things Leafstorm says."

"I'll keep you up to date on Goldenpelt's ranting and raving."

"Hey, he's not so bad," Pool replied. "He *did* save your life, and Spottedshadow's."

"Great. Now I'll have to thank him." Wildfur exaggerated rolling his eyes. "Take care of yourself, Pool. I know you'll be an Envoy someday."

Goldenpelt was keenly aware of Wolfthorn's eyes on him. He had to be, Wolfthorn thought, since he kept glancing at the pale tabby tom while pretending he didn't see his intent stare. It had become something of a game to Wolfthorn, to see how many times Goldenpelt would bother checking before he finally snapped and confronted the River-lander. The answer, as it happened, was eight.

"Is there something stuck to my fur?" Goldenpelt asked.

"Just your stripes," Wolfthorn replied.

Goldenpelt rolled his eyes. Of all their companions, Wolfthorn was easily the most aggravating. He had personal reasons to detest Wildfur more, but of the two toms, he'd take the quiet lay-about over the rakish lay-about.

"You really believe what you said, didn't you? About Spottedshadow?" Wolfthorn asked.

Goldenpelt blinked in surprise at the sudden, serious, tone. "What do you mean?"

"You called her your best friend."

Again, Goldenpelt couldn't help but blink dumbly at Wolfthorn, as if the silence was an answer in itself. He thought the answer was obvious. If not Spottedshadow, who would he call his best friend? Not Forestleaf; she was his teacher and superior, whom he had sought to serve under as Second. They were close, but not friends. Fernface was often in his company, but she was to him what he was to Forestleaf: a follower, not a friend. The same went for her brother, Volefur, who had exchanged only a few words with Goldenpelt over the years they'd known each other. Jaggedstripe was a possibility, being a pleasant companion and generally nice to everyone, but Goldenpelt had a hard time thinking of him as someone who he could share his troubles with and receive real, honest advice from. His sister, Ambereyes, acknowledged him with the same general benevolence she would show any fellow Field-lander.

Who else could possibly be his dearest friend and companion, except for Spottedshadow?

Wolfthorn looked almost sad at his lack of response.

"You aren't a bad cat. You just make bad decisions," Wolfthorn said finally.

Before Goldenpelt could ask what he meant, he trotted off to join a group of Followers who were playing a game of making a feather float in the air and pouncing on it.

The golden tabby huffed, then followed. If these cats were going to be allies, then they could stand to learn a few Field-land tricks for landing from a high leap.

Dawnfrost would never get used to the feeling of sand between her toes. Bitterly, she considered it another sign that she and Wolfthorn were never meant to be, then shoved that thought aside. There was prey to catch, and she needed to pay attention to Zephyrwillow's instructions on how best to lure down the buzzard that had been circling overhead for the better part of the morning. As the Matriarch's mate, Zephyrwillow was equally as important in the social structure of the group. Disrespecting them would be a grave mistake.

Dragonfly was not what Dawnfrost would describe as *warm* toward the Alliance cats, but Zephyrwillow was just shy of condescending. Naturally, in a land with few trees, Dawnfrost's explanation of climbing after small birds on a hunt had likely sounded ridiculous to her.

"Vultures are scavengers. They do not like to prey on anything that can fight back. You and I will stage a fight, and you will pretend to be mortally wounded while I walk away. Then the vulture will come down, and we will use its surprise that you are *not* dying to catch it." Zephyrwillow gestured with their tail to a small outcropping of rocks, some yards away. "I will hide there, then come and help you subdue it."

"I see." Dawnfrost did not like the idea of being left out in the open with the giant bird. This truly was a horrid place, where cats had to play dead to lure in prey instead of stalking and hunting. Every day that passed saw her missing the forests of home more and more. "And is there a reason why I must be the bait?"

"The vultures have seen me before. They are not fools; they talk to one another, in their way. They will know it is a lie if I am the one defeated."

Dawnfrost did her best not to bristle in indignation at the blue-gray quinn.

"You said you are the Second-in-Command of your colony?" Zephyrwillow continued. "One worries for the future of your kin."

"How dare you!" Dawnfrost hissed, unable to contain herself any longer. Matriarch's mate or not, Dawnfrost would not allow anyone to speak to her like that. "My Captain has the utmost faith in me! He would never have agreed to let me go on this quest if he did not!"

"Says the cat who cannot catch a vulture. If you cannot adapt to new ways, your old ways will die with you. Wolfthorn was wise to leave your Alliance behind, and a fool for returning when he could have had a home in Lacewing's gust instead."

"Enough!" Dawnfrost yowled.

Dust clouds billowed into the air behind her as her feet left the ground, claws outstretched toward Zephyrwillow's smirking muzzle. The quinn nimbly leapt back. Their pawsteps were aided by the wind to find sure footing without looking while sand blew into Dawnfrost's face. If Dawnfrost had looked up, she would have seen the vulture begin to descend, circling lower as it watched their squabble. Her eyes squinted against the dirt, and she paid the buzzard no mind. The wind blocked her path forward.

"Damn you! What would you know about us? What legacy do you have to defend?" Dawnfrost growled.

Zephyrwillow pounced. Her paws struck Dawnfrost's shoulders and pushed the molly down, but Dawnfrost was not so easily defeated. She ducked, moving with Zephyrwillow instead of against them, then bucked up to throw the Follower off-balance. It would have worked, had a hard gust of wind not forced Dawnfrost to her forelimbs. Before she could recover, Zephyrwillow rammed her muzzle into Dawnfrost's neck ruff with a triumphant snarl.

"Now, play dead," Zephyrwillow whispered.

Dawnfrost did not know what humiliated her more—the fact that Zephyrwillow's comments had been nothing more than a ruse to create a convincing scene for the vulture, or the fact that it had worked so well. Still seething, Dawnfrost lay still, save for the twitch of a hind leg. Her panting for breath was real enough to convince the circling raptor that she was in a bad state, and it glided ever lower as Zephyrwillow walked away.

The Follower did not need to assist Dawnfrost once it finally landed to feast on her. The Second of Oak Colony was only too happy to tear its throat out herself.

Just when Spottedshadow began to feel she could relax for the evening, Goldenpelt beckoned her away from the wind mages. As usual, he wasted no time sharing his thoughts once they were alone.

"I've been watching these cats closely, and I don't think they can help us after all. They can barely fight without their—" he rolled his eyes for emphasis, "—*magic*. Even if they did, do we really want to invite these kind of cats into our territory? Who knows what they might do when all this is dealt with?"

"We could stand to learn a thing or two from them," Spottedshadow countered. "These *stitches* they put on Wildfur have saved his paw, while we would have amputated it. If they had been around when Blackpelt—Missingfoot—had been hurt...if they had been around when *any* Field-lander had gotten hurt...who knows how many lives could have been saved? They also know how to survive in dry conditions. What if there were ever a drought? The Field-lands and River-lands would feel the pain of it most, but the Followers would be able to survive it easily enough. With their knowledge, we would, too."

Though he could see some sense in her words, Goldenpelt did not miss the sparkle of naïve wonder in Spottedshadow's eyes. "You can't let yourself get too comfortable with outsiders like this. They aren't Field-landers. They aren't even part of the Alliance. They don't have the Ancestors' Law, or much regard for any rules and structure. I don't trust them."

"Stop that." Spottedshadow stood tall and stared down into his amber eyes. "I wish I could trust *you*, Goldenpelt. I know you mean well, but your instinct to push away cats who could help us will cause harm one day. We have no reason to believe they wish to hurt us. Quite the opposite: they've fed us, healed us, and shown us hospitality. Could you say the Alliance would do the same for them?"

"There's a reason we protect our territory and they would do the same if they had anything worth protecting," Goldenpelt growled. When Spottedshadow slowly shook her head in disappointment, he softened his tone and tried a different approach. "I know you want to believe the best in everyone. I love that about you. But it's *dangerous*. Everything I've done has been to help you understand that. What do you think will happen, once Dawnfrost becomes Captain? Will you show her your belly to save your friendship if she starts letting Oak-landers have their run of the fields?"

"That hasn't happened yet, and nothing about Dawnfrost has ever made me believe she would do such a thing."

"Give it time," Goldenpelt warned. "That is an ambitious cat if I've ever seen one, and I would know. Traveling with her has only made me certain that she is willing to do anything to ensure Oak Colony thrive. Are you ready to do the same for Field Colony?" He inched closer to her. "You were given an impossible burden to shoulder. I was trained for this, and I know how hard it is. Please let me help you."

Spottedshadow stepped back. "Field Colony can thrive by making new allies. These are my friends. Yours, too, if you'd let them be."

"I have plenty of friends back home, and I don't have to worry about them betraying me. The other colonies might be our allies for now, but someday that might not be the case. We've had enemies among them before."

"Just because it happened before doesn't mean we should act like it's inevitable. We can decide to be better." Spottedshadow sighed. "Maybe it won't ever be perfect. There will always be selfish cats like Rainfall who are willing to hurt others to get what they want. But peace and unity are worth a try, and I believe Dawnfrost will be the kind of leader who embraces those ideals alongside me."

"What happens when it fails? Could you fight your *friends* then?" Goldenpelt spat in frustration.

Spottedshadow's even tone and confident glare reminded Goldenpelt that she shared blood with Forestleaf. "I've never backed down from you, have I?"

The stars shining brightly overhead reminded Wildfur of the white dots on Spottedshadow's pelt. On clear nights, he had often gazed at the sky, wondering if they would ever find a way to be together—if he would ever be worthy of her. At long last, he had made up his mind, but now that they were alone, he struggled to find the right words to express it. The rest of the travelers moved on ahead of them, their ears occasionally flicking back to make sure the two recovering cats were not falling too far behind. Wildfur knew Spottedshadow could close the distance between them if she tried, but he had asked to speak with her privately. Now he only needed to *speak*.

"What is it, my love?"

Wildfur's stomach fluttered with nervousness when she called him that. He took a deep breath and let it out slow. This was *Spottedshadow*. He could tell her anything.

"I've been..." He stammered. "Being on this journey with you, it's made me think of some things. About the future. *Our* future." He looked into her emerald eyes and patient face. "I almost lost you, and all I could think of was how much time I wasted being anywhere but at your side. I never want to leave you again. I know Field Colony doesn't take in outsiders much, except kittens, but I was hoping since you're Captain now, I might..."

Spottedshadow's eyes reflected every star in the sky. "You want to join Field Colony?"

"Yes. Marsh Colony could never be my home, because *you* are my home," Wildfur said.

Spottedshadow pounced on him, rolling the both of them over the sandy ground. Wildfur let out a moan of pain when her paw hit his bandage.

"Oh, I'm sorry!" she yelped, though her tone was still giddy. "I really am, I'm sorry, I'm just so *happy*!"

Once they had righted themselves, they curled up together, snuggling close. Spottedshadow laid her forelegs and chin across Wildfur's back, and he curled his tail around her back.

"Soon we'll get to go to sleep like this every night," Wildfur murmured, and Spottedshadow purred loudly in response.

"I can't wait for that. I feel like I could run a thousand miles, or like I could fly. We'll finally be *together*." Spottedshadow nuzzled her nose further into his pelt. "Which reminds me, there is something I was meaning to ask you about, but there was never a good time. When I received my blessing, there was a Marsh-land Spirit I didn't recognize." She looked down at his face to gauge his reaction. "I couldn't figure out who it was before, but a young calico tom...it was your brother, Patch, wasn't it?"

Wildfur closed his eyes. When they were only new-claws, he and Spottedshadow had comforted each other over their losses; her mother, his brother. He had never told her much about Patch, though. He preferred to keep those memories buried and stay away from any cat who reminded him too much of his lost sibling.

"Yes. That sounds like him."

"Oh." Spottedshadow lowered her ears at the obvious signs of his grief. "He loved you. He still does."

"I suppose, in a way, he's with us right now. I don't know if he can hear me, or how all this ghost magic stuff works, but if he can hear me—I'm sorry, Patch. You shouldn't have died so young. You deserved to be a ranger, one our parents would have been proud of."

Spottedshadow reached inside herself, searching for the light that belonged to the new-claw.

"It wasn't your fault," she said. "You were both young and inexperienced. It could have just as easily been you—but Patch and I are both glad it wasn't."

Wildfur turned his head to touch his nose to hers as a sob shook his shoulders. "*Thank you.*"

After three nights of walking until their paws ached, Dragonfly at last signaled for the group to have a break in the next ravine.

"We are nearing the end of this journey," Dragonfly announced. "It is time that I share with you what danger lies ahead of us."

Dawnfrost and Spottedshadow perked up their ears. Goldenpelt leaned forward, pushing the buzzard wing he'd been chewing on toward Shrewpelt and Pool. Lavaplume and Blusterstrike looked up from where they had been sheltering under Wildfur's thick mane.

"I do not know much about these creatures," Dragonfly admitted. "I have asked the Alliance cats about them, and from their descriptions—beasts with bodies like badgers, but faces like dogs, and dark, shaggy fur—I have come to what I believe is a good idea. Your monsters are umbra bears."

"*Bears*," Ardentwind repeated under her breath.

"Usually, bears are not such trouble," Dragonfly said. "From what other gusts have told me, cats are not worth the hassle for bears to treat them as prey. Bears can eat many things, and prefer an easy meal of fish or berries over an animal who fights back with claws and teeth. However, Dawnfrost tells me the bears did not eat those they killed, and that there are two smaller ones and one large one. This is when bears become dangerous. A mother bear will eliminate any threat she perceives to her young without hesitation or mercy."

"Oh, no," Pool gasped. "Sunfire and Breezeheart must have panicked and attacked the cubs when they first saw them, so the mother killed them to protect her babies."

"Aspenbreeze was hunting, about to make a catch. Her claws would have been out like theirs were," Dawnfrost realized.

"And my patrol chased the cubs into a corner, then into the base..." Shrewpelt winced.

"If a few cats were a threat to her young, *all* cats are now dangerous in her eyes," Dragonfly finished. "Any cat she meets, she will kill for their safety. They, too, will likely grow up to view cats as a threat and seek to remove them from any territory where they settle."

Spottedshadow curled her long tail around herself. "This is horrible. All this death, over a misunderstanding."

"Do they have any weaknesses?" Goldenpelt asked.

"They sleep for months when the weather gets cold. Does it snow for long periods of time near the Lake of Lost Souls?" Dragonfly asked.

"No. We have a few snowy days in a year, but not enough to freeze the land," Wildfur said.

"Then, no."

"All living creatures are weakened by blood loss," Zephyrwillow pointed out with a dry mew. "Focus on that tactic and do not despair. Giving up will get you nothing."

With that thought looming over them, the travelers steeled themselves for a long night of walking.

The moon was nearly full by the time the wind carried the smell of the lake to the travelers. The Alliance cats charged ahead with renewed vigor, eager to return home after so long away. By nightfall, they had reached the edge of the territory. Shrewpelt, who ran at the front of the group with some of the Followers, found the nests they had slept in on the first day of their journey—just outside the Oak-lands.

"I can't believe we're finally back! What do you think Hailstorm named the kittens? I can't wait to see them!" he yowled to any cat who would listen.

"I don't think I've ever seen you act this positive," Dawnfrost teased.

"I can't help it! It feels so good to be home." Shrewpelt splayed his forelegs like a kitten, his tail waving in the air behind him. He tousled the crest of fur on top of Ardentwind's head. "It was all worth it, though."

Spottedshadow bowed to Dragonfly. "Thank you for coming all this way. Field Colony has several suitable places for you to live, at least for a while. Let me talk to my colony first so they know you're welcome; we'll send for you tomorrow. You're free to hunt on our lands until it's time for you to follow the wind somewhere else."

Dragonfly nodded. "Followers, make camp! We'll rest here tonight."

Pool stretched his whole body. "I think I've grown! I can't wait to tell everyone about the journey." He nudged Wildfur. "I'll let Captain Hawkshell and Leafstorm know you made it back to Field Colony safely. There's no reason for you to walk all that way just to leave again, unless there's anyone you want to say goodbye to."

"Just you," Wildfur said. "I know I wasn't much of a Mentor, but I hope I taught you something."

"You taught me the most important thing of all: how to throw a pinecone." Pool laughed. "Really, though, you did teach me something important—that home isn't just where you were born. It's who you love, and where you belong. And for me, that is Marsh Colony. I know that better now than I ever did before, thanks to you."

Wildfur ruffled Pool's fur. "I underestimated you, Pool. Don't let anyone else do it ever again."

"I won't!"

"I hope you aren't underestimating Field Colony and expecting this to be easy," Goldenpelt commented. "You're going to have to earn your place, just like any other Unbound, and we aren't used to taking in adults." When Spottedshadow started to narrow her eyes at him, he added, "But, I suppose I can put in a good word. And I've missed having a cat under my wing."

"I don't know if I'll fit," Wildfur said.

Goldenpelt glared. "I'm trying to be friendly, you—"

"It's a joke!" Pool cut in. "Wildfur just *sounds* like a big jerk. He isn't, really."

"Hmm." Goldenpelt huffed, and Spottedshadow joined them to smooth over the tension. "I suppose this means you're going to be mates, officially?"

"Yes," Spottedshadow said. Goldenpelt's ears sank. "I'm sorry—"

"No, don't...don't say anything." Goldenpelt heaved a dramatic sigh. "I'll manage to carry on, somehow. For Field Colony."

"For Field Colony," Spottedshadow agreed.

Dawnfrost cleared her throat. "Word will travel quickly around the lake once we return to our bases, and I for one would like to get there sooner rather than later. We should be ready to present a plan of action. The rest of us have to tell our Captains *something* before the Moonlight Meeting."

"Tell your leader we can help you find the bear den. Any of my gust *who are old enough—*" Dragonfly gave Ardentwind a pointed look, "—may choose to join you in combat after that."

Dawnfrost nodded, then beckoned for Shrewpelt and Pool. It would be safer for the Marsh Colony new-claw to travel with them through the oak forest than to go alone, especially since they still did not know where the bears' lair was. Without speaking a word, Wolfthorn joined them, only to disappear into the forest after the group started to trot toward the Oak Colony base.

Familiar Forests

"Let us move forward into an era of peace and cooperation, in honor of our history as one colony and our unique identities as separate colonies."
Captain Elmtail the Steadfast Branch of Oak Colony

Shrewpelt struggled not to run ahead. Since they had begun the return journey, he had not stopped thinking of what his kittens might look like, or what their names could be. He was only moments away from meeting them and thoughts that had merely preoccupied him before now consumed him.

They had almost reached the Oak Colony base when they were met by Thornheart, Snowfeather, and Rowanstorm. Pool tried not to look like a scared new-claw and stood tall before the unfamiliar rangers, who hardly paid him mind.

"Dawnfrost! Shrewpelt!" Thornheart purred in greeting.

"How is everyone? How is Elmtail?" Dawnfrost asked.

Shrewpelt shoved his way forward. "How are Hailstorm and the kittens?"

"Easy," Snowfeather laughed. "Elmtail and Hailstorm are just fine, and so are the kittens."

"How many are there? Are they toms or mollies? What are their names?" Shrewpelt continued.

"We'd better get back to base as soon as we can," Dawnfrost said. "I have a report to make, and Shrewpelt is going to be like this until he sees his babies."

"Who do they look more like, me or Hailstorm?" Shrewpelt went on.

Rowanstorm chuckled. "You go on ahead. I'll see this daring new-claw back to the Marsh-lands."

"You're going alone?" Dawnfrost asked, her mew edged with worry.

"There's another group ranging out that way. I'll meet up with them." He purred, briefly brushing his muzzle against her cheek. "It's good to have you back, Dawnfrost. I missed you."

Dawnfrost cleared her throat. "Likewise." She looked to Pool. "It was nice to get to know you without a border between us. Give Hawkshell my regards."

"Same to you, and my regards to Elmtail," Pool responded.

Thornheart and Snowfeather's relaxed demeanor left with Pool and Rowanstorm.

"We'd better hurry," Thornheart said.

"I didn't want to say anything in front of the Marsh-lander, but Elmtail isn't exactly..." Snowfeather sighed.

"I understand. Let's go," Dawnfrost answered.

Shrewpelt, of course, did not have to be told twice to hurry. The moment they entered the base he raced to the nursery, while Dawnfrost climbed the cliff to see Elmtail. At once she could smell the signs of sickness—he had not been able to leave his bed easily enough to use the latrine.

"Elmtail?" Dawnfrost called out softly.

"Dawnfrost," Elmtail hardly managed to greet her without coughing. "You've returned...!"

"Of course, and with help. Our colony will be safe again soon," Dawnfrost said, sitting beside the elderly tom and grooming his shoulder and neck.

"I am glad. I hope to be able to see it. I'm not gone yet, but there's little more I can do for my colony like this." He sat up, though his forelimbs trembled. "Wrensong has been giving me herbs to bolster my strength. I only hope it will be enough, so I can die an honorable death."

"Don't talk like that! You're one of the most honorable cats I know, no matter what," Dawnfrost insisted.

Elmtail offered a smile. "I think it is time you choose your Second. In these uncertain times, it will be best if the colony knows who to rely on before they're forced to do it."

"Are you sure?" Dawnfrost gasped.

"I trust your decision."

They rested their heads on one another's shoulders, a sign of mutual respect and abiding confidence. Dawnfrost could feel how frail Elmtail had become, but she could also feel that his heartbeat was still strong in his chest. He was not gone yet, and he deserved to pass on with the assurance that his colony was in good paws.

"I think Brackenfoot would be proud of you. I know Redleaf would be."

"I'll do all I can to live up to their examples."

"Oh, Dawnfrost," Elmtail wheezed out a chuckle, "You'll do so much more than that."

They emerged from the Captain's den to a clearing filled with Oak-landers. Shrewpelt and Hailstorm sat proudly with four fuzzy kittens tumbling over their paws and batting their tails. Dawnfrost approached the landing where Captain Elmtail had once stood to make his announcements, looking to Elmtail once more for his nod of approval before she made the leap.

"Oak-landers!" she cheered, "I have returned from the Unbound-lands with good news! A colony of cats has agreed to help us drive out the beast that stalks our forest!"

A great clamor rose from the assembled cats, their eyes shining with pride and joy.

"As many of you know..." She paused to let the final shouts die down "...Elmtail's health has been declining recently. For this reason, he has allowed me to name my own Second now. If either of us meets our demise, our colony will know in whose pawsteps to follow." She took a deep breath. "Shrewpelt!"

Shrewpelt, who had been paying more attention to his kittens than her speech, bolted upright.

"Over the last month, you have shown that you have what it takes to be not only an Envoy, but a pragmatic leader. If times were different, you would have had the full season laid out by our Ancestors' Law to prove it to the whole colony. Nevertheless, if you accept, and the Council approves, I would be honored to have you as my Second."

"*If* I accept? Of course I do! I'll stand by you no matter what challenges face us," Shrewpelt answered.

"Does the Council agree?" Dawnfrost asked.

Birchwhisker hummed thoughtfully. "It *is* irregular, but..."

"Shrewpelt is a good cat," Yellowflower finished.

"Of course I think he can do it, but I'm biased," Hailstorm giggled.

Vinestripe simply nodded from her place beside Larkwing.

"Then it is decided. And..." Dawnfrost's eyes flashed. "On our journey, Shrewpelt played a key role in our success. When a young cat was in danger, he acted quickly and brought down the snake that would have killed her. It was this act that allowed us to find the other colony, and convince their leader to help us. The outsiders took to calling him Viperfang on our journey home together, and I would like to honor his courage and skill by making the name permanent. What say you?"

The rest of the Oak-landers began a raucous chant of, "Viperfang! Viperfang! Viperfang!" Even the gray tabby kitten at his feet squeaked out, "Vipafen!"

Viperfang purred. "Thank you, Dawnfrost. I will treasure this name, and make it feared by our enemies!"

While Dawnfrost and Viperfang basked in the glory of their success, Stagcharge guided Elmtail back inside to his nest. The old Captain had managed to sit without coughing for several minutes, but now lapsed into a fit that shook his whole body. Stagcharge lay beside him and comforted his mate as best he could.

If only the sun could rise on Dawnfrost's time without setting on Elmtail's.

It had not taken much time to reach the Marsh-lands, and Pool waved his tail in farewell to Rowanstorm, Finchflight, and Gorseclaw from his side of the border.

Though it was not the smartest decision, he decided to take a detour on the way home. He remembered the Envoys mentioning how they had found Sunfire and Breezeheart's bodies near the border, by the Dry Stones. Though he could not be sure of the exact place where they'd met their demise, he plucked a few stems of rose mallow and placed them at the base of the boulders. Pool bowed his head for a moment to give his thanks to their Spirits before continuing south to the Marsh Colony base.

Before he stepped inside, he took a deep breath. It felt like ages since he had been home.

"I'm back!" he called.

"Pool! Thank the Spirits. Come here, kitten." Kestrelsnap descended upon him at once, wrapping her forepaws around his neck and shoulders. She groomed every inch of him that she could reach with quick licks, not caring that the rest of the Marsh-landers were gathering around them.

"*Mom!*" Pool whined. "How's Osprey?"

"Ask me yourself!" Of course, Pool did not get the chance to do so before he was tackled by his sister. Though she remained heavily scarred, and would forever bear the marks of Iceclaw's cruelty, her spirit had clearly healed well while he was away. "Where did you go? What was it like? Tell me *everything*."

Pool affectionately shoved her off. "I missed you, too."

"We're all pleased to have you back, Pool." Leafstorm looked around, then bristled. "Where is Wildfur? Why isn't he with you?"

"Wildfur now resides in Field Colony," Pool answered plainly.

"I should have guessed! Of course he ran off on us!" Leafstorm yowled.

"He didn't *run off!* He risked his life to see the mission to its end," Pool snapped. "And we succeeded. We've brought back strong allies."

He knew Leafstorm had more to say, but she quieted when Hawkshell's shadow fell over them. The Captain loomed above the pair, and the entire base went silent. Even the crickets quieted their shrill chirps.

Hawkshell did not look well, at least from what Pool remembered. She had always been larger than life, a force of nature in and of herself. Marsh-landers were naturally large in size and sturdy in build, and Pool thought of Hawkshell as an exemplary Marsh-lander. Now her short, dense coat was ragged at the haunches, and her belly was sunken in. Her prominent cheekbones now had a skull-like quality to them, and her eyes were shadowed.

"Go on," she said.

Pool swallowed, trying not to sound as intimidated as he felt. "They're called the Followers of the Wind. We think that, with their help, we can find the bears—the beasts—and fight them together. We will overwhelm the monsters and drive them out!"

"I see." Hawkshell paused, as if trying to recall a distant memory. "Bird-flight."

"Yes, Captain?" the speckled quinn squeaked, caught off guard.

"See to it that Pool's training resumes as quickly as possible."

"Yes, Captain!"

Just as suddenly as she had appeared, Hawkshell vanished back into her den. The entire base breathed a sigh of relief as the phantom of their Captain left their sight.

Osprey shifted on her paws. "You really think we stand a chance?"

"I mean, it can't be worse than fighting three coyotes at once, can it?" Pool said.

"You did *what*?" Osprey gasped.

Indigoeyes licked them each between their ears. "Alright, settle down. I want to be able to hear Pool when he tells us all about it."

Pool purred as his family curled around him, giving him their undivided attention. He would have to regale them with a tale worthy of their admiration.

"It was high noon, and the heat was bearing down on us, but we pressed on—until suddenly, three coyotes *jumped* into our path! I raced into battle alongside Wildfur, Wolfthorn, and Goldenpelt. I used my speed and agility to confuse those mangy dogs, but there were too many! One of them nearly had me, and it would have, but Wildfur got in its way and shoved his claws right into its mouth! That was when Captain Spottedshadow arrived..."

Field and Follower

*"What good is solving Oak Colony's problem
if it leaves us unable to handle our own?"*
Forestleaf, Second of Field Colony

The brook babbled at the divide between the oak forest and the open fields, running from an underground spring somewhere in the wastes down to the lake. Spottedshadow listened to its murmurs, almost certain she could hear a faint promise of something new lying just beyond. One leap over the stream, and she would be home in a way she never had been before, with Wildfur at her side and Goldenpelt–however reluctant–supporting her choices.

She turned her green eyes to the toms standing just behind her. "Ready to go home?"

Wildfur purred his response, taking a step forward to stand at her side and twine their tails together. Goldenpelt stood to her left, muscles tensed, waiting for her signal to cross.

The Captain cleared the stream in a single leap and started running as soon as her paws touched the ground, sprinting across the soft grass beneath an unencumbered view of the sky as she had not done in ages. Goldenpelt kept pace behind her. Wildfur loped along at a slightly further distance, unable to keep up with the Field-landers, but determined not to let them get too far ahead. He had followed Spottedshadow this far, and he was ready to follow her for the rest of his life; so long as he could see her, that was enough.

She did not stop until she had crested the first hill, breathing hard—not because she was tired, but because she wanted to take in the Field-lands with her whole being. The gentle sway of dandelions in the breeze, the scurry of rabbits to and from their warrens, the enticing aroma of mustard and heather and lavender and sage. *Welcome home*, it said to her. *This is where you are meant to be.*

Yet at the same time, something was wrong. Her mind did not grasp it immediately, but her eyes and ears caught on at once. There was too much activity near the willow tree that marked the Northern Base, where the Field-landers sheltered during the stormy months of winter. They had not been gone that long; autumn had not yet arrived, let alone winter. Field Colony should still be occupying the East Base, as they had been when she'd left.

She did not have long to wait for answers. As the three began their descent toward the base, a voice called out, "Spottedshadow! Thank the Spirits, you're here!"

Stone dashed toward them, taller and broader than she remembered. Young cats grew so quickly! But there was more to it than that; his eyes had aged as well, and a ragged scar tore one ear and part of his face.

"What has happened?" Spottedshadow asked.

"Was it the beast?" Goldenpelt pressed.

The gray tom glanced warily between her, Goldenpelt, and Wildfur. "I'll escort you back to the base. Mistysnow will want to speak to you."

The two native Field-landers shared a concerned look, fearing the worst. The beasts—*umbra bears*—had caused massive destruction in Oak Colony, where the dense forest and cliffs hindered their movement. If they had reached the fields, where nothing stood in their way but the claws and teeth of brave rangers, there was no telling what damage they could have wrought. Was the East Base destroyed, or now the home of the giant animals?

Spottedshadow lifted her nose to the breeze again. There was no hint of the bears' heavy musk; she only smelled cats. Goldenpelt narrowed his eyes with suspicion as they walked on.

Although bushes and the sweeping branches of the large willow tree offered some protection from predators, especially hawks and owls that flew overhead, the grass near the North Base was not tall enough to be woven into tunnels to protect the young and vulnerable. Its location higher in the hills made it a useful shelter from severe weather that could flood the other bases; when storm season passed, the rangers of the fields were only too eager to leave the North Base behind for the East or South strongholds.

Immediately, Spottedshadow did a mental roll call of the present cats. Fernface was snapping orders at Volefur, Shadowclaw, Tabby, and Jaggedstripe. Meadowleap helped Nightpool watch the kittens, who were now big enough to charge around the clearing on unsteady legs. Missingfoot urged Fleetfoot to take one more bite of the rabbit they shared, but the lithe tom did not seem interested in eating. Mistysnow, the first to spot the returning group, was already running to greet them.

"Thank the Spirits!" She nuzzled Spottedshadow's cheek. "I've been praying for any sign that you were on your way home!"

Though Spottedshadow was never adverse to affection from the old molly, she nonetheless felt herself pulling back in surprise. "What happened? Why did the colony move bases in the summer?"

"Were we too late?" Wildfur asked in a low voice.

Before Mistysnow could explain, Fernface stomped over to them with a snarl. "How nice of you to be concerned about us *now*! Is Field Colony finally worth your attention?" Spottedshadow had no chance to reply before Fernface bowed in front of Goldenpelt, giving him the report that should have been made to the Captain. "Not long after you left on your mission, we were attacked by River Colony! I tried to do what you would have wanted, Captain Goldenpelt, and retreated with as many as I could to safety. Our patrols have confirmed that River Colony has taken over the South Base and is expanding across our territory. If we don't make a stand soon, we'll lose the East Base, too!"

Spottedshadow's heart fell to her paws. Had leaving the Alliance territory been a mistake after all? Had she made the wrong choice, and doomed the cats in her care to suffer? "How many were–"

"Do you see now?" Goldenpelt growled. "*This* is why you can't trust other cats. The moment Rainfall sensed any weakness–any chance she could take something from us–she attacked!" His claws scraped the ground. "That land is useless to River Colony, but they'll take it anyway just because they *can*, because outsiders will always push us around to prove a point!"

Spottedshadow assessed his words coolly. In the past, she would have argued that Rainfall was *one* cat, that she did not represent *all* the River-landers. It would not be easy to forgive them, especially if any Field-landers had been seriously hurt–there were many Spottedshadow did not see, and she prayed they were only ranging the territory to bring back food or information—but she would not abandon her beliefs because of one horrible act.

She could tell Goldenpelt all of that in private later. At the moment, she had more pressing issues than defending her ideals. She climbed atop a low branch of the tree. "Field Colony Council, gather beneath the Windswept Willow! I need a full report, now."

Still fuming, Goldenpelt moved to sit under the tree. Stone joined him, as did Mistysnow. The rest of the Field-landers found places around the bushes to sit or lie down, listening but aware that they were not permitted to speak unless Spottedshadow asked for their voices. Wildfur sought a place apart from them until Missingfoot waved his tail, inviting the burly tom to sit beside him. Wildfur did so gladly.

"We are all assembled, Captain," Mistysnow said.

Spottedshadow faltered for a moment. She had not left with only three Council members, and her voice shook when she asked, "Mudnose...?"

"What Fernface said was true," Mistysnow sighed. "A River Colony raid, led by Iceclaw, attacked us at our base. They were brutal in their assault. If we had not fled, I have no doubt they would have killed us all."

She lowered her head, unable to speak further. Stone, between quavering breaths, filled in the rest. "He—Mudnose—was killed, along with Swifttail, and my...and Graymist. So many more were injured, but Mistysnow saved them, except for..."

Goldenpelt started to his feet, looking around. "Where is Ambereyes?" Bile rose in his throat. First his nephew, then his mother—how would he go on if he'd lost his sister, too?

"And where is Peach?" Spottedshadow's heart turned to ice. So many skilled rangers were dead. She needed to make sure her new-claw was alright.

At the reminder of his niece's absence, Goldenpelt swayed on his paws. He gripped the thin grass with his claws to stay standing.

"Come with me," Mistysnow said. "I know you need to know everything that happened, but I don't know if this can wait."

As with everything else, the North Base's den for medicine and healing was smaller and sparser than usual for Field Colony. If it were closer to winter, the crevices would have been stocked full in preparation for the move; as it was, they were nearly empty. Inside the den, Ambereyes stood guard over Peach. The calico molly lay, barely breathing, on a bed of ferns and feathers that was soaked with blood from the long, deep gash down her belly.

"No," Spottedshadow gasped, "Oh, *no!*"

"Spot...sh'dow?" Peach mumbled.

"Don't try to talk, sweetie." Ambereyes licked the shredded remains of her daughter's ears. "You've got to focus on getting better. Your sister will be back soon with a nice, plump rabbit, just for you. Okay?"

"I waited for you, Spottedshadow." Peach's voice was clearer as she came back to consciousness, but it was punctuated with a cough that barely moved the pigeon feathers near her muzzle. "I have to tell you–I fought–"

"You fought *so* bravely," Ambereyes said, helping Peach lift her head by placing a paw under her chin. To Spottedshadow and Goldenpelt she added, "She did, she did everything right, but *Iceclaw*..."

"Oh, Peachpit, you took on that brute?" Goldenpelt crouched down to lick Peach's cheek. "I'll bet he didn't know what hit him. I'll bet you gave him some wounds to worry about. I'm so proud of you."

"I have to tell–" Peach jerked away from Goldenpelt to cough again, blood bubbling out of her mouth like foam. "Fernface!"

"Tell Fernface what?" Goldenpelt asked.

"I saw her!" Peach tried to shout, though she was almost too weak to raise her voice above Goldenpelt's. "I saw Fernface...leave her post...wanted to prac–practice my stalking...she *led* them!"

A blaze of anger melted Spottedshadow's fear-frozen heart. She whirled and asked Ambereyes, "Is this true? Was Fernface on duty?"

"I'm not..." Ambereyes blinked, trying to remember. Horror widened her eyes again. "*Yes*. Yes, and I saw that she was gone! I was woken up by Nightpool's kittens, and I went to check on them, and I thought it strange that no one was sitting on the Overlook. I remember thinking maybe Fernface had left for a moment to use the latrine, and then..."

Goldenpelt stood back, his own eyes wide with shock and–when he saw the rage burning in Spottedshadow's–guilt and fear. He stumbled out of the Healers' den and collapsed a few paces away from the roots of the ancient tree.

Peach drew Spottedshadow's attention again, her head falling limply onto her bed. The Captain forced her fury aside to comfort the young cat in her last moments. Peach's resolve to cling to life was fading now that she had passed on the truth.

"Guess what, Peach?" Spottedshadow asked, forcing enthusiasm into a purred lie. "It's the full moon tonight!"

"Really...?" Peach's eyes glimmered for just a moment.

"Really. And you're going to get to show off your new name at the Moonlight Meeting."

"What about–" Peach's voice grew weaker as her coughs rattled her entire body, "–border guard?"

"You've already proven yourself, more than any new-claw before you. You don't need to stand guard."

"That's right," Ambereyes put in. "You're going to need to rest up so you can make the walk to the island, but stay awake a little longer, okay?"

"O-okay, Mom."

Both mollies nuzzled Peach, trying to make her as comfortable as possible while still keeping her awake.

"Peach, I have been blessed by the Spirits not only as a Captain, but as *your* Mentor. I've watched you grow from an excitable kitten to a strong, capable ranger that any colony would be proud of. We are all proud of you, and how you've bloomed into such a wonderful cat." Spottedshadow had to pause to suppress a sob. "That's why I've decided your name will be Peachblossom."

"Peachblossom," the calico molly purred. "I love it. I love..." Her eyes lost focus as her eyelids slid to their final close.

"Peachblossom?" Ambereyes trembled as her daughter went still. Then she collapsed and wailed, "Peachblossom–Peach–*my baby*!"

Mistysnow rushed in to comfort the twice-grieved mother while Spottedshadow stormed out. She was not even aware of her paws moving as she scaled the Windswept Willow and stood high above the Field-landers, her lashing tail calling their silent attention at once. Even Goldenpelt's followers, who had begun to surround Wildfur with hackles raised and lips curled, stopped their meaningless antagonism.

"Fernface!" Spottedshadow roared. "Is it true? Did you lead River-landers to *murder* your own colony?" Before Fernface could open her treacherous mouth to lie, Spottedshadow continued, "Peachblossom saw you leave. She saw you meet with Iceclaw. You lead his marauders to our home!"

For once, Spottedshadow succeeded in erasing the smug look from the scarred molly's face. Her ragged ears pinned back in defiance, but her eyes were wide with fear as the colony began to murmur and cast suspicious looks at her.

Rather than answer her Captain, Fernface lowered herself before Goldenpelt. "I swear, I would never betray Field Colony! I was doing what I thought was best. It wasn't supposed to go as far as it did!"

"Fernface..." Goldenpelt found himself trapped between stepping away from his friend, or moving forward to comfort her.

"I was afraid for our colony! Afraid that we wouldn't survive without our leaders! So I made a deal, a foolish deal. I thought if I offered a small amount of territory to River Colony, they would not go further. Alliance cats are supposed to be honorable and true to their word. They tricked me! Please, believe me. Believe I would never hurt your family!" Fernface pleaded.

"*His* family? Because of you, my mother is dead!" Stone hissed at her. If not for Fleetfoot's quick actions, the new-claw would have lunged.

Volefur and Jaggedstripe stepped closer to the brown tabby molly, shielding her on either side while Goldenpelt remained still in front of her. He was aware of the eyes of the colony on him, awaiting his next words, his decision. A twisted mockery of the position he should have held.

"If you had any sense, you would have let me lead from the start," Goldenpelt finally answered the unspoken question.

Spottedshadow felt as though she had been struck by lightning. "You blame me?"

"Who else is there to blame?" Goldenpelt glared up at the Captain, his amber eyes burning with resentment. Gone was the cat who had walked beside Spottedshadow on their journey, the noble Envoy she had hoped would become her Second in time, the one she'd hoped might stand beside her and offer legitimate guidance to make their colony better.

"It's been one disaster after another from the moment you spoke at the Council meeting," Shadowclaw chimed in.

"I still don't understand why the Spirits made her Captain instead of Goldenpelt," Jaggedstripe added, more to himself than anyone else.

"*I* don't understand why Field Colony is suffering for everyone else. Let the other colonies handle their own problems!" Thrushspots said.

With a wave of his tail, Goldenpelt silenced the dissenting murmurs. "Every choice you've made has harmed our colony. *You* urged Hazelfur to accept Oak Colony's cry for help. *You* pushed him to join the battle that killed him. Our Captain! And not just him. We might be following Captain Forestleaf right now, if not for you. Timberleg would still be alive if not for you!"

"Timberleg might have lived if you—"

"*You* decided to pursue justice for other colonies while ignoring our own! What Fernface did was misguided and cost us dearly, but could she have even done it if you'd chosen differently?" Bitterly, he glared at his paws. "Perhaps this has been a test from the Spirits, or a punishment for siding with your poorly thought out plans. Regardless, it ends *now!* I cannot allow Field Colony to suffer any more losses."

He turned his burning yellow gaze on her. "I am the rightful Captain. Stand down before your foolishness causes more death!"

Righteous fury flooded through Spottedshadow. For a moment she wondered if it was coming from her, or from the Spirits who had been equally betrayed. Her rage erupted as a fierce screech. She dove at him, claws outstretched. Goldenpelt's eyes widened in shock even as he rose to defend himself, but Spottedshadow slammed into him with all her strength and bowled him over. She ripped out chunks of fur and flesh as she hissed and spat curses in his face.

Volefur, Fernface, and Jaggedstripe raced to his defense at once. Their claws were aimed at Spottedshadow, but they were intercepted: Missingfoot stomped his foreleg on Volefur's tail, pulling the dusty brown tom back so Wildfur could deliver a harsh bite to his hind leg; Fleetfoot's menacing growls and sharp nips were enough to hold off the usually gentle Jaggedstripe; Stone dared to challenge Fernface on his own.

The brown tabby had always been dangerous in battle, yet the once-timid new-claw did not back down. With a fearsome yowl of, "For Graymist!" Stone leapt onto Fernface's back, his claws scoring marks in her pelt before he sprang clear of her counterstrike. Had Fernface not been groveling moments before, he may have missed. With a furious yowl she charged at him, unwilling to let the inexperienced tom get the better of her. Her way was blocked by Clayfur, who barreled into her legs and received a nick in his ear for his trouble. Meadowleap rushed to her son's aid and used her weight to force Fernface to the ground.

On the opposite side of the scuffle, Shadowclaw shoved Fleetfoot away from Jaggedstripe. The brown tom crept away from the fighting and to the Keepers' Weave, where his kittens were crying out in alarm and terror. Volefur kicked his way free of Missingfoot and Wildfur, though the two burly toms did not give him any room to run.

"*Enough!*"

Spottedshadow had pinned Goldenpelt, her claws at the traitor's throat. Every other fight came to a standstill as cats froze, watching.

"I should kill you for what you've done. That's what you would do to me, were our situations reversed." She hadn't expected her voice to be so devoid of emotion—not when she was feeling more hatred and revulsion than she ever had in her life, than she had even realized was possible. "But that isn't the kind of cat I am, and I can't think of a worse insult than being like *you*. Your Spirit will not be allowed to walk in the Beyond with one as noble as Peachblossom, or Mudnose, or any of the other cats your ambition has killed. Now take your traitors and *get out!*"

With a final shove to prove that she *could* kill him if she so chose, Spottedshadow let Goldenpelt stand and stalk away, no better than a defeated fox slinking off to lick its wounds. Fernface picked up Dawn by her scruff and ran after him, leaving Jaggedstripe to hastily grab Dark and follow. Volefur and Shadowclaw went next, covering their retreat and hissing back at the jeers and taunts of the true Field-landers. After a moment's hesitation, Horse and Thrushspots left as well, their heads low with shame, but their hearts still choosing to believe in their teachers, Jaggedstripe and Fernface.

Only when they were gone did Spottedshadow feel the sting that their claws had left in her. She could not find the will to climb the Windswept Willow a third time, so she made her final announcement standing amid her colony as they came forward to groom the blood from her fur.

"From now on, Goldenpelt and his followers are exiled from the Field-lands and should be driven out on sight. No exceptions, no questions asked. Wildfur will join our colony when he completes the Sundown Challenge."

She waited for any cat to voice their disapproval, but even those who were wary of the former Marsh-lander knew it was not the time to be picky about new recruits. A good part of their fighting force had just turned against them, and they would need all the able paws they could muster to repair the damages.

"Wildfur, your Challenge is to go and retrieve our guests from the border. Our safety is in your paws; do not fail us."

"Of course, Captain. I will protect this colony with my life."

For the first time in what felt like his entire life, Wildfur spoke with conviction. He would not let Spottedshadow down, and he would prove to his new colony that he was worthy to be among their ranks. Despite the itch of the grass against his fur and the heat of the sun on his back, he knew he was finally where he belonged. He would put effort into removing his mats and tangles tomorrow, after he had completed the Sundown Challenge and become a member of Field Colony. Then he would catch the plumpest, juiciest pheasant for his mate and console her for her losses.

But first, the Followers. Field Colony needed numbers now more than ever, and he hoped he would not be the only newcomer to join its ranks that month.

Spottedshadow's duties were not yet done, though she wanted nothing more than to return to Peachblossom's body and grieve. "Stone, you are young, but you have proved yourself more mature than any cat your age should have to be. From now on, your name shall be Steadystone, and you shall succeed Mudnose as my Second. You'll have a proper ceremony on the next full moon, but sadly we cannot wait for that day before you fill the role."

It was perhaps cruel, making a cat so young–a cat who had only *just* received his full name–Second in Command of the colony. However, he had received a little Envoy training, enough that Mistysnow had allowed him to sit with the Council earlier. Most importantly, he was someone Spottedshadow could trust. They would have to forge their path ahead together, each compromising and learning as they went.

Steadystone was no longer a hesitant and shy new-claw. He had seen things that had aged him beyond his few seasons, and he answered with confidence, "I will serve you to my dying breath, Captain!"

The return of Lilyfire and Clayfur, each carrying prey in their jaws, signaled an end to the miserable morning. Spottedshadow nodded to Steadystone, who immediately began assigning the rest of the day's duties and tasks. Despite the awkwardness of being given orders by such a young tom, the Field-landers who remained were in too much of a shocked state to argue or question the new Second's judgment. There had been enough fighting between them, and too much Field-lander blood spilled.

Steadystone assigned himself and Fleetfoot to a medicine-gathering mission. While they were gone, they would pick a few stems of lupine and place them where Graymist had been buried, and tell her all about what had happened when Captain Spottedshadow came back to Field Colony.

Ardentwind strained her senses, searching the breeze for any hint of a sign. The wind swept through her fur passively, in silence. The sensation sent chills running across her spine. There was no spirit in the wind here; it felt *dead*, and despite being among her gust, she felt terribly alone. Where were her ancestors to watch over her? Would they refuse to get closer to the Alliance's cursed lands?

Kestrelsight smoothed her fur with long, gentle licks. Ardentwind leaned heavily against her mother's side.

"It's so strange here," Ardentwind said. Dead wind, trees blocking the sky, shadows everywhere–how did cats live in such a horrid place? She hoped what Spottedshadow said about the Field-lands was true, and that soon they would be under open sky and bright sun again.

"The winds will change eventually. We won't stay forever," Kestrelsight offered.

Ardentwind frowned. She had thought that she might stay forever, when she had journeyed together with the rangers to their homeland. It was beautiful from a distance, and she would never have to worry about going hungry again if she joined a colony of the Alliance.

Being there now, though–feeling her connection to her magic fade–she thought twice about that hope.

She shook out her fur. Eerie as it was, Pool and Shrewpelt were her friends. She would help them. Then she would leave from this dreadful place, running as fast and far as the wind could carry her.

She could tell that not all members of her gust felt the same way. Lavaplume and Blusterstrike had made a game of climbing up the branching trees and seeing how high they could go. Like them, Trueflight seemed to view the journey as one big adventure to tell other gusts about at the Four Winds Gathering. Blazewind gathered new plants and discussed their benefits with Dragonfly, oblivious to how she and Zephyrwillow warily watched over the small settlement they had made.

The Matriarch was the first to raise the alarm when she sensed another cat approaching. Ardentwind tried to reach out to the wind to tell her who it was, but received nothing in response. She hissed a curse. It was like being a kitten again, blind and deaf, helpless except to squeak in protest when touched.

The stranger slowed when Dragonfly loosed an impressive growl. The underbrush shifted gently aside, and Ardentwind let out a breath of relief when she recognized the shaggy-furred tom. "Wildfur! What news?"

"What news, indeed," Wildfur muttered. "Captain Spottedshadow has sent me to retrieve you. We will meet with the rest of Field Colony at the North Base."

"Is that where we'll be staying?" Ardentwind asked. She hoped it wasn't too close to the Lake of Lost Souls.

"Mm." Wildfur nodded. He seemed more tired than ever, his limp more pronounced than it had been since the start of their journey.

"I smell blood," Cuttingbreeze remarked, hackles rising. She looked to Dragonfly and tried to send a quiet message with her magic—*is it a trap?*—but found herself unable to do so.

"Field Colony has suffered while Spottedshadow was away," Wildfur offered. "I don't know how much she would want me to tell you, and how much she would want to tell you herself. We did not receive the welcome we had hoped for." He lowered his head and tail. "Many Field-landers are dead, and more were exiled. Including Goldenpelt."

Galerunner gasped. Goldenpelt had not been particularly friendly with any of the Followers, but Galerunner had made the greatest effort to get on the golden tom's good side. "Why?"

"His supporters were willing to do whatever it took to make him Captain. Even if it meant killing their own." Wildfur's shoulders sagged under the weight of the truth. Fernface could make up any lie she wanted, and maybe even believe it, but he knew the real reason why she'd betrayed her colony to the River-landers. "So, you will likely be staying in the North Base with the colony. There are not enough cats left to warrant sending you somewhere else, unless you prefer it." He glanced toward Dragonfly. "Of course, I can make no promises, but the less Captain Spottedshadow has to worry about at the moment, the better."

Ardentwind winced. These cats really were as bloodthirsty as Dragonfly had warned. Yet, Spottedshadow and Shrewpelt and Pool hailed from these lands, too. They could not *all* be bad.

But hadn't she thought that of Goldenpelt, too?

The young molly wished Shrewpelt were still with them, especially now that she could not feel Bravesong's spirit walking beside her in the breeze.

Unbound Magic

"Better an empty warren than a full snake nest."
Field Colony Proverb

Dawnfrost stood at the base of the ancient tree, looking out on the assembled rangers with a curious feeling stirring in her chest. Though she had been away for over a month and the full moon had come and gone in her absence, it still felt like no time at all had passed since the last Moonlight Meeting when she'd attended as a ranger. An Envoy, yes–but here, Envoys stood with the rest. There was no Alliance Council in which they could convene and discuss matters. Perhaps, when she was Captain, that could be changed. As it was, the Envoys mingled with the rest of the crowd, quieting anxious murmurs and keeping their ears pricked for any news of danger from the other colonies.

All except for River Colony, of course. Rainfall had haughtily ascended to the highest possible branch of the tree, her tail hanging down to flick in Elmtail's face tauntingly as the old tom struggled to keep his wheezing under control. Iceclaw bared his teeth in a foul grin at Dawnfrost and asked with undisguised glee, "Any deaths this month?"

"This is not the night for mourning, if we had anyone to mourn," Dawnfrost replied coolly.

"We may as well begin without Field Colony," Rainfall purred.

"The Ancestors' Law states that all must be present. Field Colony are not traitors to the Alliance, so they will be here," Hawkshell growled back.

"Being here hardly seems to indicate loyalty to the Alliance anymore," Leafstorm muttered.

Iceclaw reached a paw, claws unsheathed, toward the pale brown tabby. "Perhaps River Colony has no further need of the Alliance!"

"Now, now, brother," Rainfall cooed. "The Spirits will give us the chance to prove our superiority over these mangy Marsh-landers soon."

Leafstorm hissed, "I'll show you mangy–!"

Before the fight could escalate, a gasp and a nervous hiss announced the arrival of Field Colony. Behind them strode the Followers of the Wind.

Dawnfrost knew these cats, yet even she felt her hackles rise despite herself when Dragonfly stepped onto Moonlight Island. This was a sacred place reserved for Alliance cats only. What was Spottedshadow thinking, bringing outsiders into the very heart of the Alliance?

The ginger-pointed molly forced her fur to lie flat. Knowing Spottedshadow, she intended to seek the Spirits' blessing for all the Followers, so they could walk freely throughout the Alliance territory. It would not be a bad strategy to show they meant no harm, and she could explain to all the colonies at once who their visitors were, why they were there, and how long they would stay before leaving to pursue their windy path again.

Even more surprising to Dawnfrost was the young gray tom who came to sit beside her. He could hardly be out of training; how had he earned the rank of Envoy, much less Second? She feared the worst. Many of the Field-landers were patched with bandages and new scars, and she noted the River-landers looked especially smug.

Rainfall, of course, spoke to rub salt in their fresh wounds. "Well, look at the prey the hunter caught! And what have you brought with you? Did you have to recruit renegades to fill your ranks?"

None of the cats, whether they had been on the journey or not, expected the large golden molly to join the Alliance Captains on their perch. Even Elmtail twitched his whiskers with suspicion as the outsider took a place beside Spottedshadow, staring down impassively at the gathered rangers while her own colony stalked the outskirts of the clearing.

Spottedshadow stared ahead with single-minded determination. Her voice rang out clear and strong. "Cats of the Alliance, for the past two months I have led an expedition into the Unbound-lands to find help for our current plight. These cats who stand among you now are our answer.

They are called the Followers of the Wind, and they will speak for themselves at this meeting. Dragonfly, if you would please introduce yourself."

"Of course, Captain Spottedshadow." The golden molly adjusted her sitting position. "I am Matriarch Dragonfly, leader of this gust of Followers. We have heard of your troubles and come to aid you, in return for a boon that Captain Spottedshadow has agreed to grant us. However, while we have what we requested, we have come here to address another matter of concern..." Dragonfly pressed a paw to the trunk of the tree. "This behemoth prevents us from using all but the most basic of our magic while we are here."

"What?" Hawkshell gaped.

Dragonfly met the old molly's gaze. "You are perhaps unaware of your history, as were the cats who sought us out. Many generations ago, your ancestors used this tree to seal away magic. Its roots spread far throughout these lands, and our magic weakens the closer we get to it. Even in the furthest reaches of your territories, our powers are greatly diminished."

"Good!" Rainfall snapped, no longer playing about in the upper branches. She leapt down to confront Dragonfly. "Magic is dangerous. Magic *destroyed* the world outside once, and it will again if we don't stop it! Of all the silly things in that Ancestors' Law, that is one thing all of us have always agreed on." She whirled on Spottedshadow next, thrusting her muzzle into the dark molly's face. "How *dare* you bring these mages here? What are you trying to do, kill us all?"

"I'm trying to *save* us all, since *you* won't!" Spottedshadow snapped back, her teeth clipping the air where Rainfall's nose had been. "And don't you–don't you *dare* speak about what our Ancestors would have done, or their law." She lowered her voice to a deadly whisper. "The only reason I have not declared war on River Colony, is because you are not the *biggest* threat facing us currently. And that will soon change."

Iceclaw growled a threat, only to be silenced by a warning look from Rainfall.

"I do not understand," Elmtail rasped, looking back and forth between the other Captains. "What has magic got to do with this?"

"We are familiar with the creatures that have been terrorizing your lands," Dragonfly said. "They are called umbra bears. Normally they are not so violent, but a mother will go to great lengths to protect her cubs, and it is clear you have made yourselves a threat in her eyes." She sniffed. "Correct me if I am wrong, but you have not found their lair despite their great size, yes?"

"That is correct," Hawkshell said.

"Then they are likely concealing themselves through supernatural means," Dragonfly explained. "It is not exactly the same as how we use magic, but some bears–as far as the Followers have observed during our few interactions–can move in and out of areas undetected. *Our* magic can counter that ability to find them, *if* we are allowed to use it." She looked again at the tree. "You will need to make that choice."

"Why doesn't the tree stop these bears from using magic?" Indigoeyes asked.

"I cannot say for certain, as I was not there when the binding spell was cast. I presume the Alliance of the past did not know other animals have such powers," Dragonfly said.

Lilyfire shuddered. "Great. So that means coyotes and hawks and owls are magical, too?"

A frigid hush fell over the assembled cats. The notion that other animals had minds and souls as complex as their own–that their *prey* might have loved ones and families–did not bear thinking about for long.

"What choice?" Dawnfrost asked.

Spottedshadow met her friend's gaze. Her emerald eyes were hard with resolve. "We Captains must dispel the enchantment, and allow magic to once again flourish in our lands."

Her words were met with a series of yowls, caterwauls, and growls. Dawnfrost, too, uttered a sharp, "*No!*"

"We might as well let the bears slaughter us!" Mousetail argued.

"You are young, and so you forget yourself," Elmtail said to Spottedshadow, his eyes clouded with concern rather than anger. "The outlawing of magic in these lands is one of the oldest of the Ancestors' Laws. It has been part of our ways since the very beginning. It is what has kept us safe, made this land our sanctuary." He shook his head. "I have made many choices that have tested the limits of the Law, but I will not go this far. I will not leave our territory weak to invasion from mages."

"No one wishes to see these monsters defeated more than I, but I cannot abide this," Hawkshell answered. "We will find another way. Perhaps if the Followers fight beside us without magic–"

"Fight when? Where?" Spottedshadow demanded. "Dragonfly is right; we can't even *find* the bears, which means every battle will be on their terms, and every day we wait is a day those cubs grow bigger and stronger. We can't handle a single full-grown bear. Do you think we can stand against *three?*" She whipped her tail from one side to the other. "I understand your hesitation, I do. But this is the only way to save ourselves."

"It can't be!" Dawnfrost shouted.

"Dawnfrost?" Spottedshadow gasped.

The two mollies stared at each other, both with ears pinned back in betrayal.

"If I had known this is what you intended, I wouldn't have brought the Followers here," Dawnfrost continued. "You've gone too far this time. If you do this, you'll break the Alliance!"

"I'm doing this to save the Alliance!"

"Of course, you know my answer," Rainfall hissed. "Magic is *not* allowed here! It never will be! The Spirits are displeased!"

"Don't you–"

Kestrelsnap interrupted Spottedshadow with a loud cry. "*Look*!"

The assembled cats followed the point of her nose up toward the sky. Thick, black clouds rumbled as they formed a heavy blanket above, blocking the moon completely. Spottedshadow's heart fell to her paws. Perhaps Rainfall was right; the Spirits *were* displeased. She did not feel the weakness of any of her blessings–her magic–leaving her, but that did not mean that the rest of the Spirits Beyond approved of her plan.

"That storm is going to break soon," Leafstorm said. "Hawkshell?"

The gray molly jumped to the ground. "The Moonlight Meeting is over. Let's go home."

Elmtail was slow to climb down. Dawnfrost helped him find his footing and stayed close to him as they approached the Crossing Log, casting a baleful glance back at Spottedshadow. If the Field Colony Captain intended to bring magic back, she would have to face the consequences alone. Spottedshadow wanted to call out to her friend—if Dawnfrost even *was* still her friend—but could not find it in her to raise her voice. Whether it was her own pride or one of the Spirits within her, she could not say, but she knew she would not admit to failure just to please the Oak-lander.

"This isn't over," Rainfall spat as she led her colony home, choosing to swim the short distance across the lake instead of waiting for the bridge to be cleared.

Spottedshadow dropped her head. Dragonfly rested her tail on the Captain's shoulder.

"What now? I can't convince them to do what needs to be done," Spottedshadow said.

"Perhaps not, but you are still Captain of a colony. You have your own magic, and a connection to this land," Dragonfly offered.

Spottedshadow pressed a paw against the rough bark of the tree, the symbol of the Alliance and their ancestors' vow to seal their magic away. If she tried, would she be able to feel the power within it? Could she channel it, free it?

Her throat was dry when she swallowed. Steadystone looked up at her, offering silent encouragement. Even as the rest of the Field-landers crowded together in worry and fear, they gazed at their leader with confidence. Field Colony had lost so much; Spottedshadow would not allow them to suffer any more losses. Maybe the other colonies didn't understand, but her cats knew she was only doing what was necessary to keep them all safe.

She reached for the magic within her, the Spirits who had given her their blessings and those still in the Beyond.

Such things were beyond words. Her very soul cried out her intention.

Hear me and do as I will! Release the seal, unbind the magic!

She reached up with both of her forepaws and pressed her entire weight against the trunk. Her claws scored deep, thin lines into it as she dragged them down. The sap that emerged from the cuts ran red as blood, yet smelled sweet as a spring breeze. It glistened in the pale light of the stars. Spottedshadow blinked, and it was gone. She could not even see where her scratches had marked the tree.

A strong gust rose and whipped at her fur. Her ears flattened as she lowered her head. The clouds above grew heavier until rain poured down, pelting the Field-landers with heavy drops. At the first crack of lightning, the cats raced across the Crossing Log.

The moment they were across, the wind shifted to shield them from the storm.

The Followers and Field-landers walked home on a dry path.

The Calm Before the Storm

"Forest Colony shall reign over this land forever, tied by brotherhood and blood."
Talltree, Herbalist of Forest Colony

"Magic. She wants to use magic!" Dawnfrost paced across the forest floor, her tail flicking in irritation.

"I feel like this is something we have been over recently," Wolfthorn replied.

"Yes, but..." Dawnfrost had groaned in frustration when she couldn't find the words to express her thoughts. Perhaps Wolfthorn had not been the best cat to complain to about Spottedshadow's foolhardy plans, but she found herself less than willing to discuss her misgivings with cats who did not know the truth—and of that group, only Wolfthorn was largely unbiased when it came to the spotted molly.

In truth, she shouldn't have been speaking to Wolfthorn at all so soon after their return to the Alliance territory, but spending weeks in his company had made them reluctant to part with each other again despite their better judgments. Even now, she was drawn to him like a bee to sweet nectar. If only he could have been born in the Oak-lands, or her in the River-lands!

"It's different," was what she finally came up with. "Necromancy—which I am still coming to terms with, mind you—is at least natural to this land. It is a part of our history, whether we like it or not. The Followers' magic isn't. And who knows what other kind of mages might try to invade? I doubt the Followers would hurt us, but they aren't the only cats out there."

Wolfthorn could tell her mind had been spinning ever since the meeting, churning with possibilities and fears. Dawnfrost could not see how Spottedshadow's plan led to anything but eventual disaster. What was the point of saving the Alliance from the bears if it was soon to be destroyed by magic anyway?

"One problem at a time." Wolfthorn rested his muzzle on her head, and she leaned against him. "Bears first. When and where?"

"I'll meet with Captain Hawkshell soon to discuss it," Dawnfrost answered. "Will you stay close in the meantime?"

"I will never let you face danger alone," Wolfthorn said, his pale yellow eyes looking into hers with pure devotion.

Dawnfrost purred and nuzzled his cheek. "I love you. Whatever happens, whatever we are or aren't, I want you to know that. I love you."

"And I love you." Wolfthorn touched his nose to her before rubbing his cheek along her side. Her fluffy fur tickled his nose as he circled around her, the two of them sitting side by side so they could look out on the lake with tails entwined. "I will have to return to River Colony tonight, if only to check on Gray. I worry for him, and all the young cats." He took a deep breath. "One problem at a time. Once this bear business is settled, I will tell you everything. I swear it."

If possible, Dawnfrost purred louder and leaned against him. "We will face it together. I won't let you face danger alone, either."

Dawnfrost held the memory of her last meeting with Wolfthorn close to her heart as she neared the Marsh Colony border. Though Wrensong had all but begged to join the negotiation party, Dawnfrost had denied her request; Oak Colony only had one fully-trained Herbalist, and while Moon would earn her ranger name and begin the training soon, that fact alone made Wrensong too valuable to risk for even a moment, never mind Elmtail's worsening condition. Instead, Dawnfrost traveled with Viperfang, Thornheart, Rowanstorm, Larkwing, Oak, and Fox. The party was large for a strategy meeting, but it showed Oak Colony's commitment to the cause.

It did not take long for them to be met with Marsh Colony's border guard: Leafstorm, Halfmask, Boulder, and Tigerstripe. The unfriendly toms offered no greeting as they silently led the Oak-landers to Marsh Colony's base. Dawnfrost committed the path to memory, should she ever need to speak to Hawkshell with too much urgency to wait for escort.

"Come inside," Hawkshell said without delay as soon as Dawnfrost peered into the hollow. Marsh Colony's Council met with her rangers, welcoming them to sit and enjoy the delicacies of the Marsh-lands for the morning meal: crane liver, frog legs, and crayfish. When Viperfang attempted to follow her inside, he was met with Indigoeyes and led away to join the others.

"Just us two?" Dawnfrost asked, finding the den unexpectedly empty.

"I have already met with my Council to decide Marsh Colony's course of action. Time is of the essence, and we need to be decisive," Hawkshell replied.

Dawnfrost cursed herself; she should have done the same. Still, it struck her as odd that Leafstorm was on border duty instead of present to speak with them.

"My Council has devised a plan that best suits the strengths of our colonies," Hawkshell said. "It is risky, but we have faith it will work. We will use our superior numbers to overcome these beasts. As it is our plan, Marsh Colony's rangers will take the role of the main fighting force. We require Oak Colony's assistance in creating a distraction and secondary wave to allow us time to regroup between charges."

"With respect, Captain Hawkshell, surely Field Colony is better suited to that task?"

"We cannot expect help from Field Colony–nor will I accept it, if they insist on bringing mages," Hawkshell stated outright, her accusatory gaze piercing Dawnfrost for her involvement in guiding the Followers to Alliance Lake. "Marsh Colony will take the lead on exterminating this threat, with Oak Colony supporting us."

Dawnfrost wasn't certain what to say. Though she felt the need to defend her friend, she wasn't sure she could.

Getting help from outside the Alliance had been a risky plan to start with, but Dawnfrost had agreed to it under the assumption that they were going to have extra sets of claws and teeth to fight beside them. She hadn't anticipated a plan that would break the very foundation of the Alliance by using magic. Spottedshadow had crossed one bridge too many, and left any possible relationship between Field and Marsh Colony burned in its wake. Dawnfrost wasn't sure where her friendship with Spottedshadow stood after this decision. All she did know was that she could not let Oak Colony's standing with their closest ally falter in this pivotal moment.

Hawkshell continued with icy determination. "Summer is a bountiful season for prey. We have taken advantage of that fact to make extra kills, and we've left the remains in a hollow near Westwood Bluffs. The scent will lure the beasts in, and they will be trapped within the canyon. Marsh Colony will fight on the ground while Oak Colony uses the slopes to launch an aerial offense and clear pathways of retreat for our cats."

"You have *already* done this?" Dawnfrost bristled despite herself. Westwood Bluffs lay between Marsh and Oak Colony—a strategic location, if the cooperation of Oak Colony was assumed. Elmtail surely would have allowed it, trusting in his friend's strategic mind, but Dawnfrost was not pleased at the choice being made for her. There was no guarantee that the combined forces of two colonies would be enough to defeat the three bears they'd previously faced, and if there ended up being more than three, they were doomed. Hawkshell's idea also required constant monitoring of Westwood Bluffs, meaning that swift runners from Marsh and Oak Colony had to be stationed on the cliff at all times to retrieve rangers at a moment's notice.

It was more than risky, and there was no way for Oak Colony to back out without being abandoned to deal with the aftermath.

"There is no turning back. We must succeed, or die. That will be the motivation our rangers require to ensure victory," Hawkshell declared.

"Of course." Dawnfrost did not dare ask for clarification of who exactly Hawkshell meant by *our rangers*.

"I would recommend choosing no less than ten rangers for Oak Colony's part of the plan, divided into two groups of five—or perhaps three groups of three or four, if you believe they will tire quickly," Hawkshell said. The molly scraped a rough curve into the dust at her paws. "These squads will be placed here, here, and potentially here, while the majority of our rangers hide in these bushes. Once the bears are in the center of the clearing, we attack. Your job will be to coordinate which Oak Colony squad attacks when; two should never be on the ground at the same time or they will get in our way."

Again, Dawnfrost bit her tongue. Now was not the time for stern reminders about who, exactly, was in charge of Oak Colony's rangers and their orders. She represented Elmtail and the interests of the Alliance, first and foremost. There would be another time to address Hawkshell's view of herself as Captain of Captains.

"I will see that it is done. Can you spare an escort to return us to the border now?" Dawnfrost said.

"At once."

It was with some disappointment that Elmtail accepted Hawkshell's plan, as told to him by Dawnfrost.

"Hawkshell is a seasoned fighter. We have no reason to distrust her assessment," Elmtail told her, though she did not miss the way he uneasily glanced to his side when he spoke—as if longing to exchange words with Hawkshell himself. Perhaps Dawnfrost should not have been so eager to accept Oak Colony's role, but there was no time to argue back and forth about etiquette when cats' lives were in danger.

"Ten rangers is a lot to ask of us when they may not return," Dawnfrost pointed out.

"They must be chosen with care. And we will send non-combatants, as well." Elmtail stood on unsteady feet. "I will go."

"Elmtail—"

The old tom silenced Dawnfrost. "I must go. I am still Captain. I cannot ask my cats to put their lives on the line without doing the same, myself."

Dawnfrost nodded. "I will go, as well. Now we need eight volunteers."

"I think you will find it more difficult to narrow down the choices to *only* eight," Elmtail chuckled. "Go and make the announcement. Go and see their courage."

Dawnfrost found it easier to address the colony each time she did it. Soon, it would be no more difficult than calling for a new-claw's attention during training.

"Oak Colony, gather!"

Cats streamed out of their dens and huddled beneath her. The sight of them warmed her heart as surely as the sun warmed her pelt. Though she had been home for a few days, she had not seen everyone assembled like this in what felt like ages. Seeing them all, together, looking up at her for guidance and leadership, was like watching a dream unfurl into a reality. This was her destiny, and she was ready for it as never before.

Hailstorm stretched and rose from her nest, slinking to the edge of the nursery to listen. Mist, Leopard, Strike, and Tawny mewled unhappily as their mother, source of warmth and milk, left them. Viperfang took her place, nestling his kittens to his own side. They were so tiny, their eyes still blue.

"Don't you want to attend the meeting?" Hailstorm asked.

"I can hear," Viperfang responded, licking the top of Strike's head until the fussy red tabby quieted.

Of the four kittens, Strike and Tawny bore the most resemblance to Viperfang, thanks to their red-toned fur and darker dorsal stripes. Mist, who was spotted gray and white, most resembled Hailstorm. Leopard's golden pelt and rosette markings marked him as the odd one out of the litter, taking after Hailstorm's mother instead. Viperfang gave them each equal attention as they resettled for their afternoon nap. Once they were at peace, he was able to listen to the meeting.

"Through the conjoined efforts of Marsh and Oak Colonies, we have a plan to drive the bears out of our home and retake the forest!" Dawnfrost announced. "Elmtail and I shall lead our rangers. This is a perilous mission; any cat who chooses to join us must accept that they will be risking life and limb for Oak Colony's future. We must be able to act as one, or we will all be lost. Who dares accept the challenge?"

A chorus of voices responded. Viperfang lifted his head. He should be out there, supporting his future Captain, but his paws were rooted in place every time he looked back at his young family. Was this how Redleaf had felt when he was born? How did he ever leave the nursery long enough to become an Envoy? Yet, Viperfang was more than that. He was Second. He owed it to Dawnfrost, all of Oak Colony, and especially the four newborns to be the greatest ranger he could be.

Reluctantly, he traded places with Hailstorm and looked out from the entrance to the nursery. She returned to the nest, nudging the kittens back into place by her belly so those who had been disturbed by their father's movements could nurse.

"Take me with you!" Wrensong all but demanded. "You will need a capable healer if this plan has any hope of success. I would like Frondsway and Moon to join me, as well. We will focus on treating injuries, but we can fight if we have to."

"Excellent idea. I'd have asked you myself if you didn't say so," Dawnfrost replied.

"If Moon is going, we should, too!" Fox shouted, stepping forward with her brother, Oak. "We are nearly done with our training. Let this be our final test, and name us rangers when we return triumphant!"

"As if you'd get your names before Frost and I!" Black replied, his chest and tail lifted with pride. "We are ready to prove ourselves."

Dawnfrost hesitated before vocalizing her approval. However, though they were young, they were right; these cats had much to prove. "Fox, Oak, Black, and Frost, then. Mentors, will you join us as well?"

"I will," Stagcharge answered at once. "I wish to witness this battle, and I will keep my eye on the new-claws as well."

"Me, too!" Rowanstorm said.

"I will go in my father's place," Swiftshadow said, shooting a glance across the clearing at Tornleg. "If things go wrong, you will need a messenger to send word back to base."

More and more voices joined the clamor, each asking to represent the Oak-lands and their strengths, each giving a reason why they would be the best suited to the task. Viperfang swallowed his apprehension and raised his voice. "Dawnfrost!"

The pointed molly's icy-blue eyes landed on him. "Viperfang?"

"I..." Like a piece of bad prey, his misgivings rose up in his throat again. "I want to consider who will stay at the base. Who will protect our colony, should this not end as we intend." He sank his claws into the ground to steady himself as his colony stared at him. "Each of you are accomplished rangers in your own right. Each of you would be assets to this mission. But each of you are also needed here, to reinforce our defenses and protect those who cannot protect themselves. I ask that Stonestep, Snowfeather, and Vinestripe stay behind with the Keepers." Stonestep and Vinestripe looked ready to argue. Before they could, Viperfang added, "I understand how much you want vengeance for everyone we've lost. I do, too. But there are living cats who need your love more than your hate."

"Perhaps that is for the best," Vinestripe admitted. "In truth, I don't know that I could trust myself to retreat, if given the order. These monsters have taken so much from us..."

"Then I will be the one to avenge Aspenbreeze and Dustclaw," Larkwing declared. He brushed against Vinestripe's side. "And I will return to you, Ma. I swear it."

Vinestripe licked his ear in appreciation.

"Stonestep?" Dawnfrost asked.

"My son speaks sense. Perhaps fatherhood has granted him wisdom," Stonestep mewed. "I, too, will stay."

Snowfeather and Thornheart shared a long look, a silent conversation passing between them. The two had rarely been apart since becoming rangers, but Thornheart had been Dawnfrost's friend longer than he had been Snowfeather's mate. At last, the gray pointed molly touched her nose to his. "I am with you in spirit."

"And I carry your strength with me to battle," Thornheart answered.

"Then it is settled." Dawnfrost leapt down from the peak to stand among her rangers. "Eat and rest well, Oak-landers! Our time comes soon!"

A Mother's Pain

*"There is more to being a ranger than fighting...
But nothing tests a ranger's mettle more than combat."*
Burningwood, Envoy of Oak Colony

Thorns of anxiety pricked at Dawnfrost's skin.

She led the procession of Oak-land rangers in silence, aside from the occasional cough from Elmtail. The element of surprise was essential for this plan to work. They would only stand a chance if they were able to catch the bears off-guard and gain the advantage quickly.

The Oak Colony fighting force arrived on the eastern side of the bluff: Dawnfrost, Thornheart, Rowanstorm, Swiftshadow, Larkwing, Stagcharge, Black, Frost, Oak, and Fox. Elmtail had agreed to stay beside Wrensong, Frondsway, and Moon on the cliff. From there he would watch the battle and give the signal to retreat if the plan began to go awry. Across from them, Dawnfrost could just see the Marsh-landers hidden among the bushes: Hawkshell, Leafstorm, Indigoeyes, Kestrelsnap, Snowstorm, Falconswoop, Tigerstripe, Whitefire, Crowstalker, Halfmask, Red, Pool, and Boulder.

Roughly two dozen cats–though some not fully trained–against the three bears noisily feasting on duck carcasses below.

Dawnfrost would not let their greater numbers make her overconfident, not after seeing the damage a single bear could cause. The cubs were larger now, too; their claws longer and sharper, the muscles beneath their coarse fur more developed. They would not go down easily.

Tension rippled through the air. Every strand of fur on Dawnfrost's body stood on end, and she was tempted to look up and see if lightning might split the sky to herald the start of the fight. There was not a single cloud overhead. It would have been a beautiful day.

At last, Hawkshell gave the battle cry. "For Sunfire! For Breezeheart!"

"For our colonies!" Elmtail responded.

"Dustclaw! Aspenbreeze!" Larkwing yowled.

Bewildered by the sudden cacophony of caterwauls, the mother bear lurched onto her hind legs and looked around.

"First wave, strike!"

Hawkshell led the first charge herself. Indigoeyes, Tigerstripe, Whitefire, Crowstalker, and Pool kept pace with her. Their blows sheared away patches of dense fur from the bear's exposed underside. Overwhelmed, the bear stepped back. She staggered when Indigoeyes and Tigerstripe wrapped around one of her hind legs. Her paws flailed in the air as she fell backward.

The cubs cried in alarm as their mother toppled to the ground. Hawkshell, Crowstalker, and Pool were on her at once, while Tigerstripe, Indigoeyes, and Whitefire kept the cubs back with threatening hisses and growls. Hawkshell went straight for the bear's throat, digging at the thick flesh in vain. When the beast roared, her cubs answered, pushing through the line of Marsh-landers even as the three established rangers tried to fight them off. Tigerstripe and Indigoeyes dodged to the sides and swiped at one of the cubs. The other met Whitefire head-on and, with a sickening crunch, threw her aside. The former Second rolled into a heap, a steady stream of blood flowing from her face and neck.

"Switch out!" Hawkshell ordered.

Crowstalker and Pool moved Whitefire's body out of the way of the next attack, leaving her under a shrubby mahogany. They would have to retrieve the body later for proper burial; the bear was on her feet again by the time they reached the fallen Marsh-lander, and there was no time to carry her further.

Elmtail's voice thundered through the air. "Dive!"

Dawnfrost extended her claws as far as they would go, flexed her muscles, and leapt.

She, Larkwing, Thornheart, Stagcharge, and Fox soared down from the top of the cliff at once, their claws finding purchase on the shoulders and backs of the bears. They held on with their foreclaws and shredded the bears' thick fur with their hind claws. The bears bellowed, unable to turn their heads far enough to snap at the rangers. Before the mother bear could throw the cats from her cubs' backs, the Oak-landers let go and raced back up the side of the cliff. Furious, the bears stomped on the ground and lumbered toward the east cliff, standing again to try to swipe the Oak-landers from their safety.

The shift in the bears' concentration turned them away from the bushes, exactly as planned.

"Second wave, now!"

Leafstorm led the rest of the Marsh-landers into battle. They aimed for the exposed spots the first wave had created, claws meeting skin rather than fur.

Snowstorm cursed the lack of Field-land speed as the mother's paws came down and he narrowly avoided their crushing weight. He latched onto her leg and bit down, shaking his head from one side to the other. Any other opponent would have had a nasty tear from such an attack, but he tasted no blood, and his paws were red only from the clay-dusted ground.

The bear lifted her paw and slammed it to the ground. Snowstorm landed some distance away, and rather than launch himself back into the fight, he ran for the bushes—then the forest, then the marshes. The sounds of the battle faded into the distance as his paws moved him further and further, first toward the Marsh Colony base, then beyond it. There would be no home for him there after such cowardice.

Kestrelsnap struck one of the cubs on the nose alongside Leafstorm, the two of them battering the beast's snout first one way, then the other. Each molly put all her strength into each blow, leaving streaks of red across the thinner skin of the bear's face, until the cub was off-balance. It tried to push them back with an unfocused shove. They dodged easily enough, but the ruckus it made drew the attention of the mother and forced their retreat.

The other cub nearly snapped Falconswoop's leg in its jaws. Red thwarted its attempt with a well-timed strike, though the young tom's eyes were wide in terror. Falconswoop nudged him back to his senses, urging a retreat while Halfmask and Boulder took their places. They nipped at the cub's heels while it rejoined its mother's side, startled by the ferocious toms replacing what must have seemed like easy prey.

Once all three bears were firmly paying attention to the Marsh-landers, Leafstorm led her rangers back to the thick, thorny undergrowth. All but Boulder followed immediately; the gray tom had risen onto his hind legs, preparing to grapple with one of the cubs despite its size advantage. Cursing, Halfmask tackled his new-claw and shoved him back toward the retreating rangers. Halfmask barely evaded a slash that would have turned his flank to bloody ribbons.

The bears gave chase, and turned their backs on the cliffs. With a twitch of Elmtail's scruffy whiskers, the Oak-landers dove upon them.

A second ambush could never have been as successful as the first.

The bears may have been distracted, but they were not mindless. When they felt the rain of claws and teeth on their shoulders and backs once more, they did not flounder. Instead of tossing their heads in confusion, they shook their shoulders and dislodged Swiftshadow, Black, and Frost before the Oak-landers could get a firm grip.

The mother bear rose up to strike Swiftshadow out of the air, just as she had done when she'd killed Redleaf.

Rowanstorm dove from the cliffs with a fearsome caterwaul, distracting the beast with scratches and bites until Swiftshadow could land.

Meeting the ground knocked the wind out of the black-and-white tom. In a heartbeat, Rowanstorm was at his side, helping him toward the cliffs.

"Are you hurt?" Rowanstorm asked, leaning down.

"Just stunned. I'm okay," Swiftshadow answered.

"Then move!"

Black and Frost circled the bear, acting as a distraction. They succeeded in keeping her attention, and drawing the cubs'. One of them lifted a paw and brought it down, catching Black's hindquarters and trapping him to the ground. He struggled to get up and keep running, but the bear's hold was too strong and he screeched in pain as its claws started to dig into his side.

Frost screamed, "Brother!" and rushed recklessly at the cub. He threw all his weight and anger at it, a whirl of fur, teeth, and claws.

Though this barely unbalanced the beast, it was enough for Rowanstorm to bite Black's scruff and pull him out from under the heavy paw. With a shove, Black was back on his feet, hobbling alongside Frost to the safety of the cliff.

Rowanstorm dashed after them, but not fast enough. The cub caught his leg between its teeth.

"NO!" Elmtail rushed down the cliff as swiftly as a young cat, Stagcharge following just as fast.

Before the bears could react, Elmtail wrapped his forelimbs around the cub's neck and Stagcharge had barreled into its leg, forcing it to release Rowanstorm. Stagcharge stayed near Rowanstorm as the cream tom limped away, hissing a warning at the bears should they dare to follow. Dawnfrost met them at the cliff and helped Rowanstorm up the path to the Herbalists.

Elmtail, however, held on. His teeth were buried deep in the cub's scruff, his hind legs kicking and scratching at its throat. He could see the whites of the cub's eyes and feel it begin to struggle for breath.

The mother's roar was pure fury and hatred. She lunged for him.

Elmtail gripped all the tighter. He had already accepted that this would be his last battle, and he would die fighting.

Hawkshell crashed onto the large bear's face and slashed at her eyes, leaving it a bloody mess behind. Howling in pain, the mother bear stumbled back. Elmtail finally fell away from the cub, which trampled after its mother.

"You won't be joining the Spirits just yet, old friend!"

"Soaring Protector, indeed," Elmtail said as he found his footing.

Every able Oak-lander joined him, swiping at the bears' ears and sides on their way to the ground. Their plan had reached its inevitable conclusion. Surprise could only get them so far. Now they would have to fight directly, and hope they had done enough damage to make a difference.

"The beast is fighting to protect her babies. Use them to break her spirit!" Hawkshell declared. "Marsh Colony, keep her apart from them! Oak-landers, attack the cubs!"

It was a cruel plan, but simple enough to cling to. Dawnfrost signaled to the Oak-landers and they dove into the fray once more with the single-minded determination to cut the cubs off from their mother. She brushed against Pool as they ran into place, offering him a nod of encouragement. Pool's heart pounded so loudly that he could hardly hear anything else, but he refused to back down. He had seen so much, and faced more challenges than any other new-claw. This time, at least he had the advantage of a whole troop of rangers ready to fight with him.

Side by side, the Marsh-landers pushed the mother bear back, putting distance between her and her cubs. They surrounded the mother bear, keeping her focused on them and unable to see what was happening to her cubs. The Oak-landers drove the cubs against the wall of the canyon, where they would be unable to escape and easily overwhelmed by the rangers.

For a moment, hope filled the heart of every ranger: They could fight and win! They could reclaim their home!

Then the bear reared up again, stomped, and bellowed. She showed the gathered cats her belly—a few thin scratches and bald patches, but no great harm done. Apart from the nick in her ear and the one eye Hawkshell had blinded, she was still fit for battle. The cub Elmtail had so viciously attacked was hardly worse for wear now that it was free. The rangers were landing blows and leaving marks–but those marks were scarcely worse than brushing against a blackberry bush. Whitefire was dead; Rowanstorm's leg was likely broken; the severity of Black's injury could be anywhere from minor to permanently disabling. Elmtail started to cough. Stagcharge covered him as Oak and Fox got him back to Wrensong.

The cats put up a strong front, but Dawnfrost could see they were beginning to fail. Marsh-landers were not used to taking on an opponent bigger than them, nor did they fare well with prolonged combat that required dodging and dashing. They fought more like the bear herself: stationary, lashing out when needed, using size to overpower and intimidate.

The bear did not appreciate their similarities, nor did Hawkshell. Marsh Colony's Captain let out a wild cry and leapt at the bear. Her claws raked its muzzle, forcing it to lower its head.

"While the mother is distracted!"

A surge of Marsh and Oak Colony rangers followed Hawkshell's demand, refocusing their efforts on the cubs. They landed blow upon blow to the cubs' sides, legs, faces—yet their weakening scratches left little impression. When Dawnfrost bit into the hind leg of one of the cubs, she only choked on its fur. The Marsh-landers tried to tear the cub's eyes, as Hawkshell had done to the mother, but they turned their head and snapped frantically.

Red and Tigerstripe both stumbled away with bitten paws, trailing blood back to Frondsway and Moon. They were lucky to walk away; Halfmask had to carry Leafstorm away from the fight, her nose split down the middle. Oak narrowly avoided losing an ear the same way.

"This isn't working!" Swiftshadow hissed.

"Dawnfrost, what now?" Thornheart panted.

"I..." Dawnfrost struggled to come up with another plan on the spot. What else could they do? "We need to..." She wanted to say, "We need reinforcements." They had known going into the fight that two colonies' worth of rangers might not be enough to defeat the bears, especially now that the cubs had spent a month growing strong on the forest's rich prey. The plan had hinged upon quick attacks and exploiting a few vulnerable points to damage the bears, but the beasts were hardly more bothered than she was at fleas!

Even Hawkshell, fueled as she was by her grief, could not keep up the fight forever.

When she at last let go, Pool jumped to take her place.

He was not thinking of glory. He only knew that as soon as his Captain released the bear's face, she would be open to counter, and he could not let her die.

He dug his claws into the fresh claw marks, clinging to the bear's torn skin as it jerked back and roared. His teeth pierced her ear and his mouth filled with the sickening taste of her blood. Still, he did not let go. He could not until his family got to safety.

"Pool! Fall back!" Indigoeyes shouted.

The bear's weight came crashing down. Her jaws snapped shut, and Pool let out a howl of pain as he felt his tail rip in half. The bear opened her massive jaws again, the end of his tail hanging out of her gaping maw, and lunged for him while he was scrambling on the ground. Pool was too terrified to even close his eyes, watching those massive teeth close the distance to his head, until they were obscured by cinnamon calico fur.

Wildfur slammed into the side of the bear's head, his fierce assault hitting its mark on her injured eye. The blinding blow caused her to miss him with her claws, but the impact from her paw still sent Wildfur rolling across the ground. Pool rushed to his side and stood over him, protecting him from further harm.

Stones and branches rained down upon the bears from above. Once more confused and unable to fight back against the wind-strewn debris, the bears were distracted long enough to allow a retreat. The rangers still standing hastily returned to the bushes. Dust kicked up into the bears' eyes and noses, stopping them from following the cats to their hiding places.

"Didn't expect to see you, Wildfur!" Falconswoop commented. "Let me take him to the Herbalists, Pool. He's in no shape to fight—nor are you, for that matter."

"Then I'll walk with him," Pool said, helping Wildfur up onto three paws. "Come on, you grump. Don't make me get the pinecones."

Wildfur grunted as he got to his feet, then let out a small purr at his former new-claw. "Well, look at that. You've got your first battle scar."

Pool let out a rueful laugh as he pushed Wildfur toward one of the shallower slopes of the cliff that was sheltered by low branches and thick vines. "It hurts. *A lot.*"

Organizing Field Colony into a mercenary force had not been at the top of Spottedshadow's priority list. There were too few cats left in her care, and most of them were needed to defend the base from further aggression by either River Colony or Goldenpelt's outcasts. She had only been able to spare a few rangers, who stood beside her at the top of the hollow: Lilyfire and Ambereyes, who needed the distraction from their grief, and Tabby, whose only responsibility was to return to Field Colony and give Steadystone a report should the worst occur. Wildfur had insisted on coming too, even with his paw not yet fully healed. He had promised to stay by her side, but she did not begrudge him saving Pool.

She had been surprised at the number of Followers that volunteered for the mission into Oak Colony's territory. From the moment she had released the magic seal, they had become much more comfortable. Ardentwind had described it as the difference between knowing they were welcome and feeling like they were unwanted guests being encouraged to leave.

Dragonfly had led them, both figuratively and literally. It felt odd to follow a stranger through lands Spottedshadow was at least familiar with, but time was of the essence. The battle was already underway, sooner than Spottedshadow had been ready for, and the wind that guided Dragonfly was more reliable than her memories of exploring with Dawnfrost.

They had not meet a single Oak-lander on their way across the forest. They must have been either protecting their home or in the battle, not scouting or hunting. If all went well, Spottedshadow would send some food; their rangers were sure to be far more exhausted than her own after the fighting, and it would hopefully begin to repair whatever damage she'd done to their colonies' relations by inviting the Followers.

That would have to wait. First, the bears.

When the Field and Follower forces had arrived at the hollow, things were not looking good for the Alliance cats. An outcropping halfway down the wall was filled with injured cats. Wrensong, Frondsway, and Moon moved like bees between them, applying antiseptic medicines and patching wounds as they went. With a nod from Dragonfly, Blazewind started down the thin ledge to help them. The rest of the cats fanned out around the top of the hollow, and Dragonfly had said two words: "Hold on."

The force of the wind that followed had nearly knocked Spottedshadow off her paws. Stones and branches fell upon the bears, distracting them long enough for the cats within the hollow to retreat.

"We won't be able to keep this up for long, unless there's a hidden supply of loose stones somewhere," Dunebreak pointed out.

"Not stones, but perhaps something else." Spottedshadow scoured the ranks of Oak- and Marsh-landers for Dawnfrost and Hawkshell, having already noticed Elmtail in the makeshift infirmary. She nodded to Dragonfly before bounding down to the forest cover, waving her tail to call the two mollies over. Though Hawkshell's expression did not change, Spottedshadow could see relief in Dawnfrost's eyes.

"Strategy meeting, now," Spottedshadow said.

Dawnfrost nodded, too breathless for the moment to speak. Hawkshell opened her mouth to take the lead, but Spottedshadow cut her off.

"We will never defeat them with strength. Every ranger in the Alliance could stand here, and we would still lose. We must use our wit and skill."

"What do you propose?" Hawkshell said.

"The bears are cornered within this hollow. If we can block the exit, force them to climb out, then we claim the high ground. Gravity and exhaustion will do our work for us." Spottedshadow turned her attention to the trees at the top of the bluff. Many of their roots were exposed, intertwined with the rock face.

Dawnfrost followed her eyes. Her breathing was now even, her heartbeat steady. She had not realized how desperately she wished for her friend's presence beside her in this fight. "If we could dislodge one or two of those trees, they might bring down some of the cliffside with them. That would seal the entrance to the hollow."

"And how do we bring them down?" Hawkshell asked.

"Teamwork," Spottedshadow said. "How many are fit to dig?"

Dawnfrost swept her gaze over the remaining rangers who peered out of the undergrowth: Thornheart, Boulder, Fox, Oak, Falconswoop, Stagcharge, Frost, Swiftshadow, Indigoeyes, Kestrelsnap, Larkwing, and Crowstalker. She tried to hide her feelings but could not suppress her gasp entirely. They were down to nearly half the number of rangers who had come with them, and though many would recover, some would not.

The remaining Oak-landers followed Dawnfrost up the footholds. A few paused at the infirmary to usher those that could move into better cover; Stagcharge and Larkwing guarded the ledge. If the bears were going to come up, they could not leave their weak and injured unprotected in the beasts' path. The Marsh-landers and Spottedshadow went around, climbing the other side of the gap.

The trees were old, but sturdy. They had stood at their posts for decades, centuries.

Dawnfrost placed a paw upon the trunk of a worn oak. Then she snarled, "DIG!"

Paws attacked the earth at the base of the tree. Claws were worn down to stubs and pads cracked and bloodied. Gouges appeared in the ground while the bears, seemingly the victors of the skirmish, licked their wounds. One of the cubs dragged Whitefire's body out of its temporary hiding place and gnawed on a leg.

Spottedshadow could hardly see past the dust in her eyes. Her shoulders and paws ached from the effort of scraping away the dirt.

Just when she felt she could not scoop one more pawful, she heard a creak, long and low. She felt the roots shift.

The wind rose, stronger even than before. The Followers raised their muzzles to the sky as they channeled their magic at its fullest power.

As one, Dragonfly's gust summoned the force of a hurricane.

"Back! Get down!" Spottedshadow shouted, darting away from the edge of the cliff as the wind rose. She crouched in the safety of a camellia, sheltered beside Ambereyes and Kestrelsnap. The cats huddled close to one another, tails tucked and ears flat as the gale whipped the branches into a frenzy overhead.

Only Hawkshell stayed, watching, as the tree was torn out by its roots and clamored to the ground below, onto the cub that had dared plunder her sister's remains. Her muzzle twisted into a smile when she heard the same horrid crunch of its bones being shattered by the weight of the oak.

The mother bear wailed in anguish. Before she could move, the second tree crashed down, followed by a boulder. She and the remaining cub stared in what might have been disbelief at the severed leg of her dead cub protruding from the new barrier.

Hawkshell leapt into the clearing with a triumphant yowl. She flexed her claws against the fallen trees, the same way a Marsh-lander would mark their territory. Then she cut a scrap of fur from the cub, a gleeful glint in her eye. "I shall sleep *well* tonight," she purred.

The bear may not have understood her words, but it understood her actions. In that moment, she and Hawkshell shared the same madness. The mother bear pounded the ground with her paws and stampeded across the clearing toward the gray molly. Hawkshell deftly made her way up the cliff again, hopping from landing to landing, until she emerged at the top. The bear lumbered after her, huffing and grunting as she pulled her weight up the cliff. Once, she slipped back down, and started again without pause.

A swipe from Hawkshell's blunted claws caught the bear in her injured eye. She bellowed, giving the rest of the Marsh-landers the time they needed to bite the bear's paws until she lost her grip on the cliff edge.

Hawkshell pushed with all her might, following the bear over the side, down, to the hard ground below. Her fangs sank deep into the bear's throat on impact. A torrent of steaming blood bubbled forth.

The mother bear growled, gurgled, and was still.

"Now, the last one."

The last remaining bear let out a terrified cry and fled as fast as it could for the fallen trees.

Spottedshadow stared at the carnage in horror, eyes wide and body frozen. When Ambereyes bumped her head into the dark molly's shoulder to bring her back to the moment, she called out, "No! Leave the cub alone!"

Hawkshell was on her hind paws, ready to pounce on the orphaned cub, when Spottedshadow tackled her. The two of them rolled in a whirl of claws and teeth. Spottedshadow sprang away as soon as they stopped, narrowly avoiding Hawkshell's wrath.

"Enough!" she cried, a gust of sand and stones rising between the two Captains. "It's *over*."

"It isn't over until they are all dead!" Hawkshell spat.

"*No.*" The last words Hazelfur had ever spoke in Spottedshadow's presence echoed in her ears. With them came the relief that she had made the right choice then, and the certainty to make the right choice now as the cub wedged itself through a narrow gap. "Field-land rangers do not let cubs die. My rangers! Chase it out, but do not kill it!"

Hawkshell stood at her full height. Spottedshadow arched her back in response, ready to defend herself. Thankfully, Hawkshell left her with only a warning as she signaled to the Marsh-land rangers to depart. "If that bear ever returns, the blood of the rangers it kills will be on *your* claws. You have made an enemy today, Captain Spottedshadow. I hope the life of that monster was worth it."

On the other side of the battlefield, Dawnfrost shuddered. She had never seen Hawkshell so bloodthirsty. She could only hope that the distance between Field Colony and Marsh Colony might prevent an all-out war, if Hawkshell's desire for revenge had not yet been sated. She twitched her whiskers. Spottedshadow had chosen her den and would have to sleep in it. Oak Colony had its own problems.

She made her way down to the infirmary. To Elmtail.

The old tom lay on the outcrop, his breathing weak. Stagcharge and Rowanstorm were pressed close to him.

"Can you make it home?" Stagcharge asked, though he already knew the answer.

Elmtail could barely raise his head to shake it, "No. I will not walk away from here."

"Captain Elmtail," Dawnfrost began. She halted. What could she possibly say to him? The only words that came to mind, though they were not nearly enough, were, "Thank you."

"I wish I was leaving you in easier times, but I know you will lead them well," Elmtail responded.

Elmtail touched Stagcharge's nose with his own. His voice shook as he tried to get out his last words. "I will wait for you in the Beyond, my love."

"I will look for you by moonlight, my Captain, my mate." Stagcharge nuzzled Elmtail for the final time.

"Go in peace, Father. You were well-loved, and loved well," Rowanstorm added, his own voice quavering from sorrow.

Elmtail lowered his head and closed his eyes, managing a final purr as he breathed his last. The cats nearest to him bowed their heads before looking to Dawnfrost.

"Let's go home, Oak Colony. We have wounds to tend and mouths to feed." Dawnfrost led her colony away, and it struck her that this was truly *her* colony now. She would receive her blessings—her *magic*—that night in her dreams. At last, she would lead Oak Colony as their Captain. She only wished she hadn't lost Redleaf and Elmtail for her dream to come true, or Wolfthorn.

Claws of doubt clutched at her heart. Wolfthorn had promised he would be at the battle, whether Rainfall gave her permission or not, yet he hadn't appeared. Whatever else cats might say about the pale tabby, Dawnfrost knew he kept his word. He would not have spoken with such conviction if he had not intended to fight at her side until the very end, whether it be as mates or friends.

Why wasn't he there?

The Prophecy

*"We are the rain that forms the river,
We are the river that floods."*
Frozenpool, former Second of River Colony

Two Days Before the Battle

Iceclaw had prowled the base long after the rest of the colony had gone to sleep. He was not often plagued with thoughts of any kind, yet his mind had been troubled by a conundrum he could not solve. He had thought the most recent disaster of a meeting made it clear that now was the time for River Colony to rise up and take their rightful place as rulers of the territory. Why, then, had Rainfall not allowed him to slaughter his prey? It would have sent a clear message to any who would dare oppose them.

The sound of footsteps that he knew too well had sent a shiver up his spine. Without looking, he knew Frozenpool was passing by him, on her way to Rainfall's den. Iceclaw had never envied his sister, and might have pitied her in that moment. Almost without meaning to, he had cast his permanent glower toward the former nursery, unable to look away from the scene he'd known was about to play out before him. The larger den made it easier to meet with their closest of followers—and their *true* leader—in private.

Anyone else might have been touched by the sight of a father whispering comfort to his alarmed daughter; Iceclaw had known Fronzepool's words were anything but.

, Frozenpool had been one of the most distinguished rangers in the whole Alliance. He had fought for his recognition from humble beginnings as an outsider, reaching a place on the Council and a position as Poolglare's Second. He might have succeeded the former Captain and taken command of the colony. Now it fell to Rainfall to prepare the colony for its glorious future, and evidently, Frozenpool had not been pleased with her recent actions.

Rainfall had been trying to control her breathing in the safety and privacy of her den. Her thoughts had churned like the tide in a storm, and she had been so lost in them that she had not realized at first who blocked the moonlight from her view. She had failed to notice his narrowed yellow eyes, bright and wicked. Thus, she had spoken in the haughty tone she used to scold her rangers, "I do believe that I am owed some *personal space* after tonight's events—" Rainfall's brazen mask had faltered when she saw who had come to her den, falling away to show fear.

Frozenpool's voice had been a claw sharpened against stone. "Remind me again, why was it you decided you needed *personal space* from your colony? Your family? Was it because acting like a proper Captain became too difficult for you, so you felt the need to act *without my permission* and selfishly claim a den apart from your rangers?" His voice had dropped to a low growl. "You think your rangers have nothing better to do than build a new nursery because of your asinine whims?"

"I j-just needed space," Rainfall had stammered before looking away. "I didn't want them to see my weakness—"

Rainfall had been cut off by a wince when Frozenpool stepped closer, pinning one of her delicate paws with his claws.

"Weakness? My beautiful, accomplished, talented daughter does not have weaknesses! If she did, her brilliant father wouldn't have helped make her Captain. Right?" Frozenpool had hissed at her.

"I can't help it. Sometimes I have nightmares—" Iceclaw had seen the whites of Rainfall's eyes as she tried in vain to slow her breathing. "You're right, Father. I have no weaknesses."

Frozenpool had leaned down to stare directly into his daughter's eyes. "That's right. Now, enough of this moping like a kitten who's lost a toy. You will not show me such an embarrassing display ever again. Will you?"

"No, Father."

"Good. I have more important reasons for my visit tonight." Frozenpool had leaned in so close to her ear that Iceclaw had struggled to hear his next words. "What were you *thinking* with that little stunt you pulled in Field Colony?"

Rainfall had answered in a tone that was slightly rehearsed. "I-I saw an opportunity to capitalize on the enemy's vulnerability, Father. I thought you would approve. I had to make a decision right away, and the rangers had high morale when we set off thanks to a sign from the Spir—"

"Let me make this *clear* to you," Frozenpool had snapped. "Only *I* make such decisions, especially about your signs. Now we will have to deal with the colony being divided between two locations. How will we know our rangers are truly loyal if they can't be monitored?"

"I will send Pineclaw to oversee—" Rainfall had been cut off by a whimper as Frozenpool drew blood from her paws. "What would you have me do, Father?"

"Send Pineclaw and Gillstripe to oversee the expansion. They have proven themselves, at least. We will also divide families that have not been tested—Minnowgill, Cherryrill, and Sedgestorm."

"Perhaps," Rainfall had timidly suggested, "I might send a few younger spies, as well? Frozen and Moss could prove to be valuable assets."

"If you must."

After a silence that had dragged on, Rainfall struggling to suppress a whimper the whole time while ragged claws tugged at her skin, Frozenpool had finally relented. He'd stepped back and licked the top of his daughter's head, a poor imitation of a purr coming from his throat. "I do all I can for you, Rainfall. Don't make a mess of everything our family has worked for." When she nodded, he added in a soft tone, "See that you get some sleep, my kitten. You have been useful so far, but do not think for a moment that you are irreplaceable. Iceclaw never hesitates to follow an order, and Frozen will soon complete her training. I'm sure she will find a place on the Council before winter comes and goes."

The very mention of winter had made him cough, a hacking and horrible thing. He had never fully recovered from nearly drowning a few years before. The icy water had seeped into his lungs somehow, and cold water or high stress had sent him into a fit ever since. It had forced him to retire from being Second and pass on the position to Rainfall.

"Should I send for Orangebrook, Father?" Rainfall had asked, placing a paw on his ribs. Frozenpool had knocked her paw away with his claws still unsheathed.

"As if that oaf could do a thing!" Frozenpool had snarled. "Perhaps if you had not been so weak, Lakespeckle could have lived, but you failed to convince her of your visions. Now *I'm* paying the price for *your* incompetence."

"I'm sorry, Father."

"We will find out how sorry soon enough." With that, Frozenpool had left the nursery, coughing loudly for all to hear. The other Elders had come out of their nests as if summoned to guide poor, ailing Frozenpool back to a comfortable place to sleep.

Rainfall had sunk into her own bed and curled into a tight ball. Wordlessly, Iceclaw had gone into her den and lain down beside her. She had shifted to accommodate him, though his body remained halfway off the bedding, on the sandy floor. He had not minded. He was not a beast of comforts or luxury, as so many other River-landers were.

"Don't worry about the mages." Iceclaw had scraped his tongue between Rainfall's ears. "So the weaklings have a few new tricks. What should it matter to us? Field Colony will still fall, and we will be halfway to our goal."

"Iceclaw," Rainfall had purred sweetly, "this is why I make the decisions, and you follow the orders." Rainfall had attempted to look nonchalant by grooming her paw; Iceclaw had known she was really soothing her latest scratch. "If magic is allowed to return to the territory, we won't just be dealing with those renegades the Field-landers brought with them! We'll be fighting off mages forever. All those muscles of yours won't do a thing against cats who can open up the earth under you, or set fire to your pelt with a look. The territory will be overrun within a month, and we will never fulfill the prophecy!"

"Then let's take care of the problem now," Iceclaw had retorted. "Haven't we been waiting for the chance to declare war? Let me lead another group to the Field-lands. I'll wipe out what's left of them, and the other colonies will never dare allow a mage in the territory again!"

Rainfall had gathered the shredded moss into a ball. It was not a bad plan, all things considered. Spottedshadow had given them an excuse to invade and, so soon after the last attack, there was no doubt the River-landers would crush the weak Field-land cats.

Still, the thought of facing mages in battle had given her pause. She did not know what they could do, and she had never entered a battle she didn't know she could win. Not since Brightscale.

The snap of a twig outside had distracted her from considering the plan further. Iceclaw's fur had spiked up along his back. "Who's there?"

A frightened squeak had revealed Pine. Though the kitten was the spitting image of his father, Pineclaw, his disposition was disappointingly more similar to that of his mother, Blueriver. The brown tabby kitten had already started to sniffle and sob before Iceclaw so much as unsheathed his claws.

"Monster! I saw a monster!" Pine had cried.

"Pine!" Blueriver had appeared almost at once to scold her son and bring him back to the new nursery.

The sight of his other sister had made Iceclaw curl his lip in a snarl. She had failed to do the most basic of her duties to produce strong future rangers. Iceclaw had only sired one daughter, but Frozen was already well on her way to being an Envoy; none of Blueriver's kittens seemed fit for any greater future than being front-line fodder in the coming war.

"I apologize, Captain. Second. I won't let him get away from me again," Blueriver had mewed.

"See to it that you don't. We wouldn't want our dear little nephew getting into trouble, would we?" Rainfall had cooed. She leaned down to touch her nose to the kitten. He had squealed and run behind his mother's legs. The silver molly had stood up abruptly and snapped, "I hope Pineclaw hasn't realized what an incompetent mother you are."

"Pineclaw would have to pay attention for that to happen," Blueriver had scoffed. "It would help if Frozenpool stopped telling the kittens those horrible flood stories." She had picked up Pine by his scruff and stalked back to the new nursery, the squalling of her other kittens grating against both Iceclaw and Rainfall's ears.

Iceclaw had sneered after her. Blueriver might have grown up beside them and heard the same stories from their father, but she had never proven herself to be worthy of the truth. The flood was not a simple *story*, but a promise of a glorious future for the truly strong and loyal. She did not know, as he and Rainfall did, that *they* were the Flood that would wash the weak and unworthy from the lake territory.

The Captain had returned her attention to Iceclaw. "We will not turn into sniveling kittens about this. Acting now would make it look like we are worried. We are *not* worried. We are invincible and unconquerable, and no amount of mages will stop our plan. When we are done, no one will even remember they were ever here. The prophecy is on our side."

Rainfall had settled into her bed and let out a long yawn. "For now, we wait and bolster our forces. Then, when this crop of new-claws become rangers, we'll have all the strength we need to seize the entire lake."

Iceclaw had frowned. It would be months yet before the likes of Gray and Moss were rangers. However, if that was what Rainfall wanted, then he would see it done. That was his one and only duty.

Wolfthorn had waited until Iceclaw retreated to the inside of the Captain's new den to leave the shadows. It had always been more difficult to use his magic in the River Colony base, yet for some reason, it had been easier to slip into the shadows that evening. In his excitement, he had nearly given himself away by getting too close to other cats. If Pine had been able to detect him, then other cats would surely be able to the next time he tried it. He would have to go back to lurking in the bushes on the edge of the base. Still, despite the risk, he had learned more about what Rainfall was up to—a worthy reward.

At last, he had the names of rangers who might help him turn the tide against Rainfall and her scheming father.

It would have to wait until after the battle; he had more pressing business in Oak Colony.

The shadows had beckoned him. The darkness had shifted and twisted at his paws, welcoming him to safety and secrecy. Wolfthorn had resisted the pull of those closest to him, heading instead for the hibiscus bushes on the other side of the rangers' den. No one would be on guard there.

Or so he had thought.

"Traitor! River-landers, attack!" Pineclaw had yowled loud enough to wake the entire base. Before Wolfthorn had been able to react, he was pinned by a set of claws dangerously close to his throat.

The River-landers rushed to the commotion, eyes wide and claws unsheathed. Was Marsh Colony finally making a move against them? Was Field Colony retaliating? River Colony was surrounded by enemies; they had to stay together, had to fight back, had to defend themselves and their way of life. Even those who had resisted Rainfall's assertions of this rallied to the call, hackles up, ready to believe her at last if they had come upon such a scene.

Moss had raced to the front of the line, ready to prove herself. Swiftmask and Gray had been beside her. She had flashed them a smile, sure they would have been just as eager—only to falter when she had seen the worry and fear in their expressions. She had not been able to understand. Wasn't a chance to prove River Colony superiority what they had wanted, too? What had they trained for, otherwise? She had not liked the doubt that emerged like a worm from mud in her gut, and had looked away before they noticed her.

Wolfthorn had bitten down hard on Pineclaw's leg. When the brown tabby had yelped and pulled his paw back, Wolfthorn had kicked him off and surged to his feet. The pale tom had unsheathed his claws, ready to fight to the death. If his final stand had at last come, then so be it.

"Pineclaw, only *I* give the order for the colony to attack," Rainfall had chided. "And you, Wolfthorn. You should know that only the guilty resist. Are you ready to admit to your crimes?"

"What crime?" Wolfthorn had challenged.

"There is a curfew in place. Any ranger not on guard duty is supposed to be in their den after night patrols have returned," Gillstripe had answered from the crowd. "You would *know* that if you were ever around, which already shows you are less than trustworthy."

"Well put!" Rainfall had flashed Gillstripe an approving smile that carried the promise of a Council position if he kept it up. "Now that you've been caught breaking one rule, perhaps you'd like to confess to any others? Your punishment will be less severe if you admit your guilt."

"We both know which of us is really guilty," Wolfthorn had spat.

He had seen Rainfall's eyes widen for a fraction of a second. Then something had slammed into the back of his head and the world spun to black.

Iceclaw had stood over the tom with a vicious smile. "Shall I finally get this thorn out of our side?"

"*No.*" Rainfall's mew had been unexpectedly stern and strong. "We will take him prisoner. He may yet be useful." She had switched back to the overly sweet voice she used for the rest of the colony. "We must show mercy to our enemies, after all. We are gracious. However! Let this be a warning to all who would oppose us. River Colony will not tolerate traitors! We are united, we are strong! We are the rain that forms the river, we are the river that floods!"

"We are united, we are strong! We are the rain that forms the river, we are the river that floods!"

Iceclaw had grumbled in frustration, but had picked up Wolfthorn by his scruff to carry out Rainfall's wishes while the gathered cats cheered for their Captain.

Swiftmask had stopped Gray from going after them with a paw on the new-claw's back. He had whispered into his ear, "Wait. We'll find a way to help him, but rushing in now will only get you locked up, too."

He had not realized that Moss had been nearby, still listening.

Epilogue

Goldenpelt knew he was dreaming when he saw Forestleaf staring down at him from Captain's Overlook. His heart ached more than he realized it still could to see her standing there, the way she should have done in life as Captain of Field Colony.

Why had it been Forestleaf who died on that accursed day? Unexpected anger made him flex his claws against the sparse grass of the wastes beyond Field Colony's territory. It should have been Spottedshadow, instead of Forestleaf and Timberleg. Losing her would have wounded him just as much at the time, but Field Colony would have been better off. Now his beloved colony was a disgrace, and he was an outlaw.

In the blink of an eye, Forestleaf stood beside him. Her fur gleamed in the bright light of the fullest moon Goldenpelt had ever witnessed. She radiated power, confidence, control, all the things she had passed on to him in abundance as her future Second–had things gone the way they were supposed to. Had she ascended to her rightful rank of Captain, instead of being slaughtered without meaning or mercy in another colony's base.

He leaned into her touch, half to apologize for disappointing her and half to seek comfort for the disappointment inside himself.

She vanished from his sight, but he knew she was not gone. He could feel her determination, ambition, and cunning pulsing through his own veins. His mind was sharper, his muscles stronger, his body sturdier than before.

When he looked up again, the moon had been replaced by a blazing sun. Goldenpelt realized then what had happened. He laughed aloud, a roar of victory.

He still had friends. Fernface, Volefur, Shadowclaw, Jaggedstripe, Thrushspots—they were all fine rangers who understood what it truly meant to be loyal, and they would raise Horse, Dark, and Dawn to be the same.

So Spottedshadow had delayed him from his rightful place. So she had made foolish decisions that would endanger Field colony. So what?
He would make everything right again.
He was Captain Goldenpelt, the Scorching Sun.
And he would take his colony back.

Bonus Short - Memories of Whitebelly

Originally written by Tennelle Flowers; edited by Avalon Roselin.

Missingfoot could hear the rustling of the heather before the two youngest kittens in Field Colony tumbled over themselves and into his paws. He had been enjoying a nap in the blissful shade provided by the Keepers' Weave, until they woke him with their play-fighting. Missingfoot chuckled as Dark and Dawn sprang apart, startled by crashing into him. They were still finding their feet, and clumsily stumbled over his stump leg.

"Be careful, Dark! You could hurt Missingfoot!" Dawn scolded.

A small pang of sadness lanced through Missingfoot. He knew that Dawn meant well, but did the kittens really believe he was that weak? Though he was retired from ranging, he was by no means old or delicate. Then again, Captain Hazelfur spent much of his time around the kittens, escorting them when they ventured out of the Keepers' Weave, playing games, telling stories. Perhaps some of his beliefs had already begun to affect the young cats who idolized him so much.

Still, Missingfoot had *survived* the fox attack that took his leg. He certainly couldn't be called fragile.

Guilt followed the thought, as it always did when he remembered that day.

"I'm quite alright." Missingfoot smiled at the little tabbies, doing his best to brush his feelings aside. "That was quite a tackle, Dawn! For such a small kitten, you have the strength of a ranger already!"

"Really?" Dawn's eyes gleamed at the praise, a tiny kitten tooth poking out in a big smirk.

From the other side of Missingfoot's leg, Dark groaned. "Dawn plays too rough! She keeps knocking me over!"

"Do *not*!"

"Do *too*!"

Missingfoot could tell this argument would continue without end if he didn't put a stop to it himself.

"You know, Dark, you remind me so much of your father when he was your age." Missingfoot's ploy to distract them from bickering worked, and both kittens looked up at him with wide eyes.

"Really? Jaggestripe?" Dark mewed.

"Oh, yes." Missingfoot thought back to the days when his own daughter, Spottedshadow, had been in the nursery. Jaggedstripe—just Stripe, then—and Dark shared many similarities: dark brown tabby pelts, a small and stocky build, and a penchant for clumsiness. Though endearing at a young age, Dark would have to work hard to find his footing. The Field-lands were no place for a cat who misplaced his paws; that was how legs got broken.

Whitebelly had always thought it was unfair that the colony pushed its young cats so hard, but at the time Missingfoot hadn't agreed. Whitebelly had always had a rebellious streak against the rules of her parents, Hazelfur and Forestleaf. Missingfoot had thought, as did most of the cats in Field Colony, that their leadership's high expectations would lead to more skilled rangers. In the end, Whitebelly had probably been right; setting high expectations for Jaggedstripe had never made him a better ranger, but it *had* made it easier for him to be talked into stupid stunts to win his peers' approval.

Missingfoot turned his attention back to the current kittens. "Both of your parents caused me so much trouble when they were kittens! I remember when Fernface convinced Volefur and Jaggedstripe to sneak out of base." Dawn's eyes grew wider still with curiosity. Missingfoot sternly added, "Which was very naughty and got them in a lot of trouble, mind you." Dark rolled his eyes when Dawn guiltily looked away. "When we found out they were missing, Whitebelly and I looked everywhere—"

"Who's Whitebelly?" Dawn asked.

Familiar grief settled into Missingfoot's chest once more. He had almost grown numb to its presence, but her question had caught him off-guard.

He sighed. "Whitebelly was my mate. My best friend. She saved my life when I was attacked by the fox."

Dawn burst with questions. "Is that how you lost your leg? What happened to Whitebelly? What was the fox like? Was it HUGE? What's it like only having three legs?"

"DAWN!" Dark cried. "Nightpool told you not to ask Missingfoot that stuff! Nightpool said it was rude! You're RUDE!"

"He said it first!" Dawn stuck her tongue out at Dark, then turned back to Missingfoot with a meek expression. "Nightpool did tell me not to. I'm sorry. Can you still tell us? Please?"

After the brief shock and the ensuing argument between the kittens, Missingfoot couldn't help but laugh. Some things never changed.

"Of course you can ask me questions, Dawn. It is hard to talk about Whitebelly, but it would be harder to insult her memory by never talking about her again."

Quietly, Dark mumbled with all the sadness a kitten could feel, "Is she with the Spirits?"

Missingfoot nodded. "She is."

"You miss her, don't you?"

"Very much. We grew up together. I don't remember a day without her before the attack, and I haven't gone a day after without thinking about her."

"Can you tell us a story about her?"

Missingfoot purred. "Of course. I would love to."

"Forestleaf just won't let it go!" Whitebelly had growled. She'd been glad Blackpelt was free that afternoon, after the explosive argument she'd had with the Second. The two of them could walk freely around Field Colony and get away from the base for a while, like they hadn't done since before their kitten, Shadow, was born. The young molly had just entered field training, and had taken to it like a rabbit to a burrow. She had even found a rival in Golden, who was the leader of their little group. Whitebelly watched them with pride.

"Well, since Russetpelt died, we *are* lacking Envoys..."

"You're taking her side?" Whitebelly had turned a glare on her mate that made him jump.

"Aw, Whitebelly," Blackpelt had said softly, his expression sheepish. He had always been a shy tom, and Whitebelly had almost felt bad for snapping at him—but not if he was going to team up with her mother on this issue. When she had not relaxed her glower, he'd added, "I didn't mean it like that. I know you don't want to be an Envoy. I can see why she would ask *you*, is all."

Whitebelly had huffed, but his words had pleased her. She had gone back to complaining, sparing him her frosty gaze. "Could you imagine? Having to act all high and mighty for the colony? Having to be at my parents' beck and call? I'd rather join the Spirits Beyond, thanks! And if I became an Envoy, it would give my mother an excuse to try to control Shadow's life, the way she did to me. I won't let that happen!"

Blackpelt had sighed and offered her a knowing purr. Though he mewed only a humble, "I know," Whitebelly had seen all that he wanted to say within his soulful eyes.

They had trotted along, and though they scanned the fields for signs of prey, their minds had not been on hunting. Whitebelly had entwined her tail with Blackpelt's to apologize for her outburst. She had always known conflict upset him, but Blackpelt was a good listener. He had helped Whitebelly admit that she found the strict rules her parents enforced in the colony to be too much *because* she was just as stubborn as Forestleaf, and equally as prone to a flared temper when situations were out of her control. At least with Blackpelt at her side, she'd been able to make sense of the world again. Whitebelly could have dealt with her mother any day, as long as he had stayed by her side.

"Forestleaf is anxious. The whole colony is," Blackpelt had said, picking up the conversation again.

Whitebelly had given him a confused look. Forestleaf, anxious? She had thought of her mother as many things: overbearing, demanding, nosy. She'd had those thoughts nearly every day, in fact. But *anxious*? That had been a new idea.

She'd scanned Blackpelt's face for a sign of a joke, but he had only looked down at his feet, lost in thought.

"You and your big heart. Always worried about everyone." Whitebelly had nuzzled the dark tom. "Maybe Forestleaf should start looking outside her own circle. Field Colony has plenty of rangers who deserve the attention."

Their walk had led them toward the Oak Colony border, and the dense crop of leafless trees which the Field-landers called Shadow Forest. It wasn't the preferred hunting ground of the swift-running field cats, but sharpening her claws on the dense bark had sounded like a good way for Whitebelly to relieve her lingering frustration.

"You know how picky Forestleaf can be," Blackpelt had said, though his tone was one of agreement.

"That's her loss."

He had purred back in response. Then, as if noticing them for the first time, he'd squinted at the trees. "Climbing again?"

"Yeah. I know I'm no good at it, but it's fun." She'd given a cheeky grin. "And maybe one day Oak Colony won't be run by such a soft-heart. We might actually have to defend this area."

Blackpelt had shaken his head. "I don't think Oak Colony is interested in a bunch of dead trees when they have more lush forest than they know what to do with. And anyway—"

He'd stopped cold, his ears perked up. Whitebelly had raised her muzzle to sniff the air.

The scent of earth, and heather, and the woody smell of the bark had all been expected, but there had been something else. Something raw and bloody and *wrong*.

"*Look out!*"

Whitebelly had been shoved hard, out of the way. Screaming had filled her ears. A streak of red had smeared the ground, and when her vision had focused she saw her mate hanging from the jaws of a fox, one leg bent horribly between its teeth.

She'd shrieked and dove at the beast, praying to the Spirits that there were Oak-landers in earshot. Standing ground against an animal as large as a fox was not what Field-landers were trained for, but she would have sooner faced a whole den of them than let her mate die because she was angry at her mother.

"Can you run?" she'd asked once he was free, only to see that his leg ended in a mess of mangled flesh and viscera. The paw was gone. "Damn! Get moving, I'll hold it off!"

"Whitebelly—"

"Shadow needs you to live!"

If not for the mention of their daughter, Blackpelt would have most likely stayed and fought beside Whitebelly. Perhaps, if he had, they would both have lived. Perhaps they would both have died. He would never know.

"I love you," Blackpelt had forced out through the pain of leaving her.

The story he told to the kittens was softer and gentler, as much as a story that ends with a dead ranger can be. He had told them other tales of her life, of the mischief they had gotten up to, of the mischief that all new-claws inevitably got up to. By the time he was tired of telling stories, Dark and Dawn had curled up against his side and fallen asleep to the sound of them. He wondered if they would dream of the brilliant, brave molly they had never known, and felt at peace. He could not save Whitebelly's life, but he could keep her memory alive.

Bonus Short - Cut Prologue

This previous draft of the prologue was inspired by the short scene in the trailer for the Shifting Roots animated series of Sunfire and Breezeheart walking together, stalked by something shadowed in the foreground, then killed by the unknown assailant. The trailer served as a sort of prologue for the first episode, so I wanted to incorporate it into the novelization. This idea was ultimately scrapped in favor of using that time and space to introduce the leads individually and give the reveal during Marsh Colony's meeting greater impact. However, I still want readers to be able to get to know Sunfire and Breezeheart through more than other characters' memories of them, so here is the fully-edited scene! – Avalon Roselin

The sun rose early over Alliance Lake. The cats that lived in the western marshes rose earlier.

Two toms made their way down to the lakeshore to watch the sunrise. They placed their paws where moss grew thick on the ground out of habit, though it had been nearly a month since the last heavy rain.

The two toms were Breezeheart and Sunfire, rangers of the Marsh-lands. Sunfire held the title by blood, his large frame and thick golden pelt giving away his heritage to any cat who knew of the Alliance Lake colonies. Breezeheart was a Marsh-lander through bond, having arrived in the territory from the wastes beyond it as a young cat. He had trained alongside his brother to earn the chance to join the proud colony, and they had proven themselves true Marsh-landers by navigating the treacherous swamps alone in the dark. Though his smaller size set him apart from the natural-born marsh cats, Breezeheart knew he was where he belonged.

Sunfire led the way over the stepping stones that crossed the West River. The ground on the other side was drier, and already warm with the dawn light. The rosy tint on the horizon burned away with the eastern fields' mists, changing to a brilliant gold before Breezeheart's eyes. Summer was hurrying on its way with all the impatience of a kitten.

He snorted. "The Spirits to Come are as excitable as ever."

"They aren't the only ones today." Sunfire pointed his muzzle skyward. "Look, the full moon has risen early! The Spirits Beyond will bless the Moonlight Gathering with good fortune."

The full moon hanging in the morning sky was surely a good omen, but Breezheart did not need to see it to know there would be good news. He could hardly remember a time when bad news had been shared at a Moonlight Gathering. Perhaps an Elder might have passed, but there would be no concerns about famine or plague. He had left those worries behind him in the wastes. The Alliance territory was as prosperous and safe as his mother had promised it would be. It was for good reason that rangers trained to be worthy of their home, and protected it from those who would spoil its bounty.

In the daylight, the small island sitting in the lake was far from impressive. That night, under the light of the full moon and the watchful eyes of the Spirits Beyond, Moonlight Island would transform into a beacon of peace and prosperity for all the colonies of the Alliance.

Sunfire, however, was at his most handsome in the early morning light. When the first rays of his namesake touched his golden-ginger fur and sparkled in his blue eyes, he took Breezeheart's breath away.

"The colony doesn't leave until sundown. We have plenty to do until then," Breezeheart reminded Sunfire. Although the golden tom was an Envoy, singled out as a cat of remarkable skill and the potential to lead the colony, he was prone to kittenish behavior when there was a celebration to look forward to.

Breezeheart, however, never forgot the seemingly endless number of tasks an experienced ranger could expect in a day. No colony cat was ever still for long once the sun was up, and Marsh-landers had to work fast to complete their morning tasks before the midday heat made the humidity unbearable.

Breezeheart was even busier than most rangers—as a Mentor, it was his duty to make sure young Marsh-landers learned the skills they would need to be successful rangers.

He was not personally training a new-claw at the moment, but overseeing group practice kept him on his toes. Every ranger trained at least one new-claw during their service to the colony, but Breezeheart did not think he would recommend Halfmask or Falconswoop to be teachers again. Boulder should be having his ranger ceremony that night, but Halfmask had yet to break him of his mean streak or impart any values to the burly tom other than *might makes right*. Falconswoop was a skilled ranger, but she was awkward around young cats and didn't know what to do with Red, leading him to follow Boulder's lead more than hers.

Pool and Ice were due to begin their field training once they received the blessing of the Spirits Beyond that very night. Breezeheart had hoped to take Pool under his wing, but Captain Hawkshell had discreetly informed him and the other Mentor, Birdflight, that she intended to make Wildfur responsible for Pool's field training. As much as Breezeheart wanted to trust his Captain's judgement, he almost raised a complaint to the Council about it. Halfmask and Falconswoop were already struggling to handle their new-claws; giving Pool to the laziest tom in the colony would only make things worse.

Sensing the busy buzz of Breezeheart's thoughts, Sunfire licked his ears. "I thought we'd go by the border with Oak Colony this morning. I fancy a spar with Dawnfrost or Vinestripe if we can catch them."

Only Sunfire, who walked with confidence in every pawstep, would speak so casually of challenging another colony's Envoys to a fight. Oak Colony was on good terms with Marsh Colony now, but according to the Elders, that had not always been the case. It was Captain Elmtail and Captain Hawkshell's close friendship that had eased tensions between the two colonies, but both of them were getting on in years.

Perhaps that was why, after Whitefire retired as her Second in Command, Captain Hawkshell named young Leafstorm as her successor instead of Sunfire. While Sunfire was a promising Envoy, his relaxed attitude toward borders and mock-battles with other cats would not be taken so kindly coming from a Captain. Rather than be discouraged, Sunfire only seemed that much more determined to pursue inter-colony battle training.

Breezeheart rolled his eyes at Sunfire's antics. "And if we meet some other cat who *isn't* so keen on your sparring idea?"

"Then they'll have to catch us!" Sunfire laughed. "And besides, there are songbirds in the branches there."

The golden tom spoke as casually as ever, but the nervous sniff of his nose and flick of his tail gave away the romantic intent of the outing. He had been planning it for the better part of spring, when he first noticed the fledglings growing in their nests.

Breezeheart leaned against him and intertwined their tails. "Let's hope no Oak Colony ranger interrupts them with their yowling, then. Besides, as much as I admire your skill in battle, I prefer you with all your fur on."

"Breezy!" Sunfire huffed, though it came out as a purr near the end. He nuzzled the shorter tom. "No cat could get the best of me when I'm fighting for you."

The two walked closely to keep their tails entwined and their pelts brushing against one another until they had to part to cross back over the West River. One of its many tributaries snaked away toward the northern reach of the marshes, up to Dry Stones, where the colony sheltered during floods. The same creek made a guideline for the border with Oak Colony.

As they scouted along the borderland, Breezeheart was taken by a rush of pride in the marshes that were his home. He felt no envy for the Oak-landers' thick tangle of forest, or Field Colony's open and exposed meadows, or River Colony's too-sunny shores. Every damp pawstep of the Marsh-lands and every cat within them were his to cherish and defend, all with Sunfire at his side. He couldn't imagine a happier life, and he purred in satisfaction as he pressed his forehead to Sunfire's shoulder.

Sunfire returned his purr and settled his muzzle between Breezeheart's ears, tickling them with his twitching whiskers.

The golden tom jerked his head up. "I just remembered! Wait here, Breezy."

"Wait for what?" Breezeheart asked, but Sunfire had already rushed off into the undergrowth. With a sigh, the dark gray tom settled onto his haunches and licked a paw, swiping it over his ears to get rid of the ticklish sensation.

The sun continued to rise in the sky, its light no longer soft or playful.

Breezeheart was about to give up on waiting and call out to Sunfire, assuming he'd gotten distracted by something, when the nearby ferns rustled. Breezeheart stiffened, the fur rising along his back. Whatever shook the fronds like that was too large to be prey, and a deep, musky odor unlike anything he'd smelled before met his nose.

"Sunfire, that better be you playing a trick," Breezeheart said.

He dropped into a crouch, keeping his tail low and ears forward as he stalked toward the foliage. The crisp scent of the sparse pines that grew on the north end of Marsh Colony's territory could not completely mask the foreign stench.

What was that foul smell? It was not pungent enough to be a skunk, not earthy enough to be a badger. Every so often Breezeheart caught a faint trace of Sunfire's familiar scent, and he breathed in as much of it as he could.

"Sunfire, where are you?" Breezeheart yowled.

The ferns ahead trembled, but there was no wind to move them. The crunch of twigs and snap of branches echoed through sudden silence.

A shadow engulfed Breezeheart. At first he thought a cloud had obscured the sun, but when he looked up he did not see the sky.

He barely saw the beast before he was sent flying by a crushing blow. He rolled across the ground, struggling to get to his paws. His hind leg buckled under him, broken, and he fell against something soft and damp. He nearly choked on the smell of blood... and Sunfire. His pounding heart came to a stuttering halt when he realized he was lying on bloodied scraps of the tom's pelt. The rest of him lay not far away in a crumpled heap, a bundle of water hyacinth and rose mallow--Breezeheart's favorite flowers--not far away.

"Oh, Sunfire...!" Breezeheart cried, hobbling toward the remains of his mate. He knew he had to get back to the base, warn the colony of this strange beast stalking their land, but he couldn't leave Sunfire there. Not his brave, magnificent Sunfire.

He froze in terror as the shadow loomed over him again. The next strike came straight down, slamming him into the ground. He could no longer feel the pain of his broken leg. He tried to speak Sunfire's name one last time, only for the searing pain of his now broken jaw to stop him. The world spun out of focus, and then went dark.

Bonus Short - Relentless Storm

We knew that readers would want to see Dawnfrost receive her blessings from the Spirits. We discussed putting it at the opening of the second book, or as an epilogue, but ultimately it did not fit with the pacing. Rather than skip over such an important moment for a central character, we opted to include it here. – Avalon Roselin

Dawnfrost pressed the final pawful of dirt over Elmtail's grave. Only she, Stagcharge, Rowanstorm, and the Elders were present for the burial; the rest of the colony would grieve on the night of the new moon. There was too much to be done to stall daily goings-on with the kind of grieving a leader like Elmtail deserved.

He was laid to rest at the roots of the Ancient Oak. His body would nourish the gigantic oak, and in doing so provide food and shelter to the birds and squirrels that fed the colony. Even in death, Elmtail took care of his cats. Redleaf, Aspenbreeze, and the others were buried in the shade of the same tree, though only Captains were placed so close to the tangle of exposed roots near the trunk. One day, Dawnfrost would join him—a morbid thought, and yet it brought her comfort. Elmtail was no longer living, but he was not gone. There was every chance she would see him in her dream that night.

Stagcharge broke the silence. "There are no words to express such loss, but they are all we have." He placed a daisy atop the fresh grave. "I love you. I'll miss you."

"I don't know what the Beyond is like, but I imagine, I *hope*, that all your old friends and loved ones are there with you now," Rowanstorm said, setting his own daisy next to Stagcharge's.

"You were a good friend and a good leader," Yellowflower said.

"There will never be another Captain like Elmtail," Birchwhisker agreed. He looked to Dawnfrost. "And Elmtail would not want us to dwell on the past. The future is bright."

Dawnfrost nodded her thanks to the old ranger. She did not know how or if she would ever fill the void that Elmtail's loss had left in the colony, but she would not shy away from her duty.

Going to sleep that night in Elmtail's old den was surreal. Twice, Dawnfrost had started toward her nest in the rangers' quarters, ready to settle beside Thornheart, Rowanstorm, or Viperfang for the night. She was alone in the small cavern, set apart on the cliff so the Captain could hear any alert and respond immediately to get the colony's attention. The Keepers had cleared away Elmtail's bedding and prepared fresh feathers, moss, and ferns for her to sleep on. She was thankful for their efforts, but when she curled up, she could only think that she was in someone else's place.

She hoped that would change once she received her blessings, and closed her eyes to wait for the Spirits in her dreams.

Blue sky peeked through the thinning canopy above her head, the light shining through autumn leaves like flashes of fire. The breeze tugged at Dawnfrost's fur, pulling her along the path made by thousands of paws before hers. She started out confident, but soon her steps began to waver. There were so many branching routes, so many alternate directions. How was she to know the right way?

The moment she felt hopelessly lost, Elmtail appeared to her, resting atop a thick bough. Though still old, he was no longer unkempt, and his fur had a sheen to it that she had not seen since she was in the nursery. He beckoned her closer, before closing the gap between them himself with a single, powerful bound. When he rested his muzzle upon her forehead, the trail ahead became clear. She could not see him anymore, but she knew that he walked beside her and would not let her veer down the wrong path. She would forge ahead with his Spirit, and guide her colony to the best of her ability. That was what she had trained her whole life to do.

The next Spirit filled Dawnfrost with as much remorse as joy. Aspenbreeze rolled and played in the falling leaves, so full vigor and vitality. She had been taken from her family, the whole colony, too soon. As in life, Aspenbreeze did not hesitate to greet Dawnfrost with enthusiasm. The black-and-white molly hopped at Dawnfrost with her back arched, inviting the older cat to join her in merriment. Dawnfrost gave in. For the first time in ages, she leapt from trees for the sheer joy of the wind rushing past her face, sprang into the air to see just how high she could go. Dawnfrost was so wrapped up in the moment that she did not realize when, precisely, Aspenbreeze vanished. This time, instead of wishing she had the chance to say a proper goodbye, Dawnfrost knew that no farewell was needed. Aspenbreeze was with her, and despite the clouds gathering overhead, the forest seemed brighter than before.

Her next encounter was so unexpected that at first she did not remember who she was looking at. For one terrifying moment, the cream fur reminded her of Rowanstorm, and she dreaded the thought that he might have passed in his sleep from some unseen injury. Looking closer, she saw that the cat was paler than her friend, and a molly at that. She was Beechleaf, Rowanstorm's mother, who had passed seasons ago. Dawnfrost had only been a small kitten then, but she still knew Beechleaf by the gentle green eyes she had passed down to her son.

Beechleaf curled her tail around Dawnfrost. As they walked together, Dawnfrost's thoughts were drawn to the other cats who had shared her journey from the nursery to adulthood: Thornheart, as loyal a friend as anyone could ask for; Rowanstorm, one of the most selfless cats she knew; Wrensong, whom she trusted to always tell her the truth; Hailstorm, always able to find the light in a dark moment. There were others, too, from beyond the Oak-lands; Spottedshadow, Wildfur, Wolfthorn. Each of these cats had helped shape her. They were her family as much as Brackenfoot and Flamecloud, who she could see waiting up ahead in a shadowy clearing.

Dawnfrost stopped and allowed Beechleaf to circle her, the light cream molly fading away as the clouds overhead darkened.

Seeing Brackenfoot did not faze Dawnfrost as much as she'd thought it would. Truthfully, she had wondered if she would see him at all.

It was seeing him with Flamecloud that sent her heart tumbling over a cliff.

Like Rowanstorm, Dawnfrost had lost her mother at a young age. She still had a few memories of her mother's warmth, the scent of her milk, the rasp of her tongue over Dawnfrost's ears. Her voice had been the first sound Dawnfrost had ever heard, speaking her name with fierce love as she fought to be a part of her daughter's life for a moment longer. Brackenfoot pressed so closely against the golden molly's fur that it was hard to see where one ended and the other began. Dawnfrost wondered how different her life might have been, how different her father might have been, if Flamecloud had lived.

Dawnfrost nearly cried out when she joined them, nuzzling against her mother's chest, or her father's shoulder, it was impossible to tell. Their purrs deafened her ears.

When she pulled away, only she and Brackenfoot remained. They did not exchange words, and would not have. Dawnfrost understood Brackenfoot better in that moment than she had all her life, and she needed nothing more from him but the pride and confidence in his gaze.

Leaving the clearing brought her to the border between Oak Colony and Marsh Colony. Standing just on the other side was Sunfire. His ruffled mane was still splattered with blood, and his claws left scrapes in the earth when he walked to meet her. The warmth and comfort of her mother's love and father's pride would never leave her, not now, but the intensity of Sunfire's icy stare sent chills down Dawnfrost's spine. Her heart pounded and her muscles tensed as they did before the first strike of a battle. She tilted her ears back, listening for reinforcements within the underbrush. A growl rose unbidden from her throat.

Sunfire charged, and she returned his fury. When they met claws-first in midair, he vanished, and her blood boiled when she touched the ground.

She opened her mouth and thunder roared. She took a step and lightning flashed overhead. The sway of her tail brought a torrent of rain down upon the forest.

She was the Relentless Storm, and she would keep her loved ones, her Oak Colony, safe from any threat.

Bonus Short - Schemes in the Unbound-lands

There was a lot more going on in the background of River Colony than we could realistically show with the page count, events, and perspectives of this book. River Colony will be explored more in Shaded River, *but we wanted to provide readers with a bit more context going in. Please enjoy this "teaser" for things to come in* Shaded River! *– Avalon Roselin*

"And...there! That should do it."

Lakespeckle stood back to admire her handiwork. It was not easy to come by medicine in the wastes, but she had managed to harvest a crop of aloe. The soothing gel worked well for burns already, and she had discovered that combining it with calendula boosted its effects. Her generous application to Fennec's blistered skin had left the tom looking like he had just climbed out of a pool, but it would relieve the pain that plagued him so frequently.

"Blessings upon you, Lakespeckle. I feel like a new tom!" Fennec chuckled.

"I'm happy to help," the former Herbalist mewed. She turned toward her companion, only to see that the tortoiseshell-tabby molly was highly focused on a training session with Fennec's niece, Gosling.

"No, no, not like that! Keep your rump down!" Splash shoved Gosling's rear down with a smack from her paw.

"Hey!" Gosling protested.

"Hush up and you might actually learn something," Splash retorted. "Look how *I* do it." She leaned her body forward slowly, creeping along the ground on her belly like a snake. Her paws moved carefully in front of her, placed into careful position, while her haunches shifted back and forth to build tension without lifting her tail into the air. Then, when she was ready, she exploded forward and swept the twig they'd been practicing with into her paws before the dust could settle.

"It's not like I'll ever use this," Gosling said, though Lakespeckle had seen admiration in the young molly's rapt attention moments before. "When is a mouse going to be *sitting there* perfectly still, waiting to be pounced on?"

"It would happen more often if you weren't such a whiny loudmouth!" Splash's mew was harsh, but Lakespeckle knew that she meant well. The former Envoy's words came out as sharp as claws, but the feelings behind them were often gentle as purrs.

"Be nice," Fennec said, nudging Gosling with his unburnt paw. "I'm sorry for her attitude."

"Don't apologize for me!"

"It's quite alright. It's nice to see young cats with some fighting spirit. Isn't it, Splashmist?"

Splash hissed at Lakespeckle. "Don't call me that! I'm not a ranger anymore."

Fennec's ears twitched. "Rangers?"

Splash rolled her eyes. Lakespeckle had really put her tail in her mouth this time. They had been living in the wastes for two seasons, lurking like villains on the outskirts of their former home.

Making the decision to leave River Colony had been easy enough for Splash. She had done everything she could to prove to Rainfall that she was an excellent ranger, an exemplary Envoy, the perfect choice for Second. Instead, one of Rainfall's first actions as Second herself had been to make Iceclaw an Envoy without any great feats of dexterity or swimming prowess. Splash wasn't even sure Iceclaw *could* swim; he most definitely preferred staying dry. Then, when Rainfall had become Captain, she had promoted the brute to Second over the long-standing Envoys who had earned the rank!

The final straw had been Rainfall's decision to start swimming practice for the kittens earlier and earlier, regardless of weather conditions. Her choice had drowned two of Splash and Minnowgill's kittens. Only Ivy remained, and Splash was determined that her daughter would not grow up to serve such a corrupt colony. She urged her family to risk making a life for themselves beyond the Alliance's borders, rather than stay and be killed by Rainfall's carelessness.

Minnowgill had not supported her. When Splash had left, she'd done it alone.

She could only hope that Minnowgill had taken his own advice to keep his head down, and kept Ivy safe while Rainfall rearranged the colony like a shell collection to appease her vanity.

Splash had stumbled upon Lakespeckle not too long after taking up residence in a copse of palm trees near the shore. The speckled gray molly had been far worse for wear than Splash had been, having been forced out rather than running away on her own. The combination of Splash's resourcefulness and Lakespeckle's knowledge of plants had thankfully been enough to save her life, if only just.

Splash would have been just as happy to continue living that way, foraging and hunting while Lakespeckle defended their home, but a cat did not train to be an Herbalist out of selfishness. Lakespeckle had no sooner finished treating her own wounds when she started running a clinic of sorts for wanderers and renegades. Any cat was welcome, if they offered a piece of prey or a kind word in exchange for healing. Lakespeckle and Splash had gotten to know many of the Unbound that way, and listened to their gossip to fill their time.

"There's a group of cats that call themselves rangers gathering in Snakehole," Fennec said. At Lakespeckle and Splash's confused expressions, he added, "Pardon, that's the name we call the big pile of rocks and boulders, landward of here, about half a day's journey."

Splash's own ears pressed forward with interest. "A group?"

"I didn't put much stock in what they said before, but if you were rangers too..." Fennec trailed off. He shook himself carefully, to avoid dripping any of the aloe salve. "Maybe I will join up after all. It could be good for Gosling to be around other cats."

"Don't make decisions for me!" As much as Gosling pouted, there was a twinkle of excitement in her brown eyes.

"Did you happen to hear any names?" Splash asked.

"Golden-something. Goldenface?" Fennec nipped a flea near the base of his stubby tail. "Big yellow tom."

Splash's eyes widened. What was Field Colony's proudest Envoy doing in the Unbound-lands? And gathering forces, at that?

She traded a glance with Lakespeckle. This warranted investigation.

"If you're headed there now, we'd like to go," Lakespeckle said. "Just give me a moment to gather my supplies."

Fennec nodded. "Of course. I'm sure they won't turn away someone with your skills."

Splash's paws were lighter than they had been in months. Finally, there was a chance—a real chance—that she might be able to reclaim what Rainfall had stolen from her. Her colony, her place as an Envoy—no, her *rightful* place as leader of River Colony—and her family; all were within reach at last. If she could just convince this group of rangers to fight for her cause, perhaps revenge was closer than she had dared dream.

About the Creators

Star Cat Studio was created by Tennelle Flowers, Tiffany Pilgrim, and Audie Weiss in 2019 with the purpose of bringing their collective vision to life in the form of animation. After reaching out to Avalon Roselin of Roselin Books to assist with scriptwriting, Star Cat Studio and Roselin Books formed a partnership to also adapt the story of *The Alliance Saga* into a series of novels. Each member of the production team holds a special role within the creation of this tale and it would not be the same without any one of them contributing to the direction of the plot and characters. The cast would also not be the same without each of them finding ways to sneak their own cats into the series.

Avalon Roselin (they/she) is an educator, writer, and independent author. They primarily write and publish in the Fantasy and Horror genres, and have many more books on the way. Avalon is passionate about scary movies, the wonder of nature, and cats. She takes full responsibility for any tear stains left on the pages of death scenes and offers condolences, but not apologies, as she has pleaded with Star Cat Studio for permission to add several more deaths to this series.

Other Books by Avalon Roselin:

ALiCE
Like Falling Stars
Stellar Eclipse #1: Cloudless Rain
Stellar Eclipse #2: Dark Lightning

Discover more by visiting www.roselinbooks.com

www.ingramcontent.com/pod-product-compliance
Ingram Content Group UK Ltd.
Pitfield, Milton Keynes, MK11 3LW, UK
UKHW042211291224
452836UK00001B/34